Second Hand Out

Jeff Spanke

Boom Shadow Books

This is a work of fiction. All the characters and events portrayed in this book are either products of the author's imagination or are used fictitiously.

SECOND HAND OUT

Front Cover Photography by John Cessna

Front Cover Art and Design by G. Bradford Oman and Daniel Skubal

Back Cover Art and Design, and Boom Shadow Logo by Daniel Skubal

Edited by Taryn Lee Rex

Special thanks to John Cessna for assisting with the accumulation of the numerous epigraphs. Thanks also to the Purdue University Co-Recreational Facility and Purdue University Intercollegiate Athletic Facility for providing lovely, air-conditioned rooms in which I could type freely and drink my delicious caffeinated beverages.

A Boom Shadow Book

This book is set in Times New Roman

First printing: September 2008

ISBN: 978-0-615-25370-1

For the Distinguished Gentlemen of the 8-1-1,
for being the best friends money can buy

For Brad, for proving to me beyond a shadow of a doubt
that time travel is, indeed, possible

For Mark, without whose imagination and inspiration
this book would never have been written

For my friends, family, and all who've ever
danced the good fight

For my parents, for teaching me to research, read, and right

And for my wife, for being all a pen can never fathom

"You will not surely die," the serpent said to the woman. "For God knows that when you eat of it your eyes will be opened, and you will be like God, knowing good and evil."

-Genesis 3:4-5

Prologue
"The Beginning of Forever"

"Upon the subject of education, not presuming to dictate any plan or system respecting it, I can only say that I view it as the most important subject which we as a people can be engaged in."

-Abraham Lincoln, 1832

"For we must consider that we shall be as a City upon a Hill, the eyes of all people are upon us; so that if we shall deal falsely with our god in this work we have undertaken and so cause him to withdraw his present help from us, we shall be made a story and a byword through the world, we shall open the mouths of enemies to speak evil of the ways of God and all professors for Gods sake."

-John Winthrop, 1630

In July 2016, our nation celebrated its 240th birthday by sending me back to view its first. That single voyage ushered in the dawn of a new age of exploration, investigation, and innovation. More than crossing vast bodies of water to arrive in the new world: more than traversing the millions of miles of endless outer space to discover the heavens beyond our reach, that journey to a humble brick courthouse in Philadelphia signified the end of the old way and the beginning of forever. Never again will we be suffocated by the plaguing confines of historical conjecture. Never again will we as a people weep silently beneath a blanket of uncertainty. And never again will our society suffer from the fallacies of greed, lust, and vengeance, for we will have seen the errors our ways shown in the faces of our past selves. No longer will our children live and die having never tethered themselves to their vanished heritage. No longer will we willingly sever the ties with our own past but instead we will rise from the transgressions of yesterday to make a brilliant future for tomorrow! From the annals of history will we strip time down to its most basic truths so that all our guilt and innocence and defeats and victories as a people will be heard, studied, and honored! Our 240th birthday ventured forth an age of timeless boundaries, my friends, and though we cannot see the future for what it truly will be, I stand before you this day with the promise of prosperity, growth, and harmony not only for America, but for all mankind!

My fellow countrymen, as I watched our forefathers sign that blessed document from which all our liberties sprang, my heart cried out with the knowledge that so many lives were lost for those very liberties. That parchment--but a humble piece of paper penned by the hands of a few unassuming men--has been eternally stained with the blood of slaves, Indians, soldiers, and countless others. In the name of freedom, our sense of democracy was fractured. Yesterday's Americans could not see their corruptions, for they lacked the vision necessary to view the paths from which they came. They lacked the power, the passion, and the means to study time as you now study me: face-to-face. But rest assured, good people, the days of ignorance are gone forever. Those days are in *the past* forever. And forever more, you all *will* have the power, the passion, and the means to travel back and view those days with your own eyes! You will see as we rose to glory once again. You will see the triumphs, oh those sweet redeeming victories that served as our atonement for our years of political treachery. Time, my friends, is now literally in your hands and beauty, good people, rests just beyond the horizon.

Now I know there are those among you even now who doubt the wonders with which we have been blessed. You smirk at the prospect of time travel and you mock those who claim they have done so. You curse me for my lies and you sneer at my promises. Yet you do not flee in protest. You remain drawn to my message. You cannot, for all your mumbles of skepticism and doubt, pull yourself away from the truth despite your best efforts to shield yourself from its unrelenting light. I have seen thousands like you. I have seen your ancestors, those poor souls who doubted the future of our great nation on the very day it was born. I saw, with mine own eyes, their grandchildren, perishing 'neath the slaughter of the northern Army, blood seeping through their tattered grey coats. I saw them doubt the might of a nation whose economy crashed alongside the stock market, rendering our ancestors poverty stricken for nearly a decade. Oh, I have seen people like you in every town in every city in every state in every age since our nation began, and while I know you will never be stricken from the slate of America, I say this to you, skeptics; *nor shall our spirit*! Our path has been forged on boulders, splintering the naked feet of those who dare blaze its trail, but I assure you, time weathers all, my friends. From the past, we may now carve such a path for our future that all will prosper, all will flourish and all will triumph under the banner of our God-given right to life, liberty, and the pursuit of eternal happiness!

E.W. Harper, *President*
ClockWorks TTA
Inaugural Address
July 4th, 2018

PART ONE
The Path Now Altered

One
There's Trouble A Brewin'

"In England, at any rate, education produces no effect whatsoever. If it did, it would prove a serious danger to the upper classes, and probably lead to acts of violence in Grosvenor Square.

-Oscar Wilde

"Don't worry about it. All you have to do is follow three simple rules. One: *Never* underestimate your opponent. *Expect* the unexpected. Two: Take it *outside*. Never start anything inside the bar unless it's *absolutely* necessary. And three: Be nice."

-Patrick Swayze as Dalton, *Road House*

Will Bauer had no idea why everyone around him was speaking English. He thought he'd made it quite clear to Sherman that he wanted to go to Germany and yet, so far his trip to Bishopwearmouth had been filled with the harsh cold and unceasing rain only England can provide. Where *was* Bishopwearmouth, anyway? Will had certainly never heard of it before and though the town, at least to Will, *sounded* German, it was clear by the English worded placards and storefronts—not to mention the fact that everyone around him was and had been speaking English all day!—that he was nowhere near the destination for which he had but hours prior paid so handsomely. After mindlessly ambling around the port town for what seemed like days, Will decided that along with the setting the sun, he too would have to find a place to rest for the evening. Refusing to sleep in the gutters or on the streets with the rest of the town's vermin, he found his way to what appeared to be a somewhat lively local pub.

The plastic watch he had been given at the TTA earlier that morning had not yet begun to blink green as he had been told it would once his time began to expire. For the first time,

Will noticed that on the face of the watch—a device the likes of which he had never seen in all his years on Earth—was inscribed the word "Zemeckalian." He remembered glancing over this term when filling out his paperwork, though he could not recall the exact context: his memories now eschewed by the reality that that short, clumsy man at Harper's had single-handedly ruined his entire trip. He thought that maybe "Zemeckalian" referred to the brand or nationality of the watch's manufacturer, but those were simply guesses. Whatever the case, the chilling rain beating down on Will's now exposed forearm combined with the realization that the sun was now completely set compelled the young traveler to scurry into the unassuming pub.

It didn't take long for the patrons-- well along in their collective quest for inebriation--to notice Will's presence in their midst, which was complicated, much to Will's continued embarrassment, by his seemingly unusual choice of clothing. His dark blue denim jeans, Birkenstock sandals and faded "Suri Cruise 2064" Presidential Campaign sweatshirt didn't really match the prevailing styles of the day, but as Will found an empty stool at the bar, the same strange thought that had been plaguing him since his arrival in Bishopwearmouth began to surface yet again: *I thought they weren't supposed to see me!* To the contrary, all day people had been staring at him, snickering to themselves at his attire or his bumbling gait with a few even going so far as to throw rotten vegetables in his direction. Even more perplexing were the frantic conversations he had with some innocent passersby upon arriving in Bishopwearmouth: "Where am I?" "Where's Germany?" "Bishop-what?" "What year is this?!?" While Will understood that these questions, to any normal person, would appear strange and thus would certainly warrant, if not welcome, ridiculing remarks, what bothered him about the responses he received wasn't the crude nature with which they were delivered but rather the simple fact that they were, indeed, delivered. *They can hear me too!*

His body was finally starting to warm up from the outside cold and his damp clothes were slowly drying. *I thought I wasn't supposed to feel anything either!?* Indeed nothing seemed quite right about this, his first vacation in nearly ten years. Looking down at his watch (the face still not blinking),

Will decided he had enough time for at least one drink: a toast to a failed day. "What would you like?" the bartender asked. Not knowing the proper bar etiquette or whether or not his Modern English would translate into this town's vernacular or even what people drank in 1822 (assuming, of course, Sherman at least got *that* part right), Will carefully responded,

"What…would…*you*…suggest?" He was, for the first time since his arrival, thankful that he at least spoke *some* variation of the English language.

"Well, I 'spect you might fancy a brandy," replied the bartender, examining Will with the same scrutiny with which a father might examine his son who came home one night wearing a giant bear costume. "'Course our specialty's anything from Taylor's. He owns the brewery down the way." The bartender indicated the direction of the supposed brewery with his callused, old hand.

Will wondered whether or not he passed the brewery earlier while on his quest for his German relatives, which had occurred before, of course, realizing he was in the wrong damn country. The desire for a pint, however, quickly overcame his disappointment in Sherman and the TTA, and with a fatigued grin on his face, Will declared, "Then something from Taylor's it is!" As the bartender retreated to fill the order, Will hoped his watch would begin to blink before he would have to pay for his drink. He seriously doubted the British pub would accept either the 24 U.S dollars in his wallet or the 23 Conventionstalers he had converted before departing Indianapolis. *Thanks, Sherman!*

"'There ya are," the bartender said, sliding the pint in front of Will. "'At'll be--"

"Oh, um, I'll be having a few more," Will lied, "so, if it's alright, I'll just open a...t-t-tab?" It was more of a question than an actual assertion. *Did people open tabs back then?* Luckily the bartender merely nodded and continued cleaning schooners with the rag over his shoulder. Once he left the patron alone, Will remembered how he and his grandfather loved watching the original *Back to the Future* when he was just a little kid. *This was my favorite movie growing up,* his grandfather would always say. Will's grandfather could (and often would) always fill the room with laughter during the scene when Marty travels back to 1955 and orders a Tab at the diner only to be accosted by the bartender for asking for a tab without ordering anything first. As a boy, Will too would fall to the floor giggling during this scene even though he had no concept of the duel meaning of “tab”: he just figured laughter was the logical response to such a senseless cinematic moment. If grandpa did it, it had to be okay!

As he sat at the Bishopwearmouth bar 163 years before *Back to the Future* was released, Will found himself chuckling at the exchange he just had with his very own bartender…on his very own journey through time. Thinking about that scene from the movie, however, resonated with another thought with which Will had been grappling all day. As if lightning had just struck his mind’s very own clock tower, everything for Will became clear: “*Zemeckalian!”* Will gulped down a healthy mouthful of his drink (emptying the pint in the process), rolled his eyes, and slammed the mug down on the counter. *Sherman, you idiot, now it all makes sense!*

His moment of ecstatic comprehension didn’t last too long, however. Just as he was about to conclude how exactly he ended up seated in this British pub, two things happened: the bartender traded Will’s empty beer with a fresh, full mug and two even fresher faces entered the pub, each receiving a round of cheers and greetings from the other patrons. When Will swiveled around on his stool to see the cause of the commotion, he spied an older, distinguished looking gentlemen sporting a neatly trimmed beard and carrying a walking cane; the man moved slowly from table to table with a young boy clasped to his leg. The apparent celebrity status of the two new arrivals prompted Will to ask of the bartender, "Excuse me sir, who is that?"

"Him?" replied the bartender. "Well, 'at's Mr. Taylor, owner of the brewery down the way." Again, he indicated the direction of the brewery with his old, still callused hand. "'And 'at's 'is boy, at 'is side there." Will noticed the small child clutching to his father's pant leg. The two were making their way around the pub, Mr. Taylor greeting as many people as appeared possible. Finally, they arrived at the bar and proceeded to take a seat next to Will. Mr. Taylor began a conversation with the bartender while the child immediately took notice of Will's poor excuses for proper footwear. Unsure as to whether or not he should explain the concept of sandals, the international corporation that made them, or the internet company from which they were purchased to a four-year old British boy in a bar in 1822, Will just smiled and continued working on his second drink…

His *second* drink? No, no, he couldn't only be on his *second* drink. *Let's see, I had one when I got here...then the one when the guy...and the boy, den, um... but the other one snot here, so how come?... I don't...* He'd been seated next to the Taylor's for nearly two hours and yet, to Will's utter astonishment, there were only two drinks in front of him: one empty, the other full. *Why are my drinks evapo...ra...tating?!?* Sure enough, the damndest thing kept happening in that damn, magic British bar: Will would finish a drink, turn around to see if anyone interesting--or attractive--had entered the pub and when he would turn around again, there would be another full beer next to his empty one. He really began to hope his watch would start blinking because the only thing that would ruin a failed vacation more than not actually going to your paid destination would be getting thrown in a prison for not paying what he could only assume would be a hefty bar tab…*hehe, "tab!"*... To make matters worse, if he failed to reach his rendezvous point when the watch began to blink red-- well, Sherman never finished that part, but Will knew it probably wasn't pretty.

After Will downed yet another drink (this one, too, appearing out of nowhere while his back was turned), he simply couldn't take it anymore. His head felt as though someone had tied bricks to his ears, his stomach churned with every breath he took, and his ratty "Suri Cruise 2064 " sweatshirt was causing him to drown in his own sweat. Carefully rising from his stool, he wondered why the floor felt as though its wooden boards were now suddenly on rollers. The invisible bricks tied to his ears were weighing his head down in competing directions. His neck was getting hotter, sweat dripping from his forehead. His feet were heavy, stomach bubbling, shoulders achy: his eyes tried to find a point on which they could fixate but ultimately did nothing but roll back into his head which fell to his chest causing his entire body to collapse to the floor.

A sharp pain was still throbbing in his wrist when he opened his eyes. Will wasn't sure how long he had been passed out. When he awoke, he saw that the entire establishment had since emptied, save for the Taylor's, the bartender, and one unfortunate young man with piss-soaked blue jeans. "Took quite a spill there, my boy," came a lofty voice whose owner was seated on the same stool he had been since first arriving.

"How did it look?" Will managed to grunt, as he tried to sit up and lean against the counter. When he was younger, Will always wanted to know how his falls looked to a spectator. Sledding, diving, jumping out of trees: he could go home with three broken bones, a ruptured spleen, and a black eye to boot but, damnit, if it *looked* good, then it was all worth it. Still, after this particular fall, his head felt as though the man's son was beating it incessantly with a baseball bat cast out of pure aluminum evil. "Sorry to make a scene," Will spat out, this time directed at the bartender, "I should be going."

"You have to pay for your drinks, fella," the bartender said. "You 'spect you can just walk in here, drink all night, nearly ruin my stool and not pay a bit for it?" Mr. Taylor sat facing the bar with his back to Will who somehow had risen, albeit awkwardly, to his feet.

"Um, sorry sir, but I don't seem to have any money…" *Why won't this watch start blinking?!*

"No money!" the bartender cried, "Hear that, Mr. Taylor? Man says he hadn't any money tonight."

"Calm yourself, Joe, I'm sure there's something we can do to work this out," Mr. Taylor quietly said to the bartender. "The boy's had himself quite a night, here, wouldn't you say?"

"'Course I would say, sir, but 'at's not my problem, is it?" Joe said to Mr. Taylor, the last part glaring at Will. Then, noticing Will's watch, something struck the man's fancy. "Look at that! He's got a pocket watch on his hand, there! Tell ya what, then. You give me that there watch a yours and we'll call it even." It's amazing how quickly a guy can sober up when he's worried he'll miss his transport back to the future.

"Tell *you* what," Will cockily replied, his head nodding side to side like an early twenty-first century bobblehead. Arrogance had never served well as Will's default post-drunken-stupor mode of discourse. "*I* keep the watch and *you* can have the mystery bag inside my pocket." Apparently the prospect of missing his transport didn't faze Will to the point of taking anyone too seriously. After all, he did have the advantage of being closest to the door and, since his watch still wasn't blinking, he knew he could spend a few more minutes bargaining with Joe before he would be sober enough to at least stumble into the dark English street, hopefully out of sight of any further pursuit.

"Son, you might not want to talk to Joe like that—"

"No, it's alright, Mr. Taylor. Boy thinks he's in control now, doesn't he?" With a sinister smile matching his furrowing brow, Joe removed a large knife from under the bar and held it up so Will could see him tossing it from his left to right hand. With a gasp, Mr. Taylor's son spun around to see the reaction on Will's face. Mr. Taylor remained facing the now armed bartender. For the first time all day, Will actually felt fear. Forget the part about being in an empty nineteenth century English pub with a damn watch that didn't seem to be working and yet, ironically, offered his only hope for any kind of rescue: he was alone, he was broke, he was unable to make any kind of break for it and, damnit, his head still *really* hurt. "How'd you like to show me that mystery bag now, boy," Joe prodded. Mr. Taylor, evidently having heard enough of this feeble match of masculinity vs. idiocy, rose from his seat and with an extended right arm, lovingly pushed his son out of potential harm's way. The boy understood his father's intentions and without ever saying a word, slowly backed up to the far wall of the pub.

"Look, guys, I just wanna go home," Will said in a surprisingly articulate manner given his present obstacles.

"Ya pay, ya leave. Ain't no other way 'round it 'is time, mate," Joe retorted. *Damnit, why did he have to say "mate"?* Will was trying to weigh his options which actually proved rather difficult considering he could barely keep his chin from bouncing off his chest. Someone walking in from off the street would have perceived the situation as a living game of chess: all the remaining players were in their strategic positions on the board and it was now Will's turn to strike as his team's only remaining piece against either a 5 year-old pawn, a distinguished King or a callused, old asshole holding a knife. Will had always hated chess.

Since his watch still wasn't blinking—*damnit, Sherman*—Will decided that his best course of action would be to give the watch to Joe, wait for the situation to die down, and when the moment was right, somehow get the watch back. How he would either determine the right moment to attack a nineteenth century British man with a knife or actually proceed with the act itself had not yet crossed Will's mind. Nevertheless, the time to remain silent was rapidly coming to a close. "You can have my watch then, bro." For some reason, Will wagered that since Joe called him "mate," "bro" was just as appropriate.

"Toss it here, son," Mr. Taylor said, maintaining his position as the middle ground between Will on the main floor and Joe behind the bar. Reluctantly, Will slipped off the watch and hurled it past Mr. Taylor into the outstretched hand of Joe, the bartender. Will conceded the forfeiture of his departure ticket by bowing his head (as best he could) first to Mr. Taylor, then to Joe who was marveling like a kid on Christmas at his new toy. With his back now turned to the Taylor's and Joe, Will stumbled to the exit to try and decide how best to contact the TTA.

"What the hell?!" shouted Joe before Will had even taken three steps. Angry that Joe insisted on contending his departure from the pub, Will turned to address the bartender's complaint. He soon discovered, however, that Joe's outburst had not been directed at Will but instead was meant for the watch he had just been given. The watch that had apparently begun to sporadically blink green.

Everything next happened in a matter of seconds. Will charged at the bar with the same atavistic rigor with which a cheetah pursues its prey. Mr. Taylor planted his left leg firmly on the ground and pivoted around so that he was squared up facing Will, prepared to absorb the brunt of the charging force. Joe glanced up from the blinking magic time disc only to see Will plow into Mr. Taylor, Will's eyes piercing Joe's vacant expression. Will's momentum lifted Mr. Taylor off of his feet, knocking him backward toward the bar. Joe took a step back to avoid the inevitable collision of the three grown men while Will and Taylor began their descent to the wooden floor. Will's outstretched wrist slammed into the rounded edge of the bar, but as he began to hit the ground, he looked up and noticed something had impeded Mr. Taylor's fall: his chin was lying at an awkward angle on his chest, his eyes wide open, starting straight ahead. Lying on his stomach between Mr. Taylor's open legs, Will sat up and watched Mr. Taylor's back slump down the front edifice of the bar.

Joe peeked down from behind the counter and knew instantly what had happened. As Mr. Taylor had begun to fall, the back of his head had caught the rounded edge of the counter causing his neck to snap, killing him instantly. The force of Will's weight pulling him toward Earth only increased the force that drove Mr. Taylor's head into the polished wood. Realizing this as well, Will slowly backed away from the lifeless body of the dead proprietor and, with eyes as wide as the face on his former watch, elevated his glance to Joe who had since leapt from the bar, knife in hand. He crashed into Will, knocking them both to the ground. Without a second's hesitation, Joe straddled the shocked Will and drove the blade deep into his chest, removed it, then drove again. The pub had become a slaughter house.

Joe finished his butchery but remained saddled atop his former patron on whom so much free alcohol had regrettably been wasted. Aside from Joe's heavy breathing and Will's blood dripping from blade to floor, the only movement in the pub came from the little boy who emerged from his hiding place, wondering if he should wake his dad to inform him of the brawl. Neither Joe nor the boy noticed the blinking green watch still lying on the counter change from green, to blue, to yellow, and finally to red before finally vanishing in a flash of white light. Ironically, it was the first game of chess Will ever won.

Two
The Tardy Mr. Hinkley

"The crowning fortune of a man is to be born to some pursuit which finds him employment and happiness, whether it be to make baskets, or broadswords, or canals, or statues, or songs."

-Ralph Waldo Emerson

"We don't have a lot of time on this earth. We weren't meant to spend it this way. Human beings were not meant to sit in little cubicles staring at computer screens all day, filling out useless forms and listening to eight different bosses drone on about mission statements."

-Ron Livingston as Peter Gibbons, *Office Space*

Monstrous vermin or giant insect. Monstrous *vermin* or giant *insect*. As Sherman Hinkley awoke one morning from uneasy dreams, he found himself replaying in his mind a conversation he had with a friend the previous night. Essentially, the argument between Sherman and his fellow ClockWorks trainee, Wally Emerson, consisted of debating the significance behind two alternative translations of the opening line of Franz Kafka's *Metamorphosis.* Wally contended that the version he read in high school, which referred to Gregor Samsa as a "giant insect" was equally as valid as Sherman's version, which identified Gregor as a "monstrous vermin." The former, Wally felt, in no way confounded the overall symbolism and overarching existentialist impulse governing Kafka's masterpiece. Furthermore, the semantic nature of the debate itself only exacerbated the issue by accentuating the type of petty, monotonous human behavior against which Kafka so adamantly wrote. Of course Wally--more of a cockroach himself than an actual literary scholar-- never actually articulated his position in such poignant terms ("Shut up, dick, either way it still really sucks to be him!"), but Sherman understood what he was trying to say. Still, even as he tossed in his bed the following morning, Sherman couldn't help but think that there was something more ominous and ultimately far more psychologically scathing about being both monstrous *and* a vermin. To him, the insects of the world all got off easy; everybody just loves a cute, animated cricket.

Sherman rolled over and slapped the snooze alarm for the sixth time, still a little too nervous (and sloshed from the night before) to embrace his first official day with the Agency. *Okay, I think that was the sixth time...one, two, three—yeah, sixth time... 6x9 minutes apiece is 54...54 plus 5:30 is...* "Oh shit!" Sherman shot up and jerked his head toward the freshly slapped bedside clock which wore a jeering 6:24 upon its unblemished, digitized face. He couldn't help think the clock was mocking him as he leapt out from beneath the sacred confines of his wondrous goose-down comforter. He had exactly 36, *no 35!* minutes to shower, get dressed, eat his banana and English muffin and walk, briefcase in hand, the 1.67 miles to work. This time of day, the transit should take roughly 22 minutes, but perhaps with a slight adjustment to his ordinarily brisk pace, he could shave a few precious minutes off his time. Still, that only left him 13 minutes plus change for the remaining tasks, all of which were vital in order to achieve maximum physiological work conditions.

Believe it or not, this particular morning was not unlike the thousands of its predecessors for Sherman. He cursed his alarm clock for not being assertive enough in its one simple task of waking him up and getting him out of bed on time: the sole purpose for which its coveted "alarm" function was created in the first place. He accidentally rubbed shampoo in his eyes in the shower, dropped his washcloth and hit his head on the glass door when he blindly bent down to retrieve his paper-thin slice of *Island Springs Soap.* He burnt his English muffin while trying to figure out which shade of dark red tie would best compliment his plain white shirt and navy blue uniform pants. (He ended up choosing his default yellow tie smothered in Escheresque tessellations of the smiling sun wearing aviator sun glasses: a classic.) At least he still had his trusty banana which actually did have some specks of yellow on its peel, threatened though they were by the impending splotches of light browns and even more scary-looking darker browns. In lieu of his English muffin, Sherman brought, along with his banana, an apple from his fruit bowl: the last edible specimen of its kind. As he hurried out the door—banana in mouth, briefcase tucked under shoulder, apple in one hand and apartment keys clumsily in the other—he couldn't help wonder how it would feel to have his father take the juicy McIntosh apple and chuck it so hard at his back that it lodged itself deep inside his flesh, where it would remain until the day he died. He'd rather eat it instead, he decided. *Poor Gregor.*

If ever there came a day when Sherman Hinkley's frequent cardiovascular exercise and overall tip-top physical conditioning needed to pay off, today was it. The escapade with the ties had cost him precious time back at the apartment, leaving him with only thirteen minutes to traverse the little less than two miles to E.W. Harper's ClockWorks Time Traveling Agency, or TTA as had become the acceptable nomenclature. Luckily, he managed to arrive at his first three intersections at precisely the moment when he was granted the blinking, de-gendered human figure on the other side of the street signifying to all that it was now safe to cross. Sherman never dared cross the street before he was given electronic permission from the traffic Gods. Not only was such an act illegal, punishable by a firmly worded lecture from a law enforcement official AND a *permanent* mark on his record; it was, after all, downright dangerous! He breezed by the Indianapolis public library which had served as his surrogate home for nearly three years while he was finishing his doctorate in Forensic Psychology. He hurried alongside Lucas Oil Stadium, home of the Indianapolis Colts who just last winter had won their 19th Superbowl in 50 years. With an increased kick to his step, he glanced at the banner hanging in front of Zachary Efron Memorial Theater to see the advertisement for this season's off Broadway showcase. Sherman had never heard of "All the King's Whores," but then again, live action pornographic musicals weren't exactly his strong suit.

And thinking of his neatly pressed new suit, Sherman prayed he would arrive to work in tact and not be too disheveled by his hike to disgrace the Agency with a wrinkled pair of trousers or ruffled suit jacket. Ever since he graduated top of his class from Cross University's School for Forensic Psychology, Sherman had centered his sights on a career at ClockWorks TTA. The opportunity to explore time travel from an intellectual's perspective had enticed Sherman from the day when he first heard of E.W Harper's work with *Spontaneous Temporal Obscuring and Observing Potential,* or S.T.O.O.P. as the newspapers and journals dubbed it. With his unique cognitive skill set, Sherman just knew he could offer Harper's brainchild a refreshing insight into the evolution of human morality development, and besides, the position he now had at ClockWorks was precisely the right ticket to kickstart his career-oriented pursuits. At 45 years old, Sherman had, of course, had his share of "career kickstarts," but when the United States filed for bankruptcy in 2046, the same year Sherman earned his PhD. from Cross and nearly three decades after Harper first patented the idea for S.T.O.O.P, most Americans found it difficult to maintain their own meager jobs, let alone risk losing everything in the futile pursuit of a career in time travel.

For nearly twenty years Sherman dedicated the better part of his adult life toward earning a position with the most prestigious TTA in the world. Sure, other companies tried to emulate ClockWorks's business practices, customer relations, and techninological supremacy over the rest of the market, but as a result of E.W. Harper's somewhat mysterious death immediately following ClockWorks's first anniversary in 2019, the *International Coalition on Time Travel, Pollution, and Child Abuse* decreed that Harper's ClockWorks remain as the only operational TTA in North America. Many were pissed. Few took action. Sherman: well, he simply studied as much history as he could so when the time finally arrived for that one special interview for a much sought after trainee position, he'd appear more than qualified. After all, when all was said and done, Sherman could unpack a person's character faster and more accurately than most people could unpack a suitcase. It didn't seem to matter that he couldn't take a shower without nearly cracking his head open.

For the last eighteen months, Sherman, his friend Wally Emerson, and seven other doctors, lawyers, historians, and religious scholars had undergone extensive and highly classified training in ClockWorks's satellite facility located roughly two miles below Monument Circle in the center of downtown Indianapolis, Indiana. The nine trainees went through rigorous combat training, constant physical fitness assessments, and took classes on everything from Picasso's perception of fourth dimensionality on the astral plane to Ancient Egyptian accounting to the ethics of South African hydroponics in 1999. By far, Sherman's least favorite class of all was *Famous Canadian Wars of the Twenty-First Century,* which was taught by a belligerent old comedian turned war hero named Mike Myers. Apparently, before going completely insane in the Battle of Nova Scotia, Commodore Myers had been quite the American film star. Sherman, however, could never get past the eye patch and stuffed parrot that the Commodore insist always be perched upon his slouching right shoulder.

Of the nine original trainees, only five advanced for consideration as candidates for the four open positions at ClockWorks. At the end of the year and a half period, Harper's senior advisory committee, in conjunction with the governor and selected members of the board of trustees, proudly hired Dr. Walden P. Emerson as ClockWorks's newest Chief Head of Unintentionally Misplaced Persons. Isabelle Stowe, J.D was put in charge of Reservations, Cancellations, Finances, and Itineraries: 1600-1850. Reverend Lamar Newton slid comfortably into his new role as Chair of the Department of Supernatural and Paranormal Biblical Verifications. And Sherman Hinkley, after eighteen months of grueling preparation and almost twenty years of painstaking studies and random, low-paying jobs, was awarded his dream position: Chief Head of Investigating Malicious Purposes, Common Era Division.

That all happened last Friday. Today, Monday, Sherman arrived at ClockWorks somehow on time, though a tad, shall we say, *tired* from celebrating all weekend with Wally and the rest of the new employees. Now, as he stood at the bottom step of the magnificent concrete staircase leading up to his future, he took sight of all the types of people entering and exiting the towering building. E.W Harper insisted that ClockWorks's design reflect the innovative architectural styling of Ancient Roman temples which, coincidentally, also served as the influence of several of America's own national architectural treasures. Thus, the massive structure incorporated several white stone Corinthian pillars in the front of the building with elaborate acanthus leaves carved into the capitals and rosettes engraved at the base. Throughout the pillars, Harper's architects juxtaposed the images of classical Rome and Greece with modern portrayals of spaceships, satellites and automobiles. Harper claimed that the unique aesthetic choice was predicated upon the idea that, through ClockWorks, different eras of human evolution could potentially share in their technological and artistic advances; Harper called this somewhat anachronistic merging of ideas "an innovation conflation."

In the center of the vast outdoor forum area between the top of the staircase and the front entrance, Harper's workers installed a luscious green garden with not-too-subtle echoes of the Garden of Eden and the Hanging Gardens of Babylon. (They even included a life-size replica of an Eve-like woman removing an apple from a tree. Adam was nowhere in sight, though Sherman always liked to joke to himself that he was off with another woman.) The culminating structure of the garden was a tremendous statue of E.W. Harper, reminiscent of Thomas Jefferson's monument in Washington, D.C of which Sherman had only seen photographs. Harper's statue portrayed the brilliant scientist wearing a business suit and posed as though he was striding forward, presumably into the future. Covering the base of the statue on which Harper ran frozen in time was a large face of a clock with no minute, hour, or second hands: ClockWorks's world famous emblem. Before entering the building, Sherman always made it a point to read the plaque wrapped around the cylindrical marble base of the monument. It contained the introduction to Harper's inaugural address for Clockworks TTA entitled "The Beginning of Forever." Sherman appreciated the poetic undercurrents of the title and the epic rhetorical style with which Harper crafted the now famous oration. His first chance to travel back in time, Sherman decided long ago, would be to go back to five years before he was born and witness the historic speech the way Harper would have wanted it: face-to-face. Both Harper and Sherman shared the undying thirst for knowledge that the plaque he was now reading so feverishly preached.

He finished reading, puffed up his chest (slyly glancing over his shoulder to see if anyone would notice him enter the building and wonder to themselves what sort of important work that handsome man would surely accomplish today) and began his stroll into E.W. Harper's ClockWorks Time Traveling Agency. The day just couldn't be better.

Sherman never noticed just how big the building really was! *Time traveling doesn't require that much space, so why does this damn building need to be so big!?* His frustration was quickly climbing because as his awareness of the building's sheer girth mounted, so too did his realization that he had absolutely no idea where in God's name he was going. "*Conference Room A1-218X7-S.E.X." What floor is that on?* He only had 34 from which to choose, not including the lobby. He could've sworn he remembered something about "the archery room," but that just made no sense at all. For a brief moment he considered just spending the morning in the gift shop and perhaps enjoying a tasty frozen treat and then finding the group after lunch. He could always claim he got mugged on his way there or had a wicked case of the squirts which rendered him unavoidably detained for the morning. Besides, this particular gift shop offered some of the nicest, most expensive artificial historical relics of any ClockWorks store in the world. In fact, it offered such a wonderful shopping experience that most visitors to the TTA opted to spend their time looking for fake copies of the Treaty of Versailles to buy for their grandparents rather than actually going back in time to see the thing being signed (or at least learn what it was).

Just as he was about to pop a "screw-it-all" into his mouth, he saw Wally getting out of the glass elevator on the third floor, Isabelle and Lamar at his side. Running out into the foyer, Sherman screamed up at them;

"Hey guys! Where are you all going!?"

"The archery room," Lamar shouted back, a silent "duh" trailing the sentence fragment. *I guess it makes more sense than I thought*, Sherman sighed.

"Where ya been, Sherm?" Wally yelled down at Sherman, who still had no idea how the hell to get to the archery room or why the hell a building that books time travelers would even have a room dedicated solely to hurling arrows at little circles on the wall.

"Oh, yeah, I meant to be here on time, obviously, but um…" Sherman realized he was the lone man standing in the open foyer. "But, um, I… got a wicked case of the muggers." *Something about that didn't sound right.*

"The muggers you say, Mr. Hinkley?" soared an eerily authoritative voice directly over Sherman's shoulder. *I don't care who this guy is, I bet he knows where he's going!* Sherman turned around to find himself staring into the demonic eyes of Lt. Phineas Gage who, yes, shared a name with the famed railroad worker who, in 1848, had a three foot long piece of iron drilled through his brain, destroying his frontal lobes and nearly killing him. Of course Sherman had studied Gage (the railroad worker, not the asshole) while working on his PhD. in Forensic Psychology and after meeting the Lieutenant during training, determined that not only could the asshole also survive a skull puncturing iron bit, but he would probably remove the iron himself and then go use it to murder the entire family of the guy who made it.

"No, not…well, yes, *muggers,* sir…but, well you see, it…it wasn't like…" For a guy who had more knowledge and skill deciphering an individual's subconscious motivations and estimating their psychological tendencies, Sherman sure couldn't crack it under pressure. It didn't help either that Gage usually walked around with his moose hunting rifle strapped to his back. Sherman figured even Wally was probably scared of Gage, even though at that moment, he was three floors up protected by the religious zealousy of Newton and the three-hundred-plus pounds of Isabelle.

"You know, Hinkley, for a guy who supposedly has more knowledge and skill deciphering an individual's subconscious motivations and estimating their psychological tendencies, you sure are a little shit, aren't you." Sherman agreed with most of the assessment.

"Yes, sir. Quite little, sir," Sherman conceded.

"The littlest!" Gage declared to all in earshot, his booming voice filling the entire open concourse.

"Smallest of all shits, sir…" Sherman figured he'd give the Lieutenant the satisfaction of thinking he'd won this battle even though deep down, he personally thought it was better to go through life being only a little shit rather than a great heaping pile of feces.

"Well then, we agree. Now, Hinkley, I believe you're supposed to be with *them*." Gage pointed to the three onlookers, Wally clearly trying to hide behind Isabelle without anyone noticing he was using her fat for his gain. It wasn't like Wally was a *coward* in the John Wayne--ain't gonna protect my land--sense of the word. But to an uninformed spectator, the sheepish manner in which Wally cowered behind Isabelle's corpulence suggested that perhaps the middle-aged Agent would happily sell his own mother if it meant another day of survival, which, ironically, would also mean another day of prolonged cowardice.

"Yes, sir, I was on my way up before--" Sherman explained

"I know. The *muggers*, right?" replied the Lieutenant.

"Of course, sir."

Gage shook his head in disgust. "Hinkley, I'm going to go in there and get myself a tasty frozen treat and then I'm going to go to the archery room and if you're not there ready to begin when I arrive, you can consider this the last time you'll ever wear the distinguished uniform of a ClockWorks employee." Sherman's chest burned from the heat emanating from the smiling suns on his tie. Gage turned to enter the gift shop/chapel/hotel/public gym. As he walked away from an unnerved Sherman, he said over his shoulder, "Oh, and Hinkley: Don't ever be late again!"

Three
The William Tell Club

"It is an illusion that youth is happy, an illusion of those who have lost it; but the young know they are wretched, for they are full of the truthless ideals which have been instilled into them, and each time they come in contact with the real they are bruised and wounded."

-W. Somerset Maugham

"Youth cannot know how age thinks and feels. But old men are guilty if they forget what it was to be young...and I seem to have forgotten lately."

-Albus Dumbledore

Perhaps no other employee's legacy was garnished with such a capricious combination of mysticism, loathing, and fear than that of Lieutenant Phineas P. Gage. To the custodial staff, the man typified pragmatism and authority. To the shareholders, order and restraint. To the older ClockWorks employees, Gage personified pure hegemonic masculinity. He was the mystified Übermensch of a former era: an iconic alpha-male that never really existed, but whom served as the unattainable ideal for his lesser male counterparts. In his older years, Gage's virility had gradually been replaced by a certain social obtuseness that rendered him highly disliked by the majority of the younger staff members who would joke amongst themselves that the infamous moose hunter must have been born in a cave or raised by a pack of maladjusted, anal retentive wolves. Few believed the Lieutenant was ever actually an *infant*, of all things, and virtually everyone doubted the man's capacity for any sort of loving relationship, let alone a remote, emotional connection. He was roughly considered as romantically impotent as he was militaristically inclined. He loved his rifles but, according to Harper's legend, never got around to using his pistol save for the occasional summer night following a re-run of "When the

Sergeant's Away". During either long, arduous days as a means of lifting morale or during lulls in terribly boring days, the younger staff would sit around and gossip about what life must have been like for Gage's parents when he was a boy. Again, the prospect of him ever being younger than seven was something no one even considered. He was a seven year-old asshole from birth.

Gage loathed Agents like Sherman for their insolence and historical ineptitude. They might have *studied* history, but Gage *lived* history. He fought the battles about which miscreants like Sherman may have only read in school. He cherished the American ideals which, he claimed, had eroded over time and had since been replaced by a social dogma that preached the synonymy of freedom and equality. Gage likened the conception of freedom and equality being anything other than mutually exclusive to thinking a butte and a tributary are the same thing.(They're not.) For, if everyone is free, not everyone is equal. And if everyone is equal, not everyone can be entirely free. Thus, conceptually, Gage advocated not so much the *preservation* of democracy, but rather the mere *performance* of it, so as to keep the ignorant populous content while maintaining a concentrated system of central control. Consequently, he often found himself living not so much in the *actual* past, but in a past that he himself created so that he may always have a fabricated sense of nostalgia for a life that, in reality, never happened.

He lamented the gulf between Harper's legal obligations and the Agency's moral duties. In the mind of Phineas Gage, running Harper's TTA was no different than leading a military unit: achieve the objective, preserve life, return safely. In the recent years, Gage had grown distraught over the myriad hoops through which ClockWorks must leap in order to preserve the temporal status quo. In the early years after its inception--Gage would frequently complain--Harper's never had to worry about people abusing the system because people back then were inherently decent. *Now,* however, he felt that people, by nature, sought to abuse the power E.W. Harper had bestowed upon the world. Only exacerbating matters, was the system of checks and balances established in order to make sure no one person could preside over or control too much of any one aspect of the Agency.

Yet, Gage believed that power distributed equally among employees, while certainly democratic, ultimately threatened the stability of the company. When everyone has equal power, there's no power to be had. If Gage had it his way, he'd consolidate the Agency's sum of authority in one individual figure: albeit an elected president, nominated representative, or self-imposed dictator. Of course, Harper's *did* have an elected president, Emmanuelle Waverly, but Gage knew that Waverly's *real* power ended with his title. Waverly was a puppet leader. The real Harper's leaders were the shareholders and committee members. *Committees.* The only reason Gage continued working for Harper's after so many years stemmed from his deeply rooted fear that he was the only thing keeping ClockWorks from running the world into the ground. He was his own lone crusader: the solitary cowboy who willingly sacrificed a life of happiness for the good of all the townsfolk. Most of the time, he accepted his self-imposed, epic responsibilities with pride. In the light of Harper's newest employees, however, he'd begun to question his rationality in addition to their competency.

Lamar, Isabelle, and Wally waited for Sherman to ride the elevator up to the third floor before they all departed for the archery room. “Why’s a TTA need an archery room, anyway?” Isabelle wondered aloud.

“I’m not sure it really *needs* one, Izzy, but the manual says it’s used as a sort of holding pen for kids when their parents are taking quick trips back,” Lamar interjected. "Ya know, when the cat's away, the mice will shoot things." The other three chuckled to themselves. They all knew that one of the main reasons ClockWorks chose to hire Lamar to work in its Supernatural and Paranormal Biblical Verifications Department stemmed from a series of articles he'd recently published in an academic journal from the University of Notre Dame Press. Newton argued, rather convincingly, that despite the seemingly unending burgeoning of new technological capabilities, human beings simply have failed to evolve at a rate equal to that of their self-created technological counterparts. He claims to have charted a sort of de-evolutionary phenomenon existing in the recreational habits of children whereby rather than taking advantage of the digitized world at their fingertips, they choose instead to indulge themselves in much more archaic forms of entertainment. Such a phenomenon, he contends, began to emerge around the year 2016 and has grown exponentially more pervasive with each new generation. *Thus, our civilization now finds itself on the brink of a dramatic shifting back to the cave whence we came and in the process is inadvertently creating an entirely new allegory of which Plato himself would have been undoubtedly fearful. How will our return to darkness impair our perception of our own teleological light?*

Perhaps more so than even Sherman, Lamar Newton had already established himself as quite the well-read scholar, as well as a true asset to the ClockWorks team. Without fail, he could recite the specific pages on which all of ClockWorks plethora of guidelines, mandates, rules, and proclamations could be found. Not only that, but he could, for the most part, accurately recall verbatim certain verses from every major religious text ever written and at least three of the various versions of each. He simply had an insatiable craving for knowledge. Aside from food, the only thing Isabelle Stowe ever craved was math: pure, uncensored, raw mathematics. She loved number crunching with such an undying fervor that it came second only to her love for all things chocolate. In fact, she had been hired by ClockWorks specifically to investigate ways to cut costs of Middle Age Temporal Transportation because, for some reason, the Agency had always spent more money sending people back to Medieval Europe than virtually every other era in world history. Her other new duties included monitoring the ionic dyhydrogen monoxide chambers in which flowed the primary mechanism for time travel, as well as making sure customers' destinations were properly inspected by special ClockWorks security forces prior to the customers' arrival.

Unlike Lamar, who had three college-aged children with his wife of thirty-three years, Isabelle Stowe led a fairly secluded existence. The rumors that circulated within the group of the original nine trainees hinted that perhaps she'd lost her husband several years before in the war with Guam--a forty-six week campaign in which the United States successfully regained their right to continue free trade with the other Micronesian islands--but no one ever dared confront her about the issue. To the best of their knowledge, she lived alone in her three-story brick home off Washington Boulevard, roughly three miles directly north of Monument Circle. During training, she'd been given exemption from the majority of the physical activities due to the fact that physical health was not deemed necessary in the position for which she had applied, yet everyone knew her exemption derived from the fact that ClockWorks couldn't justify hiring her if she failed to comply with the mandatory physical standards, despite the fact that her numerical and clerical expertise were of such tremendous value to the Agency. Consequently, during those long, arduous hours when the other eight bonded over push-ups, mile runs, and blindfolded karate (an activity that strangely resembled what squirrels would look like if they ever got really pissed off and decided to fight each other), Isabelle would merely sit in a room and study forty years worth of ClockWorks ledgers and other computer files.

When she was younger, Sherman and Wally guessed Isabelle would have made a fairly attractive woman. Even in her late-fifties she didn't appear completely grotesque, though her homely countenance and acquiescent demeanor colored her more as a "long-lost-spinster-of-an-aunt" figure than someone worthy of romantic entanglements. Once in a while, she would speak up after literally days of silence only to deliver the most condescending and corrosive comment to either Sherman or Lamar. Usually, though, she reserved her nastiest harangues for Wally. This caused Sherman to question whether Isabelle's passive, "keep to herself" nature derived from an inherent fear of social connection or if it only exemplified the fact that she considered herself somehow "above" the mere peons who knew neither the function of nonhomogenous matrix equations, nor the benefits of solving them using Gaussian Elimination versus LU Decomposition. Or, she could just be a bitch.

Wally and Sherman were the only two who had known each other prior to starting their training at Harper's two years before. The friends grew up together in the small town of Tell City, Indiana located on the Ohio River on the southern border near Kentucky. Because Tell City was also the birthplace of the original ClockWorks Vice President Nicolas Covey, the only other TTA in the state of Indiana was erected there in 2020 as a way to honor his life, loyalty, and seemingly endless checkbook. Wally, a fellow bachelor of his pal, Sherm's, was a year older than Sherman and always bragged that when he was two years old, his father had taken him on a vacation back in time to 1620 to see the Pilgrims arrive at Plymouth. He never failed to ridicule Sherman for being *the only guy in the world* who hasn't ever gone back in time, and even as kids, whenever their friends would talk about vacations their families were going on, or cool trips they had just taken, Wally would bring up his trip to Massachusetts. According to Wally, he and his father were standing on the stone which would later become Plymouth Rock, waiting for the Mayflower to arrive. When John Carver took his first steps on dry land, Mr. Emerson supposedly startled the sailor by screaming, "What the hell took you so guys long? We got dinner in the oven, and the natives are getting restless!" Even as adults Wally loved telling people this story, but Sherman never relinquished his skepticism that a boy who was most likely still using diapers as a shit repository at the time had such a steel trap for a memory.

As 9th graders, the two realized they had neither the athletic prowess to pursue lucrative careers in the International Football League, the physical endowments necessary for consistent roles in adult films (the nation's most profitable industry at the time), nor the culinary expertise required of professional chefs. With no other discernible options for life after high school, the two took up the only other craft in which they had the faintest interest: crossbow hunting. (It would be another two years before Sherman realized his potential for a career in psychology and yet still another decade before seriously pondering a profession in time travel.) In school that year they learned that their town had indeed been named after the legendary 14th century marksman, William Tell: a fact that Sherman at least felt somewhat embarrassed not knowing until he was 14. It made him wonder just how many other towns were named for famous people and just how few of those towns' citizens were actually aware of it.

In the spring of their freshman year as Tell City High School Markspeople (women, it was determined in 2014, could shoot crossbows too), Wally and Sherman founded "The Club for People Who Want to be Legends and Shoot Crossbows Like William Tell Club." For purposes of flyer distribution and printing costs, they later shortened the title. With the exception of national holidays, severe meteorological anomalies, or dentist appointments, the two boys held bi-weekly meetings of "The William Tell Club" in Wally's basement. Mrs. Emerson would usually provide stale trail mix and lukewarm root beer as refreshments, while Wally and Sherman would spend the majority of the time calling their high school friends to see why the hell they weren't at the meeting. *Come on people, there were snacks!* Most weeks, they would usually wind up watching TV or arguing over the latest article in *Harper's*, a travel magazine which highlighted all the latest news and promotions of the ClockWorks TTA headquarters up north in Indianapolis. By summer, Wally and Sherman had abandoned their brief affair with medieval weaponry and in its place had formed a keen interest in the wonders of time travel. Years later, the friends would joke about how if it weren't for those meetings back in high school wherein they cultivated their ebullience for E.W. Harper's scientific legacy, there'd be no way either of them would have ever ended up working for ClockWorks. Ironically, despite their club's picture in their freshman yearbook in which they were the only figures, neither Walden Emerson nor Sherman Hinkley had ever fired a crossbow.

The archery room on the third floor of ClockWorks wasn't used for shooting at all. There were no arrows, no targets, no blood stained floors or emergency medical supplies. There were no severed heads tacked onto the wall or framed photographs of fatigue-clad grown men standing over the rotting carcass of a Colorado Elk, grinning wildly that they had *actually killed* the animal with their high-powered .600 caliber Churchill Magnum sniper rifle from 40 feet away. Nor, oddly enough, were the walls cluttered with photographs of 12 year-old Navajo boys proudly exhibiting the hides of the buffalos they killed using a hand-made bow and arrow while riding bareback atop a running stallion in the Nebraska plains. But then again, Sherman remembered, the Navajo feared that cameras would steal one's soul. That must explain the absence of the such photographs.

Everyone was surprised Lamar didn't realize that when they were told to meet in the "archery room" that morning, the directions really referred to the "Archer E" room—located down the hall from the "Archer West" room in the "Archer Corridor" of "Archer Hall." Thomas Archer was the primary architect for Harper's and, as with all of his corporate designs, made sure to designate an entire wing of the building to himself. The four new employees entered the well-decorated, pleasingly aesthetic room and were greeted with coffee, tea, and an assortment of delicious looking chocolate donuts. Isabelle was in heaven. In the front of the room stood nine or ten extremely attractive men and women, none of whom could have been older than thirty-five. Directly in front of them stood ClockWorks's President, Emmanuelle K. Waverly who kindly instructed the four to have a seat on the plush couches arranged facing the front. Around the room, there hung portraits decorating the walls which depicted past customers' vacations. Sherman and Wally each glanced at the colored photograph of Hannibal sitting on top of his lavishly ornate elephants, and Isabelle noticed a smaller photograph of Amelia Earhart walking alone on a tropical island, wreckage of a crippled plane in the background. While Lamar appreciated the abundance of religious documentation present in the room, he wasn't sure how he felt about the picture of Jesus hanging on the cross with a family of four standing in front of it, waiving. Some images needn't documentation.

"Good morning, everyone. Mr. Hinkley, I see that we hired someone whose sense of direction at least outshines his punctuality." All heads in the room turned to face Sherman as Lt. Gage delivered his greeting: the remnants of a tasty frozen treat still on his lips. "Before we open our services for the day, President Waverly and I wished to welcome you four to your first official day as ClockWorks employees and to take the time-- no pun intended-- to introduce you all to the senior members of our, how should I say it, more 'public' staff." The sexy yuppies standing in a line behind Gage wearing matching navy blue ClockWorks jackets with the embroidered handless clock emblem on the left lapel grinned in pretentious modesty at having been embarrassingly labeled "public" by Gage. Everyone knew that these models of self-absorption served as the bright glowing faces of ClockWorks, or any other TTA for that matter. While scholars and sophisticates like Sherman, Wally, Isabelle, or Lamar essentially *ran* the damn cogs that operated Harper's, these blemish-free purebreds standing in the front of the room were the people who actually dealt with the public. They were the few, the proud, the certified time travel agents of ClockWorks and the buck stopped with them insofar as making sure customers arrived at their destinations on time, enjoyed their trip, and of course, were picked up when their reservations expired. Lord help them, though, if they ever needed to explain a policy, locate a missing person, ascertain the mens rea of a potential customer or, hell, make a pot of coffee or actually *read* the contract a customer just signed.

"Thank you, Captain Gage," said obviously the most informed representative of the TTA's certified elite. Still, Sherman thought she *was* pretty damn hot. "Everyone, ladies and gentlemen, proud ClockWorks employees, my colleagues and I are ever so much looking forward to working with you. On behalf of my colleagues and me, let me introduce myself. If any of you ever need anything at all, please don't hesitate to ask any one of us. We're all here to help each and every one of you as you get estimated to life at Harper's." Here's where she just got lost. "Every now and then a company comes along that sweeps the nation's people off its feet. During those places, it's good to know we have a company like Harper's Titty-A who can make those people feel happy and take them to places you've only dreamed about being allowed to ever go to. I'm so proud to serve as a member of one of those special groups. You all now have to pleasure of working with us as we now too get to work with you also. I just know we'll all make this place the most wondrous Harper's TTA in the state of our nation. Thank you all and remember what E.W. Harper himself used to say," Sherman and Wally sunk lower in their chairs, "'There's no business like *time* business at Harper's ClockWorks TTA!'" Her fellow idiots clapped in unison. Sherman hoped that doing so would trigger the overhead lights to shut off so the four of them could make a break for it. Alas, the lights shone on.

"Did she ever introduce herself?" Wally whispered to Sherman.

"I think we've learned all we'll ever need to know about her," Sherman quietly replied.

"Mr. Hinkley, do you have anything to add?" Gage asked, somehow hearing Sherman's whisper over the still exuberant celebration of what's-her-name's epic oration.

"No, sir, I was just saying that I've never heard a speech that was so *inspirational* before. That was truly, inspiring to me, thank you. I'm inspired, sir. Really, just flat out inspired. Yup." Snickers from the sitters followed Sherman's reply. That is to say, of course, that everyone but Isabelle snickered.

"Very well, Hinkley. Alright, then, thank you again for the lovely speech, Eternity." *Yeah, that sounds about right.* Gage turned to the group of Agents and dismissed them. "You all know where you need to be. To your stations! Let's have another great day at ClockWorks. And you four," the newbies sat upright in their seats for the first time since arriving in the room, "God speed today. You all were hired to make this place run like…well, like clockwork." He paused, as if for the first time he understood the significance behind the name of his beloved company. "So go do it! Any problems, take them up with myself or President Waverly. Anything to add, Emmanuelle?"

"Just one thing, Lieutenant." Waverly seemed much kinder than Phineas Gage. "Never forget, people come here first and foremost to have fun and because they're in need of a vacation. It's *their* job to give it to them," he pointed to the door, indicating the people who had just left. "On the other hand, it's *your* job to make sure *they* don't screw everything up. So be on your toes at all times. That's all I have, Lt. Make it a worthy day, everyone!" And with that, Gage and Waverly left the room through the front doors.

The four didn't speak much as they rose from their seats but rather merely left the *Archer E.* room and proceeded to their respective sectors to begin the day. Yet as they departed in silence, each one of them came to the understanding that at least on some level, like it or not, the four of them now shared a unique and impenetrable bond: they were the new group of employees. They alone were the cogs of ClockWorks. They were the behind the scenes masterminds. They were neither the overpaid policy makers nor the unmasked and undereducated public facade of the organization. Their job was simply to sit at their desks, isolated from the rest of the world, and make decisions about time travel. They had no other friends, no other purpose. They were the new William Tell Club, minus the yearbook picture.

Four
No Business like Time Business

"If you wish to forget anything on the spot, make a note that this thing is to be remembered."

-Edgar Allen Poe

"A boss is like a teacher. And I am like the cool teacher. Like Mr. Handell. Mr. Handell would hang out with us. And he would tell us awesome jokes. And he actually hooked up with one of the students. Um, and then like twelve other kids came forward. It was in all the papers. Really ruined eighth grade for us."

-Steve Carell as Michael Scott, *The Office*

7:25. Thirty-five minutes to get it done. There was only one thing left to do before Sherman could begin his day's tasks of making Harper's a better place, one nut-job at a time. At least this time he knew where he was going. The Cognitive Restoration Lab was located just down the hall from his new office on the 17th floor of the building. In contrast with the only other primary ClockWorks division, the wing of the building devoted to the Common Era Division was the most heavily populated and highly trafficked section of the entire facility. With the exception of a few biblical zealots, most ClockWorks customers had little desire to travel back in time before Year One. Sherman knew that every position in the C.E.D had a counterpart in the B.C.E.D, but to him, it was like comparing a player on a varsity football team with a fat kid playing with a rock in the middle of an open field…by himself…in the rain…There *was* no comparison; Sherman's division *was* Clockworks time travel.

Sherman began to kick himself for not being able to complete the procedure at the closure of training like the rest of his team, but he understood the rules strictly forbade anyone who had experienced a migraine within a 14 day period from participating in the brief operation. He found the white, sterile looking doors to the laboratory, pushed them open, and signed in at that front task. Within seconds of arriving, a tall slender Asian man in a white lab coat approached him, clipboard in hand. "Mr. Hinkley?" the doctor asked. Sherman nodded. "Good morning, sir," the man smiled, "I'm Doctor Sato. Do you have any questions before we begin?" Sherman shook his head. As far as he was concerned, the only question he had was when he could get out of there and head to his office. Something about the cleanliness of laboratories had always made Sherman feel uneasy.

"If you'll just follow me, then, Mr. Hinkley, we'll have you out of here in no time. The procedure should take roughly ten minutes and then you can be on your way to making Harper's a better place!" *Could this guy read minds?* As directed, Sherman followed the doctor to a back room with a hospital bed, some surgical supplies and a large monitor for students to observe various medical procedures. (Yes, ClockWorks had its own onsite hospital as well.) Sherman began to undress himself at the edge of the table when Sato chimed in, "Oh no, sir, you don't need to do that. I will ask, though, that you loosen your tie a bit and that should be fine. And, may I say what a…festive tie it is, sir." Sherman's crimson-faced expression indicated that he should've gone with the red tie.

"Should I lie down now or…?" Sherman asked, hoping that Sato would answer the question before he would be forced to finish it himself. Luckily, the good doctor was right on cue.

"Yes, yes that's fine. Just let me make some notes here on your chart. Okay, are you ready?"

"Yup, let's do it. Ten minutes, right?"

"Should be no more than that, Mr. Hinkley," Sato said, a comforting smile blanketing his face. Sherman could deal with military people like Gage calling him "Mister." but he wondered if he should insist that Sato refer to him as "doctor" from now on. After all, he *was* a doctor, right? He continued to ponder his dilemma as Sato pressed a button on the side of the bed causing one end to slowly rise to proper operation height.

All new Harper's employees were required to undergo a basic memory modification procedure in which a microscopic, lead coated electrical device is placed directly inside the hippocampus located in the medial temporal lobe of the forebrain. It was a fairly expeditious and entirely painless outpatient procedure that was developed by E.W Harper himself as a means of ensuring that employees' memories remain in tact and in conjunction with their current line of temporal dimensionality in the case of a time traveling snafu. Sherman recalled how Lamar best explained it one afternoon during the first week of training.

"Imagine you go back in time to, I don't know, see the very first production of *Romeo and Juliet*," Lamar had said, "but when you get there, you accidentally set fire to the theater and kill everyone inside, Shakespeare included. When you travel back to the moment of your original departure, the condition of the current world would be a response to a past in which Shakespeare had died in a tragic inferno. Thus, for hundreds of years, the world would have operated *as if* a fire had claimed its greatest English writer. No one alive would have any reason to believe otherwise. *Shakespeare died in a fire!* It's just that simple. The event itself might not have altered the entire course of human evolution, but it would have certainly manipulated the memories of those affiliated in any way shape or form with Shakespeare's legacy, right? *Your* memories--the memories you had prior to traveling back in time-- would remain in tact because it's impossible for an individual to deviate from his or her own individual timeline, and even though your actions caused a change in the past which would undoubtedly alter the course of the future from that moment forward, the change itself is contingent on your arrival in the past and hence cannot affect your future memories in any way. Still, the changing of the past *would* affect the memories of anyone not directly affiliated with the catalyst for temporal alteration. In other words, everyone around you would think you were crazy if you tried to explain to them that Shakespeare never actually died in a fire. All they would have to do is Google 'Shakespeare' and discover that no document exists which would corroborate your story.

“Before Harper invented the hippocampus preservation procedure, there were stories of people returning to the Agency from a trip only to discover that what they had done in the past drastically affected our present environment. I remember hearing about one guy who came back from an afternoon in the Antebellum South only to find out that for some reason his wife had never been born. Sure, he could tell you everything about his wife, but since everyone else in the world existed on a timeline in which his wife didn't exist, they all thought he was crazy. It took some pretty convincing evidence for Harper to send an Agent back and set the course of time right again. Things like that used to happen all time. Thank God no one ever went back in time and did something that would cause Harper to never be born because the temporal paradox that would have resulted from causing a temporal alteration that would have destroyed the timeline of the person who made time travel possible in the first place would have been, well, awful! I'm not really sure what would have happened.

"What the procedure eliminates is the possibility of such an event ever occurring. Since the hippocampus plays the most important role in memory formation, by preserving the memories of all ClockWorks employees *as they exist on this dimensional time line*, we ensure that, should a disaster occur, we have the ability to identify the specific moment in which our current dimension of time eschewed to form an entirely new dimension--'the point of divergence' if you will. We can then compare our memories with the Harper's mainframe using basic forebrain scanning and then proceed to take the appropriate measures to eradicate the problem and realign the newly created alternative dimension with our own so that they are consistent with one another. So, in the Shakespeare example, assuming we all have the hippocampus implants, we'd know that our new world derived from Shakespeare dying in a fire and all we would have to do is send one of the ACHEs back to make sure he lived through the performance. Needless to say, sometimes people may get hurt, but the pain is necessary in order to protect the course of time and not risk our own present by messing with our past."

What were the ACHEs again? About half-way through the procedure, Sherman had two thoughts in his mind: he wished he could see the monitor behind him so that he could take a gander at the inside of his head and he wished he could figure out what the hell the "E" in "ACHEs signified. *Agents of Counterfactual History,* what, *Eradication? Elimination? Erection?* Either way, he knew that they were the guys who did the dirty work: ClockWorks's special policy force that would waste no time going back to kill you if you were doing so much as looking at a mosquito without permission from the Agency. And who's job was it to determine the likelihood of you actually *going* back to look at a mosquito without permission: Sherman Hinkley's. In truth, Sherman was the closet thing to a judge and jury that ClockWorks had on its payroll. No one could even *think* about taking a vacation back in time if Dr. Sherman Hinkley didn't authorize the vacation by signing off with his approval on the mandatory psych evaluation. Wally was responsible for finding people once they got lost: Sherman's job was to find the problems before they began. And he now had only a few laserized stitches to go before he could start.

"All set, Mr. Hinkley. And look at that, we have a minute to spare," Sato said as he brushed Sherman's hair over the surgical area. No one gave it a second thought anymore that what was once a time consuming, major brain surgery now could be performed in a matter of minutes. "Hopefully your first day doesn't treat you too badly, sir."

"I think I'll be okay, Dr. Sato," Sherman replied. "After all, I am a *doctor*, ya know." Sato just smiled, removed his surgical gloves and proceeded to clean up the room for the next patient.

"If you need anything else Mist--*Doctor* Hinkley, please make an appointment with my secretary and we'll see if we can squeeze you in sometime that day," Dr. Sato said as he ushered Sherman into the waiting area. With his memories now preserved and his tie re-tightened, Sherman bid farewell to the good doctor and exited the laboratory.

He had a little over twenty minutes before ClockWorks was officially open for the week, and he figured he'd take that time to review any files he might have waiting for him on his computer. *Oh yeah, I forgot!* As he was approaching his office door, Sherman remembered that he would have two other office assistants working under him. *Surely they weren't here already.* He reached his office and immediately noticed the freshly polished name plate on the door. "Sherman Hinkley: C.H.I.M.P." He never considered that as the new Chief Head of Investigating Malicious Purposes, he was, essentially, ClockWorks's newest C.H.I.M.P. *I guess that makes Wally the new C.H.U.M.P, then*, Sherman giggled to himself. Not wishing to prolong his office debut any further, Sherman clutched the brass handle to his new home-base, pushed down on it, and walked into his professional sanctuary.

"Oh shit! I mean, good morning, sir, I mean, Mister, I mean Doctor, Hinkley, sir, good morning!" exclaimed a young, collegiate looking man who shot up behind his desk the instant the office door opened. "I'm, uh, Lester Whitman, sir, your intern."

Sherman guessed that his desk was the large antique slab in the back of the room in front of the giant wall length mural of ClockWorks's emblem, a face of a clock without any hands: Harper's attempt to depict timelessness, or the arbitrariness of time, or the fact that he had no hands or something like that. Lester obviously belonged to the workstation he now stood behind, but the desk right next to it remained unoccupied. *Weren't there supposed to be two interns?* Before Sherman could ask why the desk was empty, another young man burst into the room up to his chin in manuals and other assorted documents spilling out from between the pages. "And I'm Harvey Douglas, sir, excuse me." Harvey unloaded his arms on his desk before walking over to Sherman with an extended hand. "It's a pleasure to meet you, sir. Les and I have been looking forward to working with you, Dr. Hinkley. We both have followed your work ever since your days at Cross and really appreciate your insights on the ethics of prosecution with regards to cases involving diminished capacity."

Sherman was clearly taken aback. "You've read my work? And, you app--appreciate it? Well, thank you both, very much. I'm sure I'll learn as much from you as you apparently have learned…from me," he said, clearing his throat. He wasn't used to such overt admiration for anyone let alone for something *he* had done. "How long have you two worked here?"

"Oh, well, we've each been interns for a little over a year," Lester eagerly responded. "Dr. Malcolm Poe hired us fresh out of college and when he retired a few months back, the Agency consolidated our departments and we've been working together here ever since. It's been hard, to tell you the truth, not having a real *boss* like yourself, sir, but we've managed alright. We know the Agency pretty well by now, so if you need anything, just ask us!" *A simple "year" would have sufficed,* Sherman thought, but he forgave Lester's excessive verbosity. Sherman was certainly honored to be working with two such ambitious, educated young men.

Harvey decided it was his turn to speak up next. "You have three PCs--oh, sorry, that means 'potential customers'--to evaluate by noon, but other than that, you're just supposed to familiarize yourself with the policies of the department and take some time to personalize your work space. We usually do lunch around 12:30 so if you have any sugges--"

"Whoa, slow down there, slugger!" *Slugger, really? Was this kid twelve?* "Why don't you guys just give me a second here to at least test my chair out before we start planning the lunch menus for the week?" Sherman couldn't believe how much authority the Agency had thrown in his lap. Never in his life had he walked across a room with more moxy and clout in each step than he did at that moment. He laid his briefcase on his brand new solid birch and veneer office desk complete with glass top and optional hutch, pulled out his brand new ergonomic air grid seat manager chair with adjustable padded arms, sat down, and rolled himself up to his workstation. He leaned back in his chair, clasped his hands behind his head and with a prolonged sigh of contentment, said to his--*his*--new employees, "Now, gentlemen. Tell me about these PCs." After nearly half a century, Sherman Hinkley had finally arrived.

Two hours north of ClockWorks, a young man wearing dark blue denim jeans, Birkenstock sandals and a faded old presidential campaign sweatshirt was fueling up his car for a little drive down south. He had an appointment with a Miss Eternity Alcott at 10:00 a.m. on the second floor of E.W. Harper's ClockWorks TTA in Indianapolis. Assuming the traffic on I-65 this time of day wasn't too heavy and that the impending rain showers would hold off, he would probably arrive at the

TTA right on time. He topped off the tank, looked over his itinerary for the hundredth time since booking his trip six weeks ago, said a quick prayer for safe travels, recounted the $24 in his wallet, and pulled out onto the interstate. His first vacation in nearly ten years was truly going to be a trip he'd never forget.

Five
The PhD. vs. the PCs

"There ought to be something very special about the boundary conditions of the universe and what can be more special than that there is no boundary?"
-Stephen Hawking

"Men's courses will foreshadow certain ends, to which, if persevered in, they must lead,' said Scrooge. 'But if the courses be departed from, the ends will change. Say it is thus with what you show me."
-*A Christmas Carol*

Traditionally, when a potential customer wished to book a trip with ClockWorks, the application process was a lot like applying to college for the first time; the PC would have to fill out an overwhelming amount of forms and surveys, comply with an endless list of rules and regulations, submit to mandatory medical exams, undergo an extensive psychological evaluation and, of course, qualify financially. Those were the safeguards Harper had implemented when ClockWorks first opened in 2018 to protect the organization from any ludicrous lawsuits or financial burdens, not to mention protect humanity from a life-threatening, temporal paradox. Over the years, however, with advances in time travel technology and stricter supervision by the *International Coalition on Time Travel, Pollution, and Child Abuse* (but mainly as a result of some of those snafus Lamar had discussed while in training), ClockWorks had modified its application procedures to include only a psych exam, completion of a much shorter version of the original application, and adherence to the punctilious financial requirements. After all, these were peoples' *vacations* we're talking about, not rocket science; no need to be too meticulous with formalities. Still, nobody wants a bunch of poor, crazy, illiterates traveling back in time.

Second Hand Out

Perhaps the greatest change in how ClockWorks qualified PCs for their trips was with regards to the type of clearance they now received. When Harper first developed the concept of a fully functional TTA, he envisioned two types of clearance: Dickensian and Zemeckalian. Essentially, the former would be a form of time travel very similar to the schematic framework prevalent in Charles Dickens's classic novel, *A Christmas Carol*. That is to say, as with the ghosts of Christmas past, present, and future (as well as Ebenezer Scrooge himself) the time travelers shall remain unseen and unheard while on their vacations. They would be impervious to any and all tactile or olfactory sensations such as climatic conditions or other events that would otherwise kill them (some people enjoyed seeing Mt. Vesuvius erupt, for example). Therefore, they would basically be nothing more than silent observers of the historic events unfolding all around them. The first problem to surface with Dickensian clearance came in the form of caloric consumption. Logically, since Dickensian travelers couldn't touch anything on their vacations, Harper had to create a way for them to eat while on their lengthier trips; a day back trip in time to see an event or two at the first Olympic games is one thing, but what if someone wanted to see the better part of the first Crusades? Surely they would have to eat something, or else they'd starve! To deal with this inevitable scenario, Harper devised a means by which PCs could reserve certain meals in advance of their trip which would be delivered to their destination by special ClockWorks agents. For example, if a Dickensian PC wished to see what life was really like for Anne Frank and other Jewish refugees during the Holocaust, but wanted to spend more than one leisurely afternoon in the attic, a ClockWorks Agent would periodically travel back as well, under Dickensian clearance, of course, to deliver food personally to the travelers. Obviously, the customers were allowed to bring as much food or drink back in time with them as they wished, but since most ClockWorks travel packages included complimentary meal delivery service, few refused such an offer.

The vast majority of customers fell within the parameters of Dickensian clearance. Harper felt that most PCs would appreciate any chance to go back in time *at all* and not split hairs about being unable to communicate with "the natives" or be killed in a volcanic eruption or mauled by a lion. After all, Scrooge's entire life was changed simply by seeing a poor family shed tears over an empty chair and a crutch without an owner; and he didn't even want to time travel. *Imagine what witnessing Moses part the Red Sea could do to the heart of paying customer!* Still, like Dickens, Harper recognized that attempts to travel to the future would only cast upon a traveler the shadows of things that *may be only* and not necessarily the shadows of events that *will* be definitely. Therefore, he never experimented with traveling into the future. Harper felt that no ascertainable benefit could derive from knowing what *may* happen someday; only events that have happened in the past will aid us in our shaping of the future. But was it possible to actually go back and *reshape* our past? Harper knew for a fact that it was.

And so, the second and far more classified brand of clearance was Zemeckalian Clearance, or ZC. This mode was modeled very much in the same vein as the conception of time travel immortalized in the *Back to the Future* trilogy. While Harper knew that Stephen Spielberg was arguably the most recognized name affiliated with the trilogy insofar as production was concerned, he felt it necessary to pay homage to the men who actually wrote the films: Robert Zemeckis and Bob Gale. What Zemeckalian Clearance granted (and Dickensian Clearance prohibited) was the corporeal manifestation of the time traveler in the time to which he or she was traveling. In other words, under ZC, a customer could talk to, hear, and be heard by anyone; eat, drink, and be merry in whatever time period they chose; kill or be killed. In short, with ZC, a person could really screw things up for a lot of people! For this reason, only individuals who qualified under the strictest of ClockWorks's judicial scrutiny were granted this mode of clearance. For years, Harper toyed with the notion of disabling ZC all together, as he felt the potential risks outweighed the potential benefits. However, in keeping with the vision of his "Beginning of Forever" speech, Harper ultimately continued to allow distribution of ZC as a vehicle through which scholars could interact with history's greatest figures and from them, learn as much as they could about our past as a people. Months of botched ZC trips and several near temporal catastrophes quickly flooded the headlines, however, and Zemeckalian Clearance was banned shortly before Harper's death in 2019. Only certified ClockWorks ACHEs and specified governmental officials had authorization to use ZC, and in these cases, permission had to be given by the President of North America as well as ¾ of the *International Coalition on Time Travel, Pollution, and Child Abuse.* This is why every new ClockWorks employee still was required to get the hippocampus preservation implant; better safe than sorry.

The clearance limitations on PCs nowadays sure made things easy for Sherman. Since the current timeline was no longer in any real danger of being manipulated by a rogue time crusader with an agenda and Zemeckalian Clearance, all Sherman really had to do was look out for people who may go back in time to spy on the secret location of a buried treasure or perverts who only wanted to watch famous people have sex with each other on a gondola in Renaissance Italy. These were, of course, real possibilities with real practical and ethical consequences—you wouldn't want some bad guy going back in time, find the hidden location of the Holy Grail, and come back knowing where to find eternal life now would you?—but even still, Sherman could rest easy knowing *he* couldn't screw things up too badly for ClockWorks. Brilliant though he was, Sherman never could deal well with large amounts of responsibility. Especially when his actions may have cataclysmic ramifications, Sherman tended to shy away from the frontlines of adulthood. Despite the plunging economic climate of the last twenty years, Sherman knew deep down that he could've very well found *some* job as a psychologist, even if it wasn't in forensics. After all, during times of immense economic or political strain, most people find solace in venting their concerns to an impartial listener. Sherman made up his mind long ago, however, that when push comes to shove, he would rather give people free advice with their French fries than live with the death of a single patient on his conscience. His mother used to accuse of him of only going to graduate school in order to avoid becoming a productive member of society, but he always bypassed her scathing critiques by reminding himself that he was, indeed, smarter than most people. *I'll make something of myself, one day, they'll see!* As Sherman perused his first PC of the morning, he hoped his day had finally come.

When Sherman clicked on the file labeled "Chestnut," a video box popped up on his screen and Sherman could see the taped application of what he guessed was Mom and Pop Chestnut and family. An over-caffeinated Mrs. Chestnut greeted her invisible audience while the rest of the family stoically sat and smiled at the camera. Sherman laughed at how they were all dressed in the same matching outfit for their big time travel application debut: khaki pants, white Oxford shirts, brown shoes and plaid blazers. *So last millennium,* Sherman thought. He put his elbows on his desk, rested his head in his hands and turned the volume up on his monitor, prepared to be utterly enthralled.

> "Hi there! We're the Chestnut family! I'm Harriett, hello! And this is my husband Frederick and these are our boys Irving and Nathan. We're from Sandusky, Ohio and have been wanting to come to Indianapolis to visit ClockWorks and maybe take a little vacation for about three years now. Um, oh yeah, our boys have been learning about dinosaurs in school and even though they've seen videos of real life dinosaurs from some past ClockWorks customers, my husband and I would positively LOVE to spend a day in our home town of Sandusky, about 65 million years ago. All we would need is the 24 hour package for four people. My husband works for the postal service and does have *Zemeck—is—tian* Clearance with your organization but for our trip, we wouldn't need that at all. Dickensian is fine with us! Wouldn't want to be stomped on now would we? HAHAHAHA!! If there's any chance we can book a trip for sometime before school starts, that would be great! Our number is--"

Sherman didn't need to see anymore. *I wonder how many people want to see the damn dinosaurs?!* He printed out the Chestnut's application, signed the bottom of the page marked Psychological Evaluation and had Harvey deliver it to Eternity on the second floor. Once Harvey left the room, Sherman immediately kicked himself for not using the Chestnut file as the perfect opportunity to get to know Eternity. She may be stupid, but smarts don't mean shit in the sack. Sherman took a giant breath in and leaned back his chair, raising his hands to the sky: a demonstration of sorts for his first successful psychological evaluation as ClockWorks C.H.I.M.P. Lunch was soon to come. Sherman looked at his watch to see how soon he and his—*his*—team could go out for their afternoon meal. *How can it only be 8:15!?* Sherman could have sworn auditing the Chestnut file took at least two hours, but then again, he only listened to about thirty seconds of the video. *Oh well, lunch will be here soon enough.*

The next application Sherman reviewed offered a much more complex insight into the mind of a potential time traveler than Sherman had ever anticipated encountering. Starkly contrasting the Chestnut's All-American family science trip, the second application proved that time travel serves purposes other than the somewhat idealistic pursuit of knowledge or exploration. When he clicked on the folder labeled "Jacobs" and hit the play button on the video box, an elderly woman popped up on screen. She had snow white hair, wrinkled, age-weathered skin, and the bitter consternation of a woman who'd spent her life following Sisyphus up the mountainside only to be steamrolled over by the magnificent boulder as it fell back to the beginning of its vicious, perpetual cycle. She took a sip of water, smacked her lips, and began her story.

> "My name is Eliza Jacobs. I was born on January 31st, 1979 in a little town outside Little Rock, Arkansas. Two hours after I was born, my father was killed a half-world away on the island of Morichjhanpi in West Bengal, India where he had been working as a missionary for eight months. My mother had been by his side for the majority of her pregnancy, but when the political

situation shifted from bad to worse, my father demanded that she return to America and bring his daughter into this world in safety. He never knew his wife succeeded in her task because at the time of my birth, my father was violently being evicted from the Sundarbans by a group of CPM government officials. Along with hundreds of other Indian refugees, my father was slaughtered in the evacuation. He never made it off the island or back to the 'safety' in which I was born.

Because we had no money and my mother had very little education or marketable skills, she and I were forced to move in with my dad's brother, Billy, in Atlanta. Now, I never knew my father, so all those nights when my mother would keep my awake with her violent episodes of nocturnal sobbing, I just laid in my bed trying to understand how a man who was trying to do good could have been treated so badly. I was so young. I was stupid. God knows I wanted to, but I never could bring myself to feel her pain. What I wouldn't have given to be able to take at least a shred of it away from her so she could live her life the way he would have wanted her to. He never would have wanted her working three jobs to support us in her brother-in-law's rundown shanty. He would have hated knowing that his brother would drink so much during the day that at night he would come home when my mother was working the third shift and have his way with me and beat her within an inch of her life if she were home. My father never would have wanted *Uncle Billy* to have a child with his widowed wife against her will and name it after "the missionary hero" who died over in Asia. He never would have wanted me to grow up not ever knowing the love of a father or the pain of a mother or the feeling of a home beneath my feet. He never would have wanted my mother and me to live in fear of his own blood running through the veins of a ripe Georgia monster. My father would have wanted better for his family.

But I survived. I survived that evil house and the devil that lurked behind its rotting walls. I survived the death of my mother when I was only 17 and I survived the cold streets of Charleston where I lived for two years before being accepted to an art institute in New York. I survived the financial burdens of college in the twenty-first century and *God Damn It* all, I survived my childhood. Of all my family, my "brother" included, I was the only one who survived.

So I want to go back. I want to see, with my own eyes, how it all began. I want to see the single event that stripped my soul of normalcy and condemned me to walk this Earth crippled from deep within. I want to see what my father saw the minute I was born. I want to see him die in the mangrove forest in that God forsaken island so many miles away. I want to see what he died for and I need to see-- I need to *know*-- why I should forgive him for not coming back with my mother, for not holding me when I was cold, for not--"

The video went black. *Did I hit the stop button?!?* Sherman frantically searched his screen for anything resembling a "proceed" command. He couldn't find one. The abrupt stopping of the film was like a clap of thunder in the middle of the night, waking Sherman from the subconscious spell of Eliza's saga. The woman's story wasn't like the usual time traveler's. It didn't involve recreation or useless, self-indulgent explorations. No, this woman was different. Her story was…important. It was genuine. "Lester, do you have any idea why this application just cut off like that?"

"What's that sir," Lester came bolting over from his intense game of desert solitaire, "Oh, yeah I see. Well, there're a couple of explanations. Most likely, whoever this was accidentally hit the stop button on her computer while she was recording."

"No, that's not it, she didn't move at all," Sherman replied. *How did he know it was a "she"?*

"Hmm. Well, there is a maximum time limit for video applications. Maybe the system just shut her down after the time expired. How long was it?" Lester asked. Sherman looked at the clock again.

"I don't know, five, six minutes tops. I really need to see the rest of this if I'm going to make an informed decision about her!" Sherman demanded. He was dying to know what else she meant for someone to hear.

"Of course, sir, let's see, here," Lester examined the screen with the precision of a surgeon seeking a tumor on an x-ray. "Well, I don't see anything here that suggests it's the camera or the computer. The only other thing I can think of is that, for some reason, she was deemed psychologically unstable for time travel and they vetoed her file. But that's only happened, like, one time ever, I think." Upon saying that last part, Lester's eyes bulged from his skull the way a man's do when he accidentally lets it slip that he's been having an affair with the maid for six months. Sherman couldn't believe what he was hearing. Did Lester just tell him that someone *else* could veto a PC based on psychological instability? Wasn't that Sherman's job? Why the hell was he hired then? What was he supposed to *do* with those applications if he didn't have full authority to authorize or reject them?

"*What* did you just say? What do you mean someone can—who has the—is this woman going back or not? I NEED TO FINISH HER EVALUATION!" Sherman was furious. Harvey had just returned to the office from delivering the Chestnut application to Eternity and immediately could tell something was wrong.

"Everything okay in here, guys?" he cautiously asked, his words falling on broken eggshells.

"No, Harvey, everything is *not* alright. Lester here was just about to answer some questions for me and I'd like for you to stick around to see if you can help him out." Both of the interns gulped. "Lester, is she or is she not going back in time *per my recommendation as this agency's only certified Forensic Psychologist* to witness her father's murder?"

"Actually, sir, probably not," Harvey interjected from across the room. Sherman couldn't take his flaming eyes off of Lester who stood in his place shaking like a boy who just got both hands cut off in the cookie jar.

"Why the hell not, Harvey!?" Sherman screamed, still piercing Lester's stare with his raging pupils. The video's importance exponentially grew with each second Sherman failed to retrieve it.

"Sir," Harvey replied. The monosyllabic pseudonym operated as a sort of remedy which brought Sherman out of his heated trance. Sherman relinquished his visual stronghold on Lester and turned to face Harvey. "Sir," Harvey repeated, "there's nothing we can do about that now. That woman—Miss *Jacobs,* was it?—she was denied her request for a vacation not because she was deemed *psychologically unstable*," Harvey shot a disgusted glance toward Lester, who diverted the subliminal message by turning his sights to the floor, "but for reasons that have nothing to do with you, your position with the TTA or your current status as our resident CHIMP."

Sherman didn't understand any of this. *Who did this guy think he was? How did he know Eliza's name? Why did it take him so long to get back from Eternity's? Didn't it take him a really long time? It did, right? And why the hell was her file sent to his computer if he was never supposed to have anything to do with it?* "Then why--"

"Let's just say that it's personal, Dr. Hinkley," Lester declared, clearly trying to redeem himself with a still disgruntled Harvey.

"*Personal*, Lester?" Sherman sneered; Lester, he could handle.

"Personal, sir," Harvey swung back as calmly as ever. "As far as we're concerned, it's just personal." Despite all of Sherman's years training himself to accurately read situations and decipher peoples' inner psychological motivations, Harvey's mind was as still as a lake on a winter's morn. "But the good news is you now have only one more PC to review before lunch. The file should be all ready to review on your computer. It's a good one too: real hottie from Chicago. Wants to go back and see some of history's greatest nude beaches for a college term paper she's writing on mating habits or some shit. I skimmed her app when it came in last week. She is *fine*, yo! Hope you don't mind me lookin' at it, sir."

Sherman had never seen someone switch on and off so effortlessly between being an abrasive, secretive government conspirator and a 21 year-old fraternity boy. He was completely dumfounded; Was the Jacobs issue still up for discussion? Had the entire argument ever even occurred? *One minute we're discussing occupational integrity and "personal" agendas, the next we're joking about boobs in pop culture vernacular. And when the hell is lunch?!?* Sherman took a second to consider his options; He was standing in the back of a windowless office on the 17th floor of a military run time travel agency with two younger men who'd each worked at ClockWorks for a over year standing between him and the door. He could call his boss, who hated him, and confess that within his first—*twenty?*—minutes of work he'd encountered a situation that he couldn't handle. He could dismiss the entire situation and simply continue with the Chicago hottie file but, in doing so, would establish an unwanted precedent of unequal power distribution between him and his interns. He could run to Wally and cry about Eliza Jacobs and have Wally just hold him for the rest of the day. Or, he could grow a pair and fight back!

"Which way to the bathroom?" Again, Sherman was never sharp under pressure.

Harvey looked at Lester, and Sherman knew that the smile on both of their faces signified their shared perceived rhetorical victory over their new boss. "Just down the hall to the left, sir. You can't miss the sign right next to the IDM Room. That's the Ionic Dyhro--"

"I know what it is, Harvey, thank you!" Sherman snapped back. What nerve this little bastard had: explaining to him, *Dr. Sherman Hinkley,* what the Ionic Dyhydrogen

Monoxide chambers were. “Thank you both so much, but if you’ll excuse me, I’ll be right back!” Harvey stepped aside as Sherman hustled out of the room, loosening his tie in the process. He knew exactly what he was going to do. As soon as he’d left the building, he’d get into his car and drive the seventy six miles north to his mom’s house and have her make him some cookies. He did it forty years ago on the first day of kindergarten when no one was nice to him at snack time and damnit, he’d do it again today! *Forget this place! Forget Harper’s!* Sherman had already had enough of his illustrious career as a TTA employee. It was time to retire. As he charged out of his office, though, and took a step toward the elevator, he slammed into the body of an unsuspecting yet strikingly attractive young woman.

“Oh, Dr. Hinkley, excuse me, sir, but I was coming up to look for you,” said an out of breath but beautiful blond woman wearing a nametag bearing the name ‘Eternity Alcott.’

“For me? Well, why would *you*—what, what can *I*—well, here I am! Ya found me!” Sherman comically proclaimed, throwing his arms in the air in a mock exhibition of submitting to police capture. As a courtesy, Eternity giggled at Sherman’s lame attempt at a joke.

“I see that, yes. Dr. Hinkley I was wondering if you could, like, do me a huge favor--”

“Love to, Miss Alcott, really I would, but you see, I um, am sort of late for an appointment!" Sherman began to dash for the closing elevator at the end of hall.

“Whadya think of that second application?” Eternity shouted at the fleeing doctor. Sherman froze in mid stride. He turned to face the Agent who repeated her question, this time with the look of a prosecutor who just found the hole in a witness’s testimony. “What did you think of her, doc? Did you think she was pretty? Did you think she was *sexy*?” *How did Eternity know about Eliza? Weren’t the psych evaluations supposed to be confidential? Sexy?!* Sherman scanned the hallway for onlookers as he slowly walked back to Eternity.

“Uh, no, actually, I couldn't finish watching it because it went blank." Sherman whispered. “Do you have any idea why it just shut off like it did? How did you--”

"What do you mean it just shut off? She told me she previewed the video before she turned it in and it worked fine…" Eternity responded, visibly puzzled.

"Uh, no it shut off right before she was about to explain why she wanted to see her father murdered."

"Her *what*?!? Dr. Hinkley, what the hell are you talking about? I'm talking about the *second* video…the one after the Chestnut's…with the girl from Chicago?"

"Oh yeah, that one. No, no, I haven't watched that one yet. But what about--"

"Pity, isn't it, Sherman," Eternity cut him off. *Sherman*? "Oh well, I'm sure you'll enjoy it later. She's a friend of mine and she's just *dying* to, like, come here and see what I do and stuff." Sherman nodded in place, growing more and more aware that he had absolutely no idea what any of these TTA people were thinking. "Oh well, at least that's all you gotta do before lunch. Long mornings, aren't they?" Eternity complained, her face consumed by the same vacant facade that she wore during the welcoming meeting. "Gosh, Sherman, isn't it, like, so cool that *I* can send you whatever psych evaluations I want to? I mean, like, even though I can't read the files myself, like somehow I just *know* which ones you'll so love to review. It's like I'm psychic or something!" Eternity was two seconds away from twirling her hair around her finger and blowing a monstrous bubble of pink gum out of her mouth. She restrained, however, and the pause in the conversation made Sherman want to ask her if she knew anything about the Jacobs file. Before he could muster the words, however, Eternity asked again "Now, Sherman, how about that favor."

"Yeah, what is it? No wait, before you tell me about that, what do you know about the Jacobs file?"

"The Jacobs file? The Jacobs…the *Jacobs* file? Uh, I never sent you any Jacobs file, Sherman."

"Yes you did! I had three psych evals in my inbox this morning and one of them was this application from a woman named Eliza--"

"Three?" Eliza interrupted. Sherman was getting tired of being cut off. "I only sent you two this morning."

"What? Well then somebody else must have sent it to me. One of the other public agents…" Sherman guessed.

"Mmmm, no, no that couldn't happen because *I'm* the head PA and I have to sign off on everything that gets sent to you." *Why the hell would* you *have to sign off on anything,* Sherman racked his brain. "The only other person who has access to the applications is Gage--"

"GAGE!" Sherman proclaimed. It was now his turn to butt in. "But that makes no sense," he said aloud to himself. "Why would Gage purposefully send me a secret application that he himself manipulated. And I thought he hated me…it doesn't make sense…"

"Yeah, whatever, Sherman, listen I'm in a hurry, okay, so how 'bout that favor, huh?" Eternity prodded.

Since Sherman woke up this morning he had been rendered perpetually speechless by the day's various circumstances. It started with his drastic oversleeping, continued with his late arrival to work and the ensuing encounter with Gage in the foyer--*Gage!* – had persisted during the welcoming meeting, lasted into his confrontation with Harvey and Lester and remained as he stood there outside his closed office door staring into the beautiful yet mysterious sky blue eyes of Eternity Alcott. "Sure," was all he could manage to muster.

"Cool! You rock!" Eternity exclaimed, her spirit instantaneously rejuvenated. "See, I have this appointment scheduled at 10:00 with some guy from Crown Point. But here's the thing, I forgot I have a hair appointment at 9:30 in Westfield and there's just no *way* I could make it back here by then. Since all he's got left to do is the psych eval, I was hoping you could just do that face to face, give him his watch, explain the rules and all that and take him to the IDM Room to send him off?" *Did she just bat her eyes?*

"Um, why can't anybody--"

"Everyone's swamped with other appointments, Sherman! I asked Wally and Lamar and that new fat lady but they all have stuff to do too! Please, you're my only hope, Sherman!" *DID SHE JUST BAT HER GODDAMN EYES?!*

Sherman had no intention of helping this woman at all. Truthfully, he had no intention of ever doing *anything* for the

ClockWorks organization again, especially after the episode in his office with Lester and Harvey and now this fiasco with Eliza Jacobs and Gage. He was about to let Eternity down gently when a family of four got off the elevator at the end of the hall. A clean shaven, muscular man wearing form fitting khaki pants and the official ClockWorks Agent's jacket was escorting the family to IDM Room, tremendous smiles on everyone's faces. It took a moment, but Sherman soon recognized the family. "Aren't those the Chestnuts?" he leaned in and asked Eternity as the family walked past them.

Eternity rolled her eyes, "Yeah, that's them. The mom drives me crazy, but the kids are cute, though. Since you signed off on their eval, they're headed back for their trip now. Can you imagine: a whole day with *dinosaurs*? Boring! It pisses me off how some people just wanna do boring school stuff here. Like, *hello people*, we're a *travel agency!* Seriously, take a vacation once in a while!"

Seeing the anticipation and uncontained excitement seeping through the pores of the Chestnut children reminded Sherman of how thrilled he used to be about the prospect of time traveling when he was younger. Despite what Eternity was mumbling on and on about, he knew that what this family was doing was exactly what E.W. Harper had invented the TTA for in the first place. Even though the Chestnuts were a little on the obnoxious side, at least they were taking the opportunity to use ClockWorks as a way to learn about the world. And the fact that they were doing it as a family made Sherman feel all the more eager for a career with the Agency. In a period of sixteen minutes, ClockWorks's newest CHIMP had gone from dedicated employee, to threatened boss, to disparaged victim, to object of a young woman's love (maybe), and all the way back to empowered, renewed, and loyal public servant. All it took was seeing a family on vacation: a vacation that wouldn't be possible if he hadn't earned a PhD. and used it to authorize their trip. Only at a time traveling agency can complete mental revolutions happen so quickly.

"Tell me more about this Crown Point kid, Eternity. I think I can clear my schedule by then."

"Oh my God, thank you soooo much, Sherman, I love you! It'll be so easy, I promise, any idiot could do it!" *I don't doubt that,* Sherman thought. "Besides, I already called him and told him he'd be meeting with you instead so it would totally suck if he thinks I lied!"

"Don't worry about it. It's my pleasure." He modestly replied. "How hard could it be to a give a guy a watch, right?"

Six
Time, it is a Changin'

"I smile when I'm angry, I cheat and I lie. I do what I have to do to get by. But I know what is wrong and I know what is right, and I'd die for the truth in my secret life."

-Leonard Cohen

"You got heart, but you fight like a god-damn ape. The only thing special about you is ya never got your nose busted - well, leave it that way, nice and pretty, and what's left of your mind...Hey kid, did ya ever think about retirin'?...You think about it."

-Burgess Meredith as Mickey Goldmill, *Rocky*

"Did you guys hear Sherman's got his own office and two interns working under him? Lucky bastard, he must be havin' the time of his life!" Unlike Sherman's cushy digs up on the 17th floor, Wally, Lamar and Isabelle were given a renovated hotel suite to share as an office. Because Sherman was the only member of the team who had a direct influence on whether or not an application was approved, Harper's management deemed it prudent for him to have his own office. The other three, by contrast, were stuck on the first floor of the building, wedged between the honeymoon suite on their left and the free-weight section of the ClockWorks gym on their right. It wasn't all bad though; they did have their own bathroom and occasionally they were told room service would mistakenly deliver meals to their door, but no one was holding their breath for that one.

As ClockWorks's latest CHUMP, Wally's morning had turned out to be about as work-filled as Sherman's. Since Zemeckalian Clearance was now banned to all but a select few…and since very few of those select few ever managed to actually get lost in time…and since when someone *did* get lost in time, it was up to the ACHEs to actually go back and retrieve them, Wally's job responsibilities as Chief Head of Unintentionally Misplaced Persons were fairly limited. Essentially, they entailed finding the occasional lost puppy running around the building or locating a wandering toddler if his parents were at the bar drinking their vacation away on delicious Midwestern microbrews. A professor of Chemistry from the University of Michigan, Wally Emerson had always envisioned that his decision to abandon academia for a career at Harper's would elevate him to mythical and uncharted realms. Instead, at 46 years old, he now sat in a former hotel room with nothing but eight or nine feet of concrete separating him and his eclectic colleagues from the Indianapolis public sewer system.

Lamar and Isabelle, attempting to at least make the most of their unorthodox surroundings, had been hard at work since they arrived in their "office." Isabelle immediately began crunching ClockWorks's first quarter numbers, paying extra close attention to the Division of Medieval Inquiries. Lamar had spent his morning planning potential day-trips for local school children. At one point, Wally managed to catch a glimpse of one of Lamar's ideas. Apparently, Reverend Newton carried deep in his heart a special affinity for the ancient religions of South America and had coordinated several possible afternoon excursions to witness a few Incan rituals of animal sacrifice and sun worship.

"I'm sure he's doing just fine, Walden," Lamar said, keeping his eyes focused on his itineraries.

"You do realize, of course, that anything you write over there has to be okayed by me, right?" Aside from budgets and ledgers, Isabelle's other responsibilities included ensuring that any new travel package or itinerary fell within the ClockWorks patented "policy of excellence." Personally, she took pride in knowing that on her watch, no travel package would be authorized that involved mundane trips back to Iowa in 1956 to watch corn grow. The packages had to be exiting and intellectually worthwhile. Even though no one in their right mind would ever *want* to go back to Iowa in 1956 to watch corn grow, with Isabelle Stowe at the helm, they'd never even be granted the chance.

"Yes, of course, Isabelle, I realize that. I was just drawing up some basic schematics of what I would like to do if and when you do okay my plans," Lamar calmly replied.

"Schematics?" Wally butted in. "Jesus, you make it sound like you're designing a satellite!"

"The name is 'Lamar', and if by 'satellite' you mean 'a manner by which people can see more of the world than previously possible,' than I guess that's exactly what I'm doing." This exchange of witty repartee was getting on Wally's nerves.

"Yeah, well, my job is to find 'misplaced persons' and frankly, I don't see too many people getting lost around here." In times of great boredom, Wally had the emotional stability of a twelve year-old girl who just found out the boy she liked was moving to Alabama to marry his cousin.

"*You* seem to be almost losing it, Walden," Lamar returned.

"*Excuse* me?" Wally volleyed back.

"Oh please, would both of you just stop it!? Do you have any idea how difficult it is to work when you two are bickering like a couple of rabid hyenas?" squawked Isabelle.

"No," the guilty parties answered in unison.

"Well it's pretty gosh darn annoying!" Isabelle yelped.

"Whoa careful, Stowe, that's some pretty PG-13 stuff, there--"

"Walden, why don't you go for a walk and see if you can find some misplaced honeymooners or something," Lamar said in an effort to preserve whatever shred of amicability their work space possessed.

Wally took a deep breath. "You're right, Lamar. I'm sorry, Isabelle. I'll be back in a little bit." And with that, Wally was out of the room and on the prowl. His first order of business: a post-breakfast, midmorning, pre-lunch snack.

With ClockWorks officially open for business for the week, the foyer bustled with the traffic of tourists and time travelers alike. In the concourse area, Wally found the line to the breakfast buffet—complimentary to any of Harper's hotel guests—and took his spot behind the last person. *I am technically staying in a hotel room,* Wally thought to himself. As the line quickly shortened and Wally wound his way around the sausage and egg cart, his ears took notice of all the conversations happening around him. An older couple evidently had just returned from being guests at their own wedding fifty years before. They were holding each other and joking about how much skinnier they used to be. Over by the entrance to the *Harper's Museum of Popular World History*, a group of teenage girls were discussing the first stop on their spring break vacation. Wally couldn't tell exactly when they were planning on traveling but he did hear one of the girls rambling on about how they'd get to see Maddox Jolie-Pitt take his shirt off on set. He guessed they were going back to watch the filming of one the senator's early films, but with kids these days, who the hell knows for sure?

A familiar voice hollered at Wally from over at the pancake and waffle counter. "Don't you have better things to do than spy on people?" Wally spun around on his seat to see Sherman approaching, a full plate in each hand. "I couldn't wait until lunch," Sherman said as he sat down across from Wally at their quaint table near the edge of the foyer. The glass paneled ceiling of ClockWorks flooded the entire lobby with a splendid array of natural, unrestricted light, and while they sat there enjoying their snack, Wally and Sherman each secretly wished they were kids again outside playing baseball…or at least playing a baseball video game in Wally's basement.

"Long morning?" Wally asked, swallowing a mouthful of scrambled eggs in the process.

"Ugh, the longest," Sherman sighed. "I've had, like, *thirteen* or so files to approve, two interns to train, and an enormous office to organize. You?"

"Hell yeah!" Wally ignored the last part about the office. "I can't believe all the stuff they got me doing here. I thought working for Harper's would be fun, but since I got here, all it's been is 'find people, find people, find people'!"

"I know, right! Eternity said she asked you guys about her little favor and you all were too busy to help her or something." Sherman poured another gallon of syrup on his waffles/pancakes hybrid.

"Wait, what? Eternity? The girl from the meeting? I haven't seen her all day," Wally said, his confusion similar to that of a four year-old learning about sex for the first time from the kids at recess.

"You haven't? Well, that's weird. She said she asked you all to meet with her client at 10:00 this morning."

"Nope, not us. Why would she ask us? She's got a whole crew of people who are trained to deal with people. We're just the behind the scenes guys. Yeah, that doesn't make any sense at all."

"That's what I said," Sherman argued, "it makes *no* sense, right?" Wally nodded as he cut up one of the thirty-three pieces of sausage on his plate and stuffed it in his mouth. "Anyway, I said I'd do it," Sherman continued. But then he remembered Eliza and his mood immediately turned more serious. "Ya wanna hear something kinda weird though?" When Wally and his full mouth simply nodded in affirmation, Sherman wondered if he was paying attention to anything he was saying. "So basically my entire job is to watch these video applications and perform a psych eval on each one to determine if they're fit to travel back in time, right?" Another nod from Wally indicated that Sherman should continue. "Well I get this one earlier from an old woman who, like, wanted to go back and watch her father get killed or something. Yeah, I know! Anyway, it really freaked me out to see the pain in her eyes and the desperation she had for getting this…*closure*, I guess…on her life."

"I bet, Sherm, that's rough," Wally mumbled. *Shut up, Wally, grown-up talking.*

"Yeah. So that was really weird. But what *really* freaked me out was that the video just went blank and ended before she could finish her application. It was almost like someone had gone in and pulled the plug on her. I have no idea what the rest of it said. When I went back into my office from talking with Eternity, her file was deleted from my computer. I don't know if they delete automatically when they're done or not. If not, then one of my interns—who are both complete tools, by the way—must have deleted it when I was in the hall."

"But, wait, didn't *you* train your interns? Man, Sherm, you must really be lacking basic management skills," Wally joked. Sherman had already forgotten his lie from two minutes ago. Mentioning Eternity, however, jogged his memory.

"OH, and the thing that's really strange about the whole thing is, ya know how Eternity is in charge of all the applications here because she's head travel agent or PA or whatever? Well, *she* claims she never saw this file I was talking about. She says Gage must have sent it to me because he's the only other person with clearance to manipulate PC's applications."

"Yeah, that is weird, man, I'm sorry." Wally attempted to sympathize but was distracted by how hot the girls by the museum looked from where he and Sherman were seated across the foyer. *They have to be in college at least.*

"What about you? You save any lost souls today?" Sherman asked. Now it was Wally's turn to lie about his morning.

"No not really," Wally started. He learned as a child that it's never a good idea to lie right off the bat; you always want to build into to the charade in order to 1) convey an image of modesty to your audience which in turn ups your credibility and 2) give yourself plenty of time to think about what you're saying first so you don't get caught up in the web of you own deceit. Wally had certainly proven himself to be a liar with a thousand faces repeatedly throughout his life. Over time, however, due to his own perceived invulnerability, his lies became more and more intricate—and, hence, more likely to unravel—that by the time he was on his third marriage, it only took his wife four months to realize he'd been cheating on her with yet another undergraduate coed.

To men like Sherman and Wally, lies had evolved into a sort of discursive second nature, an alternative system of language through which they competed with each other for intellectual supremacy: a mechanism for coping with the harsh realities of an unforgiving world. For years, lies served each of them well as a means of protection from unwanted responsibilities, status elevation and self-assurance. Where honesty lacked a certain degree of finality with matters of dispute or controversy, lies granted the friends a common springboard from which they may loft their discussions into other, more conceptual directions. Instead of admitting, for example, that he hadn't read a certain book, studied a specific scholar, or seen a given movie, Wally would lie and say he had, merely in an effort to not alienate himself from a potential conversation. Since he knew that he would never be held accountable for knowing any of the subtle plot details of a movie or book or be asked to quote directly from any of the scholar's texts because people, by nature, tend to believe others when they say they've done these things, he never had any problems passing as a man well-versed in all matters literary and cinematic.

As he advanced in his carefully crafted enigmatic condition, he exerted great effort to familiarize himself with the vast range of topics circulating within his current milieu, thus insuring his ability to at least carry on a conversation with any*one* about any*thing*. When the conversations exceeded the capacity of his makeshift knowledge bank (as they usually did), Wally could charismatically steer the topic at hand to something with which he was more familiar. Granted, like Sherman, at Wally's core lie the intellect and keen thirst for knowledge characteristic of a true scholar, yet for some reason, he always seemed to rely more heavily on knowing how to convince others he knew the facts than actually knowing the facts themselves. The present conversation with Sherman was no exception.

"No, my morning's been pretty slow. Well, there was this one guy who, get this, missed his transport back from being on Noah's ark and so, like, I guess he had to spend all night watching two of every animal shitting all over the place and what not. Good thing he couldn't smell anything otherwise it would have been pretty nasty. It took me and Lamar like 45 minutes to find him so we could send the ACHEs back to get him." *Shit!* Despite his best efforts, Wally had just broken rule number one of basic lie telling: Never involve someone else without consulting them first! Oh well, it was early. Wally still had the whole afternoon to spit out flawless canards. "So how have your eval's been?"

"Not bad. I haven't really been paying attention. One annoying family wanted to see dinosaurs and the only other one-- besides that old lady-- was this hot chick from Chicago who wanted to go see nude beaches. I just put it on mute and signed off anyway. She seemed harmless."

"Nice," Wally chuckled, "but I thought you said you have like 13 or so to do before lunch?" Part of the game of lying was trying to catch the other in his own logical fallacies. Ironically, it was, more or less, a moral victory to be the "better liar" because you then had the opportunity to call the other person out on his malfeasance. Sherman usually was the loser of these cognitive bouts in which he and Wally would constantly engage, but from his point of view, he pitied Wally. He silently wept for Wally's inability to hold down a decent job, a decent woman, or a decent sense of self. In Sherman's mind, it was ultimately better to be a bad liar but a good person than a bad person with a penchant for skilled deception. Though both men had their histories of spinning wild yarns for no discernible purpose whatsoever, other than perhaps as a means of escaping their own mechanized existence, Sherman never felt he was doing anything other than indulging Wally in his little game: similar to the way a loving father plays action figures with his son even though he'd rather be watching football or bangin' his wife. *It's just part of being a loving father.* Sherman's sense of paternal affection allowed him to justify his personal laziness and lying because he truly felt his presence aided Wally's moral development, even though in reality all it really did was mask his own insecurities and doubt. While Wally acknowledged, often with a hint of arrogance, his slimy, lascivious nature, Sherman rested comfortably believing that no man with a PhD. in Psychology could ever be anything other than morally infallible. His narcissistic tendencies allowed him to dismiss his shortcomings without ever striving to correct them; *they weren't really character flaws as much as they were reflections of the residue left over from associating with Wally's moral corruption.* How unfortunate that Sherman never turned that clinically trained, critical lens on himself. Where Wally willingly thrived in the annals of his own shortcomings, Sherman remained convinced that his life had purpose: that his mind was meant for something extraordinary. No one had ever taught him any better.

"What? Oh, no, I do have 13, well, actually now only 10 left to do. I couldn't do anymore without coming down here and getting something to eat. My interns were driving me nuts," Sherman conceded. *And I'm bored out of mind because I have no work to do.*

"Cool, so hey, tonight ya wanna go see the new Jodie Sweetin fil--"

"Hey Lamar, over here!" Sherman was standing up halfway from his seat, waiving to Lamar who just walked out into the foyer. *Damnit,* Wally thought. A sign of a great liar is when he ever does make a mistake, he keeps a mental note of it so when the time finally comes to rectify the wrong, he's ready. Wally turned around and seconded Sherman's summons.

"Yeah, Lamar, come sit with us. We were just talking about that guy who got stuck on Noah's ark." Ameliorating a flawed lie is a two step procedure. Wally wasted no time checking the first step off his list by confirming to Sherman that Lamar had indeed taken part in the Noah's ark ordeal. He held his mental pen ready to scratch off step two.

Lamar sat down on a seat located on the third edge of the square table facing the foyer. He let out the nervous chuckle of a guy who had no idea what kind of conversation he was walking into. "Yeah? The guy who--"

"Whoa, shit, look at that!" Wally yelped, pointing to a balcony on the fourth floor. Sherman and Lamar jerked their heads in the direction of Wally's outstretched pointer finger.

"What? What are you looking at?" Sherman begged, a note of concern in his voice.

"Oh my God, I thought I just saw Eternity Alcott standing up there naked!" Wally said, pretending to be hyperventilating at the mere prospect of seeing the voluptuous blond in her birthday suit.

"Eternity?!" Sherman said, looking down at his watch. *9:40*. "She's supposed to be in Westfield at a hair appointment by now."

"A hair appointment? Doesn't she have clients today?" Lamar buzzed in. Wally didn't care to hear the rest of Sherman's epic narrative. As far as he was concerned, he could now scratch off step two: divert the attention of the conversation away from the primary lie making sure it will not return to the original topic. When he heard Sherman say "Gage," Wally knew that he was already filling Lamar in on the whole story of the old lady who wanted to murder her father or whatever. He leaned back ever so slightly in his seat, exhaled in relief and continued to watch the hot college girls in front of the museum argue about what to wear on their trip. *Mission accomplished.* Ironically, while liars like Wally spend their whole lives making sure they never get caught, neither Lamar nor Sherman cared either way. The details of Wally's lies were so minute and inconsequential that no reasonable adult would spend their precious time verifying them. The lack of recognition for a beautifully orchestrated verbal maneuver put Wally on the same pedestal with other men who dedicate themselves for a life's purpose knowing full well they will never receive their much deserved credit. To Wally, his ability to weave his way in and out of lies with impunity likened him to other artists who, though brilliant aesthetes, seldom transcended the confines of their medium.

Roughly fifty yards away from where the chimp, the chump, and the preacher were sitting, a young man strolled through Harper's front entrance having made excellent time on his drive thanks to the abundance of sunshine and no rain in sight. His Birkenstock sandals flip-flopped against the marble flooring as he crossed the foyer and approached the Currency Exchange booth on the far end of the concourse next to the museum. Since ZC was banned, there was very little need for people to exchange currency for purposes of time travel. In fact, in recent years the booth often sat open all day without a single customer save for those select few with special ZC authorization or the occasional souvenir hunters who wanted to own some coins from 14th Century France or bills from 1934 Canada. "I'd like to exchange some Indiana Dollars for Deutschmarks please," the chipper young political activist said to the less than sprightly, non-voter behind the counter. Ordinarily the Currency Exchange booth was operated electronically; in recent months, however, Harper's staff thought it more socially beneficial to hire actual human beings to deal with the public. There still were some problems to work out, though.

"When are you going?" The woman—*Edna Fitzgerald*—asked.

"Germany," responded the eager young man.

"Not *where; when* are you going?"

"Oh, uh, does it matter?" The young man asked, now realizing he only had a few minutes before his appointment with Eternity, *no, wait,* Sherman *Hinkley?*

"Nope. No, I guess it really doesn't matter at all, sir. Of course, you want Deutschmarks, right, since you're going to Germany? And since Germany was invented the same exact year as the Deutschmark, you should be all set then, right? Yup. There's *noooooo waaaaaay* you could ever go back in time to the landmass currently known as Germany and *not* be able to use those Deutschmarks as a form of currency, right?" The young man wondered if she was being sarcastic.

"Uh, well, I'm going back to 1822, if that helps." Edna entered some information into the computer.

"Well, bad news. If you want to back to 1822, you won't find any Germany. Nope, the country of Germany wasn't unified as a modern nation-state until 1871. You're a little early on that one, sir." Now he knew she was being sarcastic.

"Okay, then, how's this? I want to go to the Province of Brandenburg in 1822 in what is *now* modern day Germany." He was learning how to play this woman's mind game.

"Well, now, that helps quite a bit now doesn't it?" She typed some more information into her computer whose monitor teased the young man with only a slight viewable angle from where he was standing. "We can do that sir, but Deutschmarks won't do you any good then, sir. Those are *Germany's* currency, and remember--"

"I know, I know," *three more minutes to go!* "Look, just please can you give me whatever form of currency *did* exist in the Province of Brandenburg in 1822?"

"Of course, sir, whatever you'd like!" the elderly woman smiled as though her grandson just asked her to be the guest speaker in his second grade class's "My Hero Day." She performed some brief calculations and then asked, "How much would you like to exchange, sir?"

"Um, I guess whatever this can get me." He removed some loose change from the pockets of his dark blue denim jeans: mostly small bills and assorted coins. Edna took the cash and performed the appropriate conversions.

"That will get you exactly 17 Conventionstalers, sir. Will you be requiring anything else for your trip, sir?" In a strange way, Edna's facetiousness was growing on the young man. However, when he glimpsed up at the clock above the booth, he realized he was running late for his appointment.

"No, this'll be fine, thank you!" He grabbed the Conventionstalers with his left hand, did a triple body tap with his right (butt for wallet, left pocket for keys, right for cell-phone), turned around, and sped away from the booth. He almost had a clear line to the elevator when, from out of nowhere, he was blindsided by a tiny little man wearing a mismatched suit and a butt-ugly sunshine tie.

"Oh my God, are you alright?" The fashion criminal winced as he picked himself up from lying on the floor.

"Jesus, man, you almost killed me. What the hell?! You gotta be more careful!"

Sherman was taken aback by the overly rude nature of the young man. "I know, I'm sorry but next time why don't you *not* be such an asshole and run out in front of me like that! You made me late for my appointment." Of course Sherman didn't realize that if he would have left the table a few minutes ago instead of leaving three minutes *after* his appointment, the collision never would have occurred.

"What?! Whatever man, I'm outta here. I got an appointment too," the young man said as he turned and headed toward the elevator.

"Psshaw, *whatever,* yeah whatever to you too, *man*! Hey, you can take off the sweatshirt now; she lost, okay! Get over it." The two were now neck and neck in their vigorous pursuit of a ride upstairs.

"Oh, I get it! I should've known you were a *Moses* fan."

"Hey, President Martin has been doing an excellent—what floor?" Sherman asked. The two were now standing alone in Harper's world famous glass elevator.

"Seventeen, thanks. I swear if I'm late because of you…"

"Oh calm down, son, it's not like it's a matter of life and death, ya know." The door closed in front of them. The two men rode in silence to the 17th floor where each was running late for a very important appointment.

Seven
Mondays with Sherman

"Of course! November 5, 1955! That was the day I invented time-travel. I remember it vividly. I was standing on the edge of my toilet hanging a clock, the porcelain was wet, I slipped, hit my head on the sink, and when I came to I had a revelation! A vision! A picture in my head! A picture of this! This is what makes time travel possible: the flux capacitor! It's taken me nearly thirty years and my entire family fortune to realize the vision of that day. My God, has it been that long? Things have certainly changed around here. I remember when this was all farmland as far as the eye could see! Old man Peabody owned all of this! He had this crazy idea about breeding pine trees."
-Christopher Lloyd as Dr. Emmett Brown, *Back to the Future*

"Mistakes are the inevitable lot of mankind."
-Sir George Jessel

As President Moses Martin was nearing the end of his first term in office, he often found himself basking in the glow of his own popularity. His approval rating had never been higher and it appeared as though a landslide victory the following November was inevitable, despite the fact that under Martin's administration, teenage pregnancy reached all time highs, along with rates of illiteracy and inflation. Martin's economic policies left the nation in fiscal peril and on several occasions he'd gone on record saying he was avidly opposed to any form of minority hockey players. And yet, notwithstanding his racist tendencies, budgetary recklessness and general disregard for the sanctity of human life, the American public adored the man, for it was also under his administration that TTAs like Harper's became publicly funded. No longer did Waverly have to disgrace himself by pleading with private donors for funds necessary to instill the future of his little company. With Martin's backing, TTAs around the world not only received the funding they needed to remain in full operation, but their renewed visibility prompted a tidal wave of time travel enthusiasts, the likes of which Waverly had never seen, who flocked to the Agencies in swarms to book their next vacation through time.

Not long after Martin's 2064 inauguration, everyone, at least to some capacity, recognized the name E.W. Harper, and children on all corners of the globe knew that the only way to get to the beginning of forever was to look for the watch with no hands. The Clockworks emblem became as pervasive and synonymous with Harper's as the two round ears on the black hat were with the Disney Corporation. Almost overnight, Indianapolis became the mecca of temporal research and exploration with Harper's reigning as the world's frontrunner in all things time travel. Waverly's salary tripled while the influx of new employees at his disposal cut his overall job responsibilities in half. Indeed the Harper's family enjoyed three unprecedented years of prosperity and affluence. But as with the sons of Jacob, ClockWorks too would eventually experience a nearly crippling financial famine.

To make sure he could cover the astronomical costs of his 2068 campaign, President Martin allocated government funds to pay for his commercial advertisements, international goodwill missions and journeys to the moon to speak in front of the seven U.S colonies established 2.56 km south of the Copernicus Crater. The gauche redistribution of funds caused organizations like Harper's and the EPA to absorb heavy financial hits which, in turn, threatened to shut down the respective companies. Only through the ingenious strategic plan of Stanford economist, Maxwell Clemens, could Harper's weather the dust storm caused by Martin's second run at the presidency. Needless to say, toward the end of Martin's first term, the relationship he once enjoyed with President Waverly had evolved into a slapdash charade of cheap promises and cheesy smiles. Martin, however, vowed that when reelected, he would handsomely reward Harper's for its perseverance when faced with adversity and unwavering support of Martin's dream for America. Waverly still wasn't quite sure what that the dream was, but as long as Martin kept footing the bills, he really didn't care.

Few moments in life are as awkward as walking into an elevator with a man whom you just took it upon yourself to hate, then walking down the hall with that same man, only to stop at your office door and realize he's the guy you're supposed to have an appointment with for which you are late…because of that man. Indeed, this was an awkward moment for all parties involved.

"*You're* Dr. Hinkley?" the young man asked, hoping to God the name on the door referred to another man waiting patiently inside for his tardy arrival.

"One and the same. You must be," Sherman just realized Eternity never mentioned his new client's name, "tired from your trip from Crown Point." *That was a close one.*

"Not really. A little sore though from when you ran into me downstairs." *First Harvey and now this punk; What was it with kids today?!*

"I'm sorry, I didn't catch your name."

"Will." The young man had just exemplified author Tom Wolfe's sentiment that beginning around the turn of the millennium, last names no longer served any practical social purpose.

"Ah yes, *Will*, of course. Well, then, Will, why don't we step into my office and…" he wasn't sure what exactly he had to do. All Eternity said was something about finishing up paperwork, "do this thing." *Really? Did he just say that*?

Sherman was pleased to see that Harvey and Lester were gone. The good doctor escorted his first ever live patient to the rear of the room where they both had a seat at Sherman's desk. After Sherman opened Will's file on his computer, he looked at the young man and began. "So, Mr. Bauer, it says here you wish to go to Germany…traveling with one of our nine hour packages this time, I see. Good choice, they're on special this month!" Sherman was treating this as if he were selling the poor boy toilet paper and a can of tuna. *On special this month? Where the hell did that come from?*

"Yeah, I know, look, I already went over all of this with Eternity. All I need is my psych eval and my watch thing. I've already paid and everything and I'm ready to go: so, like, can we just skip ahead?" The watch thing…the watch thing…*Oh shit!* Sherman had forgotten where the watch things were. He suddenly found himself missing the aid of his two interns, tools though they were.

"We'll get to those matters in a second, Mr. Bauer. Do you…I mean, did Eternity mention what type of clearance you'll be given for your trip?" Sherman assumed the PhD. next to "Hinkley" on his name plate would ward off any potential suspicion from Will that he was, in fact, a moron. Will's blank expression, though, didn't do much to enhance Sherman's confidence. "Where do you work, Will?"

"I work for the Justice Department for the State of Indiana. Is there a problem or something?" Will was getting pushy. Still, he did have a government position and from what Sherman remembered from training (as well as his discussions with Lamar) people who work for the government were awarded Zemeckalian Clearance. *Right?*

"No, no problem at all, Mr. Bauer. And why is it that you want to travel back to…Germany with us today?" Sherman was confident that Will had no idea he was totally winging this whole thing! "Special Indiana State government business, I imagine?"

"Uh, actually no…look, it's all in the file right in front of you." Rather than wait for Sherman to figure out where, indeed, these minor details were, Will sighed and proceeded. "I want to go back to watch my great, great, great, great, great, uh, great grandfather write in his diary. That's all! I know it sounds boring as hell, but he had this diary that kept track of all my family's land and financial history and all our family tree too, and some pages from it are missing. No one in my family knows where they are, but there's this gap on June 14th, 1822 and, well, my dad would go back himself to see—it's probably nothing—but he thinks it would be good for me to go and, ya know, see the family and what not. So, yeah, that's pretty much it. Just a diary."

After the third "great," Sherman's mind began thinking of what he and Wally would do once they left work for the day. He didn't pay attention to a word of what Will was saying. The kid looked harmless enough. He didn't exhibit any of the classic signs of a pathological sociopath or child predator. Why he needed Zemeckalian Clearance was beyond him, but hey, rules are rules. Will was entitled to all the benefits ClockWorks could provide. Sherman inhaled deeply and scrunched his face as if he had just eaten a sour grape; the way pediatricians do when they're pretending to be serious with their patients but really are about to tell them only to be nice to their parents and eat plenty of vegetables. "Well, Mr. Bauer, I see no reason why I shouldn't give you my fullest recommendation for a trip back in time to see your family's dairy farm." Sherman failed to see Will's confusion. "So, let me just print off your approved file here and deliver it to--" Sherman realized that neither his interns nor Eternity were available to take Will's file. "Well, hell, I'll just keep it here on my desk for now. Why don't we go get your watch now, how's that sound?" *Don't forget your sucker at the nurse's desk.*

Sherman and Will left the office and walked down the hall to the entrance of the IDM Room. Aside from the requisite Harper's tour on the first day of training so many months ago, this was Sherman's first time near the temporal chambers. The custodial staff was cleaning up from the last transport which must have included several people because water was spilled everywhere near the submersion tank. The IDM Room contained two vast tanks of water similar in size and appearance to the dolphin tanks most zoos used to have before dolphins became extinct. One tank was labeled "Departures" the other, "Arrivals." E.W. Harper had devised a system of time travel that functioned as a product of cognitive energy, tremendous amounts of electricity and nearly ice-cold water. In 2010, he began experimenting with chimpanzees in his laboratory at Purdue University in West Lafayette, Indiana. After thousands of preliminary trials, he eventually discovered that even in chimps, when the brain processed a neurological code consisting of a specific time, date, and location at precisely the moment an electrical current was sent to the part of the brain that processed the code; and as long as the external conditions of the chimp itself were such that they could serve as a viable conductor of that supplied electrical current and the brain waves that responded to the original message, the chimp would be transported to the exact time, date, and location of the neurological code.

Since there was no way to ensure the chimp would process or "think" of the TDL (time, date, and location) in the same manner a rational human would, Harper and his researchers had to create a way to make sure the chimp would travel to the TDL of their choosing. Using the available technologies of the day, Harper would send digitized signals directly to Area 4 of precentral gyrus in the chimp's primary motor cortex. Simultaneously, Harper would also send massive amounts of electrical current surging through the chimp's brain. This technique accomplished very little aside from angering a great deal of innocent chimpanzees and eliciting the wrath of PETA, the FDA, and NATO.

It wasn't until February 10th, 2016, after nearly six years of failed trails and when Harper was at the end of his third grant that he made the discovery of a lifetime. As with many unprecedented historical breakthroughs, this one too was born from a brief tryst with Miss Serendipity. Harper's latest chimp, Abraham, was seated patiently in his chair, hooked up to dozens of loose electrical wires attached to his brain, waiting to be shocked into oblivion. In the corner of the room, one of Harper's assistants was preparing a piece of toast for breakfast. When Harper called her over to help begin the experiment, she forgot her toast was still being cooked. The billowing smoke emerging from the top of the toaster eventually set off the above sprinklers at exactly the moment Harper and his assistant triggered the switch to jolt Abe's brain with the digital TDL and the electrical volts. Abraham vanished in a brilliant flash of light and an ear shattering crash. It took him several minutes to reappear on the other side of the room, perfectly intact though, Harper thought, a little embarrassed by the looks of him. E.W. Harper had done it; he had successfully teleported a living specimen across an underground research laboratory. But did the chimp go into the future or did the transport simply take longer than anticipated? The answer, Harper would discover, was found in factoring in the temperature and volume of the surrounding water; *that* was the missing variable!

Harper's first successful *time* travel experiment came nine months later in the aquatic center in Purdue's Co-Recreational Facility. Abe, still in good ole' spirits, was harnessed into all the appropriate apparatuses; over the better part of the previous year, Harper's team constructed a sort of dipping mechanism similar to the anti-shark cages of the twentieth century. Only these were entirely enclosed and water tight. Once the chamber was completely submerged in 33.33 degree water, a TDL code would be sent from the command center through the wires, down into the water, through the carefully sealed hole in the top of the chamber and directly into the subject's brain. At the same time, the chamber itself would become electrified via the command center, and, like an item in a microwave, everything inside the chamber would undergo an intense chemical reaction culminating, *unlike* a microwave, in the transportation of the chamber's contents to the previously determined TDL. The event would conclude with, essentially, an implosion of the chamber resulting in a terrific splash of freezing water out of the tank; the whole process always reminded Harper of the last scene in *Jaws* in which the mechanical shark explodes in the water, sending hundreds of gallons of Amity Island ocean to be hurled into the cool summer's air.

On Christmas Eve 2016, Harper's dream was realized at last. The theme of the day: success. The mission: send Abe back in time ten minutes into a locked closet on the other side of the pool. Harper realized that if his experiment was successful, all he would have to do is walk over to the janitor's closet on the pool's opposite end, unlock the door, and find a version of Abe sitting there, ten minutes older than the one who was sitting in the chamber prepared to be dunked in the pool. In an effort to not spoil the surprise, Harper vowed not only to fire anyone who unlocked the door before the experiment was complete, but to fire *at them* with the WWII Navy deck gun he supposedly owned and kept in his den at his home in Lebanon, Indiana. Needless to say, everyone stayed near the command center.

When Harper flipped the switches, Abe's chamber imploded, water flew from the tank and onto the floor of the natatorium, lights flashed, and sparks flew. When the action finally subsided, an empty chamber bobbed peacefully in the freezing pool water. (Harper's engineers designed the chambers to withstand their own implosion so that they may be used on more than one occasion.) Harper didn't wait for the applause to stop; he leapt down from his elevated platform, ignored the cries from the custodial staff to not run by the pool, sprinted over to the janitor's closet, inserted his key, and flung open the door. Inside sat Abraham, clearly miffed that it had taken Harper *ten minutes* to let him out of the dark closet.

Fifty years later, the IDM Room on the 17th floor of E.W. Harper's world famous ClockWorks TTA still stood at the precipice of human technological imagineering. On average, the tanks next to which Sherman and Will now stood sent and received about 175 chamber loads a day. To return to the IDM Room from a trip back in time, Harper's team had to create an alternative means of time travel; history, after all, offered very little insofar as the availability of mechanized, electrified imploding chambers submerged in tanks full of freezing water. To overcome this obstacle, Harper developed a prototype for the *STOOPING Piece:* a watch-like structure that essentially served as a homing device that was electromagnetically tethered directly to the departure TDL which almost always was the IDM Room. Conceptually a glorified GPS system, the STOOPING Piece—SP—didn't require freezing water or a connection to brain tissue to be transported through time. Instead, it was programmed with the traveler's return TDL code, and when the command center (which stored the *original* TDL) emitted a homing signal formatted specifically for each respective SP, the SP would begin to blink green. The blinking lights on the SP warned the traveler that the SP would soon be "pulled back", so to speak, to the original departure TDL. If the traveler was standing in their designated location when the SP began to blink red and, of course, if they were wearing their SP, both the device and the traveler would be safely transported back to their return TDL where they would land inside the IDM chamber in the "Arrival" tank on the 17th floor of E.W. Harper's ClockWorks TTA. It's all just as simple as that.

Well, this just doesn't make any sense at all! Sherman was confused. "What do you mean it's already in the system?"

"It's, um, already in the system, sir. Mr. Bauer's TDL has already been programmed and we're just waiting on the Departure tank to be cleaned before we can begin. It should only take a few minutes. Though Sherman couldn't argue that the IDM Room employee was acting in a courteous and professional manner, he had no idea how Will's file had already been sent to the IDM computer system and been programmed. *I thought I left on my desk?* Sherman assumed he would have to explain Will's itinerary manually to the IDM staff and yet, when he approached the command center to report Will's destination, he was told it had already been programmed into the system. *Lester or Harvey must have done it,* Sherman realized as he climbed down to greet an anxious Will.

"Everything alright, Doc?" Will asked.

"Oh yeah, everything's fine! I just needed to make sure the chambers were still watertight. Last week a girl nearly drowned on her way back to the 1893 World's Fair in Chicago." *Where the hell did that come from?*

"Oh…thanks," Will said, unsure where the hell that came from. "Don't I get a watch or something?"

"Oh yeah, of course, your special ZC watch. Here it is." Sherman removed the watch from his pocket and handed it to Will. Sherman couldn't believe the fuss the guy's upstairs made about giving *a government official* Zemeckalian Clearance! *Don't they know the rules?* Will had every right to talk, hear, and do whatever it was a guy with ZC could do while on his vacation. Will apprehensively accepted the watch and put it on his wrist. He rolled the sleeve of his sweatshirt over it, never giving it another glimpse. "Now remember," Sherman said, "when it starts to blink green--"

"I know, thanks; I can read, ya know." *Out of the mouths of babes and sucklings,* Sherman thought to himself. "What time should I expect it to do that though?" Will asked.

"What, blink green? Um, well you paid for a nine hour package so," Sherman quickly did the math. "I'd say right around 7:00 or so. That should give you plenty of time to see how they milked back then." Again, Sherman failed to see Will's utter confusion.

"William Bauer, please report to Departure Deck 1, your chamber is ready," said a soothing female voice over the IDM Room's loud speaker. Saying "Departure Deck 1" had a certain appeal to it, even though, in reality, there *was* only one departure deck. Will climbed the stairs to the top of the platform and entered his IDM chamber. Once seated, a crew of Harper's employees strapped him into his cushioned captain's chair and placed the electrodes on the appropriate sides of his head. When Harper himself would do this procedure fifty years prior, the placing of the electrodes was an arduous and time consuming process; the slightest millimeter off could have jeopardizing effects on the life of both the experiment as well as the subject. However, the process now had become such second nature to the Agency that the employees almost threw the wires unto Will's head with a casual air that made even the naïve Crown Pointer somewhat nervous. The employees checked to see that the electrical cords were running smoothly through the sealed hole in the top of the chamber so that the necessary voltage would reach Will's brain. Lastly, they strapped Will's feet down to the bottom of the chamber so that when the vessel itself became electrified in the water, the energy would run up his body as well as down from his brain, thus guaranteeing a full anatomical transport.

When they were done with the initial checklist, one of the employees patted Will on the shoulder, gave him a single thumb up the way NASA engineers would give Apollo astronauts a thumb up before takeoff, stepped out of the chamber, and sealed the door shut. Sherman watched from the command center as Will's chamber dipped into the chilling tank of water. He could hear the engineers behind him going through some basic procedural measures before they began their countdown. Rather than prolonging the anticipation of their guests, IDM technicians were taught to begin their countdown with three. Seconds later, the engineers flipped their switches and two waves of energy—one containing a departure TDL code, the other bearing thousands of volts of electricity—flowed through their wires into the IDM chamber. A third wire electrified the chamber itself, and moments later, Will's time machine vaporized in a blinding coruscation and deafening crash. Water shot into the air and landed on the observation deck as if a giant orca had just splashed into the tank. When the currents in the water finally ebbed and eventually stilled, IDM technicians rushed to retrieve the now empty but fully operational chamber floating in the middle of the tank. Will Bauer was now safely back in 1822 Germany.

The last thought running through Sherman's mind as he departed the IDM Room was how the German citizens would react to Will's faded "Suri Cruise 2064" Presidential Campaign sweatshirt. *Stupid, kid,* Sherman chuckled to himself; *I wonder why he didn't wear something more conducive to a German dairy farm.*

Eight
Halleluiah, It's Noon at Last!

"It contributes greatly towards a man's moral and intellectual health, to be brought into habits of companionship with individuals unlike himself, who care little for his pursuits, and whose sphere and abilities he must go out of himself to appreciate."

-*The Scarlet Letter*

"The quest stands upon the edge of a knife. Stray but a little, and it will fail, to the ruin of all. Yet hope remains, while all the company is true."

-*The Lord of the Rings*

With Lamar, Wally, and Sherman congregating in the ClockWorks Food Court for the second time since arriving at work only five hours ago, Isabelle Stowe was once again left with nothing but her work and her appetite to keep her company in the office. Already that morning she had accomplished the primary task for which Harper's had hired her in the first place: coming up with more cost efficient methods of transporting people back to the Middle Ages. It turned out the algorithmic complexity of a Medieval TDL code was such that the command center mainframe took 1.56 times longer to process that particular destination than virtually any other time period. Thus, as Stowe uncovered, each trip cost Harper's exponentially more money for really no reason at all. To bypass the problem, Stowe transmogrified the Medieval TDL code to something much less complicated in order to shorten the time it took the command center to process the transport. The entire project had kept Isabelle occupied until 10:15. She killed the next two hours examining past ClockWorks brochures and berating them for their lack of aesthetic appeal and poor choices of persuasive verbiage. After 45 minutes of that monotony, she evaluated three of Lamar's proposed field trip packages (all of which she despised) and when Lamar and Wally left for lunch around 12:03, she realized she was not only done with her work for the day, but with every assignment ClockWorks had assigned to her for the next three months. After five minutes of sitting alone in her cramped workspace, she decided it was time for her afternoon meal.

For a Monday at noon, the ClockWorks "Cuisine Emporium" was packed. Hundred of people flooded the foyer on their way to vacations, the museum, the gift shop, or the bathroom. Almost as if they'd never left, Lamar, Wally, and Sherman sat at their square table near the edge of the atrium area across from the museum and elevator. When Lamar saw Isabelle leaving the buffet line, he guessed she had neither a place to sit nor the nerve to ask for one. "Isabelle! Over here!" Lamar shouted much to the chagrin of his co-workers.

"Why the hell did you do that, Lamar? She hates us!" Wally protested under his breath.

"She may hate *you*, Wally, and I must admit her sentiments are justified with how you've been treating her lately," Lamar responded, calm as ever.

"I've been *ignoring* her lately, Lamar! I can't stand her ever since she got the fast pass through training because she's too fat to run a fuc--"

"Afternoon, everyone," Isabelle declared as she placed her trays in the fourth spot at the table. Wally thought it best not to finish what he was saying.

"Hi Isabelle, have you had a nice morning?" Sherman asked.

"Oh yes, yes. I'm already done with all my work for the quarter, so I'd say it's been a pretty productive day!" *The woman is just useless,* Wally thought.

"Wow! That's great, Isabelle," Sherman replied genuinely, "Sounds like you and Wally have had great mornings. What, with the Noah's Ark guy and--"

"Sherman have you seen Eternity since she got back?!" Wally interjected. *Shit! That was close.*

"Uh, no, but I should probably go and find her. I'm sure she'll wanna meet her client before he goes back home.

Assuming, of course, that he's still here..." Sherman plunged his sandwich into his mouth.

"What do you mean? The guy who left this morning? He's already back? That was a fast trip!" Lamar said, clearly surprised.

"Well, no, it was a nine hour package, but they return right away, right? I mean, like, if you go back in time, it really doesn't matter how long you're back there because when you come back, you'll come back to the moment you originally left, right? So it'll be like you never left even though you could've been away for weeks." *Damn, I'm good,* Sherman thought. And yet, no one at the table said anything. They just stared at Sherman as if he had just confessed he thought he had a chipmunk camping in his large intestine.

Lamar and Isabelle spoke at the same time, stomping on each other's words:

"Uh, no, Sherman, that's not how--"

"Wait, what was the name--"

Like the gentleman that he is, Lamar conceded the conversation to Isabelle. She proceeded. "Thank you. Sherman, what was the name on that PC?"

"Um, Bauer. Will Bauer, why?"

"Because he owes me money, that's why! What are you doing sending people off anyway? Isn't that Eternity's job?"

"Well, yeah, but..." At least Sherman *thought* it had been a great morning. "She said she asked all of you--what's going on--what did I--*Will* do to owe you money?"

"He only paid for a nine hour package but his TDL Codes are for a 16 hour package. He owes ClockWorks *a lot* of money, Sherman!"

Now Sherman was really confused: Will left at 10:00. His SP would go off at 7:00. That's nine hours. Yup, no mistake here. "Um, sorry Isabelle, but I think you're mistaken. You see--"

"What was the return TDL code?" Isabelle demanded. This apparently was no joke.

"The return T--"

"Yes, Sherman, the return TDL code! What was it?" Sherman's face went blank. He never entered a departure or return TDL code. Lester or Harvey must have, but now, Sherman had no idea how to respond to Isabelle's grand inquisition.

"I, I don't really know. I'm assuming it's 7:00 because that's nine hours after he left, so--"

"7:00. You're *assuming* it's 7:00. Sherman, do you even know what a TDL code *is*? It's the exact TIME, DATE, and LOCATION of the time traveler's arrival and departure. It can't just be *7:00*!!" Isabelle looked like a volcano preparing to burst.

"Sherman," Lamar interrupted. *At last, the voice of reason and comfort.* "You can't just send a person back to a random time. You need all three components to constitute a viable TDL code," *Duh!* Sherman thought. "When you say *7:00*, do you mean 7:00 Eastern Standard Time? Greenwich Mean Time? Keep in mind, of course, that the time zones we know and use today weren't even invented until the later part of the nineteenth century, so any destination before that has to have a very specific TDL in order to be successful. Now, Sherman, is it *possible* you sent him back to 10:00 his *destination's* time but programmed his retrieval for 7:00 *our* time?" *It's possible, dad, thanks for the talk.*

"I didn't program any of his codes…"

"WHAT?!?" Mt. Stowe officially erupted in an awesome display of bread crumbs and magma.

"No, no, no, someone else did," Sherman declared. *Don't worry mom, Jimmy's watching the baby!* "One of my assistants! Lester or Harvey: one of them took care of it!"

"Lester or Harvey? LESTER OR HARVEY?!? *TOOK CARE OF IT?!?!*" Mt. Stowe still had some fire to spew. "Well whoever *Lester and Harvey* are, they sent him back for a 16 hour package because *they* are obviously too stupid to understand anything about time zones or TDL Codes or ANYTHING at all!"

"Isabelle, Lester and Harvey are very responsible--" Sherman apologetically proclaimed.

"Sherman." Lamar said, waving his hand in front of his face and shaking his head, signifying that it's best if Sherman didn't continue.

"Well, I guess I just don't get it," Sherman continued to plea his case. "Why can't we just go to the IDM Room and find Will and get him to pay his fee?" At this, Isabelle shot up from her seat, consolidated her trays into one massive heap of sweet roles, croissants, and mashed potatoes and left the table, ash still pouring out of her skull.

"Because that's not how things work, Sherm," Wally said, finally entering the conversation. Sherman's head turned to face Lamar who had a look of disappointment and shame, the likes of which Sherman had never seen.

"When someone goes back in time, Sherman, the trip is in *real time.* A nine hour package means a person is gone *for nine hours*. That's just how the system was created. That's why the return TDL Codes are so important because they're different than the departure codes: in some cases, dramatically different. Harper made the system this way to give people the sense of an actual *journey*. Think about it: you wouldn't want to go back in time for a three week vacation and come back two seconds after you left. You wouldn't feel like you accomplished anything. The world would've just been put on pause while you were away and nobody wants that. A vacation is a time for the world to go on without you so when you come back, it's not as if time stood still. Also, say you went back for an extended period of time and returned to the exact moment of your departure. Your body would be that much older than the rest of your fellow humans who never took the trip. My twin could go back in time for a month and come back two seconds after he left and he'd actually be *older* than me. Make sense?"

"You have a twin?" Wally asked. Lamar just ignored him.

"So you see, Sherman, we can't *get* Will until it's his time to return which, according to Isabelle just now, will be in about…14 hours, or 2:00 am tomorrow morning." Papa Newton's wisdom was vast and deep.

Sherman sat at the table and shrugged. *Why didn't he know any of this?* He went through training just like everyone else. He loved time travel and studied it ever since he was a kid. Why now after so many years of research and study was he so far out of the Harper's loop? As he racked his brain with a morning's worth of questions, three answers got off of the elevator at the other end of the atrium. Lester and Harvey were walking with Lt. Gage over to the buffet line.

"Excuse me guys, but I gotta go ask my interns over there some questions." Wally and Lamar glanced over and saw Gage standing in line next to two younger men who they assumed were Sherman's interns.

"See ya later, Sherm. Good look with Isabelle if you see her again," Wally said, the voice of a true friend. Sherman rose from his seat and clamored over to Lester, Harvey, and Gage, unsure of whom to interrogate first.

"He thinks you did it, sir. That's what Lester told him," Harvey was whispering to Gage. Sherman's presence had not yet been detected by the three buffet line occupants.

"And did he believe you?" Gage replied, the concerned countenance of breeched national security on his face.

"I think so, Lieutenant. I'm not entirely positive but he seemed to lose all interest in the matter when he came back into the office from talking with Miss Alcott," Lester replied.

"Ah yes, and what is the word on her?" Gage asked.

"Still nothing, sir, but we're working on it," Harvey assured his boss.

"Eternity? She had a hair appointment in Westfield this morning. She should be around here somewhere by now," Sherman chimed in. The other three simply stared at him, examining him from head to toe, wondering how long he'd been standing there and how much of their conversation he'd heard.

"How long have you been standing there?" Gage demanded.

"How much of our conversation did you hear?" Lester and Harvey followed.

"It's rude to eavesdrop, Hinkley. You're always bound to miss some vital information," Gage prophesized.

"I know, I'm sorry, I just heard Eternity's name that's all," Sherman said to Gage. Then to his interns, "Hey, which one of you programmed the TDL Codes for the Bauer file?" Sherman had never seen faces similar to the ones Lester and Harvey expressed in response to his question. It was a mixture of utter confusion, fear, embarrassment, anger, and a smidgen of condescension, with just the slightest hint of insolence. Sherman knew that his expression must have looked the exact same way.

"The *Bauer* file? Oh, I'm sorry, sir, that was me. I sent the codes to the IDM Room before Harvey and I left for our meeting with Gage. *G-Germany* right?" Lester finally replied.

As if disciplining a small child for sneaking out of the cafeteria to go to the bathroom, Gage said to his employee, "Next time, Lester, be sure you inform Mr. Hinkley here--"

"*Doctor*, Hinkley, sir." Sherman couldn't believe his ears. Had he just corrected Gage in front of subordinates? Sherman didn't know much about the military chain of command or anything like that, but he did know that you never question, correct, or interrupt a superior military officer in front of expendable peons like Harvey and Lester.

"I beg your pardon, Mr. Hinkley?" Gage said. *You did* what *to my car?!*

"Excuse me, sir, but I am a Doctor. That's all. I, um, just wanted you to know that I am, in fact--"

"Mr. Hinkley I served under General Burgess C. Breckenridge in the Alaskan Revolutionary campaigns of '23, '24, and '25 when you were still sucking milk out of your evidently poor excuse for a birth mother. I watched countless friends and loved ones die in those battles, but I'll be damned if the General didn't grab me by the balls and throw me out onto every frontline advance he could muster. He appointed me Lieutenant because of five separate accounts of bravery and courage on the Fairbanks battlefield. Therefore, I *earned* the right to be called 'Lieutenant.' *You*, Mr. Hinkley, have done nothing with your life but read books and write essays which, I might add, are poorly worded, argued weakly, and often contain little or no relevance to our current cultural climate. You depend on your so-called 'PhD.' as a means to somehow transcend yourself above your own circumstance, but rest assured, Mr. Hinkley, you are no more a *doctor* than I am a chimp like you. The sooner you can realize how little your worthless degree means to me or this agency, the better."

"Is that why you destroyed the Jacobs file, sir?" Sherman firmly asked. *Nobody messes with my mother!*

"The Jacobs file should have never been sent to you in the first place, Hinkley," Gage replied. "It has nothing to do with you, your position with the TTA or your current status as our resident CHIMP." *That sounds familiar,* Sherman thought. Then Gage leaned closer to Sherman than either one of them considered appropriate and stared deep past his frightful eyes back into his soul. "It behooves you to not concern yourself with that woman's file any longer, Mr. Hinkley. Do you understand?" Sherman nodded. "Good. Mr. Douglas, Mr. Whitman, shall we bring our lunches up to my office? And don't forget, men, no more sending over Mr. Hinkley's TDL Codes without notifying him, first." Lester and Harvey nodded at the Lieutenant's order. The three proceeded through the buffet and up the elevator to Gage's lair.

When Sherman's gaze returned to his table on the other side of the room, he saw that it was empty. Wally and Lamar had since left to return to their afternoon's work in their suite. As Sherman stood alone in the bustling foyer, his heart winced thinking about the events that had just transpired in which he had been heavily outnumbered and antagonized not only by his asshole boss but by the very people who were supposed to be on his side. Sherman didn't care about the Jacobs file; he didn't care about the TDL Codes. What mattered most to Sherman at that moment was how quickly Gage's comments had eroded away his sense of validity and self-worth. How dare Gage belittle Sherman's accomplishments like that! Who the hell did he think he was? Who was he to criticize anyone? What did he know about forensic psychology or assessing competency or malingering and deception? True, Sherman had never testified in court or evaluated a single client or even sat in on a sentence mitigation proceeding, but Sherman *knew* how to do all of those things! He received a doctorate from the most well-known forensic psychology program on the east side of lower Indianapolis! *He was a doctor, for crying out loud!* Traditionally, Sherman's default method of coping with disparaging comments was to deny the validity of everything said and retreat into his own private space in which his degree *did* have merit. He *was* an accomplished doctor from a prestigious university and his employment at Harper's was *not* some bureaucratic fluke, but rather reflected his unique abilities to single-handedly make the company prosper. As he effortlessly slid from self-loathing to self-loving, his nostrils detected the familiar scent of female body wash.

"Psst, Sherman, over here." Sherman recognized Era Howells immediately from the welcoming meeting earlier that morning. In the Archer E. room, Era had been standing directly behind Eternity while she was giving her moving speech. and from the moment Sherman saw her, he was smitten with just how beautiful she looked. She seemed somewhat different now, though, than she did during the meeting: her hair was tussled across her face and her once neatly pressed outfit had accumulated a fair amount of unsightly wrinkles.

"Busy day, Era?" Sherman playfully asked as he walked over to the pillar she was leaning on.

"What? Oh yeah," Era said, realizing he was referring to her disheveled appearance, "I've been moving furniture all day in my office. I guess we're losing somebody so we had to do a little housekeeping. Listen, have you seen Eternity lately?" *Why was everyone asking about Eternity?*

"Um, no, but she had a hair--"

"Yeah, I know, a hair appointment in Westfield at 9:30, but is she back yet? Have you seen her?" Suddenly Era seemed much more agitated. Her eyes darted around the foyer, and for a second Sherman thought she was trying to hide between him and the pillar.

"Uh, no I haven't, why? Is everything okay?" Her eyes were still scanning the room.

"What? Oh yeah, everything's fine. Listen, when you see her, could you give her this. She left it in my apartment last night and she really needs it today for an appointment she has this afternoon." Era gave Sherman a sealed file folder which she insisted he keep close to his chest. *What is it with these people?* Sherman thought. *Why can't anybody do their own work around here? This is, like, my third favor today.*

"Sure, Era, yeah I can give this to her if I see her. But I don't really know when that--"

"Thanks, Sherman! I gotta run. I'll talk to you later!" And run she did. Once again Sherman was left standing alone in a crowded foyer surrounded by people who had no idea just how chaotic and stressful life at ClockWorks really was. *Lucky bastards*, Sherman thought, as he tucked the file under his arm and walked toward the elevator. Peering out the glass elevator on his way up to the 17th floor, Sherman spied an alluring young woman enter Harper's through the front door. He recognized this woman too, but he couldn't pinpoint the exact context. One thing was for sure, though; this chick was definitely a hottie.

Nine
The Traveler from the North

"All men should have a drop of treason in their veins, if the nations are not to go soft like so many sleepy pears."
-Dame Rebecca West

"To die, to sleep;
To sleep: perchance to dream: ay, there's the rub:
For in that sleep of death what dreams may come,
When we have shuffled off this mortal coil..."
-Hamlet, Act III Scene I

When Sherman entered his office, he found his interns hard at work. Lester was on the phone with what Sherman assumed was a new PC, while Harvey was apparently working on a project for Gage. Sherman walked to the end of the room and plopped himself back in his comfy office chair. His post-lunch relaxation time didn't last too long, however, for seconds after Sherman began to adjust himself in his seat, there came a knock at the door. Sherman motioned to Harvey to answer it which, of course, he willingly did. When Harvey pulled open the door, his jaw looked as though it was about to plunge to the floor. There, standing but inches away from Harvey Douglas was the Chicago hottie in the flesh!

"Is this Dr. Sherman Hinkley's office?" the girl asked.

"Uh, y-yes it is, r-right this way," Harvey stuttered. *Ah, young love*. Harvey escorted the girl over to Sherman and announced to his boss that he had a visitor. "Dr. Hinkley, a Miss…?"

"Hi, Dr. Hinkley, I'm Leslie Rowlandson, I believe we have an appointment?" the girl asked. *Appointment? What appointment*?

"Uh, I'm sorry, Leslie, I don't have any appoint--"

"I was told you would already know about the change. A woman called earlier today and told me when I got here, I should come to you and you could help me with my trip." *She just batted her eyes too!!*

"A woman?" *Eternity?* "Oh yes, of course, she told me you were coming," Sherman lied, "Why don't we have a seat here and, uh, get started on your trip. Nude beaches was it?"

"Yeah, that's right," Leslie giggled. "I know it's a little embarrassing, but it's something I have to do for this paper I'm writing for this class I'm in at school."

"Oh yeah? What school do you go to?" Harvey asked from across the room.

"Um, Loyola of Chicago," Leslie replied, unsure why the strange boy was listening in on their conversation.

"Harvey," Sherman simply said. *Quiet, son, grown-up time again.* "So, Leslie, uh," Sherman was clueless about what he was supposed to be doing with her. Where was Eternity? Why hadn't she mentioned *two* PCs? "I'm sorry, give me a second, I--I wasn't expecting you for a while…" Leslie sat in her seat and smiled at Sherman, who looked as though he was trying to decide whether or not to run for the exit. *I wonder if I should just get the hell out of here*, Sherman thought to himself. Suddenly he realized he still had the file folder Era had given him in the atrium. Maybe the file was meant for Eternity's meeting with Leslie. "Leslie, you said someone called you and told you to talk to me?"

"Yes, I think her name was Sara, or something…"

"*Era,* maybe?" Sherman suggested.

"Yeah, yeah 'Era', that's it," she replied. *Perfect!* Sherman knew he had the right file. He tore open the folder and found a few random documents and a computer disc. Ignoring the scattered papers, Sherman removed the disc and inserted it in his computer's CD-ROM drive. Dozens of folders filled his screen. They ranged in labels from "Documents" and "Destinations" to "Whereabouts" and "Aliases." With absolutely no logical rationale informing his decision, Sherman clicked on the folder marked "Aliases." Two columns then filled the screen: one labeled "First names," the other labeled "Last names." As if it jumped right off the screen onto Sherman's pupils, he noticed the name "Jacobs." Out of curiosity, he was about to click on it when he noticed "Rowlandson" three names down from Jacobs.

"Here we go," Sherman said. "Sorry that took a second. These computers are running a little slower today because of a new program we installed over the weekend." *Wally would have been pleased.* Sherman double clicked on "Rowlandson." No sooner had he released his finger from the second mouse click than an excruciatingly loud alarm began going off in the office. Sherman and Leslie slammed their hands over their ears.

"What's going on, Dr. Hinkley?!" Leslie screamed over the roar of the alarm. The fear on her face was not the usual fear one would expect in a situation like this.

"I don't know! Lester, Harv--" Sherman couldn't finish his sentence. When he turned his head to ask his interns if they knew anything about the alarm, he saw Lester and Harvey standing in front of their chairs wearing earplugs, pointing guns at Sherman and his Chicago hottie.

"Whoa!" was all Sherman could get out. He had never had a gun pointed at him before.

Harvey raised his right hand to his mouth and spoke into the cuff of his sleeve. "Sector Alpha Juliet 17 Charlie Echo Delta contained, suspect apprehended."

"Harvey, what the fu--" Sherman began to walk towards his intern.

"Freeze, Dr. Hinkley!" Lester cocked his gun and authoritatively aimed it at Sherman. "This doesn't concern you, sir." *Nothing here concerns me, damnit!* Sherman snarled to himself.

"Okay! Okay! But what's the deal with the alarm?" Before anyone could answer Sherman's question, Leslie reached into her purse and yanked out a device that looked as if it could possibly be a remote control. She was frantically pressing buttons when Harvey pulled the trigger on his gun, sending a jacketed hollow point bullet whizzing past Sherman and into Leslie's shoulder. She dropped the device and fell to the ground, collapsing first on her roller chair before finally hitting her face on the carpeted office floor.

"Stay where you are, Doctor," Lester insisted, anticipating Sherman's retaliation. Sherman had never longed for a crossbow (and the skill and precision necessary to fire one) more than at this moment.

"Wha--What the--You sonofabitch!" Sherman cried at Harvey. At that instant, several armed men broke through Sherman's office door, clearing the area. Each man was dressed in all black with matching helmets and visors pulled over their eyes. Woven into their interceptor body armor were the letters ACHE. The Special Forces had been called into action. As seamlessly as a choreographed ballet, the ACHEs spanned the perimeter of the room in less time than it took Sherman to check his pants for any unwanted discharge. Behind the surge of soldiers, two men entered the room: Emmanuelle Waverly and Lt. Gage.

"Sir! President Waverly, Harvey just shot--" but he couldn't finish. ClockWorks President Emmanuelle K. Waverly shot Sherman from across the room with an officially licensed Harper's Model 6400X tranquilizer air pistol. The last image Sherman had before his mind went blank was the look on Waverly's face as the ACHEs closed in on Sherman's location on the floor: the same look Travis Coats had right after he shot Old Yeller, minus the adolescent tears.

Sherman was back at his apartment. His alarm was going off on the nightstand on the left side of his bed and Lt. Gage was screaming from the kitchen for Sherman to shut the damn thing off. Sherman tried to roll over to terminate the tortuous reminder to awake but his armor-plated back and ridged, segmented body rendered such a task impossible to complete. Unable to bare with the agonizing chirping of the digitized time piece, Lieutenant Gage charged into the bedroom, his moose hunting rifle in hand. Without the courtesy of a final warning, Gage opened fire on the bedridden Sherman. Instead of bullets raining from the barrel of the rifle, however, large, juicy apples aimed directly at Sherman's head assaulted across the room. Utilizing one of his six legs, the doctor formerly known as Sherman ascended his bare walls and scurried up to the ceiling. Gage continued to barrage the room with apples; some skidded safely past Sherman, others he was able to successfully dodge altogether. Sherman's malice only furthered Gage's masochism until finally, after what seemed like hours of endless artillery, Gage landed an apple deep in Sherman's backside. From out of nowhere, Eternity Alcott and Leslie Rowlandson arrived on the scene, both in shock of the condition of the room as well as the weakened state of their friend, Sherman who maintained his hold--albeit with tremendous effort--on the ceiling. Upon seeing the apple embedded in Sherman's shell, Leslie fainted and fell onto the bed. Eternity, on the other hand, began to remove what Sherman considered to be an excessive amount of clothes. When she was completely naked, she sprawled herself on Sherman's bed, looked at Gage, and insisted that instead of continuing to shoot at Sherman, he join her for a little afternoon delight. Placing his rifle on the floor, Gage smiled the smile of all men about to be unjustifiably pleased, looked up at Sherman, and said to Eternity, "Alright, babe, I'll stop. He's just a giant insect anyway!"

"Giant insect!" the monstrous vermin of a Sherman thought to himself as the scene faded away into nothingness. The next thing Sherman knew, he was in an empty land surrounded by nothing but trees and a large lake to his left. He no longer had the body of a giant insect, or monstrous vermin, or whatever the hell he was, but he wondered why there were no people around him. From off in the distance, Sherman heard a loud roaring sound reminiscent of the climatic scenes in the monster movies he used to watch as a kid. Within seconds, a herd of Ornithomimus dinosaurs came stampeding over a nearby hill. Three veloceraptors were chasing the dinosaurs straight into Sherman's path. "Hey, up here, hi!" an obnoxious female voice called from the branch a giant oak tree. Sherman ran to the tree, found his footing, and climbed up to an available space on the occupied branch on which the family of four was sitting. He only narrowly escaped being trampled by thousands of pounds of extinct animal weight.

"Aren't you the--"

"Yup, that's us, the Chestnut family, hi!" The woman said. Her husband and children just sat on the branch and smiled.

"But what are you doing here? What am I *doing here?" Sherman pleaded.* Where was Gage? What happened to Leslie?

"Don't worry about it, Sherman, it doesn't involve a little favor. It has nothing to do with you, your position with the TTA or your current status as our resident CHIMP," Mr. Chestnut said. But it wasn't *Mr. Chestnut; it was Gage! Gage is married to Mrs. Chestnut!*

"Don't worry about it, Sherman, it's already been programmed in the computer," one of the Chestnut children said.

"The muggers, Sherman? A case of the Jacobs file muggers?" said the other child.

"Don't I get a watch or something? I know, I already paid and everything. When can I go to the dairy farm," Mrs. Chestnut asked. The Jacobs file!

"What do you know about the Jacobs file?" Sherman demanded. He looked down from his branch and saw Era Howells undressing by the tree's trunk. When she was completely naked, Eliza Jacobs walked into frame and started to sob uncontrollably. Sherman plunged from the tree in an effort to both stop Eliza from crying and to grab whatever he could of Era's naked body before hitting the ground. He failed on both accounts.

He awoke in Bill's basement. He had never been to Atlanta or to Billy Jacobs's basement but he just knew *that's where he now was. He also knew that Eliza's mother was working the third shift and that at any moment Billy would bring Eliza downstairs and have his way with her. Sherman strapped on the crossbow lying by his foot. Wally was sitting on the couch calling his friends on the phone asking them why the hell they weren't at the meeting. Sherman ignored the 14 year-old Wally; his mission was to kill Billy when he walked down the stairs and listen to whatever Eliza had to say. The blinking, de-gendered human figure at the bottom of the staircase signified that it was safe for someone to come down. Slowly the door at the top of the stairs opened and Sherman could hear footsteps creek down the old, wooden Atlanta stairs. He loaded his crossbow with the aid of William Tell himself, who was standing right behind him. Sherman was relieved to see it wasn't Billy who was carefully descending the stairs but Eliza Jacobs herself. Except, even though Sherman was positive it was Eliza, for some reason, Eliza was walking in Leslie's body which, Sherman freely admitted to himself, was not something he was prepared to complain about.*

"I want to see why he wasn't there for my mother, why he didn't hold me when I was cold. I'm cold, Sherman, so cold. I'm cold, Sherman, hold me, I'm so, so cold. I survived the cold. The cold. I survived this place. He never would have wanted me to be cold. Hold me, Doctor Hinkley, I'm cold. I need you." Eliza's voice was growing more and more ominous (and it was Eliza's *voice!) as she slowly crossed the damp basement floor, nearing Sherman. When she was only a few yards away, Eliza, who was still trapped in Leslie's young Chicago hottie body, began to strip in Billy's basement. "Open the file, Sherman," she moaned. "I need you to rip open the file, now. Fill my file, Sherman, I need you to fill my file!"*

"What do you mean a nine hour package? Lester and Harvey?" Wally was saying on the phone. Sherman reached out to grab Eliza's/Leslie's naked body when Wally threw the phone at Sherman. When it hit him square in the face, though, it broke into a million tiny pieces and fell to the floor like drops of water. Sherman's face was wet. "Sherman!!" Wally screamed. "There he is! He's coming back. SHERMAN! There ya go, Hinkley, you're alright now!"

"There ya go, Hinkley, you're alright now," Emmanuelle Waverly said as he lightly dabbed Sherman's forehead with a moist cloth. It took a moment for Sherman to recognize his surroundings; He was back in the cognitive restoration lab surrounded by Waverly, Lester, and Harvey. Gage was seated in the corner of the room polishing his rifle. Even though its presence was as clear as day, no one spoke of the massive erection protruding from Sherman's wrinkled slacks.

"At ease, son," Waverly said, "nice dreams then, eh?" Lester and Harvey snickered.

"What time is it? How long have I been out?" Sherman groaned, his entire body seething with stiffness and pain.

"It's almost closing time, sir. You've been unconscious for nearly four hours," Lester replied. *Four hours?*

"Wha--" Sherman tried to sit up on his hospital bed. "What happened to Leslie?" All eyes in the room searched for someone to answer Sherman's question. Ultimately, they all fell on Gage.

"The woman you know as 'Leslie Rowlandson' is actually named Kristen Lapham," Gage rose from his chair and proclaimed to the room. "We've been expecting her to make an appearance at Harper's for some time. She's a member of an anarchist commission with whom this organization has been fighting ever since its inception almost fifty years ago.

"An aunt ark--" Sherman muttered.

"*An anarchist* commission, Sherman, yes," Waverly piggybacked Gage. "When ClockWorks first went public in 2018, not everyone condoned the idea of organized time travel. From day one, we've had our share of protest rallies, political campaigns, and even malicious threats, all demanding the immediate dismantling of Harper's and any other functional TTA in the country. With the *International Coalition on Time Travel, Pollution, and Child Abuse* decree of 2019, which mandated that Harper's be the only functional TTA in North America, obviously Harper's received the brunt of public scrutiny. These rogue sects of people have been trying to infiltrate our Agency for years. Their primary goal is to convince the public majority that what we do here has no moral foundation or ethical validity. They seek a means to prove that we have no *real* control of time travel by messing with the very fabric with which our institution has been woven in the first place. They believe that if they can demonstrate, through a botched exhibition of our services, that a TTA is conceptually flawed and has no actual moral, ethical, and practical societal concerns, they'll then be able to shut us down for good."

"So Miss L-Laf--?" Sherman was trying to understand what Waverly was saying.

"Kristen Lapham was one of them," Gage pronounced. "She's the first *real* threat we've had since I started here back in '37. Usually one of our ACHEs can triangulate the location of the next potential attack wave and thwart the threat privately and quickly." *Thwart the threat, thwart the threat, thwart the threat,* Sherman tried to think to himself. "This one, however, somehow knew we were coming for her and made it here anyway. She broke through our system, undoubtedly with help from the inside. She knew about the ACHEs and the standard system of protocol we implement in case of eminent danger." Gage's voice was growing increasingly concerned. It was almost as if he returned home to find his own house burglarized.

"Why didn't you just stop her at the door then? Or flag her when she made her video application?" Sherman challenged.

"Because we have no idea what they look like, sir," Harvey announced. "Trust me; I feel awful right now knowing that I almost let her slip through my fingers."

"What do you mean you don't know--"

"Think about it, Sherman," Waverly said in anticipation of Sherman's question. "We communicate with dozens of different people throughout our daily routines nowadays that live on the other side of the planet. We'll never meet them face-to-face, nor is there any need to see them electronically when we actually do business with them. As long as the business gets done, it doesn't matter anymore what anyone looks like, does it?" *No dad, I never thought of it like that.* "If someone wished to dedicate their life to tormenting our little company here, they could accomplish a great deal without ever having to show their face. Of course, knowing this, our defense department has made certain…contingencies…that protect us from these faceless terrorists."

"The ACHEs?" Sherman posited.

"The ACHEs, yes, are trained and authorized to detect phantom threats and pursue the swift eradication of those threats with the fullest backing of Harper's TTA." *Eradication! I knew it!* Sherman thought to himself as he sat up straighter in his bed. He wanted to ask about Eliza Jacobs and her file and why it was destroyed and why it was sent to him in the first place, but his head was feeling heavier and his mind was still groggy. He slumped back down in his bed.

"But not even the ACHEs could detect Lapham," Gage asserted. "No, sometimes it takes a special type of person to read through all the lines of code and crack a person for what they really are. I don't know how you did it, but you're a hero, Doctor Hinkley. You may have just saved the world." Though Gage still wasn't smiling, he picked Sherman's right hand up and shook it proudly: the sort of congratulatory gesture reserved only for a soldier returned from battle. *Did he just call me 'doctor'?*

Gage stepped away from Sherman. His four hospital guests started to collect themselves in preparation of their encroaching departure. Sherman still had so many questions: where was Leslie, or *Kristen*? What happened to Eliza Jacobs? Why the hell couldn't Wally have seen him get shot? How did Eternity's hair look? Why did Era give him that folder? When's dinner!? ERA! ETERNITY! Era was the one who tipped Sherman about Rowlan—*Lapham's* file! But Kristen was supposed to meet with Eternity this afternoon; or was she? Why didn't Eternity mention that meeting when she and Sherman talked earlier about Will? She did *mention* her friend, but that was it, right? Was there a meeting scheduled or did Era just make that up? But if she made it up, how did she have that file and why would she give it someone like Sherman? Why couldn't she have just met with Lesl—*Kristen* herself? As these ponderings raced through Sherman's blurred consciousness, Lester, Waverly and Gage bid their farewells and exited the hospital room. Harvey stayed behind to give Sherman one last problem to munch on before dinner.

"I called Dr. Emerson and told him what happened. He said he'd stop by before he left work for the day. The doctors say they want to keep you overnight for observation, sir. I'm sorry. I guess those tranquilizers are pretty strong stuff." He was fidgeting with his fingers and looking down at the ground in avoidance of Sherman's eyes. "Sorry if I scared you back in the office by shooting Kristen. I was just doing my duty."

"I know, it's okay, Harvey. I'm sure I would have done the same thing." Sherman's lies carved deeper into his mind's bedpost.

"I'm sure you would have, sir," Harvey said. He turned and walked to the door. Before he exited, though, he stood with his back to Sherman and said over his shoulder, "Oh, and sir; sorry again about sending over those TDL Codes to the IDM Room earlier."

"It's okay, Harvey. I'm sure Lester won't do it again," Sherman dismissed Harvey's apology as a workplace formality:

speaking for the team instead of letting a coworker take all the blame.

"Oh. Right. Lester," Harvey paused. "Yeah, he sent them over." Another pause. "Well, sorry anyway, sir." He pushed through the door and left Sherman alone on his bed, a combination of questions and chlorpromazine hydrochloride flowing through his veins.

Ten
Briefly at the Bistro

"When did Noah build the ark, Gladys? Before the rain."
-Robert Redford as Nathan Muir, *Spygame*

The stubborn clouds finally decided to come out and spill on the people below. After the most beautiful Monday the people of Indianapolis had seen in nearly a week, the sun was now falling, the sky was now darkening, and the rain was now pouring. In a quiet bistro seventeen miles north of Harper's, two women sat at a table, engrossed in conversation. "But you're sure she's okay?" one of the women asked.

"I haven't actually been by to see her, obviously, but yes, I'm told she'll live," the other responded.

"And what about him?"

"He'll be fine. He's being kept for observation all night but his condition hasn't worsened at all so he thinks that by tomorrow morning, he should be as good as new."

"We were so close this time, you realize. Do you think we got too greedy? Was I too careless with the file?"

"No, I don't think so. How could we've known she'd turn on us like that? Was her mom the same way?"

"Of course she was: always taking sides, making alliances and then breaking them to suit whatever flavor she had at any given moment. I just hope she didn't discover too much. Which one of you handled the codes this time?

"I did, and don't worry; I'm not sure how she found the file but there's no way she could know anything about the codes. That part of the plan is working like clockwork."

"Stop it! You know I hate when you do that."

"Of course I do!"

"Just like your mother. So where did you send this one? I swear, if you sent him back to 9/11 again, I'm never going to trust you--"

"Relax! I didn't send back to 9/11 *or* to the Titanic or anything like that. I'm grown up now, remember. I sent him to some town in England: Bishop something."

"'*Some town in England?'* Did you check it out first? Is there any way he could—oh, I know I know, I'm sorry. I trust you. It's just, this used to be easier. All of it. The whole project was supposed to be so simple. Hopefully he'll turn out to be as good as we originally suspected so we can just end it all."

"I have a feeling about this one. There's something about him: something almost childlike. He hides behind his credentials, which I'm not sure he realizes aren't that impressive, but behind the walls he puts up, he's the most genuine one we've ever worked with. His friend may come in handy too."

"Right now let's just concentrate our efforts on getting him on our side. I fear his time with them this afternoon may have swayed him more than we can handle. It will be extremely difficult to convince him to join us if he's already pledged his loyalty to them. He may be genuine, but he's also naïve, idealistic, and arrogant, and based on my experience, that's never a good combination."

"Maybe you could meet him this time? Did you ever think of that? You can't just spend your life teasing these guys with a file! If you want to change things you may have to get your hands dirty, ya know. God knows I have. Oh I have too! You don't know what it's like parading around in there like their little lapdog all the time. You could never understand the way they look at me. Nothing I say or do could possibly matter less to any of them."

"*I* couldn't understand being belittled? Thought less of? Have you *seen* the monument? Have you *read* the speech? Do your research and then come talk to me about what I would or would not understand. You may have to deal with them looking at you all day and dreaming about you all night, but until you've lived a silenced life, you can't talk to me about struggle! If I want to meet him, I'll meet him. After all, it was my idea to track this one in the first place. But I can't easily go strolling through the front door and just ask to go upstairs, now can I?"

"I didn't mean to upset you. I just thought that we have a real chance of doing it this time and I know we won't be able to without his full cooperation and your help. You need to pull your weight this time."

"I know you think it's as simple as that, but now it's complicated. Again, you wouldn't understand. I can't just write off my child with the flick of a wrist like that. I devoted the better part of my life to her, so I'm sorry, but it's not always easy for me to want to risk my life killing her! I lost my husband for her for Christ sake!"

"You could always go back--"

"NO! I will not! That is NOT why she's here and you know it. Shame on you. How dare you even suggest such a thing? That's precisely the reason why we need to--"

"I know, I'm sorry. I didn't mean to suggest that we take advantage of her. Do you think I should go back tonight and check on everything?"

"Absolutely not. They'll be looking for someone to come in and talk to him. You stay away from there whatever you do and go in tomorrow like nothing ever happened. I can trust you with this, right? I want to make sure you understand how vital this is. Stay away from there tonight!"

"I will. I promise. Nothing's going to happen there anyway. I better get going. It's not smart to spend too much time with you. Hopefully this storm will blow over soon and I can get some sleep. Will I see you tomorrow?"

"Hopefully not. Goodnight."

Eleven
Some Last Minute Visitors

"I firmly believe that if the whole material medica, as now used, could be sunk to the bottom of the sea, it would be better for mankind-and all the worse for the fishes."

-Oliver Wendell Holmes

"The ignorance and general incompetency of the average graduate of the American medical Schools, at the time when he receives the degree which turns him loose upon the community, is something horrible to contemplate."

-Charles Eliot, President of Harvard University, 1869

Personally, I never appreciated the moments in popular culture when a young couple agrees to go on a date simply by naming the date and place. "How about the pool hall on Friday?" or "Let's go see a movie tomorrow night!" Rather than continuing along the conversation's logical progression and have someone *ask what time the agreed upon engagement will commence, the directors of these bastardized versions of adolescence felt it believable that the two would simply go on their separate ways only to miraculously meet up again at exactly the right time at precisely the right place. I always wished that just once I would see a television show in which, after acquiescing to her basketball playing boyfriend's request for a date at the bowling alley, the cheerleader would arrive three hours after her boyfriend had left, angry at having been stood up. In a fictional world where temporality assumes such a non-diegetic form as to almost not exist at all, one would imagine such a scenario occurring rather often. And yet, alas, in the realm of television, no one takes the time to consider the preposterous absence of time itself.*

When I began teaching Aeronautical Engineering at Purdue University in 2009, years before I developed the concept of Spontaneous Temporal Obscuring and Observing Potential for which I am now ironically immortalized in the history books, I decided to conduct a little experiment on my first year students. Whenever one of them needed to meet with me I would (assuming I was available) offer my assistance and provide them with two out of three of the following bits of information: time, date, and location. Shockingly, upon receiving their incomplete appointment with me, virtually every student would inquire about the missing component. If I told Dick I would meet him at the library at 3:00, he would make sure he knew what day I was talking about. If Pauline was told to meet me on Thursday at 4:00, she would ask where. The concept of time proved an integral and highly influential component to their daily activities. In retrospect, this revolution makes perfect sense. After all, in everything we do we must make special contingencies for the burdens and realities of time. For example, I know that I can drive to the bank in 20 minutes during my lunch break. However, it takes at least 30 minutes during rush hour and even longer on home football game days. I therefore make the proper adjustments so I can accommodate the fluctuations in the time it takes to complete respective tasks.

Thus, despite the constant distance from my house to the bank, the time it takes for me to travel between the two points remains a function of other, shifting factors. In my seventh year at Purdue, I read an older article written just around the turn of the millennium. The author describes the process of throwing a baseball from a midway point between the pitcher's mound and home plate. Logically, it would take a certain speed for the ball to travel a certain distance in a certain amount of time. Still, if the thrower wished to cast the ball from the pitcher's mound to home plate in the exact same amount of time it took him to complete the throw from a point several feet closer, the speed of the throw would obviously have to increase. Thus, speed functions in response to desired distance and time. Speed, though a desired constant, served as a product of personal agency; the ball went faster because the thrower threw *it faster. Similarly, the decision to determine the initial points of each throw was also a product of the individual's cognitive processing. I extended the position of the article further to wonder if, since speed and distance could, under the proper circumstances, serve as byproducts of the individual human mind, could the same be said for time? In other words, if speed remained a constant, to what extent could time and/or distance be altered simply through our personal desire for it to be so?*

E.W. Harper's personal diaries were stored in the ClockWorks Archives which just so happened to be conveniently located down the hall from the hospital in which Sherman was now staying. Towards the end of the day, Sherman got tired of playing chess with the nursing staff and requested that one of the aids please go to the library and bring him back some reading material. When the nurse returned, she brought with her a few old magazines, some books on Aztec architecture, and one particular volume she thought Sherman would find especially intriguing. As it turned out, this particular book contained the most intimate thoughts of Sherman's childhood hero, E.W. Harper himself! He shooed the nurses out of the room and insisted that he be left alone so that he may devote himself entirely to his reading of Harper's 2010-2015 diary. He had just completed an inspiring section Harper's initial hypotheses regarding STOOP when Wally snuck inside his hospital room.

"Sorry to bother you, Sherm, but one of your interns called me and told me what happened. I meant to be here sooner but I've been swamped all afternoon." In truth, Wally had indeed been swamped: swamped by the seductive clutches of one of ClockWorks's junior PA's with whom he had been gallivanting around downtown Indianapolis all afternoon. The pair managed to catch a movie at the local cinema, visit the historic Civil War Museum located at the base of Monument Circle and even made it back to Harper's in time for a quickie in the employee's lounge behind the Harper's petting zoo. "How ya feelin', bud?"

"Like a rusty old shit shot me in the chest with a tranquilizer gun, how the hell do you think I feel?" Sherman replied, annoyed at both Wally's lack of urgency at hearing his friend was in the hospital as well as the interruption of Sherman's reading.

"I hear ya, man, you've had a rough first day. Listen, I'm gonna head on home, but I just wanted to stop by and make sure you were okay. Do you need anything?"

"No," Sherman declined, "I'm fine. All I have to do is yell and someone will come in to make sure I'm not dead or anything. How was *your* afternoon?" Sherman asked, hoping that Wally would respond with the customary "fine" and leave him to rest.

"Oh, ya know…fine." *Excellent, now get out of here!* "Except I had this guy go missing in the arctic and it took me and Lamar like--"

"Yeah, ya know what, that's great, but I really don't care. No offence, I've just had a really long, hard day, and I kinda just wanna lie here and rest for a bit before tomorrow."

Sherman couldn't believe how honest that was. Not only that, but Wally almost seemed to *respect* it!

"No, that's cool, Sherm, I get it. I'll leave you alone. You take care of yourself and if you need anything at all, just yell." Wally patted Sherman's knee, smiled at his sickly pal, and walked out of the room.

Sherman resumed his study of Harper's diary. Flipping through the pages at random, he came across an entry from May, 2019 that caught his eye. He pulled the book up to adequate reading height and scanned the cursive lines. *May 10th, 2019: Today I lost all faith in humanity. Damn them all.* And that was it. Sherman turned to the next page and discovered it was blank. He flipped to the next page; it too was blank. In fact, as Sherman soon realized, the last written account of E.W. Harper's legacy was a damnation of "them all." Who could "them all" be referring to, and why was Harper apparently so loathsome of their actions? Sherman had always considered E.W. Harper a man of unwavering character and moral fiber. However, this diary entry in no way correlated with the image of Harper as man above corruption, free from doubt and cynicism. The E.W. Harper he knew would never damn anyone, let alone lose his faith in of all things, humanity! *This can't be real*, Sherman thought. Surely some pages were missing from this diary that would otherwise explain his macabre sentiments.

"I see they brought you my book," an emollient voice floated into the room.

"Era? What are you doing here?" Sherman said, growing excited all over. Hospitals inevitably invoked a certain fantastic element into an otherwise gloomy situation whenever an attractive woman entered them.

"I came to see that you received my book. Well, maybe not *my* book, but I told the woman working at the archives to bring this to you when I heard you were going to be stuck in here all night. I thought you might enjoy it. Harper was a pretty interesting character," Era remarked.

"He sure was. I loved when he was talking about STOOP and what originally got him thinking about time travel, but this last page is pretty interesting. Here, check it out."

Sherman gave Era the diary and watched as she read the last brief entry, her eyes widening with each passing letter.

"Damn!" the PA articulated, "this is kinda dark, isn't it?"

"That's what I thought!" Sherman agreed. "It doesn't really sound like Harper to me."

"What doesn't look like Harper?" Eternity Alcott wondered aloud as she entered the room. *This just went from 'R' to 'NC-17'*, Sherman thought to himself.

"Hi, Eternity," Era snapped. "You have fun playin' hooky today?"

"Your hair looks great, Eternity," Sherman lied. He couldn't notice a difference.

"Thanks, Dr. Hinkley," Eternity smiled warmly at the poor, innocent, defenseless patient who was all alone in the big scary hospital where no one could hear him scream if they decided to experiment on him. "Hi, Era. I wasn't playing hooky today! I had an appointment in Westfield and then had some other business errands to run this afternoon."

"Oh, I see. I don't know if you heard but that client you had this afternoon was flagged as a PTT—Sherman, that's a *potential time terrorist*—and Harvey Douglas had to put her down. Right in Sherman's office, too!" Era exclaimed.

"You're kidding!" *The fish was how big?!* "I wonder how she got flagged, Era. That just doesn't make any sense, does it, Sherman?"

"Uh, no, I guess no, not really…" Sherman thought the whole exchange between the two sexy PA's was very disconcerting. If they weren't going to strap him to his bed and ravish him, he actually preferred they both just leave so he could finish his reading.

"Eternity," Era said, "I forgot to tell you Gage and Waverly were looking for you earlier. I think they're still in their offices right now. You should stop by and see what they wanted. I'm actually on my way out, so we can go together if you want. I have some things to talk to them about it."

"That's okay, Era, thanks. I'm not on the clock anymore. I'll just see them both tomorrow at work," Eternity said. Era looked at Sherman then at Eternity. She said goodbye to each of them and started to leave the room when Eternity cut her off. "Oh, Era; While I was out today I saw your grandma walking through Westfield. She told me to tell you thanks for everything today and she's doing well? I think that's what she said…Oh yeah, she said she'll be seeing you soon."

"She said that?" Era said in disbelief. "That's weird. I didn't know she was back in town yet."

"Well, I'm pretty sure it was her. She said something about a code or something? I don't know! It was a quick conversation and it's been, like, the longest day ever!" Eternity affirmed.

"Well, thanks for telling me, Eternity. I'm sure she liked seeing you. She always does," Era mentioned. "Goodnight, you two. Sleep well, Sherman."

"You too, thanks, Era," Sherman replied. *God, she's beautiful!*

"Sherman, er, Dr. Hinkley, I better be going too. It's late and it's still storming outside. I don't think it's going to hold up for a while." Sherman had never seen Eternity this sincere and compassionate. She walked over to his bed, leaned over, and kissed him on the cheek: the corner of her mouth barely caressing the corner of his. The unexpected sign of affection forced Sherman to perform a brief self-adjustment so that Eternity didn't notice anything when she rose to leave the room. "Thanks again for helping me out today," she whispered in his ear, "I really appreciate it." *Baseball statistics, glaciers, baby seal poachers, Schindler's List, ghosts of small children staring at me while I sleep at night*. Nope. Sherman's body was still open for business. Luckily, Eternity never noticed a thing. She merely turned, gathered her umbrella and left the hospital room. Sherman shut his eyes and went to sleep. The last thought he had before his mind stripped itself of any coherence was of Will Bauer. *I sure hope he's learning a lot about Pasteurization,* Sherman thought. And then he was away.

He was standing outside the main ClockWorks entrance on a gorgeous summer's afternoon. Thousands of people gathered on all sides as foreign dignitaries and government officials claimed their seats on the stage. The front of the *building looked spotless: the glass windows seemed as though they had not yet been touched by mortal hands and the grand garden at the top of the staircase sent the liberating aroma of the American pastoral through the crowd. From where Sherman was standing, he could clearly see the hand-carved capitals at the top of the ClockWorks's Corinthian pillars and the engraved floral arrangements near the columns' bases. A colossal hanging curtain blocked the public's view of the inside of the building, and in the center of the outdoor concourse leading up to primary entrance stood a prodigious statue, partially covered by a massive tarp. This was our nation's 242nd birthday. This was ClockWorks inauguration day. In his slumber, Sherman had journeyed back to his dream destination.*

An uproarious thunder of applause elevated from the crowd as E.W. Harper took the podium. He stood tall behind the microphone sans the hubris or overt egotism indicative of a man out for mere fame and exuded the esprit de corps only an accomplishment such as time travel can elicit. As he spoke, his message was clear; his words rang like bells within the boundaries of the masses. Those who were gathered hung with bated breath on every syllable. Every pause brought forth with it a round of cheers from every member of the thousands present. From now on, people will divide history into two parts: The Beginning of Forever and everything that came before it.

When Harper was about to close the speech by invocating a truly American axiom, the curtain and tarp fell to the ground, thus revealing Harper's vision to the eager world. Sherman watched as Harper looked up at the sky and a solitary tear seeped from his eye, ran down his cheek, and fell to the ground. Harper began to weep. His world famous ClockWorks TTA, the corporeal realization of his life-long scientific pursuits, melted into the ground behind him. Flames shot from the sky above and the earth opened up to swallow its trespassers. In the midst of the unbridled carnage, Harper took hold of the microphone, looked directly at Sherman, and whispered three simple words: Damn you all.

Sherman wasn't alone in his hospital room when he abruptly awoke from uneasy dreams. In the midnight shadows, he felt the presence of another. He could hear the syncopated breathing of himself and someone else over by the door. Whoever this was, they had already made themselves comfortable in the chair in the front corner of the room.

"Miss Lapham is in stable condition, Dr. Hinkley," the man's rough voice said. *Where have I heard this guy before*? "She'll be ready for interrogation and sentencing in the morning." Only the man's legs and lower torso were visible: the rest were masked by the shadows cast down from the drawn hospital curtains. "The Agency requests that you serve as primary witness for the prosecution by testifying that Miss Lapham's psychological condition makes her a threat to herself and to society."

"Dr. *Sato*?" Sherman asked. "Dr. Sato, is that you?"

"The Agency wishes to inform you that should you decline your position with the prosecution in this case, your future employment at ClockWorks may be…questionable. Furthermore, I've been asked to relay to you that failure to comply with the Agency's request may…complicate your status as a twenty-first century citizen."

"Complicate? What the hell does *complicate* mean?" Sherman protested.

"The Agency wishes to offer you another opportunity for compliance, however, should your current condition render you unable to perform the necessary tasks of a forensic psychologist by morning," the voice declared.

"Yeah? What's the offer?"

"Provide the name and whereabouts of the person who gave you Kristen Lapham's file."

"Dr. Sato, I don't know who gave it to me! It was on my desk when I got back from lunch!"

"Your falsities will not award you much leniency, doctor. Your interns testify that you had the file with you when you returned from lunch this afternoon." *Wasn't Era on her way to see Gage when she left here?* Sherman tried to remember the conversation. Was it Eternity or Era who left to go see Gage? Sherman knew he couldn't tell Sato that Era had given him the file.

"I can't remember right now, Dr. Sato. Is there any way I could think about it and let you know in the morning? First thing in the morning?" Sherman begged.

"Very well, then. First thing in the morning, Dr. Hinkley. I shall return and pray you have a more refined memory than you have presently." With that, the owner of the voice rose. "By the way, do try to recall the right name. From what I'm told you were quite the hero this afternoon. You have pleased the Agency with your courage and willingness to bring a wanted traitor to justice. We wouldn't want you to disappoint everyone by not remembering a silly name now would we?" *No, mom, I guess not.* For the fourth time since entering the hospital room earlier that afternoon, Sherman was left alone.

Before he returned to his state of dreaming, Sherman made a mental checklist of everything he had to do before morning. He knew he had to come up with a way to avoid reporting Era while at the same time making the Agency think he was cooperating. He knew he had to find the missing Jacobs file and uncover the end of her message. He knew he had to find Eternity and confess his love for her. He also knew he had to find Era and confess his love to her. And if he had time, he'd go see Kristen and apologize for getting her shot…and maybe confess his love to her. He had started the day later than expected and now, lying in his vacant hospital room, he realized it was hours past his usual bedtime. His metamorphosis into a real life ClockWorks CHIMP had officially begun. A smile curled onto his face as he dozed off, dreaming of all the people who'd be begging for his help in the morning. And what better man to aid them in their quests than Dr. Sherman Hinkley?

Two hundred and forty six years earlier, a young boy and bleeding bartender sat alone in a Bishopwearmouth pub looking for a mysterious time piece that had somehow vanished out of sight.

PART TWO
The Realist Mystique

Twelve
A Dissonant Carroll

"Well, if I eat it, and if it makes me grow larger, I can reach the key; and if makes me grow smaller, I can creep under the door: so either way I'll get into the garden, and I don't care which happens!"

-Alice in Wonderland

"All the meanness, all the revenge, all the selfishness, all the cruelty, all the hatred, all the infamy of which the heart of man is capable, grew, blossomed and bore fruit in this one word, Hell."

-Robert G. Ingersoll

"Please, Mr. Dodgson, tell us another story!" exclaimed the voice of 8 year-old Edith Liddell. Across the pond, the United States were celebrating their 86th birthday in style by mourning the lives of those lost in the Peninsular Campaign which ended only two days before. Floating down the Cherwell River near Oxford, however, the Reverend Mr. Charles Dodgson was relishing the tranquility only a sunny, placid day on the water can offer. His crew consisted of his colleague, Reverend Robinson Duckworth, as well as three young sisters: daughters of the Dean of Christ Church, Henry Liddell and his wife, Lorina. Though Lorina, especially, questioned the sanctity of Mr. Dodgson's relationship with her three young daughters, both she and her husband—an educated and highly respected Greek instructor—reluctantly granted him permission to take the girls for rides on the river, where he would entertain them with tales of magic and fantasy they so clearly enjoyed.

"Another story, you say? Why, I've already told you three!" Mr. Dodgson jestingly protested.

"Oh please, Mr. Dodgson!" Edith's older sister, Alice, proclaimed. "It isn't nearly time to go yet!" Alice Pleasance

Liddell served as the inspiration for so many of Dodgson's stories. An expert mathematician, logician, and Anglican, Charles Dodgson was also an avid and skilled professional photographer who spent many an afternoon posing the Liddell's in various positions and costumes. He first took up the relatively new art form known as photography only six years prior to his current nautical adventure with the sisters, but in the little over half a decade since, he'd established quite a respectable name for himself throughout the upper echelons of English social circles as a gentleman-photographer.

Mr. Dodgson knew Alice's assessment of the time was accurate. They'd only been on the river a little over an hour, and yet, he had already exhausted all of his best stories on the three yearning children. Combing through his literary lexicon, he realized he did have one story he could tell them: a story with which he'd been meddling for the past five years ever since he met the man responsible for the most disturbing play he'd ever witnessed. "So you all wish me to tell another story?" he asked playfully.

"But of course we do, Mr. Dodgson! You always tell the most wonderful stories," Alice replied.

"Very well, then. I seem to recall one particular tale I have yet to tell you. Though, I must warn you, it isn't wonderful or gay in the slightest. Rather, it is a murderous tale of danger and vengeance!" Dodgson now had the full attention of the three sisters.

"Oh, do tell us, please, Mr. Dodgson. It sounds terribly thrilling!" Edith said, speaking for the rest of the ship's crew. Dodgson got comfortable in the boat and began recalling the events of his friend's story to himself, as best as his memory allowed, save, of course, the most lugubrious details. As he formulated the story in his head and began crafting it in a way conducive to a children's audience, his mind began to wander back to when he first met the man who inspired his macabre tale.

Five years before Dodgson told the girls the chronicle aboard their boat, he attended the opening night performance of a one-act play entitled "A Sheep in Wolf's Clothing Who Kills Other People's Fathers" at London's Royal Olympic Theater located at the junction of Drury Lane, Wych Street, and Newcastle Street. Even though, since its inception in 1806, the theater usually specialized in premiering comedic plays, "A Sheep in Wolf's Clothing Who Kills Other People's Fathers" was one of the venue's few attempts at running a dramatic piece. Neither Dodgson nor any of the other audience members were remotely surprised by the complexity of the play's narrative; it was about a sheep who dresses up like a wolf and, yes, kills other people's fathers. (At one point, the sheep killed someone's mother, but that was only because, due to a case of mistaken identity, he thought his victim was male.)

When the play was concluded and the house spilled out onto the streets faster than if the building were set ablaze, Dodgson embraced his civic duty to remain seated until the company at least exited their dressing rooms (if, for no other reason, than to warn the cast and crew in the case that the building had, in fact, been set ablaze by angry patrons). He hoped that if he could just meet the playwright, he'd be able to determine if the theatrical offence to which he'd just born witness was the product of a competent author or an imbecilic illiterate. Dodgson was shocked to discover, however, that not only was the playwright extraordinarily competent, but he was also actually one of the most well-known and beloved playwrights of the contemporary London theater scene. Apparently, the man wrote under the nom de theatre *J. Noakes, Esq.* and had produced some of the most dramatic and angst ridden works England had seen in the last hundred years. He too was a learned mathematician, an accomplished journalist and stage manager, and earned both a B.A and Masters Degree from Trinity College at Cambridge University. He drew a significant crowd as he departed the theater, but Dodgson was able to dart his way through the mob to extend an arm and introduce himself to the owner of the fluke theatrical failure. "Excuse me, sir, I enjoyed the performance," Dodgson lied. "My name is Charles Dodgson."

The bearded man smiled, looked down at Dodgson's extended hand, and shook it firmly. "Taylor," he replied. "Tom Taylor."

Over the proceeding months, the acquaintanceship between Taylor and Dodgson evolved into a semi-professional relationship predicated upon frequent letter writing and the occasional afternoon visit. The two would solicit one another for suggestions for titles of works, narrative themes, or other, more personal advice. Dodgson, however, never pressed Taylor about the source of his inspiration for the exceptionally morose plays he wrote and yet the theater world so oddly adored. As an artist himself, Dodgson appreciated that one's muse ought never to be publicized, for doing so risks corrupting the essence of the end product.

Despite Taylor's elusive constitution, Dodgson's correspondence with the playwright did yield some light—albeit dim and foggy—on why, perhaps, the man's works were governed by such a xenophobic impulse and nationalist undercurrent. Dodgson knew that Taylor lost his father at an early age: that much was public knowledge. Mr. John Taylor owned a brewery in Tom's home town of Bishopwearmouth and from what Dodgson could ascertain, the family never wanted for wealth. Years before the cholera epidemic of the 1830's in which an estimated 32,000 Englanders lost their lives, Mr. Taylor's brewery had an unexpected visitor. Dodgson knew only that it was this strange encounter which altered the course of young Tom Taylor's path. No one could know in which direction he would have steered his life had his father not been murdered in his own pub late one rainy summer night.

Nevertheless, once Taylor matured and enrolled for two sessions at the University of Glasgow before heading off to Trinity College and eventually entering the publishing business, his mind was deeply entrenched in all matters foreign and domestic. Dodgson found Taylor's strongly rooted investment in American politics especially mysterious, for the publisher had neither traveled to America nor, to the best of Dodgson's knowledge, had a familiarity with any American citizens. The manner in which Taylor described Americans' clothing was always particularly interesting to Dodgson; no pictures Dodgson had ever seen even remotely coincided with the style of dress Taylor swore was customary to American men.

Through his correspondence with Taylor, Dodgson also noticed that the former apparently suffered from some sort of obsessive compulsion (though, of course, he didn't recognize it in those terms) whereby he would cover the margins and backsides of his letters with rough sketches of a small, round time piece with straps on each side. When asked about the drawings, Taylor insisted that Americans had a technological supremacy over the rest of the world and it was only a matter of time before they would "harness their discs of destruction to destroy mankind." Ironically, not long after Taylor expressed these fears, Americans were in the middle of destroying themselves with revolutionary submerged boats and other innovative land-based forms of weaponry.

"The rabbit *talked* to her?!" Edith Liddell asked Dodgson, puzzled. Dodgson had only been telling his story for a few seconds.

"Of course he talked. It is surely a *magical* rabbit. Isn't that right, Mr. Dodgson?" Alice retorted.

"Dear girls, if you wish to hear the rest of the story, you best sit quietly so that I may continue. Indeed it was a magic rabbit and thus, yes, it spoke to a girl sitting on the bank of the river." Dodgson replied to both girls. The three sisters gasped at the prospect of a talking rabbit, whispered to themselves, giggled slightly, and resumed their attentive positions listening to their private orator.

For reasons to which most can relate but few can explain, for the remainder of that July afternoon, Charles Dodgson forgot he was in the presence of children. His story began well enough; A girl sat on a river's bank with her sister. She was bored and looking for something to do. A rabbit comes up and tells her to follow him, so she does. That part was fine. That part could have been a classic. Where his story took a more unconventional turn, however, is when the child protagonist descends into the depths of Hell where she marries three of Satan's sons, carries to term their demonic spawn, and watches from her lava throne as angels descend to kill her children's fathers.

Distraught at having been thrice widowed, the heroine—who is still very much a girl—decides she best return to Earth in order to unite forces against the evils of Heaven with the hopes of engaging in a cataclysmic, epic battle with God himself. Satan refuses to grant her safe passage to Earth, but allows her to make the journey at her own risk. Satan's verbal dare, essentially, serves as the impetus for a series of ensuing events in which, among other things, the girl becomes an elephant, flies to the moon to destroy its face, sets London on fire with her own breath, grows an extra arm, drinks the Atlantic Ocean, and, as a grand a finale, defecates living cats. The Liddell sisters wished they were in America.

Dodgson, on the other hand, was elated by his own words. Never before had he borrowed so intricately from such a variety of literary and philosophical texts to create a story with more insight and raw passion than the yarn he'd just spun! For far too long, his days with the Liddell sisters had been spent delighting them with stories meant for *children:* stories, which, of course, indeed have an audience and could potentially—though not bloody likely—lead to a lucrative career and immortalization within the canon of children's literature; but alas, this was different. This was *exciting*! Dodgson quickly wrapped up his story by making the freshly defecated cats do something with some guy and there was a tree or something and this cow who gave milk that saved everything, and then he told the girls it was time to go. He ignored the tears streaming down each of the girls' faces, dismissing the sobs as indicative merely of their desire to stay out just a little bit longer. Even the most olfactory impaired dog could have smelled their fear. But Charles Dodgson was no dog. He was a man: a man who just thought of a damn good story, courtesy of his friend Mr. Tom Taylor.

That night, after returning the still weeping babes to their perplexed parents, Charles went home, prepared to spend the evening committing to paper his consummate opus. Upon arriving at his door, however, he saw that during the afternoon, he'd received a letter from none other than his friend and inspiration, Tom. Because Dodgson desired nothing more than to transcribe his homage to Taylor's childhood loss, he felt it only proper to read Tom's letter before he started to write. He went inside, tore open the envelope and began reading.

June 1, 1862

Dear Charles,

I trust this letter finds you in good health and keen spirits. Let me assure you that I have been exerting my best efforts to produce plays of equal quality to that of my previous pieces. Recently, I've been working on a project entitled "The Ticket-of-Leave Man Who Has No Father." My readers tell me it's rather ambitious in scope, but ultimately lacks a certain emotional tenet that would otherwise make it an instant success. Alas, I shall continue writing.

So far I'm told the run of my fifth play has been well-received. I still find it difficult to imagine that of all people, I would grant an American venue the rights to perform one of my works, but I feel as though it is necessary for the citizens of that country to expose themselves to their own potential fate. I also have trouble realizing that almost four years have passed since first it premiered in New York. My good friend Miss Keene frequently writes to speak of the enthusiasm she still receives from patrons who so enjoyed her theater's production and inquire when it will return. She vows that the show has already broken new ground in American theater as the only show of its kind to run with such success for so many years. Having already thrived for these past four seasons, she hopes to trace its career to its extension in order to see if history will deem it in any way significant. I certainly doubt it will ever prove to be anything other than a forgotten work by a worthless playwright, but only will time will tell. I have enclosed clippings of its Philadelphia premiere last month. The critics praised it once again as a truly haunting glimpse into our deepest anxieties. They clearly missed the point.

I thank you for continuing to send me photographs of the lovely Liddell sisters but warn you against venturing too close toward impropriety. You are quite older than the three of them, and I grow weary at the thought of your relationship verging on the grotesque. Do be careful.

When next we meet, we must discuss the latest writings of our own Mr. Darwin. As I'm sure you're aware, the second anniversary of the great Oxford evolution debate is fast approaching and I'm told Mr. Darwin has occupied himself lately with a the early stages of a new theory which applies his previous studies to human evolution, specifically sexual selection. It is indeed a very exciting time.

Your friend,
Tom

Charles placed the letter on the corner of his desk and removed his steel dip pen and notebook. He wrote feverishly throughout the early evening and into the night. His thoughts flowed like the Thames as he emptied his mind onto the blank pages. Satan's spawn, the elephant, the drinkable ocean: it was all there! He remembered every minute detail of the story he told the Liddell girls earlier that day. He flooded his manifesto with vivid imagery, illusionary characters, and rich, moral dilemmas. The petty children's stories he *used* to write were good; this was the stuff nightmares were made of. When he finished with the first draft, Dodgson scanned the top of the first page and noticed something was missing. The only remaining ingredient needed to make his opus a sure fire recipe for literary fame was a title. He wiped the sweat from his brow, squinted his eyes and thought. And thought. And thought. After what seemed like hours of pondering the right syntax, the perfect syllable count, the precise wording, it finally came to him. He struck the pen to his paper and scrolled across the center of the top of the first page his creation's signifier: "Alice among the Demons of Hades" by Lewis Carroll.

Back across the pond, a dashing, lean, athletic looking man took a step off his train. Along with his 5'8" frame topped off by a full head of jet-black hair, the man carried with him a travel case in one hand and his rapier in the other. He'd been traveling for three days from St. Louis aboard the first class car, and after a roughly mile walk from the train station, was now standing in front of his final destination: Laura Keene's Theater in New York. He'd planned to arrive several weeks sooner, but after being arrested in Missouri by a provost marshal earlier in the year, he was forced to postpone his departure in order to tie up a few loose ends before traveling to the North. It was early in the evening and since it was not only a Friday night, but also the 86th birthday of those grand United States, Keene's Theater was opening a new original musical extravaganza written by Keene herself and featuring music by Mr. Tom Baker. The man standing outside the building had little interest in the variety show, however; he was there on business.

As with Mr. Dodgson some eight years earlier, this American theater lover waited until the end of the performance with the hopes of stealing a minute of the proprietor's undoubtedly precious time. Near the show's finale (a horribly elaborate and chaotic dance number involving three poodles, seventeen clowns and, yes, one fat lady), the man rose from his seat in the back of the theater to claim his spot by the backstage entrance. When the show concluded, and the house emptied and the company exited, a beautiful, well-dressed flamboyant woman took notice of the loitering man and approached him.

"Evenin', sir, show's over. I have to ask you to leave. Don't you know there's a party goin' on outside." The man just stood there and smiled. "May I help you with somethin', sir?" she asked.

"Pardon me, mam, but I was looking for Miss Laura Keene. I'm interested in auditioning for a role in one of her recurring productions."

"Oh, and which production would that be, sir?" the woman asked.

"Why, none other than the work by Mr. Tom Taylor which premiered at this very theater about four years back. I'm interested in one of the lead roles, ma'am."

"Well, I'm terribly sorry, sir, but unfortunately at this time we're not casting for primary roles in that particular show. Mr's Sothern and Jefferson have proven themselves more than ideal for the two male leads. Perhaps you'd like to audition for one of the minor roles?" At this, the handsome man scoffed.

"Madame, pardon me, but might I say that perhaps you'd like to see me read before you cast me away like that? I've traveled a long way and I intend on having my talents assessed before I journey back home. I come from a theatrical family, ma'am, and therefore have the utmost confidence that I can surely blend well with the cast you've already formulated. I implore you, do not send me away without hearing me read. I'm sure you won't be disappointed." One thing was for sure; this man had charisma.

"I see. And what, may I ask, are your credentials?" the woman demanded, torn between frustration and lust.

"I've worked extensively with the Philadelphia Arch Street Theater's stock company, the Richmond Theater in Virginia, and several various Shakespeare troupes. I have training in fencing, pugilism and dance and, frankly, will do whatever you say to take part in Mr. Taylor's play. It is quite simply the most ingenious portrayal of human desperation the modern stage has ever seen." He smiled at the woman, who blushed in return. He had her at 'pardon me, ma'am.

"Well you certainly are versatile, aren't you? Alright then, I suppose we could find some time to hear you read. Come back tomorrow at 12:00 and have something prepared. No need to meet Miss Keene," the woman continued. "You already have."

"Pleased to meet you, Miss Keene, I figured as much," the man smiled back.

"And who should I tell the rest of the cast is auditioning tomorrow for their roles?" she asked, slyly grinning.

"The name is Booth, ma'am. John Wilkes Booth."

Thirteen
Sherman's Folly

"A man of genius makes no mistakes. His errors are volitional and are the portals to discovery."

-James Joyce

"It was the best purchase ever made."

-Richard Nixon, *on the purchase of Alaska*

On July 8th, 2068 at 2:03 a.m., Eastern Standard Time, E.W Harper's ClockWorks TTA went on emergency lock down for the first time in over twenty years.

Dr. Sherman Hinkley was sleeping peacefully in his bed in the hospital wing on the 17th floor of the building when his dreams were interrupted by a swarm of ACHEs barging into his private room. The ACHEs ripped the covers off Sherman's bed, grabbed the chimp by his arms and legs and hurried him out of the room, into the dark hallway. The flickering emergency lights and roaring siren circulating throughout the building didn't do much to boost Sherman's awareness of his surroundings as he was being dragged through doors, down stairs and finally into the office of Lt. Phineas P. Gage who was yelling to someone on the other end of his secure office telephone.

"Goddamnit, get them down here now! We'll need everyone working on this one. She's really fucked things up this time!" Gage yelled. At the sight of Sherman, Gage slammed the phone down on his desk, crossed the room and punched Sherman across the face with a deadly right cross. "Where is he, you little bastard!? What did you do with him?!?" Gage's rage vibrated the walls. Sherman struggled to his feat after the sucker punch. In the past ten hours, Sherman had been shot with a near lethal dose of tranquilizers, had his job threatened, his integrity denigrated, and now his face broken. And it was barely even his second day of work.

Gage reached under Sherman's arms and lifted the beaten doctor to an upright position: an impressive task given the Lieutenant was in his sixties. The accomplishment didn't last long, however, because once Gage had Sherman standing straight, he drove a fist deep into the little bastard's lower abdomen. As Sherman hit the ground for a second consecutive time, Wally and Lamar entered the room behind him, each forcibly escorted by armed ACHEs who shoved the two new agents into the center of the room where Sherman now lay cowering on the ground.

"What's going on, Lieutenant?" Lamar asked, clearly agitated that he had been woke up in the middle of the night and transported back to ClockWorks. Sherman cracked open his left eye and noticed that both Wally and Lamar were still wearing pajamas.

"I'll tell you what's going on, Newton; Sherman here's been fucking with TDL Codes and PCs, that's what!" Gage hollered back. Another agent threw a STOOPING Piece into Gage's hands. Sherman recognized the agent from his encounter with him earlier in the IDM Room. It was the same man who informed Sherman that Will's TDL Codes had already been sent down to the command center. Gage got down on one knee and shoved the SP into Sherman's scrunched face.

"You see this, you little shit? This is what happens when you send someone back to the wrong goddamn place!" Gage threw the SP at Sherman's head as he stood up to resume his pacing around the office.

"Sir, still no sign of Alcott or Howells," Harvey gasped as he ran into the room trailed by Lester. "We've notified President Waverly and sent out another ACHE team to recover Agent Stowe."

"And the rest of the guests?" Gage asked.

"The entire first floor has undergone TMA and has been evacuated. The building is secure. There's no one here but agents, sir."

Hearing this news calmed Gage slightly. "Very well, then, Mr. Douglas. Now we just have to determine the extent of the damage Mr. Hinkley here has caused us."

"Sir, excuse me," Wally interjected. "Would you mind telling us what Sherman did?" *Thanks, Wally,* Sherman thought.

"Certainly!" Gage yelled in reply, his back to the rest of the cramped office. "For some reason, our own Mr. Hinkley took it upon himself to not only send a client back to the wrong country, but he also decided to give him Zemeckalian Clearance! When the command center sent out a signal to retrieve his SP, guess what returned? THAT!" Gage irately shot a finger at the STOOPING Piece lying on the floor next to Sherman's throbbing head. Throwing his arms up in the air and stomping around his desk, Gage continued. "So somewhere in *1822* there's an American kid from Crown Point walking around with no hope of getting back, no clue where he is, and no idea how much he's already fucked up the future of the entire world!"

"What's happened, sir?" Lamar insisted. "What did he do? What's changed?" Upon hearing Lamar's questions, Gage went silent. Luckily Harper's President Emmanuelle K. Waverly had just arrived to pick up where Gage left off.

"That's the problem, Reverend Newton." He said, walking into the office with his hands in his pockets and his face peering at the floor. "In the past, whenever something like this has occurred, we've been able to consolidate our collective memories and corroborate them with the ClockWorks mainframe to determine the precise moment in which the traveler forged an alternate temporal path."

"Exactly," Wally said. "That's how Cole solved the crisis of '42."

David Cole was Harper's first CHUMP. He worked under Harper himself when the company launched in 2018 and continued his dedicated service until his death in 2046 when he committed suicide after losing everything when the United States declared bankruptcy. In 2042, while he was walking home from work one day, Cole noticed a sign posted in a store window that made the hair on his Dutch neck stand on its end. The sign read "NO WHITES ALLOWED." Without warning, Cole then heard a gunshot and the sound a bullet whizzing by his ear. Within seconds, an angry mob of American Indians and Blacks were chasing Cole through the middle of downtown Indianapolis. He dodged the vile horde and took refuge in a dark alley where he hid until nightfall. When the coast was clear, he sprinted back to Harper's and locked himself in his office where he spend the next three days filtering through the mainframe to determine what could have possibly driven the good minorities of Indy to such maliciousness.

After sifting through every PC's application for the last fiscal year, Cole finally uncovered the culprit: Julius Wharton. Wharton had purchased an eleven month, multi-stop time travel package the year before: a trip that would take him to early Mesopotamia, the Fertile Crescent around the year 8,000 B.C.E., 10,000 B.C.E Africa, and sixth century North America. Packages of this nature were cornerstones of Harper's pedagogical philosophy: why limit people's exposure to knowledge by restricting their travels to simply one place at one time? (After the crisis of '42, however, Harper outlawed these particular itineraries.) Cole discovered, via the aid of four ACHEs (who all received US Presidential Commendations for their efforts in the Wharton Campaign, as it became politically dubbed) that Julius had illegally traveled back in time with Zemeckalian Clearance to assist early American Indian and African clans in the cultivation of their agricultural and linguistic skills. He educated these primitive people on matters of seamanship and metallurgy and taught them essential combative tactics they could use in future wars. Cole ascertained that Wharton must have had extensive anthropological training, for he had little difficulty knowing how and what to communicate with these primitive people in order to effectively alter the course of mankind's history.

He also exposed the American Indians to a cornucopia of various diseases so that when it came time for the European explorers to arrive, the bodies of the savage natives would have already had centuries to develop immunities to the European illnesses and thus would be impervious to both germ warfare and European firepower because they too would have gun manufacturing capabilities. In short, Wharton had single-handedly rewritten history's saga of white supremacy and European Imperialism. And in only eleven months to boot. This was something David Cole just could not allow.

Cole personally sent a specialized force of ACHEs back in time to precisely five minutes prior to Wharton's original TDL code. When he arrived in Ancient Mesopotamia expecting to see the dawn of early human civilization, he instead found an elite military force with automatic guns pointed at his heart. Even though the command leader had yet to give the order, a rookie ACHE named Austin Corbett fired first at Wharton. The others immediately followed. Wharton's life was over thousands of years before it ever began. The ACHEs returned to the TTA as heroes. Austin Corbett eventually had three Indiana streets and a library named in his honor. In 2043, the Indianapolis Public School system opened Austin Corbett Middle School where for twenty-five years, thousands of inner-city Black kids learned all about slavery, the middle passage, and the Jim Crow South. A copper bust of David Cole commemorating his years of loyal service to Harper's was kept on Wally's desk in his apartment. Cole was to Wally what Harper was to Sherman: brilliance personified.

"Very good, Dr. Emerson," Waverly responded. "But this time around things are a little different. Sometime in the last few hours, someone has interfered with the primary Harper's mainframe and dismantled all of the TDL Codes for the last six or seven months. There's no way of knowing when or where our PCs have been transported and therefore no way of telling which, specifically, is responsible for the temporal alteration. However, we have managed to successfully retrieve all clients from their trips except a Mr. William Bauer from Crown Point, Indiana. His SP came back, well, without him. We estimate something happened on Mr. Bauer's trip which has resulted in an exponential change to our way of life, but until the system is up and running, there's no possible way to determine how our ACHEs can fix the problem or even when it occurred."

"How bad is it, Mr. President?" Lamar asked.

"It's too early to tell, Reverend," Waverly replied. "We have Reconnaissance Agents deployed presently, but they have yet to return with their reports. Unfortunately we may all just have to wait to see how bad Dr. Hinkley's damage really is."

"Looks like he's comin' around, sir," Lester called to Gage, noticing Sherman attempting to lift himself off the ground. "What should we do with him?"

"Lieutenant, is it really necessary to do *anything* with him?" Wally pleaded. "I mean, he's obviously secure. It's not like he's going to do any more damage. Why not just leave him with us so you can carry on with your…work?"

"If I wanted your opinion I'd--"

"I see no problem with that, Lieutenant," Waverly interjected. Gage snorted and turned his head away from the group. Even grown-ups pout when they don't get their way. "Lamar, Walden: You take Dr. Hinkley down to Archer E. Room and wait there until further instructions. Lieutenant, you stay with me. Misters Douglas and Whitman, keep us informed on the status of Agents Howells and Alcott and let us know when the ACHEs have returned with Agent Stowe. She may be able to shed some light on this entire situation. Lieutenant Gage and I will be in my chambers."

The trek from Gage's office to the Archer E. Room reminded Wally of traipsing through old haunted houses during the weeks preceding Halloween when he was younger. In order to combat his seemingly endless list of phobias, Wally often embraced a psychological technique known as "exposure" through which he attempted to identify the cognitions, emotions, and other forms of physiological arousal that ordinarily accompanied a situation that caused Wally to be afraid. Through habitual exposure to the fear-inducing stimulus, Wally was able to ward off several of his more minor anxieties: spiders, snakes, public speaking, jumping. Yet one particular condition that plagued Wally through the better part of his childhood and early adolescence was an acute form of monophobia: the fear of being alone. It wasn't necessarily the fear of being *left* alone, but enveloped any situation in which Wally could potentially find himself by himself. Consequently, when he was old enough to take the bus home after school before his mom got home from work, Wally would rarely enter his own house. Instead, he would simply stand outside the front door ringing the doorbell and peeking through the tiny windows on either side of the blue door to make sure no robbers who may have been inside were startled by the ringing bell. Even if he was outside by himself, the open space to run provided Wally with a small degree of comfort. Claustrophobia combined with monophobia is a potent and deadly mixture.

Some nights, Wally would lose sleep trying to figure out a means to combat his monophobia through exposure. How do you expose yourself to solidarity gradually? Start in a room of ten people than slowly have them leave until it's only you remaining? What made matters worse for Wally was that his friends quickly caught onto his need for perpetual companionship. What they once simply dismissed as Wally's adolescent, clingy nature, his friends soon discovered that his desire to maintain a close proximity with anyone stemmed not so much from social awkwardness but from a deeply rooted fear of solitude. It didn't take long before they realized they could have a good deal of fun with their fear-proned friend. And at virtually no cost to them!

Near Wally's thirteenth Halloween, a group of his friends convinced him to go with them at night to a nearby old building that was supposedly haunted. When it was still in operation, the Ridge Side Hospital served as a full scale assisted living facility for the Tell City sick and elderly. Since being condemned nine years prior, the building sat vacant in its ironic location on the west corner of town, nowhere near a ridge of any sort. Dozens of daring teenagers claimed to have heard strange noises coming from the building, particularly from the psych ward, where a few witnesses testified to having seen illuminated specters banging their vapid heads against the walls late at night. Wally had long ago vanquished his fears of ghosts, goblins, and dark places by watching countless movies featuring ghosts and goblins…which he watched in dark places…with the company of several other people, of course. No one was surprised, therefore, that the invitation to tag along with his spook-seeker friends one night was one which Wally quickly accepted. He wuddn't afraid of no ghosts.

The other kids told Wally to meet them by the main gate to the hospital at 9:00. The front gate was really about a quarter of a mile away from the hospital's front door and set back several dozen yards from the main road. To get to the gate from the street, one would have to veer off the pavement onto a gravel pathway which led to the wrought iron barricade. From there, a once beautiful cobblestone road lined on each side by impeccably trimmed mature oak trees led the way to the Ridge Side entrance. When Wally arrived at the gate at 8:55, the cobblestones appeared as residual proof of a long-ago earthquake: broken and crumbled with tall, unkempt grass poking through the cracks into the cool night air. The oaks had grown so wildly that they provided a wholly enclosed canopy around the entire pathway leading up to the main entrance. As a tableau, the scene seemed creepily like a perversion of an Ambrose Bierce story. Despite the menacing essence of the structure, at 9:15, Wally considered that perhaps the group meant their rendezvous point to be the main entrance of the building and not the front gate. Gathering his courage, Wally ran to the front door and waited for the arrival of his friends who never came.

The following Monday at school, everyone wanted to hear about Wally's weekend excursion to the old Ridge Side Hospital. Much to their dismay, however, instead of coming to school with an air of fully justifiable hostility, Wally showed up in the locker bay before first period with an MP3 player, headphones, and a humongous grin plastered on his face.

"Have a good weekend, Wally?" asshole friend number one asked.

"Screw you, Asshole," Wally retorted. "Good joke leavin' me there like that, though. Laughed my ass off about that one."

"We thought you'd go crying to your mommy or something," dickhead jabbed.

"You wish, Dickhead! I actually went into the building and walked around." The ridicule gently subsided.

"You did?" fucker asked.

"You bet I did, Fucker. And check this out. I wanted to film some stuff to see, ya know, if I could catch any ghosts or anything on tape."

"Did you!?" Jen asked.

"No, I didn't see any ghosts, Jen." Wally always liked Jen. "But check this out. I also recorded some of the ambient noise to see if I could capture anything. When I went home to play it, at first I didn't hear anything. But when I adjusted the volume and levels and stuff, I was able to isolate *this*!" Wally gave Asshole the headphones and turned the volume all the way up. At first there was nothing but loud static and the sounds of someone slowly walking through what sounded like rubble. But then, faintly beneath the sounds of the wind and footsteps, Asshole could hear an angry raspy woman's voice saying, "*There are people here. Get out!"* He literally jumped up from his seat and ripped the headphones from his ears. Everyone else begged Wally to let them hear the haunting noises from beyond the grave which he graciously allowed. In a forty-eight hour period, thirteen year-old Wally Emerson had successfully conquered his monophobia, borrowed a microphone, went to the new Ridge Side Hospital on the east side of town, and recorded the voice of one of the sweetest old women he'd ever met. She was much obliged to assist in his little trick. Asshole, Dickhead, and Fucker never messed with Wally again. And now, years later, as he and his team were making their way through the makeshift Harper's funhouse, Wally wasn't the least bit scared.

The ClockWorks corridors were pitch black, save for the flickering emergency lights which cast amorphous shadows upon the barricading walls. The eerie vacancy of the evacuated building filled the minds of the three team members with a sense of desertion and impending doom. With his arms thrown around the necks of Lamar and Wally, Sherman was able to limp along the hallways, down the stairs and into the Archer Wing of the building. As he tried to locate his bearings amidst the chaos of a world turned upside down, his mind frantically surged with the desire to find Eternity or Era, if only to ask them what the hell was going on. Oddly enough, Sherman began to miss his private hospital bed and the seemingly endless array of pesky night visitors that only hours before had tried to steal from him a night of uninterrupted sleep.

When they arrived at the door to the Archer Room on the east side of the Archer Wing, Lamar entered the digital code into the security lock, and the three men lumbered inside and flopped themselves on the leather couches, still in their arrangements from the welcoming meeting the previous morning. Sherman was now finding it easier to keep his head from bobbing up and down, though his jaw still throbbed from Gage's right cross. Luckily the tranquilizers had almost completely worked their way through Sherman's body.

"We'll just wait here until they come and get us, then, I guess," Lamar said after a few minutes. The three sat in silence in the dark, abandoned room in the dark, abandoned corridor. The pictures hanging on the walls around them appeared more ominous than they had when the men arrived on their first day of work. The shadows dancing off the pictures of Hannibal resonated with a burgeoning fear in all the men that they too were about to be conquered by something greater than themselves. Lamar noticed that the family smiling in front of Jesus on the cross seemed to be doing so with a greater degree of hesitation than the previous morning. It was almost as if their enigmatic happiness masked a deeply entrenched fear that perhaps they were meddling with something with which none ought meddle. Indeed, Hell hath no fury like a man who longs for self-preservation. After all, what are photographs but the manifestation of one's desire to immortalize a moment in time?

"How bad do you think it is, Lamar?" Wally asked after what seemed like hours of silence.

"Like Waverly said, it's too early to tell. Maybe it's nothing, Wally. Maybe this kid Sherman sent back didn't do anything at all and we'll walk out into the world tomorrow morning and find it's the exact same place it was when we left last night. Or, maybe it's worse. It could be a lot worse. But that's why we work here, gentlemen. I, for one, have confidence in the Agency's ability to cope with tragedies of any magnitude. They've certainly done it before. In the early years, before ZC was banned, things like this happened all the time and ya know what? It never amounted to anything at all! The ACHEs went back and fixed the problem. It's as simple as that. I'm sure this will be no different. I just wish I was back home with my wife and girls. They'll be leaving for school again soon and I can't bare the thought of spending any more time here than necessary."

"What do you mean *more time*?" Sherman asked, his first coherent sentence since he'd been nabbed from his cozy bed. "How long do you think we could be here?" All eyes were on Lamar.

"Well, if I remember correctly, the longest it's taken the Agency to decipher the precise point of divergence was two and half weeks." Sherman and Wally gasped. "But again, that was in the early years when the technology wasn't as good and the ACHE's ethics weren't as, how should I say it…lenient?"

"Lenient? What the hell does that mean?" Sherman begged.

"Well, when Harper first started the company, he rejected the idea that it should be anything other than epistemological. In other words, he hated suggestions that the Agency in any way be affiliated with the military or government. In the situations when military action was deemed necessary, Harper insisted that absolute caution be taken in bringing the culprit to justice. Thus, for the first couple of years, it took the ACHEs a while to *find* the time criminals, let alone capture them and ameliorate the situation. When Harper died, though, the Agency realized that in order to prosper, the ACHEs must take swifter and more decisive action in order to ensure we stay on our path, so to speak. The irony is, of course, that in their efforts to maintain our coordinates on our temporal path, they completely compromised their moral path. I promise you both that with this situation, lives will be lost if they haven't been already. I'm sorry, Sherman, but I have a bad feeling things are going to get much worse for all of us."

"Or they could get better, right?" Wally exclaimed. No one gave much credence to his optimism, however. "No, I'm serious! Isn't it possible that, like, whatever happened could have made our world better? Like, if this guy did something to, I don't know, cure famine or make it so a tyrant ended up being a bus driver or something. That could potentially *save* lives, right, not end them?" *How cute they are at this age.*

"Wally, yes, of course, you could very well be right. But unfortunately that's just not how it usually works with these types of situations. In a way, this whole damn place functions in response to sort of a...a distortion of the human capacity," explained Lamar, whom Sherman noticed was no longer looking at anyone in particular but instead, through the darkness, was staring at a picture hanging on the wall: a picture he had apparently not seen before.

"A what?" asked Wally. Lamar rose from his seat and felt his way to the mounted photograph on the far wall on the other side of the room. Sherman turned to watch Lamar as Wally kept up with his grand inquisition. "What do you mean a...distortion of the human condition?"

"*Capacity*, Wally, the human *capacity*," Lamar answered, his back now to his coworkers. Wally glanced at Sherman. Both shadows of men shrugged their shoulders in anticipation of Lamar's explanation for his ambiguity. Such an explanation, though, never came. Rather, Lamar placed his forearm against the wall and leaned in, trying to harness all of the room's present light to gaze at the photograph. On the opposite side of the room, both Sherman and Wally heard Lamar mumble quietly to himself, "Come ye, therefore, let us go down, and there confound their tongue, that they may not understand one another's speech." Ambiguity, Wally and Sherman learned that night, is often an ends to itself.

A door creaked open and a stealthy figure snuck inside. "It took longer to find you than we thought. They hid you well."

"I knew they would this time. I see something happened tonight. Do we know how big the damage is?"

"Nobody knows anything yet. Three out of the four are sequestered in the Archer Wing, and ACHEs have been sent to bring back the woman. The mainframe is dismantled and the building is locked down. All the customers have had their memories temporary altered and have since been evacuated. The building's now empty except for agents and us. I think she'll be proud this time. This is exactly what she wanted."

"I know it is. I didn't think I'd end up in here, though. I thought you and I took care of everything this time. I didn't think he'd turn on us like that."

"No, it wasn't him, it was *her*. Somehow she found out you were coming and sabotaged the whole thing. He actually took a bullet for it. A tranq, but still, I guess it knocked him out pretty good."

"Have you seen him? Is he still with us?"

"I think he is, yeah. I saw him earlier tonight. But she's worried that he might sway to the other side like the others. She's worried he sympathizes with them and won't want to fight for our cause. I tried to convince her he's different but you know--"

"Have you seen her lately?"

"Yeah, I met with her last night for a little bit before I continued with the operation. She still doesn't want to interfere but I think that after everything's that happened, she'll change her mind this time. I have a feeling this is the last chance we're going to get. They're onto us. If we fail this time, she's finished."

"I agree. Well, are you going to get me out of here or what? I'm not exactly looking forward to what they might do to me once the excitement dies down."

"Shut your mouth, of course I'm here to get you. She's actually outside around the corner ready to say congratulations on a job well done."

"How bad is it out there? Can you tell anything's different yet?"

"No not yet, but it's still early. Hopefully it won't be too bad though. We wouldn't want things to get too horrible before they go in and fix everything like they always do."

"Yeah but still, another screw up and I think we've got 'em. I think the world's had enough of all of this. It made sense at the time, but once they see just how wrong it is--"

"I know, I know. Alright, what can't you move here?"

"I'm a little sore in the shoulders, so if you could avoid those, I'd appreciate it. I can walk if you need me to, but I'm assuming we're just going out the window."

"Yup. Okay, let me strap you in here. There we go. It's good to see you again. I'm glad you made it down here. You ready to go?"

"I'm ready. You comin' back tomorrow?"

"I have to, right. It's my job isn't is? I can't just *not* show up. They *think* I'm involved somehow but if I don't show up they'll come looking for me."

"Maybe they'll have other things to look for. Besides, how long do you think it will be before they connect me to you?"

"I bet they already have. I told you, they've gotten a lot smarter this time around."

"Then why the hell would you risk coming back tomorrow?"

"I have to. If she gets to him before we do, the whole thing is over. Trust me. Sherman Hinkley is our only hope."

Fourteen
Stowe Away

"It is the retention by twentieth-century, Atom-Age men of the Neolithic point of view that says: You stay in your village and I will stay in mine. If your sheep eat our grass we will kill you, or we may kill you anyhow to get all the grass for our own sheep. Anyone who tries to make us change our ways is a witch and we will kill him. Keep out of our village."
-Carleton S. Coon, *The Story of Men*

"When two cultures collide is the only time when true suffering exists."
-Herman Hesse

The three-story brick home on the west side of Washington Boulevard was hardly abuzz when four ACHEs landed on its roof at quarter past 2:00 on July 8th, 2068. The Head ACHE instructed his team to clasp to the gutter before rappelling off the roof and into the master bedroom of ClockWorks Agent Isabelle Stowe. Shattering through the glass with cocked guns in hand, the ACHEs quickly realized that the schematic layout of Stowe's master suite differed from the photographs Harper's Intelligence had provided them. Instead of a king-sized bed lying flush against the south wall, there was a queen bed butting out from the west wall. Instead of one woman sleeping alone, there were two men. Was Isabelle Stowe hiding something from the Agency? Could it be that by day, Stowe was an obese, unwed, king-sized bed loving mathematician who moonlighted as an evidently physically fit homosexual thirty-something who preferred to downsize beds when lovers slept over? And where on Earth was the giant painting of Da Vinci's *Vitruvian Man* that supposedly hung over the dresser? And what's the deal with the baby monitor next to the bed? And why the hell didn't anyone *hear* the team rupture through the windows? *Whose house is this?* thought the Head ACHE.

The Agents swiftly maneuvered around the room, securing its perimeter as they had done with Sherman's office the day before. When the room was secure, two ACHEs moved out into the darkness of the foreign hallway, still convinced that this was indeed Isabelle Stowe's residence. The other two ACHEs maintained their position in the master bedroom, guns pointed at the sleeping men. Suddenly, one of the sleepers rose from beneath his covers and began walking around the room. His eyes were open but the ACHEs could tell he was unaware of his actions. He mumbled to himself as he bumped into walls, went to the bathroom only to flush the toilet, sat down in the recliner in the room's corner and exited through the door, descending the staircase. In addition to being a gay man, Isabelle Stowe was now apparently a somnambulist.

The other man rolled over onto the now vacant, yet still undoubtedly warm side of the bed. Feeling around for his companion, the man first noticed his absence, then detected the unexpected presence in his room. "Who's there?" the man asked with a trembling voice. From the cadence of the man's inquiry, the ACHEs ascertained that he, in fact, was deaf. This, of course, explained his inability to hear the crashing of the windows. Truly, the entire experience couldn't be further from their assigned mark; instead of easily retrieving Isabelle Stowe, somehow the ACHEs invaded the private residence of two hearing-impaired homosexual men, one of whom walked in his sleep and both of whom, it appeared, had adopted at least one young child.

Unsure as to quite how they should reply to the deaf man in the dark, the two ACHEs merely remained positioned in their respective spots throughout the room. The somnambulist returned to the room after a few minutes of rummaging through the kitchen. He was followed closely by the other ClockWorks Agents. The Head ACHE instructed one of the others to turn on the overhead light using the switch by the door. The Agent did as he was told and as fast as electricity could flow to the light bulb, the room was now fully lit. The deaf man rustled his partner who awoke standing by the edge of the bed. Both men were terrified of the intruders in the room. Both were speechless. The Head ACHE lowered his weapon and removed his protective visor. He pointed to the embroidery on his chest and indicated the Harper's emblem sewn into his right sleeve: a watch with no hands. The two men exhaled simultaneously, indicating that they at least understood who these men were, though clearly couldn't comprehend why, with all the things to do on a Monday night in Indianapolis, they would want to go to all the trouble of breaking into their quaint home on Washington Boulevard.

One of the ACHEs approached the nightstand where he found a pad of paper and pen. He picked up the items and wrote down a solitary syllable: "Stowe?" The men looked at each other and shook their heads. Another not so patient ACHE on the other side of the room screamed at the two men, "Where is Isabelle Stowe?" Because the ACHE didn't bother to remove his visor, the men simply ignored his question and remained fixated on the Agent holding the pad and pen.

"They're deaf, Franklin," the Head ACHE told his soldier.

"Where the hell is Isabelle Stowe," the man called Franklin yelled again, eleven times louder. Again, no one said a word.

"Captain, you don't think we got the wrong place, do you?" one of the Agents suggested.

"Denning, ask them how long they've lived here," the Head ACHE demanded. The man called Denning wrote the required words and handed the pad over to the two men.

"Six years," the sleep walker replied aloud.

"Carlisle, run a check on this address using the public mainframe," the Head ACHE ordered.

"But captain, we ran a check before we left using the Har--"

"I know, damnit, I want the *public* mainframe: the one that's subject to change with temporal alterations. Something may have happened in the past that affected Agent Stowe's residency at this address, and the only way to know for sure is to verify this address with the public mainframe." The man called Carlisle did as instructed.

"Sir, according to the public mainframe, this address is currently occupied by a Mr. Jeremy Diddler and Dr. William Dean Hughes. Before that there was a woman named Gilman and before that, sir, a man named Jewett. But that was nearing fifty years ago, sir. No one's ever lived here named Stowe: at least not in the last half century." The Head ACHE absorbed this news in silence. The Harper's mainframe had never been *this* wrong before. Was it wrong now? What else could have happened to the city? To the world?

"Sir, what should we do with them?" the man called Franklin asked, still audibly agitated that the deaf men hadn't responded to his threatening questions.

"Sir, is it safe to leave them? How should we handle this, captain?" asked the man named Denning.

"I'm not sure anything's safe anymore, men," the Head ACHE uttered. "But I think, yes, it's safe right now to leave them. Let's move, men. Up and out." The Head ACHE nodded at the man called Denning who wrote down one more message on the sheet of paper. As the rest of the coalition ascended the roof, Denning balled the paper in his hand and hurled it onto the bed as he was pulled up to their departure point. Mr. Diddler unfolded the paper to read the ACHEs note. All he had written were two simple words: "Do good."

"I wonder what's taking them so long to get Isabelle," Sherman wondered aloud as he, Wally and Lamar sat in the Archer E. Room. "Doesn't it seem like they've been gone a really long time?" Lamar nodded.

"Who cares where she is? I can't stand that woman! She's disgusting and rude," Wally whined. "I hope they never find her. Or if they do, I hope they fire her ass for being a fat…ass." Wally could lie with the best of them, but insults were never his specialty.

"She *is* pretty much the only one of us who actually did any work yesterday, Wally," Sherman noted.

"That's true, Walden," Lamar added. "The three of us essentially just sat around all day talking, if you'll remember."

"That's not true!" Wally protested. "I did a ton of work yesterday!" He was actually upset at Lamar's accusation even though it was a hundred percent accurate. Rather than arguing with Wally, however, Lamar simply smiled at the man the way a good father does when he knows his son will eventually realize how full of shit his argument is. Luckily, in this case, it took about two seconds. "Well, I still hope she never comes back!" Still, Sherman couldn't help but think that the ACHEs had been gone an awfully long time.

"Do you guys know anything about her at all?" Sherman wondered, a hint of genuine curiosity sprinkling his query. Wally shook his head in defiance of the whole subject matter.

"I remember her telling me something, or me reading something, or *something* about her being a descendent of William the Conqueror," Lamar recollected, "but that's about it. I know she lived alone a few miles north of here, and I know she never married."

"Yes she did," Wally chimed in. "Her husband was an astronaut and divorced her to be with some Russian woman."

"No, her husband was an author and killed himself because he could never get a book contract," Sherman tried to recall.

"Or because he married a walrus," Wally joked.

"Well, yeah, that too," Sherman conceded.

"No, sorry guys, but I'm pretty sure she never married. Sure, there are a lot of rumors about her, but I don't think we should pay any attention to any of them. Why don't we just ask her next time we see her?" Lamar posed.

"Deal," Sherman and Wally replied in unison.

Without warning, the door to the Archer E. Room swung open and Waverly entered, followed by Gage, Harvey, and Lester. *Why don't these guys go home?* Sherman thought, regarding his straggling interns.

"We need you to come with us, gentlemen," Waverly demanded curtly. The three were escorted through more dark hallways and shadowy corridors, down more deserted stairwells and vacant chambers to a secluded room at the end of the fourth floor. Without hesitation, Waverly unlocked his office and ushered the group inside, locking the door behind him. Four ACHEs were already standing in the room, waiting for the return of their commander and employer.

"Gentlemen, we seem to be having some trouble locating Agents Stowe and Alcott," Waverly cried. *Did he say 'Alcott'?* Sherman's eyes perked up at the president. "When was the last time any of you have seen these women?"

The three new employees looked at one another. Finally Lamar spoke, "Uh, sir, the last time we saw Isabelle was at lunch yesterday, sir."

"And the last time I saw Eternity was right after you shot her client in my office for no reason yesterday," Sherman replied, courage evidently a byproduct of tranquilizer bullets. Gage looked as though he'd kill Sherman if he had three minutes alone with him. Alas, with Waverly present, Sherman's life was temporarily safe.

"Dr. Hinkley, have you been in contact with anyone regarding Agent Alcott or her client since the…incident yesterday afternoon?" Waverly asked. Sherman tried to recall the details of thc conversation he had with *Dr. Sato, was it*? about Kristen but his mind was unable to process the particulars. However, given the circumstances, he felt it prudent to be honest.

"Not that I can recall, sir, no." So much for candor.

"Bullshit, Hinkley!" Gage roared. "I know for a fact you had a visitor last night!"

"He had a lot of visitors, sir," Wally protested. "I was one of them." Waverly's office phone rang before anyone could reply to Wally. The room fell silent as Waverly rushed to his desk and lifted the receiver.

"Yes. Yes. Well, why the hell--uhuh…I see. *The morning!?!* Why, that's still--I understand…but, yes, well…how hard can it be to find--*deserted?* What about the grand--yes…WELL, DAMNIT SHE'S AROUND HERE SOMEWHERE! What about him?...Of course not! The mainframe's still--yes…yes, he's right here…all three of them…uhuh… I understand…They'll be right down." Waverly hung up the phone. He walked over to Gage and whispered something in his ear. As Waverly was talking, Gage's upper lip snarled and he turned to face Wally and Sherman.

"But, sir," Gage argued.

"It's the only way, Lieutenant," Waverly said. Gage shrugged.

"Dr. Emerson, Dr. Hinkley, Reverend: you three have a job to do. Since our mainframe has been damaged, it's now impossible to process any new TDL Codes, which means there's no way of knowing for sure what happened to Mr. Bauer or Agent Stowe. You three are going to spend the remainder of the lockdown in the library doing as much research as you can to see if you can uncover the truth. The computer in the library has access to the public's mainframe which will reflect the current state of our world *after* Bauer did whatever he did in the past. You should be able to find some answers there. Remember, no one leaves this building until the lockdown is complete. When our timeline has been breached, as is evidently the case here, the building automatically shuts down for a minimum of five hours. When the sun rises, the building will open its doors as always and we will have our first opportunity to see our changed world, God help us. Until then, stay put! It's just too dangerous to leave now, even if we wanted to.

"Here's what we know about Bauer; he was sent back to 1822 England to a small port town called Bishopwearmouth. He missed his TDL retrieval because he was in the wrong location. His STOOPING Piece returned unoccupied. That's it. As for Agent Stowe, we have no idea. She could be anywhere. This is what we trained for, gentlemen. This is why you were hired. We could be at war now, for all we know. It's up to you stop it: to find the source of the conflict and squelch it. This is the business you've chosen. If our doors don't open tomorrow morning as scheduled, it could mean the end of your careers with Harper's. We are a dying breed. Time Travel as we know it, is on the brink of extinction. It all depends on Agent Stowe and Mr. Bauer. Gentlemen, find them. You have until dawn."

"I think I counted four," Wally said as he and his crew journeyed to the ClockWorks Library.

"I don't know, I got five," Sherman said. The friends were counting the number of clichés Waverly spewed out in the speech he made before they were dismissed from his office.

"Yeah, but are you counting the whole 'this is the business you've chosen' thing?" Wally asked.

"Of course! That's pretty cliché, don't you think?"

"Not really, it's kind of a direct rip-off some old movie. I forget which one.," Wally argued.

"*The Godfather*," Lamar interjected.

"What's that, Lamar?" Sherman asked.

"That line: it's from *The Godfather: Part II,"* Lamar replied. He'd been acting oddly ever since they left the Archer E. Room earlier that Tuesday morning.

"Everything alright, Lamar?" Sherman wondered.

"You grew up around here, right Sherman?" Lamar asked pensively.

"Uh, no, Wally and I grew up down in Tell City, Indiana."

"Oh, Tell City. *Tell City*, eh?" Lamar asked. "Tell me, guys, what did you all do for fun down in *Tell City*?" Sherman and Wally were taken aback. This line of questioning seemed strangely out of context given their current predicament of having to save the entire world by sunrise.

"Uh, well, we used to, um, what *did* we do, Wally?" Sherman asked.

"There's nothing really *to* do, Lamar. We basically spent most of the time back then just watchin' TV or talking on the phone." Wally said.

"You doin' okay there, Lamar?" Sherman asked again. Lamar stopped in the middle of the stairwell. He was standing two steps above his coworkers who saw nothing but a blackened silhouette caused by the emergency lights at the top of the stairs when they turned to face him.

"Say for second that I'm not from here. Pretend that someone brought me back from one of their ClockWorks vacations or, hell, say that I'm a traveler from a faraway land that no one's ever heard of. Say I just asked you that same question about what you used to do down in Tell City. How would you answer it?"

"There's nothing really *to* do, Lamar. We basically spent most of the time back then just watchin' TV or talking on the phone." Wally said, this time slower and more emphatically. Apparently all foreigners are also retarded.

"*TV? Phone?* What are you talking about?" Lamar begged. "When I was a kid we played outside and threw rocks at squirrels. You're tellin' me you just sat inside all day? Even in the summer?"

"Oh come on, Lamar, you know what we're talking about. Let's go to the library and do our jobs." Sherman and Wally turned again and continued down the stairs. Lamar remained on his step. He yelled down at the descending pair.

"So you mean to tell me that for the better part of your childhood you two just sat down and watched images on some artificial box? Or talked to other people on some voice transportation device? This is what you're saying? That was the life you both chose for yourselves?"

"Yeah, Lamar!" Wally shouted, his frustration mounting. "That's exactly what we're saying! That's what people *do,* okay? It may not make sense to a guy like you, but that's who we are and that's all we've ever known. It's just what we do. That's it. There's nothing wrong with it. *You* abused defenseless animals when you were a kid and you got the balls to criticize the way we spent our childhood? Personally, I'm tired and a little pissed that instead of spending the night in my nice warm bed, I gotta spend it here with you two assholes, so if you don't mind, why don't we just go down to the library and try to figure out where the hell Stowe could be. You got a problem with that, Lamar?!"

Lamar took a few steps down the stairs and passed Sherman and Wally. As he walked by Wally, Lamar looked at him and simply said, "Maybe we all should." Sherman didn't know why, but for the first time in his life he felt shame for the William Tell Club. Wally, on the other hand, wasn't going to let this one go without a fight.

"Hold on a second, Lamar! Alright, whatever, you don't like technology or whatever--"

"That's not what I'm saying, Wal--"

"Well, fine, whatever, I don't care! You tell us now--same thing--you tell us what you did in *your* childhood to make you so goddamn special, huh. Go on! I'm dying to hear why I should feel bad about the way I was raised but *you* don't need to.

Cuz all I'm hearin' is that you were some little masochist or something as a kid, right?"

"It's not that simple, Wally. I did most of the same things it sounds like you both did. I watched TV, still do. I talk on the phone all the time. And no, I was just kidding, I never threw rocks at squirrels or any other animal for that matter. Of course, I did open up a book once in a while and actually read something, but I'm sure you did too. I doubt you spent your entire time in Tell City watching TV or talking on the phone."

"Damn right we didn't! So what's your point, then?"

"I'm not sure really what my point is, Wally. I'm not. But it seems to me that this empty building we're now winding our way through has been here longer than you've been alive and certainly as long as I can remember, and no one's ever really given it a second thought. It's our culture, after all. It defines who we are."

"Damn right it does! That's why I'm working here. Everybody knows that if ya wanna make some noise, ya work at Harper's!"

"But that's just the problem, Wally, don't you see! All this place *is* is noise. It's just white noise! Like your TV or phone, or my conferences and articles or TDL Codes or the IDM Room. It's just noise. Sure, the noise floods the city with excitement and fervor at first, but eventually people get so used to it that the same noise that was once deafening and earth shattering overtime becomes nothing more than its own mode of silence. No one cares. No one questions. No one hears. Well, until something goes wrong, no one hears. Just ask anyone who's ever stayed in a hotel with its own air conditioning unit; eventually you'll fall asleep.

"But that brief detection of sound doesn't derive from genuine interest in the sound itself, but rather exists solely in the primal recognition that *something isn't quite as it should be*. That's the extent of our curiosity! We say to ourselves, 'Hmm, something doesn't seem right. I wonder what it is.' It's like when you wake up in the middle of the night and aren't quite sure why. Maybe a flash of lightning from a far off storm woke you up. Maybe something fell in your closet and caused you to temporarily abandon your slumber. Whatever the impetus of your wakened state is, it occurred while you were asleep and was gone once you awoke. Since you can't put your finger on it, and it's still dark outside by the way, you just say 'fuck it' and go back to sleep!

"And so ClockWorks, which once stood on the precipice of human innovation, now serves as a means onto its own demise. The necessity which led to its invention which led to yet more necessity has finally destroyed its own capacity for progress. We've abandoned our pursuit of the source of the noise and have instead grown complacent in its mere presence. We've grown so complacent, however, that we can no longer recognize its presence or the social, moral, or ethical justification for its presence in the first place. It's just there. It's always been there. *It's just what we do*. Now, it's only a matter of time before all will crumble to the ground."

"Alright, *Lamar*, very good, you've obviously given this a lot of thought," Wally sardonically commented. "And *my God,* you're wordy! Just answer me one question, though. If you hate this place so much--*and after one fucking day at that*--why the hell did you want to work here in the first place? Why!? You could've done anything in the world? Why sell yourself so fundamentally short by applying to a corporation whose moral foundation in no way coincided with what you feel is right? Why? And what's up with this whole necessity versus invention bullshit, anyway?"

Sherman stepped in to answer the last part. "They say that necessity is the mother of all invention. We needed a way to study history more decisively than books or articles so Harper invented time travel. He responded to a public need."

"That's right, Sherman," Lamar added. "But as Jared Diamond once argued, invention also can serve as the mother of all necessity. Once Harper invented time travel, we suddenly had so many more needs for it: needs that never existed prior to its invention. Think of the telephone. Before Bell unveiled his new invention in 1876, sure, there was a burgeoning need to communicate with people from far off distances. The world, after all, was expanding at an unprecedented rate and Bell was simply responding to this growth. But think of how many needs rose *from* the invention of the telephone. Before too long we needed cordless phones, so we wouldn't have to get up to make a phone call. Then we needed answering machines so we wouldn't have to answer the phone even when it did ring. Then we needed text messaging so we would never even have to talk on our phone at all. Of course these aren't *real* needs in the sense that we couldn't function as a species without them, but all the same, try stripping a kid today of his cell phone and see how well he does at recess without being able to chat with his cyberfriend in Tokyo."

"You still haven't answered my question, *Lamar*. Why are you here? Why bother placing yourself on what is obviously such an inferior pedestal when you appear to have the ability to enter into any field of your choosing. Why?" Wally demanded.

"I guess it's because of the same reason you chose to work here, Wally. Because somewhere along the line, someone told me--and I don't know who and I don't remember where--but someone told me that the only way to get on the path to the beginning of forever was at E.W. Harper's world famous ClockWorks TTA. All I had to was follow the watch with no hands."

Sherman's heart sank. A voice from his childhood crept into his mind when Lamar uttered this final sentiment. They were the words of his former Sunday school teacher, Father Daniel Norris who used to stand on his old wooden desks during Lent and proclaim to the attentive students the Passion of the Christ. *"When Pilate saw that he was accomplishing nothing, but rather that a riot was starting, he took water and washed his hands in front of the crowd, saying, 'I am innocent of this Man's blood; see to that yourselves.'"*

Fifteen
Second Hand Out

"Marriage is wonderful when it lasts forever, and I envy the old couples in *When Harry Met Sally* who reminisce tearfully about the day they met 50 years before. I no longer believe, however, that a marriage is a failure if it doesn't last forever. It may be a tragedy, but it is not necessarily a failure. And when a marriage does last forever with love alive, it is a miracle."

-Peggy O'Mara, *Mothering*, Fall 1989

"The father who does not teach his son his duties is equally guilty as the son who neglects them."

-Confucius

When Era Howells awoke in the middle of the night, she rolled over to see how much longer she could sleep before having to get up and go to work. *Weird,* she thought. *Where's my alarm clock?* Thinking perhaps she had knocked it off sometime while sleeping, she leaned over the right edge of her bed to see if the clock was somewhere on the floor. It wasn't. *Why did I wake up in the first place?* When she rolled back over to lie on her back, she caught a glimpse of something in the corner of her right eye. It was a tiny red glowing light at the edge of her bed. Era slowly turned her head and saw her alarm clock sitting on the nightstand on the left side of her bed. It said the time was 5:30. She had fifteen minutes before she had to get up and go to work. Fifteen minutes to find out who moved her clock to the opposite side of the bed.

Era heard a toilet flush coming from the master bathroom. *The master bathroom?* She didn't have a *master* bathroom. She shared a bathroom with her roommate and fellow ClockWorks PA, Stacey Mather. But this was definitely not

Stacey coming back to bed. This was certainly a man: a man who, apparently, didn't think there's anything wrong with kidnapping a strange woman in the middle of the night and bringing her back to his place, ravaging her, then taking a piss break before hopping back into the sack to do it all over again. Well, *this* man wasn't going to have his way with her again!

"Sorry, did I wake you, babe?" The man could tell Era was wide awake. Yet, the voice sounded familiar. No, it couldn't be. *This must be a dream.* It's impossible.

"Go back to sleep, sweetie, we still have a few more hours to go before the plane leaves," the man said, rolling over to his side of the bed--*the left side*--before going back to sleep.

"C-C-Casey?" Era stuttered. She was terrified. She didn't turn to look at him but rather stayed perfectly still with the blankets pulled to her face and her eyes glued to the ceiling: a ceiling from her past.

"What is it, babe?" the man mumbled into his pillow.

"W-w-what am I--what are *you*--how--?" Era was at a loss for words. Casey, however, handled her staccato, intermittent questions with shocking calm and composure, as if he'd performed this role thousands of times. He rolled over and engulfed her in his muscular, bare arms.

"Shhh, honey, go back to sleep. The doctor will help us tomorrow, remember? He's going to make you all better. You'll see. Trust me, go back to sleep." *Where am I? Where's Kristen? Where's Sherman? Gotta get back to Harper's! Something's wrong! Really wrong! Help me!*

The man called Casey then leaned in and kissed Era on the lips: the wet, passionate, loving kiss of a sworn protector. Her body tingled with a sensation she hadn't experienced in four years, six months, three weeks, and two days. Her toes went numb. Her eyes filled with tears. Casey rolled over and reentered his dream world while Era silently wept. She didn't know how she got there, but at that moment, she didn't care. Whoever this doctor was that they were supposedly going to see tomorrow, she knew he couldn't make her feel any better than she felt at that moment. As she wiped a tear away from her face, she scratched her cheek with the diamond ring she wore on her left hand. This was no dream. She was in her *own house* at 5:30 on a Tuesday morning, lying next to her husband who had died four and a half years before. The world was finally as it should be.

"This is ridiculous!" Wally exclaimed. "How the hell are we supposed to find anything about Isabelle without the ClockWorks mainframe? We don't even know where to begin!" Sherman and Lamar closed their respective web browsers in concession of Wally's point. The three had been slaving over years of Harper's employment applications and print articles in a relatively futile attempt to crosscheck those with anything on-line to determine if they can match any shred of Stowe's past with *something* in their current world. So far, nothing had come up. According to public records, Isabelle Stowe simply didn't exist.

"She's got to be *somewhere*, right? I mean, you can't just *disappear* like this, can you? We have proof she was hired by ClockWorks! We all *know* her! She was here yesterday!" Wally continued.

"Well, then something must have happened during the course of the night to alter the path of her temporal line. As far as the world is concerned, she was never born," Lamar claimed.

"But how can that be, Lamar? I mean, we all have the…hippo-implant thing, right? So all of our memories can't be altered? So she should still *be* here, shouldn't she?" Sherman posited as if he were a kid trying to rationalize the existence of Santa Clause to a six year-old Jewish boy.

"No, Sherman, that's not how things work. The hippocampus implant, yes, makes all of our memories impervious to any alteration in the temporal path which is why nobody here can determine how our society has changed: because we have only memories from the *old* timeline," Lamar explained.

"Right, and Isabelle was *on* that timeline, right?" Wally argued.

"Indeed she was, Wally," Lamar continued. "But the hippocampus implant is only effective if the person who received it was born in the first place. Something must have happened which caused Isabelle to never be born. In other words, because she was never alive to undergo the procedure, its effects on memory can't possibly apply to her."

"I don't understand, so someone can just...*not be born*?" Sherman begged.

"In a word, yes," Lamar replied. "If something was changed in the past which interfered with the formation of that person's family tree." Sherman and Wally stared at each other, each silently wondering if anyone else they knew might not exist anymore. "Another thing that can happen, though, I've never heard of it before, is someone sort of...coming back from the dead. You may walk out of here this morning and bump into your dead dad, Sherman or your dead grandmother, Wally."

"Whoa, what?!" they both asked. "How's that possible?"

"Well, imagine that your father died in a car crash when you were a child. Say, he was killed in a head on collision by a drunk driver named, oh I don't know, Larry. Well let's say that someone goes back in time and somehow interferes with Larry's ancestral line--accidentally kills Larry's great, great grandpa or something. Well, that change would spark a series of events which would render the current world Larry-free! With no drunken Larry around to kill your father, Wally, there'd be a chance he could still be alive today. The instant that time traveler veered the current timeline off its path, the world would change and exist as if your father was in it. If you or I or anyone else with a hippocampus implant were standing around, there's a chance we might see your father just...appear....out of nowhere and carry on just like he'd been doing for years. The entire process would probably look very similarly to how Ebenezer Scrooge flashed between points of his past; one minute he's there, the next minute he's somewhere else. One minute your father's dead, the next he's been in your life all along.

"Of course the problem is, because of your implant, *you* wouldn't remember having your father around. You would only have memories of a life spent without him: the memories present on *your* temporal plane. This would result in a paradox of astronomical proportions. Your father would have memories of a life spent raising a son who's perpetually convinced he died when his son was a young boy. So, I guess, following the flash in which everything changes, you may find yourself locked up in some asylum somewhere. Your father would be alive, but the world would think you're insane."

"I don't get that last part," Sherman said, confused. "Explain that again: *why* would people think I'm insane?"

"Think of it this way. I'll use dates this time. Okay, say you're father died when it was, um, 2040. Okay, you're five years old in 2040 and your father is dead. For, 28 years, you've lived your life without him, okay? Now, let's say someone messes with Larry's timeline causing Larry to never be born which means he could never kill your father in 2040. This new timeline--the one in which the world now has your father living in it--would begin to branch off in 2040: the year Larry's life would have directly interacted with your life. Now, of course the timeline would *really* begin to branch off the second Larry's ancestor was killed, but chances are that wouldn't directly have an impact on *your* life until 2040 when Larry kills your dad. Make sense? Okay, anyway, your memories up until 2040 would be in accordance with the timeline *as the rest of the world now knows it.* Thus, everyone would be able to talk with you about your early childhood and everything else that happened in the world before 2040. But because you have the hippocampus implant, everything that happened *since* 2040--everything in the last 28 years--would be completely foreign to you because your father would have been around.

"Now, everyone around you today, in 2068, would have memories of your father. They'd be able to talk with you about how he helped you get your driver's license or got you drunk at your college graduation or things like that. *You,* on the other hand, would have no concept of what the world has been like since 2040. Well, you *would* but your memories would reflect a life spent without your father: the only life you've ever known, the *original timeline*. Of course, you could still form new memories. In other words, once 'the great time shift' occurs you'll be able to remember everything that happened to you. You would merely have a gap of about 28 years where you'd have no idea what happened in the world. Consequently, for 28 years, you would have been a zombie: a zombie with which your family would have had to cope for nearly three decades. So, when that time traveler in the past ruins Larry's genealogical progression--the *instant* that happens--you would be simultaneously transported to wherever it is a guy would be who's convinced his father died when he was a kid even though he really didn't. For most people, the world wouldn't have changed that much. But for you, the results could be horrific."

"So, when we walk out those doors…" Sherman began.

"There's no way to tell what could be waiting for us," Lamar concluded. "We don't even know for sure that this building is even ClockWorks TTA anymore, at least as we recognize it. It may look entirely different for all we know. We may not even be in *Indianapolis* anymore. We may be in Ohio somewhere or Mexico or who the hell knows where?"

"But the ACHEs came to get us in our own homes this morning, Lamar, so we know we're still in Indy," Wally retorted, silencing Lamar. Sherman couldn't believe it: Wally actually said something that made sense. And made Lamar speechless at the same time! "And besides," Wally continued, "chances are nothing has really changed that much. I mean, seriously, how much could some guy in 1822 England really do to affect our lives over 200 years later? Seriously." No one wanted to admit it, but even Wally recognized the ominous, foreshadowing implications of his last quip.

"I guess I still don't get it though," Sherman said. "Why would Harper's risk institutionalizing its own employees by giving them this memory implant? It seems that the risks far outweigh the rewards."

"It would seem like that, Sherman. But you have to remember that things like this don't happen very often. And when they have, ClockWorks has always relied on people who can accurately recall the way things *were* so that they can make everything normal again," Lamar explained.

"Yeah, but it seems to me like that's putting way too much emphasis on the integrity of a select group of people. I mean, how do we know that these people can be trusted? What if someone with an implant lies and changes the past to fit his or her own private agenda?"

"Nothing, I guess. Nothing except the endless system of checks and balances Harper himself implemented to make sure something like that doesn't happen. Remember, Sherman, *you're* one of those people trusted to make the right decisions. We were all hired to ensure the future of the company against all enemies foreign and futuristic."

"Okay, just stop--both of you!" Wally snapped. "The world isn't going to suffer because Isabelle Stowe was never born. The world will be fine. We'll *all* be fine, okay? So let's just give the bosses some bullshit explanation of why she's never born and move on, alright?"

"Think they'll find anything, sir?" Gage wondered aloud in Waverly's office. "I'm betting they'll all just come up here with some bullshit explanation for why she's never born and move on."

It was the irony of ironies that in the building with perhaps with most technological capabilities and intricate computing systems of any facility in the Western Hemisphere, the remaining Harper's Agents were literally locked within their own walls, forced to wait until the building released them with the rising of the sun. While Lamar was educating Wally and Sherman on the mysteries of the universe down in the library, Gage and Waverly sat nervously in the President's office, anxiously awaiting the return of the reconnaissance ACHEs, or at least a report from the three new Agents. Barring the commencement of World War IV, however, all Gage and Waverly could do was wait and contemplate the condition of their brave new world.

"Frankly, Lieutenant, I don't give a shit," Waverly snorted. "This world will live on just fine without that poor excuse for a woman stomping on its tender surface. Alcott and Lapham are who I'm worried about." Gage nodded in agreement, simultaneously taking another swig of his brandy.

"Do you think the Bauer boy's dead, sir?" Gage asked.

"I should hope so, Phineas!" Waverly replied. "Death, we can handle. Death is swift. Death is quickly forgotten. Death becomes myth, and myth will always remain simply that: a fable embraced by the eccentric minority, the anti-truth. What concerns me is the possibility that he's alive. He's young, Phineas. There's no limit to what a young man can accomplish if he's left to his own devices in a foreign land." Waverly finished his drink. "Make no mistake, Phineas, death is the only way we can ensure our survival."

Waverly picked up a framed photograph sitting on the corner of his desk. The black and white image captured behind the glass depicted a line of military men standing in front of a pile of wreckage in the middle of the desert. The men all wore smiles indicative of some sort of accomplishment though, to a layman, no discernible feat could be ascertained solely from the photograph alone. Waverly never spoke of the photograph and even Gage didn't know to which of the rumors circulating around the Agency regarding the picture's narrative he should subscribe. Gage had examined the photograph a number of times with the fleeting hope that maybe he would deduce that Waverly was one of the men pictured. There were, after all, stories floating around the annals of ClockWorks' lore that suggested Waverly was born in 1903 in a small town in North Dakota and had been brought into the future to run the Agency, but Gage never believed such campfire tales. Still, anyone who'd ever been around Waverly knew that of crimes one could commit, none was more deplorable than tampering with his coveted desktop photograph.

"Did I ever tell you about Sam and Max, Phineas?" Waverly asked, carefully repositioning the frame in its rightful place on the corner of his desk. It was the type of question that automatically necessitated a negative response. Whether or not Gage had in fact heard of Sam or Max was inconsequential compared to Waverly's undeniable desire to tell Gage a story. Obliging his employer with courtesy (and honesty, for Gage had indeed never heard of Sam or Max), the Lieutenant shook his head and prepared himself for the story to follow.

"I'm sure you're familiar with the Biblical accounts of strange lights appearing in the night's sky or flying discs hovering over Jerusalem or Egypt?" Gage nodded in uncertainty. "History liked to aptly write these phenomena off as UFO's--unidentified flying objects, and frankly, that name makes sense. Where the affiliation with extraterrestrials came about, I can't be terribly sure, but to me, it always seemed appropriate to identify a flying object which is unidentifiable as such. What people don't realize, however, and what only a select few have ever known for certain, is that what history embraces as evidence of life outside our planetary realm is actually our own fingerprints peppered throughout time: the residual traces of our ClockWorks voyages.

"Some years after Harper's death, the Agency began experimentation with a new form of time travel, one that involved not the cumbersome IDM chambers we currently use, but rather a form which utilized speed and energy, as opposed to water and energy. Harper's engineers harnessed the prevailing aviation technology of the time to create, essentially, a flying time machine. Before you say anything, I want to remind you that this program never, pardon the pun, *took off* as I personally hoped it would. The investors were all on board and patents were in the process of being finalized, but we had to maintain absolute secrecy from any and all employees to protect our liability. You understand, sir, of course. We had several successful initial trials, all automated, mind you. We didn't dare send back living specimens at first, not even descendents of Harper's dear subject, Abraham.

"Our first successful trial came about after I had been with the company for a little over three years. We sent a capsule back in time to, well, it was *suppose*d to be Mexico in 1565 but because of a problem we encountered adjusting the TDL Codes to a wireless medium, the capsule went back much earlier than anticipated: to Ancient Egypt. We retrieved the capsule five minutes later and since it had been equipped with a video surveillance unit, we knew we had succeeded. Well, at least we knew the damn thing went *somewhere* that resembled Ancient Egypt. I guess it *could* have been Mexico, but anyway…

"Over the next three years, while our program maintained its top-secret security classification, we successfully sent back six hundred and sixty five air-based time capsules, over two hundred of which were flown by ClockWorks pilots. They went everywhere from Aztec Mexico, to Ancient Egypt, to Pre-Christian Jerusalem, to indigenous upstate New York to several visits to the early nineteenth century American Old West."

"So, the Pyramids--" Gage interrupted.

"Exactly," Waverly wryly replied. "Let's just say that a couple of our pilots *ignored* their retrieval TDL Codes and decided to stick around for a while before coming back. Ever wonder what Moroni looked like when he visited Joseph Smith?"

"Uh, not really sir."

"Well, for some reason, I'm told he looked a lot like my first intern. But that's neither here nor there."

"So what happened, sir? Why did Harper's stop production--"

"I'm getting to that, Phineas! Do you have somewhere to go? Am I keeping you from something?"

"No, sir, I apologize, carry on."

"Thank you," Waverly refilled his brandy glass and proceeded. "When I was younger, my wife gave me two sons. She was beautiful, Lieutenant, and I loved her with all my heart. Unfortunately, complications arose during the birth of our second son and she was taken from me. She left me with two baby boys and a company to raise into maturity. It just so happened that my boys came into this world at the height of our aviation research program. They loved hearing me debate with my engineers into all hours of the night and watch as the capsules would return home safely from their voyages. The oldest, Sam, he especially was fascinated with the flying aspect of the program. Max was the time traveler, Sam was the pilot; that's just the way it always was. Of course, they were both still too young for me to consider letting them go on their own voyage, but when the capsules were stripped of their TDL processors during routine maintenance, I would shadow the boys on quick little flights around the base. They loved those afternoons with me! I never saw Sam happier than when he was behind the wheel of an official Harper's time capsule with Max in to the co-pilot's seat plotting his next trip to see a pirate battle on the open seas. They understood, though, that for me, the company came first. I know it sounds harsh, but it's because of the Agency that they even knew about time travel in the first place. If the Agency goes, we all go; it's that simple, and they respected that. You must understand this, okay? They respected-- they *honored*-- that code.

"On Sam's thirteenth birthday, I gave him the present of his life. For the months leading up to his big day I'd been soliciting the engineers and investors for permission to allow

Sam and Max a solo flight through time. Of course, it would be under direct Harper's supervision and to a remote location where there'd be no chance they could alter our timeline. I requested they use a prototype vessel--a cruder version of our more developed, technical capsules--for their journey, so as to ensure that no insurmountable debt be incurred by their trip. I vowed to take all necessary precautions and forfeited all rights for a rescue mission; I trusted my boys, Gage. I *trusted* them. The only request I made of the Agency was that Sam and Max be allowed to paint their capsule prior to departure. You know, a way of personalizing their vessel. Leaving their mark, so to speak, the way all good pilots do.

"The final clearance came two days before Sam's birthday. He expected I had gotten him something spectacular but when I informed him that he and his brother would be going on their very own journey through time in a real life flying time capsule…well…few parents have had prouder moments, I assure you. I told my sons that their first duty was to decorate the exterior of the capsule however they wished. I provided them with adequate supplies for the task and left them for the afternoon to aesthestisize their capsule. Of course, we planned on cleaning it once they returned but they neither needed to know that, nor would have cared either way. For that special day, that was *their* capsule.

"We wanted to choose a location that would be remote enough for them to avoid any suspicion or detection but not long enough ago that they couldn't survive on their own on the off chance they get into trouble. That was my stipulation. Safety first: fun, a distant second. My engineers and I chose a tiny patch of desert in New Mexico in 1947 as the destination for their trip."

"Sir…" Gage said, his voice trembling. Waverly didn't say anything. His hand reached for the photograph on his desk again.

"You ever put a town on the map before, Lieutenant? I have," Waverly said, gazing at the picture. "Nobody'd ever heard of Roswell before that day. Nobody."

"Sir…" was all Gage could utter.

"I can't say exactly what happened, Lieutenant. No one can. Sam…just…crashed…It's as simple as that. Of course, as you know, the crash didn't kill them. No, sure it ruined their capsule, but both he and Max were healthy enough to crawl out of that goddamned….out of the vessel and try to find help. It's all they could think to do. They didn't know where they were or what to say to anyone once they found help. They were so young. What you probably *don't* know, Lieutenant, is that it took about eight and a half minutes for local RAAF officers to converge on the scene. Believing my boys were a threat to national security, the officers shot each of my sons, killing Sam instantly and wounding Max in the lower sternum. The officers then rushed in, collected Max and carried him back to their base. They left the wreckage and the rotting body of Sam, the birthday boy, to roast in the scorching desert.

"Apparently, those fuckers didn't think to come back and clean up the sight of their massacre because a few weeks later, one of Roswell's farmers, a man named Mac Brazel, uncovered Sam's decomposing, little corpse and the remains of the capsule's infrastructure that hadn't already been blown away into the desert. The rest, as they say, Lieutenant, is history."

"But, sir, excuse me, but why--"

"Don't!" Waverly pronounced. "Don't you dare ask why I didn't go back! Don't you think I wanted to? Don't you think it killed every ounce of me knowing that I killed my sons? I *killed* my sons, Gage! But I couldn't go back. I forfeited my rights to a rescue mission. The Agency would never allow it."

"Oh, sir, surely you of all people--"

"I couldn't, Gage."

"But *would* you?"

"I beg your pardon, Lieutenant?"

"Begging *your* pardon, sir, but surely you *would* go back if you had the chance. Surely you would go back to…save…but you've *had* the chance…sir? You could have gone back anytime since then? Why haven't you?" Gage was dumfounded. Waverly stood up from his chair and began pacing around the room, his framed picture in hand.

"We dismantled the aviation program the following week, Lieutenant. We returned all time traveling operations to their rightful place: the way Harper designed it, in the IDM Room. Life is precious, Lieutenant. My time with my wife and my boys was the greatest gift my life has ever given me."

"I realize that sir, so why--"

"It's a *gift*, Lieutenant," Waverly calmly said, raising a finger in a gesture beseeching Gage's silence. "But it isn't a handout. We must be accountable for the decisions we make. For no other industry in the world is this philosophy more incumbent. It is imperative that we accept the consequences of our own actions and the resulting condition the world bestows upon us. We must find a way to live with whatever *our world* is like right now because of whatever Mr. Bauer may have done in the past. His death will make it easier to carry on with our own lives. His death will be a gift, sir: a gift of continued life. But we mustn't ever mistake it for a handout. With handouts come a sense of entitlement that curses everything for which this Agency so proudly stands. With gifts, merely a sense of appreciation for what life has granted us." Waverly tossed the frame into Gage's lap and turned to pace in the opposite direction.

Gage examined the photograph yet again. He remembered hearing stories of the Roswell incident as a child and since then had always been fascinated by the entire UFO cultural phenomenon that spawned from that desert so many years ago. He now viewed the photograph with a new, refined lens of a father witnessing his son's burial: the lens of a guardian to a land of unwarranted pleasures and unbearable pains. The officers surrounding the alien wreckage smiled at a task well done in successfully eliminating a threat to their nation. If only they knew all they did was murder an American child on his birthday.

Lieutenant Phineas P. Gage noticed something in the picture he had never seen before. Some Roswell reports speak of strange and phantom markings on the casing of the alien ship's wreckage: signs and symbols that seemed to have derived from a foreign system of linguistics, an alien language of sorts. While Gage sat in Waverly's office early that Tuesday morning, all he could decipher as he squinted at the faded black and white photograph were two distinct markings on the outside rim of one of the shattered pieces of debris: a barely perceptible pair of eagle's wings and what appeared to be an eleven year-old's rendition of the Jolly Roger, a pirate's insignia. Alien characters indeed.

Sixteen
Dawn

"Let us go to war. The world has become stale and insipid, the ships ought to be all captured, and the cities battered down, and the world burned up, so that we can start again. There would be fun in that. Some interest, — something to talk about."

-Editorial in the *New York Journal of Commerce* (August 1845)

"Happiness in this world, when it comes, comes incidentally. Make it the object of pursuit, and it leads us a wild-goose chase, and is never attained. Follow some other object, and very possibly we may find that we have caught happiness without dreaming of it."

-Nathaniel Hawthorne in *The American Notebooks* (1851)

The sun still rose that July morning in Indianapolis. The world had not been destroyed during the night. Hoosiers drove to their respective places of business as they had done the day before, several enjoying their second day back from a rather lengthy holiday weekend. Planes took off from the Indianapolis International Airport, buses carried anxious transients to their destinations, and pedestrians flooded the streets on their way to the market, the Children's Museum, or the Indianapolis Zoo. Summer camps ran in full swing with lines of minivans frantically speeding into bustling parking lots, making sure their children had everything they needed for lunch and afternoon craft time. Parking garage attendants raised their gates in preparation for a lucrative morning. Victory Field employees arrived early to clean the baseball stadium for the evening's moderately publicized match-up against the Columbus Bulldogs. Indy police casually patrolled bank entrances and hotel lobbies. And slightly south of Monument Circle, E.W. Harper's

ClockWorks TTA was officially open for business. The sun had indeed risen that glorious Tuesday morning.

Sherman, Wally, and Lamar stood in the foyer facing the Harper's entrance. They could each sense stirrings of the city as they awaited further instructions from their superiors. During the course of the night, neither of the team members uncovered a single trace of Stowe's existence. She had simply vanished from any and all temporal paths. Wally, especially, felt no inclination to inform Gage or Waverly of their shortcomings; Stowe was, after all, a worthless employee, and he for one didn't believe anyone would miss her. If her absence is the worst thing to evolve from Sherman's folly, Wally personally thought Sherman deserved a medal of honor.

Gage and Waverly emerged from the glass elevator at the far end of the atrium. Behind them marched four ACHEs and, Sherman was unnerved to see, Harvey and Lester. "Well, gentlemen, I trust you came to some conclusion regarding the whereabouts of Agent Stowe," Waverly asked.

"Yes, sir," Wally answered. "We estimate that due to some sort of alteration in Stowe's timeline derived, of course, from Mr. Bauer's malfeasance in the past, her existence was rendered, um, well…non-existent." *We're dead,* Sherman thought. Gage looked at Waverly who in turn examined the countenance of the ACHEs and Sherman's trusty interns. After several moments of silent contemplation, Waverly finally declared,

"Yes, we figured as much. Well done, you three." Sherman was shocked. Lamar was ashamed. Wally couldn't have been prouder. "Now that we're all here, gentlemen," Waverly proceeded, "I feel it necessary to implore you to be on the look out for Agent Alc--"

"Sorry guys, didn't mean to be late," Eternity said as she came rushing into the foyer from a door at the rear end of the concourse area. "I thought we'd be meeting upstairs like always. I didn't realize yall would be down here." *Did she just bat her eyes again?*

"Agent Alcott," Gage sneered, "so kind of you to join us this morning. I'm sure you're aware by now that we've had a little catastrophe on our hands all night. But now that you're here, we may leave those matters to the professionals and you, Dr. Hinkley, President Waverly, and I can proceed with the deposition of your client, Miss Lapham." *Kristen!* Sherman's eyes nearly bugged out of his skull. He had completely forgotten about his duties this morning of testifying against Kristen's psychological competency.

"Lieutenant, I'm afraid that isn't going to be possible," Lester uttered.

"And why not, Mr. Whitman," Waverly said, turning to face the trembling boy.

"Uh, well, you see…" Lester mumbled.

"We thought we could get her back, sir," Harvey stepped in.

"Get her *back*, Mr. Douglas? Get her back from *what*?" Gage snarled.

"She, during the night she…she escaped, Lieutenant. She's no longer in the building," Harvey confessed.

"I see," Waverly whispered. Sherman likened the conversation to when Peter Brady had to confess to Carol and Mike that he broke his mom's favorite vase by playing ball in the house. Only in this case, the hourglass figure was made of porcelain flesh as opposed to clay, and instead of shattering from the impact of a poorly thrown basketball, she apparently just ran away. "I suspected there might be an attempt to rescue Miss Lapham, but I didn't think it would come this soon. Agent Alcott, I don't suppose you know anything about this…*escape*…do you?"

"No way, sir! I've been sleeping all night. I don't even know who you're talking about. The only clients I had yesterday were Will Bauer and Leslie Row--"

"Her name is *Lapham*, Alcott, and you damn well know it!" Gage screamed. "Now where is she?!"

"I promise, sir, I can't be sure where my friend is, but I do know her name is *not* Lapham or whatever it is you said."

"Agent Alcott, why don't you go with Harvey and Lester upstairs so they can ask you just a few more questions to see if you can remember anything about your *friend* that perhaps we have yet to hear." Waverly suggested. Everyone present, though, knew that this was no suggestion. It was a direct and indisputable order.

"I'd be happy to do that, Mr. President, but what about the Agency? None of the other PAs have arrived yet, and I'm worried that if we got busy, these guys wouldn't know what to do. It's only their second day, after all." The William Tell Club felt slightly embarrassed by Eternity's lack of faith in their managerial skills, though secretly they realized she was right. They'd be sunk without the assistance of Public Agents.

"You needn't worry about *them,* Miss Alcott," Gage sneered yet again, "They won't be working in the office this morning."

"I beg your pardon, sir?" Lamar protested. Had they all been fired sometime during the night and not been told yet?

"That's right, Reverend. Today ClockWorks TTA will begin offering its traveling services at precisely twelve noon. The building, of course, will be open for public visitors and we will administer our usual tours and operate according to our standard gym, restaurant, and museum hours. Only the IDM Room will be closed until noon for our quarterly maintenance. Thus, we will not be sending people on their trips until noon. It's important we make sure none of our technology is sub par, is it not?"

"Since when is being *sub par* a bad thing?" Wally whispered to Sherman. "I thought the *goal* was to be below par. That's how you win, right?"

"Anything to add, Emerson?" Gage growled.

"Uh, no sir, I was just wondering how often we're going to be doing these quarterly maintenances?"

"Hopefully never again, Agent Emerson. Hopefully never again," Waverly replied.

"Excuse me again, sir, but if we're not working here this morning, do you want us back by noon or what should we be doing exactly?" Lamar wondered.

"Excellent question, Reverend," Waverly announced. "Gentlemen, you three are going to do some surveillance work for us. Our public mainframe here in the building only grants you so much into the workings of our new society, however it has changed. I need you to go out into the city. Look around.

Read the newspaper, go to a museum; *learn about the world.* The reconnaissance report from this morning indicates no discernible alteration to the world, but then again, during the night their visibility is fairly limited. Essentially, I want you to tell me what is different about the world today compared to yesterday. We can only assume that since Mr. Bauer's STOOPING Piece returned unoccupied, it means he's dead. That should make things easy for us. When the Harper's mainframe is up and running, we will be able to send Agents back to 1822 and get him the hell out of there, but until then, I want to know first hand what in God's name we're going to be dealing with out there.

"Mr. Douglas and Whitman, please escort Agent Alcott upstairs for further questioning. ACHE Team, proceed with your search for Agent Howells and for God's sake, someone find Miss Lapham. You three, good luck out there. Be careful. Keep your wits about you. Watch out for the other guy. Report back here by 11:30 at the latest. If you're not back by 12:00, consider your employment with Harper's terminated. Stay together at all times and God's speed!" With that, the three were dismissed. Gage and Waverly retreated back upstairs to Waverly's secure office after deploying the ACHEs. Sherman's loyal interns escorted Eternity back upstairs, and Wally, Lamar, and Sherman began to count to themselves the number of Waverly clichés from the last tirade. *Someone should be writing this shit down.*

"Do *we* know anything yet, grandma?"

"No. It's still too early to know anything for sure. Eternity hasn't been able to find out much either. There's still no sign of your cousin. Eternity tried to go to her house after the change, but she wasn't there. I'm worried about her, child."

"I wouldn't be. She double crossed us. She deserves what she gets. When this whole thing boils over, I swear she'll never be part of this family again. The whole plan was almost ruined because of her. Thank God he's such an idiot. Do you think we'll have any use for him now that it's almost over? I mean, we only needed him to send me back and even though that part didn't work, he still managed to screw up with the Bauer kid. Why the hell he gave him ZC is beyond me, but it seems to have done the trick. Gage and Waverly are terrified that people will find out what happened."

"That's good, dear, very good news. I'm not sure how much more use we'll be able to extract from Dr. Hinkley. Based on what we just heard I'm not convinced he realizes he's had anything to do with this. None of them appear to grasp the situation for what it really could be."

"And what's that grandma? What *could* it be?"

"I'm not sure yet, dear. I'm really not sure. But all my life I've worried that abuse of the system will only result in tragedy. But what if it doesn't? What if the world is actually better because of Dr. Hinkley's mistake? Nevertheless, our first priority is to contain the doctor. I have a feeling he may try something foolish. I can't be sure why, but something tells me this all just won't go away anytime soon. I think it's time you bring him to me. I want to meet this one."

"Listen, she told me she thinks that's a good idea, but I'm not sure. With her being questioned right now and him thinking I'm some sort of criminal, I'm not sure it's such a good idea to go and bring him here and have you explain everything. He won't *believe* you for one thing. And the last thing we need is for him to think you're a liar. Then we'd really be lost."

"We may be lost anyway. It's important he realize why we chose him: if, for no other reason, than to give him the sense of purpose for which he's spent his entire life longing. I'm tired of worrying about this whole mess. I'm tired of everything. Eternity won't be able to help. They're onto her. You can never show your face around there again. Nor can I. And your cousin, assuming she's still alive, may have no recollection of ever working for ClockWorks in the first place. If something still needs to be done, Sherman Hinkley is the only person who can do it. We need to bring him here. He needs to hear the rest of my story."

There were no rag-clad gangs of rambunctious boys on jetpacks. No talking dogs gambling their owners' savings away in a mindless game of five card stud. There were no purple trees or chocolate rivers or bleeding clouds in the heavens. There were no burning buildings, crater holes, screams of distress, naked children, cursing geriatrics, sewers with green smoke percolating out their covers, or soot covered adolescents hurling canonical texts into ginormous bonfires. There were no horsemen hovering above the masses or scrolls of destruction being read by air-born devils. There were no lines of soldiers marching down the street or armored giraffes running amuck in Circle Center Mall. There were no planes flying overhead dropping bombs on the city nor people leaping from buildings. No one appeared to have any sort of super powers and absolutely no one appeared to be doing anything out of the ordinary. Indianapolis was consumed by the excesses of Monday, and ostensibly nothing more. Normalcy had persevered.

Still, despite the lack of catastrophic anomalies, Sherman and his partners detected a sense of*...pleasantness....*imbuing their fair city. As they slowly descended the grand stone ClockWorks staircase to the city streets, a feeling of joy overcame them. Perhaps it was because, for the first time in several hours, they were outside. Perhaps it was relief that world had not, in fact, gone to hell in a fucking hand basket. Even so, something *was* different. Something was *nicer*. Lamar observed that there seemed to be a lot *more* people walking around. Indy mornings were usually a populated affair, but this seemed eerily like an immense overcrowding. Maybe everyone was in town to see "All the King's Whores," or perhaps, due to some fluke geographical modification, Indy was now the nation's capital. In addition to the suspected surplus of people, both Wally and Sherman took note of the tremendous amount of elderly citizens: not *old* in the decrepit, socially burdening manner, but old in the "my grandparents still go rock-climbing and parasailing on weekends" way. Indeed, after they voiced their sightings, Lamar agreed that the senior population of Indianapolis seemed happier, healthier, and in greater numbers than any of them remembered.

After several trips in and out of a variety of their favorite stores, restaurants, and other businesses to see if anything inside was different, Lamar's nostrils picked up a pungent aroma he'd not smelled in years. As they were walking around the downtown capital building, Lamar asked his co-workers, "Did you guys notice that everyone back there was smoking?" Indeed

Wally and Sherman detected a strange and distant aroma but couldn't quite identify the source. Upon hearing Lamar's concern, they immediately realized what it was.

"Yeah, Lamar, I did!" Sherman eagerly replied. "That *is* weird isn't it? It's so early and yet so many people are already smoking."

"Yeah, but not only that Sherman, think about it. They were smoking *inside*. This country's been smoke free for over a decade." In fact, Lamar was right. The United States passed the much contended *Statute of Anti-Smoking Regulation Ban Law* in 2056 making it illegal to smoke any form of tobacco in *any* public place without the expressed written consent of a public notary or sanctioned religious official. Consequently, Americans rarely smelled smoke anymore because most people decided that getting up and going outside to light up was too much effort to continue the habit.

"It's weird that there's still so many healthy looking people around with everyone smoking," Wally posited. The others nodded in concurrence. What could a kid from Crown Point do in 1822 England that would change American laws in 2068? *What other laws have been changed*? With each step the three took as they continued to meander around the city, seeking clues which they hoped would indicate Bauer's role in their current world, a part of their collective consciousness began to rest easily. The absence of a centrally located orgy of golden calf worshippers at the base of Monument Circle seemed to effectively convince the team that God himself or, in keeping with the analogy, *Moses,* wasn't going to strike them down anytime soon. As far as they were concerned, life actually seemed pretty good, even though none of them had any idea how it ended up that way.

How the hell did everything end up this way? When Era awoke earlier that morning, the evanescent state in which she found herself (combined with the fact that she was lying next to her long lost love) resolved any shred of animosity or anguish she felt toward the world. For those ephemeral moments in the sweet morning's infancy, she cared nothing for the explanation for her husband's presence or the whereabouts of the rest of her family and friends. The corrosive clutches of destiny had, in one foul swoop, relinquished their suffocating hold on her after half a decade, and as she fell back to sleep, she knew that at last she was free. That was then. Now, however, Era began to wonder why her husband was no longer dead and what effect his prolonged existence may have had on her own life.

Casey Howells was finishing loading their car as Era sat nervously in the front seat. The two were about to depart Indy and fly to New York where Era supposedly had an appointment with a world renowned neurologist who specialized in rare cases of extended anterograde amnesia. In contrast to retrograde amnesia in which the patient cannot recall events which occurred prior to the amnesia's onset, anterograde amnesia refers to the loss of any memories formed *after* the onset of the disorder. Typically patients can remember, with varying degrees of accuracy, memories before the onset of amnesia but lose virtually all ability to remember later events for any more than a few brief moments. Era's case, though, differed slightly from the textbook cases of anterograde amnesia, and after four and a half years of emotional turmoil and marital dissipation, Casey Howells decided he had had enough. Having studied extensively on the latest research into anterograde amnesia and damage to the hippocampus region of the brain, Casey managed to locate an Indian doctor specializing in cases very similar to Era's. Based on email and telephone correspondences, Casey was hopeful that Dr. Ajay Nagheenanajar could aid Era to a quick and relatively painless recovery.

The primary trait of Era's condition that deviated from the textbook classification of anterograde amnesia was that in addition to being unable to form new memories, she had, for some reason, formed in an entirely new set of memories in her mind: memories that had no bearing whatsoever on the life she and Casey lived. Furthermore, and what kept Casey awake most nights, Era's condition didn't seem to have a logical catalyst. Most patients with either type of amnesia acquire the disorder from either a self-induction of benzodiazepines (or other drugs) or some traumatic brain injury. In Era's case, neither of these seemed applicable. She was neither a drug user nor, to best of Casey's knowledge, had undergone a shocking blow to the head.

She merely woke up one morning and couldn't remember where she was. But it wasn't as if she simply *forgot* things either. According the fourth edition of the Diagnostic Statistical Manual, forgetfulness would at least fall under the criteria of amnesiac patients. No, Era most certainly didn't forget. Rather, she remembered *specific details* of a life that never happened. She was convinced that she worked for ClockWorks TTA which, even though early in their marriage they had discussed such a career, Era never had the courage to pursue. When pressed, she would frequently assert that her cousins and grandmother were trying to sabotage the company and it was up to her to stop them from doing so. Recently, she would even toss violently in her sleep, mumbling something about a Sherman Hinkley.

Casey ran back from having re-checked to see if the front of their house was locked and hopped into the driver's seat. To get to the airport from their home, the Howells's would have to cut through downtown Indianapolis before taking I-70 west to I-74 North. Casey knew, however, that this early on a Tuesday morning, traffic should be no problem. They should arrive in New York sometime in the early afternoon, leaving them plenty of time for their appointment with Dr. Nagheenanajar later that evening.

The couple pulled up to a stoplight at an intersection cattycorner from Lucas Oil Football Stadium. Era rested her head on the passenger side window and gazed thoughtlessly at the myriad championship banners hanging off the massive structure's edifice. Suddenly, she saw three men in the rear view mirror approaching her car from a distance. Without pondering the dangers of oncoming traffic, she released her seatbelt, unlocked the door manually, and flew from her husband's car, sprinting toward Sherman and his team.

"Era?" Sherman said to himself as the flailing woman sped toward him. He could tell she was truly horrified. "Era, what's wrong? What is it?" she was shaking in his arms when she arrived. Wally and Lamar stood behind Sherman and let the scene unfold before them. They had only seen the frightened woman a few times in their lives prior to this freak encounter while she was in the company of her fellow ClockWorks PAs.

"Sherman, Sherman, I need your help! It's him, he's back, he's taking me away, Sherman--"

"What, who? Who's back?"

"My husband, Sherman, he's back, but he died, but now he's back, and he's taking me to New York to see some doctor but I don't want to go, I need to get back to Harper's. Sherman, I thought it was a dream, but I'm scared of what he'll do to me, Sherman." Now Lamar and Wally shared in Era's terror.

"Whoa, okay, calm down. Your husband…*died?*...but he's back?" Sherman shot a glance at Lamar. *Hadn't they talked about something like this earlier?* "And he wants to take you to New York? Why?"

"I don't know. He says he's worried about me, but I don't see--"

"Era! Era, sweetie, come back. It's okay, honey, I got you. You're safe now," Casey soothingly declared as he ran to his wife, engulfing her in his arms. If only he could see the fear plaguing her pupils. "Sorry, guys, she gets a little scared sometimes. I'm, uh, Casey Howells and this, um, this is my wife Era."

"I'm Sherman," said the doctor. "This is Wally and Lamar."

"Sherman huh?" Casey responded. *I didn't think that was a common name…*"Nice to meet you all. Thanks for keeping Era here safe while I swung the car around the corner. She could've been killed running out like that. You guys work around here?"

"Yeah," Wally answered, "We work at Har--"

"*Hardee's*!" Lamar abruptly interrupted. "We're managers of Hardee's restaurants. There's a conference this week at the Hyatt over there. Big, national, conference…thing." Wally and Sherman stared at the Reverend, obviously confounded. "She, uh, your wife there said something about a doctor…in New York? Mind if I ask which one? I have several good friends up there in the medical field."

From Casey's expression, the three couldn't tell if Lamar was out of bounds with his considerably personal inquiry. It wasn't any of his business who the doctor was. Casey had every right to ignore the stranger's intrusive question and be on his way. *And what was the deal with Hardee's?* "Uh, yeah, sure,"

Casey finally replied. "His name is, uh, Dr. Nagheenanajar. He's a neurologist in Manhattan."

"Ah, never mind then. Never heard of him," Lamar brushed off Casey's reply.

"Fair enough. Well, there are a lot of doctors these days. Can't hardly tell 'em apart anymore, they're all over the place, right?" Sherman and Wally smiled. "Anyway, uh, thanks again guys, but I gotta get this one on a plane and get her better. You all take care now and good luck with thee, uh, conference thing, okay?" With his arm still wrapped around his trembling yet still strangely attractive wife, Casey went back to his car and the Howells's drove off to the airport.

"Man, I sure am hungry guys," Wally said to the others, all of whom watched contemplatively as the car vanished over the horizon. "Maybe we could go and get some Hardee's before our conference this morning."

"Yeah, seriously, Lamar, what the hell was that all about?" Sherman whined. "Why couldn't we tell him we worked at Harper's?"

"Because Era works at Harper's too," Lamar mumbled.

"So?" Wally complained. "What the fuck does that mean?"

"Ya know, *Walden*," Lamar snapped, "I'm not sure what's more upsetting: the fact that you seriously don't know what I mean *even though we talked about this very issue just a few hours ago* or the fact that when faced with an unfamiliar situation, your first reaction is to get angry and malignant. Or, maybe you're just a complete asshole who really *does* know what I mean but instead of stating your own opinion and carrying on--oh I don't know, *a conversation*--you'd rather frolic around as an intellectual impotent, masquerading under a banner of self-induced naiveté. You pride yourself on the illusion of stability that you so meticulously fabricate for yourself but when push comes to shove, you're nothing more than a coward, a disgrace: the embodiment of nothingness."

Wally wanted to retaliate but possessed neither the full comprehension of Lamar's harangue nor the sophisticated vocabulary needed to combat it. Sherman estimated that Wally's embarrassment and burgeoning sense of inferiority resonated with a similar rhetorical bout in which the two had been engaged while juniors in high school. As Tell City High School Markspeople, Sherman and Wally led fairly secluded lives. With the exception of their aforementioned extracurricular club, the two ran in moderately sized--if not miniscule--social circles and rarely exceeded more than one option for weekend gatherings. While the majority of their lot as high school students stemmed from their awkward appearance and general cultural ineptitude, a portion of their social isolation derived from factors over which they had little control; both families lived on the outskirts of town, and both sets of parents passionately subscribed to a rather antiquated meritocratic conception of parenthood. As a result, upon turning sixteen and finding themselves immersed in an environment where the vast majority of their peers not only had cars but often several makes and models at their disposal, Sherman and Wally quickly grew disdainful of their parents' archaic Protestant work ethic. They were both *Catholic,* for crying out loud. *Gimme a damn car!*

Content with pissing into their proverbial sea of self-pity in lieu of getting a job and earning enough money so they could actually *buy* a car, the friends spent their mornings and afternoons either on the bus to and from school or, on nice days, riding their Schwinns across the town square, over the river, and through the pedestrian path in the Tell City conservation area. Depending on the weather on any given day, the trip would usually take anywhere between twenty and thirty minutes to complete: enough time to sufficiently berate their parents for not handing over the keys to their very own automobiles. On one such occasion, as the pair was nearing Sherman's house on the southwest corner of Tell City's limits, they heard from deep within the woods, the hardly audible cry of a young girl. The blood-curdling screams immediately prompted Wally and Sherman to investigate their source. What they found would torment the good doctors for the rest of their natural lives.

Ashley Marx, the four year-old daughter of Tell City's District Attorney and recent runner-up in the Southern Indiana "Little Miss Cornstalk" Pageant, was cowering behind a rotting log in a tiny clearing in the woods. An irate and inbred pit-bull was circling the stump, snarling and barking in sync with each of

Ashley's cries for help. From the angle at which Sherman and Wally arrived, they saw that the hostile canine was positioned between them and the defenseless little child. Making sure to not draw premature attention to themselves, Sherman reached down and grabbed a sturdy stick lying next to his feet. Wally reached into his pocket to retrieve his cell phone but upon flipping it open, he found that not only did he have no bars from where he was standing, but his battery was also dead. (Sherman made it a point to never bring his cell-phone to school out of a paranoid anxiety that someone would steal it from him). So there they were. The castle had been stormed: the village pillaged. The knights were now alone in the woods, inhaling the smoke fuming from the evil dragon: a prepubescent damsel in distress, a trusty saber and two Schwinns parked three yards away.

Despite the epic imagery of the scene, the pit-bull soon reminded the boys that they still were very much alone in the Tell City woods with the life of a little girl hanging in the balance. Verisimilitude would once again prevail over the otherwise pervasive tenets of a Romantic narrative. When the dog attacked Ashley Marx, the mythical hauberks the boys wore weathered away into the vast abyss as if they were phoenix feathers, leaving the young men cloaked solely under a thin veneer of their own terrors. They were mere boys once again.

Sherman threw his stick at the dog which, upon getting clunked in the head by a flying shred of wooden shrapnel, merely brushed off the minor inconvenience and continued to gnaw at the whelping child's upper torso. The boys stood and watched, neither one prepared to accept the consequences of a failed rescue attempt. The entire attack--from the beast's first pounce to having its side blown in by a nearby Good Samaritan packing heat--lasted all of forty-five seconds. After firing two rounds into the dog, the man sped into the woods and removed the animal's carcass from the body of young Ashley. She was so close to death that Sherman wasn't sure if the man was going to carry her away or bury her on the spot. He gathered her up in his arms and ran back to his parked truck, the keys still in the ignition. Sherman and Wally remained in the woods, gorgonized by the sight of the slain monster, killed at the hands of another's blade.

Ashley would live. She'd be deformed though: cursed to schlep through the remainder of her crippled life scarred with both the memories of a shattered youth and the markings of adult negligence manifested. But she would survive nonetheless. The owners of the dog were prosecuted in a criminal court and the two Tell City Markspeople received special thanks from Ashley's parents in the form of a hefty financial reward ($100) as well as enough cookies and brownies to feed a small continent. The driver of the pick-up truck who ultimately disposed of the savage dog by puncturing its abdomen with two 62-grain Bulk .223 Remington rifle bullets told the authorities that had he not seen the two abandoned Schwinns tossed into the bushes outside the entrance to the woods, he never would have rolled down his windows and heard Ashley screaming. Something about the whole scene seemed fishy, he told reporters. "When I saw them bikes, I knew somethin' wudden right. Then I heard the scream, grabbed my rifle, and done took care of biness." For unsuccessfully throwing a stick at a dog that was eating a girl, Sherman and Wally became heroes. Sherman relished in his new found celebrity status. Wally, on the other hand, merely wore the mask of stardom. Behind closed doors, his fifteen minutes of fame proved to be worth about sixteen days more than most kids ever dealt with.

In the wake of the Ashley Marx affair, Wally's step father quickly deduced that his wife's son was no hero: that Hinkley boy, maybe, but Wally, not a chance. For weeks immediately following the incident, Wally's step father would come home from work, drunk as always, and after flipping through the plethora of local TV spots centered on Wally and Sherman's act of selfless altruism, would proceed to beat the boy to a living pulp for not having the courage to save the poor girl himself. For Russell Brimley, cowardice was something that could be smelled a mile away and, like the dust on an old rug, was an abhorrent parasite that could only be exorcised by a harsh and unrelenting pounding. The painstaking task of reconciling his peers' admiration at school with Russell's leather belt at home proved enough to make Wally repress the entire event from his mind. Juxtaposing hospitality with hostility is something few of even the most self-reliant individuals can achieve, and Wally was anything but self-reliant. And so it went in the Emerson household. Whenever a random fan or reporter or kindly neighbor wished to congratulate Wally on a job well done, Russell made sure to always be waiting behind in the shadows, anxious to congratulate his wife's son with some fresh markings on his back: tokens earned from a dishonorable duty. Ironically, in striving to ward off any sense of cowardice plaguing his teenage son, Russell Brimley effectively accomplished nothing more than ensuring that Wally would forever lack the courage to confront any form of opposition. Sherman could tell that the current verbal challenge with Lamar was no exception, even if Wally did understand what all those big words meant.

"He's her *husband*, Lamar," Wally tried to argue. "Don't you think he knows she works at Harper's? I don't get why you had to lie to him…" Despite the irony of Wally, of all people, expressing this particular concern, Lamar lowered his head and took a few steps away from his inquisitors. *Era's husband was dead. But now he's back. New York... Dr. Nagheenanajar... where have I heard that name...now he's back... New York...New York... Nagheenanajar...and now he's back...*

"Lamar?" Sherman curiously asked. "You okay? Tell us what you're thinking…"

"Something's wrong, guys," Lamar realized. "Something is *very,* very wrong. That man is not supposed to be here. Who knows how long he's been gone from Era's life? This is bad. We need to get back to Harper's. I need to do some research. *Nagheenanajar.* I know I've heard that name before." The three did an about face and commenced their trek back to headquarters. They'd covered nearly the entire city and were now only a few blocks from Sherman's apartment building *(if, indeed, it was still his apartment building).*

The familiarity of the walk back to ClockWorks comforted Sherman. The town may have been filled with an abundance of aging, healthy smokers and dead people, but dammit, Sherman at least still knew how to get from A to B. They passed the library, and Sherman was reminded of studying during graduate school. They passed the football stadium and again, Sherman was reminded of studying during graduate school. Two blocks later, however, is where Sherman's universe collapsed upon itself.

"I love life-action pornographic musicals," Wally said, acknowledging the advertisement for the season's traveling Broadway productions. Sherman's eyes, however, were drawn toward the sign plastered on the front of the building. With brilliantly lavish brass lettering serving as a testament to the structure's namesake, Wally, Lamar, and Sherman found themselves standing in front of one of Indianapolis's most famous landmarks: the wonderfully ornate and architecturally mesmerizing "John Wilkes Booth Memorial Theater." Harper's had never seemed so far away.

Seventeen
Inside the Booth

"The fate of the country does not depend on how you vote at the polls — the worst man is as strong as the best at that game; it does not depend on what kind of paper you drop into the ballot-box once a year, but on what kind of man you drop from your chamber into the street every morning."
-Henry David Thoreau

"Woe unto you when all men shall speak well of you!"
-Luke 6:26

"So, how close *are* we Mr. Douglas?" Waverly had been on the phone with Harvey for ten minutes and still didn't know the status of the Harper's mainframe. Gage sat casually in one of Waverly's office chairs, slightly reclined so as to more efficiently utilize the light emanating from the lamp behind him in order to read his book. Until the mainframe was repaired or the Agents returned from their surveillance of the town, Gage and Waverly could do nothing but wait.

"That's good to hear, Douglas. You call me the instant it's repaired. The sooner we can control this thing, the better." Waverly hung up the phone, returning his attention to Gage. "What the hell are you reading over there, Lieutenant?" It was the type of question that so many people ask, but about which so few actually care. Waverly had no desire to either hear Gage's reply or to discuss the book Gage was reading on the off chance he'd ever heard of it before. On the surface, questions of this magnitude--*What song are you listening to? What's your article about? How was Luxemburg? What are you studying in school? What can you do with a degree in that?*--deceitfully imply the genuine interest of their creator though often embody little more than the pitching of the social hot potato: lines of inquiry mindlessly tossed from one person to another in a futile attempt to establish an emotional bond with another human being while at the same time signifying that *you don't really want to know anything about me and are just trying to be polite, so why don't you just admit that you won't understand what I have to say and move on?* Nevertheless, Waverly removed the needle from the record, thus stopping the party music and leaving the proverbial spud in Gage's sweaty palms. If he acknowledged Waverly's lack of interest in his chosen text by refusing to answer the question or perhaps merely dismissing it as *oh just some book,* Gage would come off as the asshole: the arrogant literary snob whose taste in art could never be matched by the likes of a prosaic mortal such as Waverly. If, however, Gage did choose to respond with the title, he realized such an act would result in simply a polite nod of feigned acceptance from Waverly before the conversation immediately shifted to other, more accessible topics. Waverly would have been better off throwing an eraser at Gage's head to get his attention. That, at least, would have involved some physical activity.

"Nothing, sir," Gage responded, closing the book in his lap. "Just some book." *Like clockwork.*

The phone rang again. Waverly answered it. "This is Wav--yes…uhuh…excellent…what is it?...the *what* theater?! Oooookaaayy…but they're still there? Fine, then, make sure you keep them in your sight. Yes, uhuh, I see…Right, keep me informed, thank you." Waverly held the receiver in one hand and hung up on the call with the index finger of his other. With a fresh dial tone, he pressed three numbers and was connected to what Gage could only assume was the IDM Room. "Yes, Douglas, we need that mainframe, *now*! Three minutes? We'll be right down. No, no, no, we're coming." Once again, Waverly laid the phone to rest.

"What is it, sir? Anything the matter?" Gage wondered.

"I'm not sure yet, Lieutenant. Apparently the chimp, the chump, and the Reverend are standing outside the John Wilkes Booth Memorial Theater right now trying to get in."

"Was that one of the ACHEs on the phone?"

"Of course it was, Phineas. You don't think I'd let those three idiots go around this city without having them followed do you?" In fact, that was exactly what Gage thought. "Of course not!" Waverly continued. "Come with me. Douglas says the mainframe will be ready to go in three minutes. It's time we see exactly what Agent Hinkley did to this world."

"You don't understand, sir, we're ClockWorks Agents on special assignment from President Waverly himself!" Lamar protested to the Booth Theater security guard. "You must let us in the building. Lives could be at stake!" For the past fifteen minutes, the three Agents had been squabbling over their admission price with a kindly old soul of a public servant reminiscent of Deputy Barney Fyfe's great grandfather, who claimed that in order to enter the building without a membership card or hotel room key, each guest *has* to pay the full price of the theater admission: $45.75. Wally and Lamar, however, were still clad in their sleepwear from the night before, and Sherman made it a point to never carry around more than ten dollars in cash with him at any given time. And he left that in his office back at Harper's. The three were broke, and Wally and Lamar were realizing for the first time all morning just how ridiculous they looked walking around downtown in their pajamas. The threat of total world destruction had apparently distracted them from being conscious of what they were wearing.

"If you want to visit the museum, you have to pay full price!" The crusty old fart kept repeating.

"But we don't want to actually *go* to the museum," Wally contested, "We just want to go to the museum and see…why this place is named after…we just want to see some stuff in the museum!" *Well said, Emerson.*

"Look, if you won't let us in, can you at least, like, give us some brochures or something so we know what we're missing?" Sherman pleaded. "It's very important to us!"

"I can see that, son, but I'm afraid the brochures are in the gift shop, and the gift shop isn't open yet," the Fyfe declared.

"Well when does it open?" Lamar begged.

"Eight O'clock every morning, sir, on the dot," Captain Dick said proudly.

"Well, it's...*it's 7:55 right now!* Can't you go open the doors and get us a brochure?"

"Afraid I can't do that, sir. Someone has to watch the entrance, ya know, and make sure no one tries to sneak in."

"IT'S 7:55 ON A TUESDAY MORNING!! Who's gonna want to sneak into this place?" Lamar screeched.

"You mean besides you three? Who knows? But it ain't gonna happen on my watch, no sir, that's for darn sure."

"We don't want to *sneak* in, we just--"

"You would if I wasn't here."

"Well, that's true, but only because we need to see--get, rather--we need to *get* some information."

"Oh? And what type of information do you need?"

"Again, you wouldn't understand, but if you let us in, I promise you we won't be a bother."

"Your promises mean about as much to me as my ex-wife's," the belligerent old kook asserted. "I can't just *let* you in and that's it! Now, if you don't go away *right now* I'm going to have to call the police and have them escort you off the premises."

"The *police?* You're going to call the police on us? For what?"

"For disrupting the busiest week of the year. Can't you people read the signs? It's the annual celebration of the start of Mr. Booth's final theatrical run! It's a major occasion for thespians everywhere to celebrate!"

"Well, uh, we're thespians. Don't you have any sort of discount for the children of the stage?"

"Course we do! It's free admission all week in honor of Mr. Booth's memory!"

"Well if it's free admission, *why can't you let us in!?"*

"Because it's only free for guests who arrive during normal operating hours. All other guests must pay full price."

"I see, and when again are normal operating hours?"

"Monday through Friday 8:00 a.m. to 6:00 p.m., sir." Lamar looked at his watch as did Oz's gatekeeper. "Well, would you look at that, it's time to open!" The pitiful excuse for volunteer law enforcement slumped out of his cushioned throne behind the plexiglass booth and reversed the sign on the front door which originally said "CLOSED." He waddled back into his chamber of solitude, climbed his chair once again, and swiveled around, facing the three perturbed Agents. "Good morning, gentlemen. Welcome to the John Wilkes Booth Memorial Theater. Because of our celebration of the commencement of Mr. Booth's final run on the American stage, admission this week is free to the public. Enjoy the museum and please, consult the concourse message boards for future show times and upcoming events. Have a nice day!" As Lamar, Wally, and Sherman silently walked past the reigning Wizard of Indy, Sherman chuckled at how appropriate it was that the main security guard for the John Wilkes Booth Memorial Theater was such a douche bag.

Similar to ClockWorks, the Booth wasn't simply a theater. The entire Booth complex included a Booth library, Booth tanning salon, Booth gymnasium, Booth restaurants, Booth hotel, Booth museum, and somewhere in the back, the actual Booth theater. Almost as if the establishment was an homage to a fallen U.S. President, the inside of the main lobby was decorated with enormous sepia photographs of Booth from different productions in which he played the lead, as well as early childhood renderings of Booth with the rest of his famous theatrical family. The lobby also contained interactive Booth games and offered a fine variety of Booth-themed clothing accessories and refreshments. Booth hotel guests were winding between the giant Indiana limestone statues of Booth, each echoing in girth and style the statues of Revolutionary War heroes or historical inventors. Sherman felt nauseated. Lamar felt confused. Wally was hungry.

After breakfast in the "Meals with Booth Cafeteria" in which the three demanded they sit at the counter, their first stop was the museum. They needed to know how on earth John Wilkes Booth went from sharing a circle in Hell with Judas Iscariot to having four city blocks erected in order to preserve his legacy as a great American. Sherman, especially, needed to know why exactly this dramatic transition evolved over night. As an extracurricular yet avid scholar on all matters American historic, Sherman had a duty to seek the truth and rectify the past as soon as he could. Lamar was trying desperately to make some connection between the surplus of elderly Indy citizens, the exponential rise in smoking, the vanishing of Stowe, the re-birth of Casey Howells, and now the deification of one of history's most vile traitors. Wally, by contrast, never noticed the irony that as Harper's newest Chief Head of Unintentionally Misplaced Persons--the man solely responsible for finding people if they were lost in time--he had no desire to locate either Agent Stowe or Kristen Lapham. Deep down, he was simply along for the ride.

In the center of the main museum entrance stood a floor to ceiling model of John Wilkes Booth made of pure bronze and beaming with the majesty reserved only for Greek temples or Roman coliseums. Sherman's heart ached at how similar the statue was to E.W. Harper's iron likeness in front of the TTA. Over the statue hung a banner that read, "When I leave the stage, I will be the most famous man in America." It was clearly meant to be metaphorical. At the base of the indoor monolith, Sherman noticed a modest 24" by 36" plaque containing a brief overview of Booth's life which in turn offered the justifications for his massive Indianapolis memorial. Sherman skimmed the first several paragraphs searching for any details that seemed out of place. He already knew most of it by heart: John Wilkes Booth…born May 10th, 1838…American stage actor…large theatrical family from Maryland…*yeah, yeah, yeah*…Confederate sympathizer…*Confederate Sympathizer?!?* When Sherman read those words on the statue commemorating Booth's life, he felt a rippling concern for his friend Lamar. *Had they seen any Black people that morning? Why is a Confederate Sympathizer being honored? Is Lamar in danger? What have I done!?* Praying the remainder of the plaque would yield some hint as to what happened for Booth in his life to warrant future praise while at the same time wishing that the Civil War still ended the way it *needed to end*, Sherman continued reading. *Okay "Confederate sympathizer...confederate sympathizer... confederate sympathizer"...There it is!* Sherman found his place and pressed on. He made it to the last paragraphs where, with each engraved word, his heart skipped a beat:

Second Hand Out

Nevertheless, Mr. Booth's southern allegiances came to an end soon thereafter as a result of a trip to New York in 1862. On the Fourth of July of that year, Booth met Laura Keene who, upon witnessing Booth's unparalleled theatrical prowess, immediately cast him as the leading role in "Our American Cousin," a dramatic play by renowned English writer Mr. Tom Taylor. With Booth at the helm, Keene's production toured the nation for three years, gaining critical and public acclaim before making its final resting place in Washington in April, 1865. Booth's swansong came just three days after his arrival in the city. On April 14th*, 1865, "Our American Cousin" premiered at Ford's Theater in Washington and included a sell-out house of celebrities and political dignitaries ranging from Secretary of State William Seward to President Lincoln himself. After the performance, however, is when fate made its final curtain call for John Wilkes Booth's life.*

Booth and several of his friends and fellow cast members were having a party at a local boarding house owned by Mr. John Surratt and managed by his wife, Mary. Sometime during the late evening hours, the lower levels of the house caught fire, trapping many of cast members and Mary Surratt herself. In the midst of the inferno Booth successfully evacuated four men from the burning building including his friends David Herold and Lewis Pane before reentering the house for the last time. In a matter of seconds, flames consumed the remainder of the structure, leaving John Wilkes Booth and nine others stranded inside. Witnesses testify that before Booth ran into the building to retrieve more victims he yelled "E Pluribus Unum!" which is Latin for "out of many, one." Scholars maintain that this was Booth's parting acclamation of the democratic American spirit against which he had fought for so many years of his early life.

"What an amazing man, kids," a father declared to his young children who were nudged on either side of Sherman, all pretending to read the plaque and admire the statue.

"Daddy, is John Wilts Boof, um, was he, uh, was he a president of the Unided States?" asked one of the little tykes.

"Haha, no son, he wasn't a president," the father replied. *They really do say the damndest things!* "But he probably could've been if he wanted to."

"What happened to him, daddy? Why did he not become da presamint?" the other little squirt whined. *Control your children, for the love of God!*

"Well, you see kids, it says it all right here on this plaque," Papa Lion told the cubs. The kids looked at the plaque in awe as if it were the single most amazing thing they'd ever seen in all their months on earth. That plaque held all the answers. To them, the plaque was grown-up Jesus, their father, Santa Clause, and the guy down the street who can dunk a basketball all rolled into one flattened piece of bronzed magic. The plaque's powers were great. Sherman wondered how the kids would react to the Booth Ice-Cream Parlor if they pissed their pants at seeing a bunch of writing on a piece of metal, but he didn't want to wait around to find out.

Sherman found Wally and Lamar in the "Booth's Final Act" section of the museum. Lamar seemed haunted by a Mathew Brady photograph of Booth in full costume on stage at Ford's Theater. A speck of humanity in one of the balconies was labeled "President Lincoln." On the bottom right corner of the photograph, Brady had penciled "April 14, '65."

"Okay, two things…" Sherman whispered to Lamar and Wally. They needed to take extra special caution not to draw attention to themselves by saying things out of the ordinary. As far as the rest of the guests were concerned, everything in the museum was common knowledge, the salience of which cluttered history books and lectures of school age children around the world. These were the new historical truths.

"Two things?" Wally whispered back.

"Yeah, two things: One, Booth was never *in* 'Our American Cousin', and two, that play was a *comedy,* right?" Sherman begged of his peers.

"Yeah, you're right on both accounts, Sherm," Wally answered. "But what *I* want to know is if Booth died on April 14th, what, 1865, when did *Lincoln* die? Who killed him?"

"Maybe he wasn't killed at all," Lamar posited. "Maybe he just died like any other president." Since entering the building, such a thought never occurred to Wally or Sherman.

After a few moments of silent contemplation, Sherman continued with his original position. "But what about the play? It's a *comedy*! How the hell would it suddenly become a drama, and why the hell would Booth suddenly be in it?"

"Excuse me, sir, I don't mean to interrupt, but I couldn't help hear that question you just asked: about why Mr. Booth was cast in Mr. Taylor's play," an old curator said: the older, less attractive distant cousin of the crusty old fart at the front desk. "Funny you should ask about that."

"Why's that?" Wally retorted.

"Well because most people don't know of that play. In fact the only reason its legacy has lasted this long is because it was Mr. Booth's final production and he was, after all, the greatest American stage actor of the nineteenth century! He was, well, the *Zach Efron*--to use a name from my childhood--of his generation." Only Sherman appreciated the irony of standing in the building that was once dedicated to Zachary Efron only to have *this fucker* compare him to its current namesake.

Of the three, Sherman was the only one who'd actually read "Our American Cousin" in its original comedic transcription. His freshman year of college, Sherman wrote a report on the Lincoln assassination conspiracy and chose to focus his critical gaze through a theatrical lens. He compared the plot of "Our American Cousin" with Booth's perception of Lincoln's presidency and noted the pervasive undercurrents of xenophobia, homoeroticism, and ostracism common in both texts. The piece culminated in a cogent and persuasive argument suggesting that if Lincoln had not been present at Ford's Theater that evening, there's no way he could have been shot while sitting in his balcony suite. It took twenty-five double spaced pages to reach that conclusion. Sherman failed the assignment for reasons ranging from rampant spelling errors to lack of sufficient research to overall wasting the time it took to read it. Still, despite the minor academic setback, Sherman had indeed familiarized himself enough with the play enough to know that it was, in fact, a comedy. Probably. Maybe.

"Okay, so tell us... *Vern...* why did Booth want to be in *this* play?" Wally asked.

"It's complicated. You said you knew what the play was about?" Vern asked Sherman, who nodded in an uncertain display of approval.

"I'm afraid *I* don't know much about the play, Vern. Perhaps you'd like to tell the rest of us?" Lamar suggested, referring to himself and his trusty sidekick, Wally.

"Certainly, sir. Well, you know that the play was written by Mr. Tom Taylor of England. It contains three acts and is, well, billed as a drama, but if you've ever read it, you'll agree it's more of a tragedy. It centers around a cocky, estranged nephew of an aristocratic British brewery owner who comes to visit his English family during the summer of his twenty-first year. The boy is an egotistical, austere youth who epitomizes American arrogance and pride, as well as the strict moral compass which governed much of nineteenth century society. He makes no friends, but rather accumulates a wealth of enemies while staying abroad. The play ends with the boy murdering his uncle after a heated dispute over the boy's inheritance from his late grandfather. It premiered at Miss Laura Keene's Theater in New York in 1858 and ran for almost four years before Mr. Booth joined the cast as the lead role of Lord Dundreary, a tight-fisted, stern aristocrat who rules over the boy's moral development and ultimately condemns him to death by hanging for his role in his uncle's death.

"Initially, the play failed to receive a warm reception from its American audiences, particularly those in the southern states who despised its insinuations that all Americans are murderous vultures or capitalist fiends. Eventually, however, the northern states especially grew to adore the play as a testament to America's struggle against the immoralities of slavery manifested through the south's economic dependence on slave labor. The south viewed the character of the American youth as the personification of the north's reliance on industry which, according to southern plantation owners, served as a placeholder for the north's own breed of human cruelty, while the north recognized the boy as representing all that was wrong with the lower half of the country. Unbeknownst to Mr. Taylor, the play became a political weapon over night and quickly became the hottest ticket on the American stage. Michael Moore would have been proud."

"Michael *who*?" Wally wondered.

"Never mind, I'm sorry," Vern said. "So, surely you can appreciate why Mr. Booth was so inclined to be involved with such a poignant political drama." All nodded in agreement though none truly agreed. "The conflation of this play with that actor made its production the single most exciting spectacle of the antebellum period. The symbiotic relationship shared by Taylor's work and Booth's talent not only solidified a national ethos but also marked the beginning of the uniquely American Cult of Personality. This was it, gentlemen! This *was* America! Booth was our nation." Excusing Vern's hyperbole and clearing the vomit from his throat, Sherman loosened his sunny tie which he too forgot he was still wearing.

"Well, thank you, Vern. You've been very helpful," Lamar expressed his earnest gratitude that the old man took the time to inform the three of what the hell was going on.

"That's what I'm here for. Enjoy your stay!" And with that, Vern was gone.

"We have to get back to Harper's," Lamar proclaimed. "None of this makes any sense."

"I agree. This is kinda fucked up." Wally tactfully responded. "I mean, old people are one thing, but something about this doesn't seem good for me."

"Which part?" Sherman mocked. "The murderer turned hero, the Agent on her way to an asylum, Stowe gone? What?"

"Well, Stowe gone for one, but that's--"

"Yeah, fine, I shouldn't have--" out of the corner of his eye, Sherman saw the face of a young woman he knew. *From where*? He pivoted around Wally and Lamar and looked out into the main lobby of the building. Through the crowds of families hurrying to their bus tours and the line of wheel-chaired grandparents speeding to the exit ramps, Sherman saw her: a slender, beautiful, *brunette?*, wearing thick, black-rimmed glasses and a sling over her right shoulder. *Kristen Lapham?* From across the rooms, the two made eye contact causing Sherman to black out all other sensorial distractions. She was not supposed to be here. And yet, it certainly appeared she was here…for him.

"That okay with you, Sherm?" Wally asked his comatose partner. "Sherman?"

"What? Yeah, no, that's fine guys. Listen, I'll meet you, uh, *there*…I just need to go to the bathroom real quick."

"*Where* are you going to meet us, Sherman?" Lamar asked feebly, confused.

"Sounds good, guys, see you then," Sherman left his friends and exited the museum exhibit, went through the museum concourse, followed Kristen down the stairs, over the Booth greenhouse, through the Booth chapel, followed her into a stairwell marked "Private" and finally down three more flights of stairs before reaching the fleeing Lapham and demanding some answers. All he got was a kiss on the mouth.

"Good to see you, Sherman," the wounded fox moaned.

"Uh, yeah, you too. Um, what are you doing here?"

"There isn't a lot of time. You're being followed. They probably saw you come in here with me, and if they didn't, they'll be following Lamar and Wally anyway."

"Followed? What? Why? When? Where are we going? I need to get back to Harper's!"

"That's where we're going. We need to get Eternity and get the hell out of here."

"Eternity? Wha--why? When?"

"Just shut up and follow me, Sherman, we gotta go!"

"But why Eternity? If things are so bad, why can't we just leave right now?"

"We need her, Sherman. She knows things that neither one of us know. She'll be able to help us make everything better," Kristen wheezed, grabbing hold of Sherman's hand and leading him down the dark and scary hallway. "And besides, she's my sister."

Eighteen
Dr. Hinkley, I Presume

"Everybody loves a hero. People line up for them, cheer them, scream their names. And years later, they'll tell how they stood in the rain for hours just to get a glimpse of the one who taught them how to hold on a second longer."
-Rosemary Harris as May Parker, *Spider Man 2*

"Hunters for gold or pursuers of fame, they all had gone out on that stream, bearing the sword, and often the torch, messengers of the might within the land, bearers of a spark from the sacred fire. What greatness had not floated on the ebb of that river into the mystery of an unknown earth! . . . The dreams of men, the seed of commonwealths, the germs of empires."
-Heart of Darkness

"Ya know, you guys could at least turn on the air conditioner down here. I know you have one. I pay the bills for it every month." In lieu of taking Eternity upstairs for further questioning, Harvey decided that the company would benefit more by having her confined to the Harper's prison. Yes, ClockWorks even had in its repertoire a minimum security prison facility buried three stories beneath its main lobby. When Thomas Archer originally drafted his blueprints for ClockWorks, E.W. Harper insisted the building include a jail in which to imprison any reprimanded threats or known assailants of the time travel industry. He modeled the compound in the style of the eighteenth century French Bastille, save, of course, for the fact that it was to be built underground and would contain neither the expansive courtyards nor the grand towers. Pragmatically speaking, the prison functioned as more of a storage facility than an actual detention center. In the rare occasions when the prison needed to be used for the purposes for which it was initially constructed, the mere sight of the authentic guillotine or iron maiden was often enough to coerce the guilty parties into full confessions. Harper, of course, would never dream of using these tortuous instruments on actual people; he just thought they spiced up the place.

While Harvey tended to the mainframe repairs in the IDM Room, he assigned Lester to stand guard over Eternity's cell: an 8 foot by 8 foot slab of dirt-covered stones containing a thirty year-old cot and a bucket, presumably functioning as a toilet. After the situation the previous evening in which Eternity may or may not have played an integral role, Harvey and Lester concluded her situation necessitated containment: domestication from the wilderness of anarchistic time travel. Once in her bunker, however, Eternity wasted no time before complaining about everything from the drab dungeon décor to the stifling heat and stagnant odor.

"Look, I'm not going to turn on the air, and that's it. So please just shut up and be quiet so I can read, okay?" Lester declared. *Jeez, ya give a guy a gun...*

"Oh come on! Lester...*Lessy*...I know you wanna help me, Lessy. I know all about your feelings for me. Don't you want to see my cold and shivering so you can come over and keep me warm?" In truth, Eternity had no idea how Lester felt about her. The primary contingency of her proposal was that she'd never been turned down before in her life, leastwise by a gawky, frail, clumsy, virgin bibliophile like Lester Whitman.

"Listen, you can hit on me all you want, but I am not coming over there so you can sink your vicious woman fangs into me, okay? So just shut up!"

"But what if I told you I can help you fix the mainframe?"

"They've already fixed the mainframe. They're fixing everything right now."

"Well, if they've already fixed everything, then why do I need to be here? Why do I need to be locked down in this grimy, humid, disgusting excuse for a basement?"

"I told you: I can't leave my post until I have clearance from one of my superiors."

"At ease, soldier," boomed the authoritative voice of Dr. Sherman Hinkley as he took his final step off of the damp, winding stone staircase. Why Harper's never invested in an elevator down to the prison was beyond any of its employees' comprehension.

"Dr. Hinkley!" Lester exclaimed. "You're back! Are you, uh, where are the rest of you…guys? How did you--why are you down here?"

"I've been ordered to replace you, Mr. Whitman. You've done a fantastic job, but now you're to report to the IDM Room for a special classified debriefing of our reconnaissance mission while I remain here and guard the prisoner." Lester studied Sherman's face for any sign of deception, but there was nothing to convince him that Sherman was telling anything other than the truth. He then turned to examine Eternity who appeared almost *disappointed* that Sherman was replacing him as her guard. The combination of Eternity's blasé countenance and Sherman's stoic demeanor was sufficient enough to compel Lester to relinquish his position.

"Alright then, sir. She's been a bit of a bitch so far. Make sure you keep the A/C where it's at and be careful not to get too close to her cage over there," Lester warned. "She's a lusty cobra, that one." He nodded at Eternity and flew up the castle-like stairwell. The changing of the guards had ended.

"Hey, Sherman, thanks for comin'," Eternity whispered as she slipped through the open gate. *Oh, she definitely batted her eyes that time!* Sherman hoped that the insertion of a long, hard, ribbed key into the tight, moist, secure lock and the twisting and pushing that would culminate in an evitable release would move Eternity to greet him in a similar fashion compared to that of her sister. Maybe even more. All he got instead was a hug. A fucking hug.

"Your sister's outside," Sherman pouted at Eternity's carnal denial.

"No, she's not," she smiled in return. "If she's any good at her job, she's long gone by now." Sherman's turbid stare elicited further chuckles out of Eternity. "Don't worry, Sherman. She's not *gone,* gone. I'm sure she's made it to the rendezvous point by now. She gave you the remote, right?"

"Yeah, but --"

"There's no time to explain. Give it to me," Sherman acquiesced to her demand. "We have only have a few minutes before they realize you're not with Lamar and Wally, and when they find out they'll--" an earsplitting alarm filled the entire building and within seconds, Sherman could feel the vibrations of dozens of large, armed men, traipsing down the stone staircase. Eternity yanked the remote control from Sherman's hands. *Why does that look so familiar?* She began rapidly punching numbers into its microscopic computer.

"No, don't do that! She already did that!" Sherman yelled over the blaring alarm.

"No, she didn't. She only did enough to get you here!" Eternity screamed in reply. Sherman could hear the echoes of men hollering down the stairs as enlarging shadows began to consume the stone cellar walls. "SHERMAN! PUT YOUR THUMB ON THE PAD!" Sherman and Eternity each placed their thumbs on the tiny pad located toward the bottom of the remote control device. Eternity hit a green button at the top of the remote just as two ACHEs reached the bottom of the staircase and lunged toward the unarmed conspirators. Suddenly, a radiant burst of light filled the room as a tumultuous clap of thunder knocked the ACHEs to the solid stone floor. Only when they composed themselves did they realize that their suspects had vanished completely from the room.

I'll be right back, daddy! So sang the sweet voice of six year-old Shauntell Newton. It was 2051, and Lamar had taken his family of five on their annual week long summer vacation. As a special treat, the good Reverend and his wife decided that year to take their family on a cruise of the Greek Islands. They flew from Indianapolis to Chicago to JFK Airport in New York to Frankfurt, Germany before finally arriving in Athens after nearly 26 consecutive hours of flying and scurrying through international terminals with luggage spilling through their arms. A vocational pedagogue by trade, Lamar designed the trip to include both the requisite Grecian tourist sites, as well as the myriad historical hotspots bearing any theological and/or geopolitical significance. After surveying the Parthenon ruins, the Theater of Dionysus and the Temple of Zeus in Athens, the family boarded their Hellenic cruise vessel set to embark on a majestic voyage throughout the Mediterranean and Aegean Seas. On day three, they reached the island of Patmos, one of the northern most Grecian islands of the Dodecanese complex in the southeastern corner of the Aegean archipelago. For Jasmine Newton and her children, the island was just another rock in the middle of the ocean littered with overpriced yet aesthetically pleasing postcards and fanatical yet odoriferous Greek cab drivers: just another mountain to curse while climbing. For God's servant, however, the island claimed tremendous relevancy for Judeo-Christian dogma; in biblical times Patmos served as the place of exile for John the Apostle who, while sitting in his cavern of solitude after having been banished by Emperor Dometian, reportedly dreamed the dream he would later immortalize in the Book of Revelation. Indeed, Christianity and the island of Patmos are inextricably linked, as the latter remains the Mecca of the former's apocalyptic vision. The Newton family pilgrimage of '51, while granting the Midwestern clan ample quality time to learn and grow with one another, also provided Lamar with his own sort of apocalyptic revelation.

To get to the Monastery of Evangelist and Apostle John the Theologian, Patmos pilgrims must climb a series of steep and uneven inclined roads carved into the side of the island leading up to the top wherein the Reverend Christodoulos first built the temple in 1088. The Sacred Grotto of John the Devine, considered by locals to be the most important sanctuary on the island, also sits atop the island's hill and can be seen from any point on Patmos, as well as from far off at sea. Those who don't truly appreciate the value of "the experience" can rent cars or tour buses to scale the mountain, but for the Newtons, experience is what makes learning fun. At least to Lamar, anyway. The kids made it about half way up the dirt roads before starting to get fussy: little whines under their breath at first which escalated into shoving, rock throwing, sitting in the middle of the road, and screaming at the top of their lungs, "Get away from me! You're not my mother. THIS WOMAN IS NOT MY MOTHER!" Jasmine and Lamar always loved that one.

When they finally made it to the Monastery and were about to descend the 43 steps into the sacred cave, Lamar's youngest daughter, Shauntell, realized her bladder was about to burst. Having already trekked to the peak of the island and shut all cell-phones and cameras to their off position--electronic devices of any kind were prohibited inside the cave so as not to damage the iconography or spoil the reverent ambiance of the surroundings--Lamar asked the gentle old Orthodox monk guarding the cave's entrance for the location of the nearest bathroom. (Jasmine thought the real reason they weren't allowed to take pictures inside the cave was because no one wanted to see a sweet old Turkish woman so blinded by the flash that she hit her head on a rock, stumble up the stairs, get blinded by the sunlight, roll off a cliff and die. True, no one wanted that.) The monk informed Lamar that there was a small rest area just outside the Monastery with a modest souvenir stand (mostly copies of "The Revelation" in assorted languages as well as various Greek icons) and a unisex water closet. Since Lamar's oldest daughter, Jacquie, possessed a strong intestinal urge to purge herself as well, he instructed her to take Shauntell to the bathroom. The two girls stepped out of line, excusing themselves as the stepped on the toes of their fellow travelers, and skipped back up the stairs to the Monastery exit. "I'll be right back, daddy!" little Shauntell cried out. It was a promise that took four hours to fulfill.

Jasmine was the first to notice anything was wrong. She, Lamar, and their middle daughter Shannyn, had been in and out of the cave with still no sign of Jacquie or Shauntell. *How long were they in there?* It seemed like hours and yet, the girls still hadn't returned from the bathroom. After expressing her concerns to her husband, the three Newtons abandoned the remainder of their guided tour and ran to check the souvenir stand and water closet. Lamar was the first to spot his oldest child sitting on a rock bench overlooking the water below, reading a French translation of John's dream. She could sense that her father was worried and after looking at her mother and sister, noticed something was indeed wrong. "Where's Shauntell!?" Lamar and Jacquie asked at the same time, confusion blanketing the latter's tone: sheer terror blanketing the former's. Jacquie explained to her frightened parents that when she and her sister went to go relieve themselves, Shauntell demanded that she not be babied and asked her sister to let her go to the bathroom by herself. Jacquie let her baby sister have her way and left to go browse the gift shop for any unique and moderately priced cultural relics. When Shauntell never came to meet her at the stand, Jacquie assumed she had simply returned to her parents. That was about fifteen minutes ago. Suddenly Lamar wished he would've paid more attention studying Greek in college.

In the ensuing years, Shauntell grew into a mature and intelligent young woman. Granted, she and her parents had their share of arguments over curfew, less than ideal weekend dates, choices of clothing and public signs of affection, but all in all, she was a good kid. All the Newton women were. Lamar and Jasmine had taught them well. Jasmine instilled her motherly intuition into all of her daughters, and Lamar taught them the importance of questioning precedents and pursuing an education. He smiled with pride whenever he unscrewed the training wheels from their bikes. He cherished the experience of watching them blossom in a world that judged them by the content of their characters formed, in part, by his own paternal influence. Lamar peered through the kitchen window at the bus on each girl's first day of high school. He shed a silent tear after dropping each one off at college for the first time. He gut drunk on bourbon when Shauntell came home at seventeen and told her parents she was engaged and toasted with his wife when the relationship ended three weeks later: a salute to their parental stamina. Sure he worried about them while they were away at college: it's what fathers do. At times the relationship between Lamar and his daughters was like a pesky toe nail: piercing and painful and sometimes even managing to ruin a perfectly good pair of socks. Still, as with even the most obtrusive toenail, no matter how hard his daughters tried to sever their bond with their father, whenever times got tough, it always grew back. They always do.

That afternoon in Patmos, though--Lamar could shake off a scrape on his daughter's knee, a curfew violation, a sketchy boyfriend or a hidden pack of cigarettes in one of Shauntell's sock drawers. He could deal with racism against his family, the protest rallies in which his daughters marched, Shauntell's pregnancy scare, and other forms of typical teenage rebellion. He tolerated the occasional speeding ticket, and though he was furious when his baby girl got a tattoo of a treble clef on her left breast, the fact that she didn't come down with hepatitis somehow ameliorated his anger. But when he thought he had *lost* his baby on the other side of the world (as well as on the wrong side of an insurmountable language barrier), suddenly St. John's vision seemed as arbitrary as the stone on which he had it. Nothing mattered. Lamar's fear masked his confusion which masked his anger which masked his guilt which masked his shame. In the four hours in which the island's police searched the area for the lost girl, Lamar went through all but one of Elizabeth Kubler Ross's five stages of grief. When they finally found Shauntell playing with some older kids on a secluded beach at the base of the island, the joyous frenzy was such that Lamar quickly resolved his internal struggles and tended to the immediate needs of his beloved family. Shauntell was safe. She was unharmed. She was pure. She was still his child innocent, the darling apple of Newton's eye. The festive reunion spilled over into the evening as the ship--which was gracious enough to remain docked until the girl was found, delaying their departure by nearly an hour--put on an impromptu celebration in the main deck's entertainment hall. It had certainly been a revealing afternoon.

When the girls were sleeping that night, Jasmine rolled over to her husband. In the darkness of their cabin, she whispered in his ear, "I never lost hope. I knew she was out there." She kissed him on his cheek.

"Me too, sweetheart. Me too." Lamar muttered soothingly. It was the only time he could remember ever lying to his wife. What he never confessed to anyone and rarely processed himself was that he had indeed gone through all but one of Kubler Ross's stages of grieving: all but the bargaining phase. He went through denial. *This is a joke, right? She's with you, right?!* He was certainly angry at Jacquie for leaving her sister alone in a foreign country. He was depressed at the thought of having to inform the world of his failure as a father as well as having to sleep next to the mother of a dead child for the rest of his life. He had even come to accept that his daughter was gone forever. It didn't take him long to reach that conclusion. Lamar always felt that accepting the inevitability of a situation was a whole lot easier than grappling with its potential solutions. Why delay his pain? Why prolong whatever shred of futile hope his weeping soul possessed? His daughter was gone. They'd find her tattered body in a bush at the bottom of a cliff. Nothing could ever assuage the bereavement of a lost child, so why the hell bother hoping for the best? Acceptance was morosely simplistic for Lamar. What he could not bring himself to do, however, was bargain for his daughter's return. Not to God or St. John or Buddha. Not to the police or the phantom hostage taker. Jesus didn't save John while he was in exile, why would he save a little black girl from Ohio? And so, for seventeen years Lamar Newton lived with the shame of knowing that when his baby girl was missing in Greece in the summer of '51, for four hours all he could think about was how the world would view *him* as a father. Rather than hope for a quick recovery, his first reaction--the *very first thing* that came to his mind--was that his daughter's disappearance would make them miss their boat's departure. It was a transient thought: one that he banished from his head the instant it lurked inside. But it was a thought nonetheless. It was his greatest hour of weakness.

From that moment forward, everything he ever did as a husband, a father, a Reverend, and a man was done as atonement for the most despicable display of narcissistic lunacy he'd ever enacted. The fact that he never told anyone about his transgressions only exacerbated his anguish. His discretion made him his own judge, jury, and executioner. At least with uninhibited aggression there comes a sense of purging. But Lamar was never aggressive. He was never contentious. His role as iconic family man could never accommodate such deplorable tenets. Rather, he lived a constrained life, a law-abiding life. He could neither afford to release his demons to the world nor bring himself to appreciate the therapeutic merit in doing so. He'd written off his daughter in less time than it took to conceive her. For that single act of dismissal, he would never forgive himself. To be sure, he was a terrific father both before and after the Patmos affair. And his paternalistic impulse informed much of his decisions later in life. Over time he verged on fully subjugating his moment of weakness on that island so many years ago, but a part of him would always wonder why, even for a split second--even if he was sure he wouldn't get an answer--why he never turned his head upward and asked God to watch over his baby girl when she was missing.

When Sherman Hinkley never came back from the bathroom, Lamar swore he could hear his daughter's cry.

“Must’ve really had to go,” Wally commented on Sherman’s prolonged potty break. He’d been gone nearly fifteen minutes.

“Something isn’t right, Wally,” Lamar whispered. “Did you see the way he ran out of here? It was almost like he was looking for someone.”

“Probably thought he saw his dead grandpa or something. Wouldn’t put it past this new place, that’s for sure. When he gets back we should head back to Harper's. I think we've seen enough here."

"Yeah good idea. I need to look up some stuff on that doctor in New York, and I'm sure Sherman will want to find out some more about this play. He seemed pretty upset about the whole thing."

"I'm afraid Dr. Hinkley will not be returning, Agent Newton," said a bulky young man in a business suit. Embroidered on the lapel of the man's jacket in calligraphy was the Harper's logo. Underneath the handless clock were the words "Special Division of Head ACHEs." Lamar and Wally looked around the room and spotted three similarly dressed men at various strategic locations by an exhibit door, stairwell, and emergency exit. They were surrounded.

"If you come along quietly, there'll be no need to use force. You're not to be harmed, but if you challenge us, we have orders to take you down."

"*Take us down?*" Wally mocked. "I'm sorry, but where's Sherman? Lamar, let's just go find him and get out of here--"

"Your colleague returned to the Agency and proceeded to aid a convicted felon in a violent escape from Harper's prison. He injured three agents in the process, severely bludgeoning one over the head with the severed limb of a baby horse. He is considered armed and extremely dangerous. It behooves you both to suspend all further contact with him, as any future correspondence will qualify you as accessories to terrorism." The great and powerful Head ACHE had spoken.

"*Terrorism?*" Lamar begged.

"*A baby horse?*" Wally followed. "Why the hell would you have a baby horse in a prison? And why the hell would Sherman--*do you know Sherman*--use it to hurt anybody?"

"And how the hell did he get back to Harper's, wound three agents, escape, and leave you time to get here to retrieve us? He's only been gone a few minutes?" As Lamar asked the last part, he realized that they'd been followed since the beginning. Even though the man in front of them wore sunglasses, something in his eyes told Lamar of Waverly's treachery.

"All excellent questions, gentlemen," said the mid-life crisis accountant on steroids. "And if you'll follow us back to ClockWorks, I'm sure you'll find your answers." What choice did Lamar and Wally have? Aside from the occasional meaningless dispute, Wally's spine divorced him years ago, as had Lamar's endurance and high school state championship speed. They'd never make it to the exit. Since neither wanted to see how painful messing with the Head ACHE could be, they decided to submit to their orders. The suits swarmed the two distraught men, and as a cluster of polyester, silk, and an airy cotton blend, the clan marched out of the John Wilkes Booth Memorial Theater. A black car parked outside on the curb was waiting for the group. As Lamar was being shoved in the back seat next to Wally, the chump whispered to the Reverend, "Have you ever read *Dreamer's Syndrome?* It was written before we were born by some guy from Purdue, but have you ever read it?"

Lamar shook his head. "No, I've never heard of it."

"This whole thing reminds me a lot about it."

"Oh yeah? What's it about?"

"Well, it's been a long time since I read it. I had to write a paper on it for a class I took in college over great American books of the twenty-first century. It's basically about this guy and girl who wake up one morning and the world is, like, totally changed. Not because of time travel or anything, but because God decided to grant everyone's childhood wish of what they wanted to be like when they grew up. So, like, the guy is a pirate I think, and the girl is a princess or something. And there's monsters and dinosaurs and Satan has a kid and all sorts of wild shit happens but, yeah, basically all because God decided to take a holiday and let everyone, sorta, *just do* whatever they wanted to when they were kids."

"God took a holiday? Why?"

"Because he got so frustrated that he couldn't build a rock big enough that even he couldn't lift it. He tried and tried and tried but he just couldn't do it. He could always lift the rock. So he got pissed and let the angels run things for a while, but they fucked everything up and the world went to shits."

"But he *succeeded* then, right? He could always lift the rock…"

"No. By lifting the rock he failed to create one big enough that he couldn't lift. *That* was the task: not lifting the rock."

"Sounds like a pretty good book."

"I liked it."

"But what does it have to do with any of this?"

"You mean besides the fact that everything seems to have changed? I guess I was just thinking that in this case, *we're* God. And maybe our infinite strength and power has finally gotten us to a point where we just decided to fuck it and let the world fall on its ass."

"Okay, but according to your assessment of the book, God *has* limits. His powers aren't boundless. He can't create a rock that he can't lift. His inability to do so is a form of limitation."

"I guess. But *we* don't have any limits. We *can* do anything. So I guess that's the only difference between us and God. Sorry I brought it up; this whole thing just reminded me of that book, that's all."

"No, I think you were right the first time, but not for the reasons you said."

"Why then?"

"For the reasons I said."

Faster than he could secure his hideous tie, Sherman and Eternity found themselves standing under an outdoor staircase in the center of a posh-looking apartment community. From the surrounding landscape, Sherman could tell that he was no longer anywhere near downtown Indianapolis. There were no tall buildings, no Superbowl Championship banners. There were no walls of bumper-to-bumper, eco-friendly automobile traffic or museums dedicated to the scum of treasonous lore. The absence of the ambient sonances of interstate traffic combined with the tranquil affluence of life in the Hamptons prompted Sherman to pinch himself to make sure he hadn't been knocked out in the Harper's prison. *Where am I now?* Eternity handed Sherman the remote control as she stepped out from under the staircase and peered at a second floor window. "It's red, Sherman, we can go up." A thread of relief wove through her exclamation. She looked over her to shoulder to make sure Sherman was following close behind as she ran up the stairs to apartment B4. He noticed a tiny red light bulb in the corner of the window pane. "This is us, Sherman," Eternity muttered once they reached the top of the stairs. She knocked three times on the door, paused, knocked twice, paused, bent down and faintly knocked five more times. On the fifth knock, sounds of chains and locks vibrated through the door until finally it swung open to reveal a smiling Kristen Lapham.

"Nice work, Sherman," Kristen grinned.

"I know, right?" Eternity seconded, stepping across the threshold into the temple of uncertainty. "He did great! Lester never suspected a thing. Come on in, Sherman. We won't bite." For the first time since lying in bed the previous evening, Sherman's trousers began to tighten.

The inside of the apartment was like something out of one of those old movies about serial killers or guys who like to blow up school buses. The walls were systematically cluttered with news clippings and other assorted articles, the shades were drawn, and dozens of flat-screen computer monitors filled the living room. Peeking around the apartment's décor, Sherman spied various maps of the ancient world, timelines, genealogical charts, assorted mathematical equations, constellation diagrams, and replicas of several famous historical documents. At least

Sherman *thought* they were artificial. One bedroom was filled with nothing but books, some torn and tattered, others impeccably preserved in their tidy dust jackets. Similar to the Archer E. Room back at Harper's, the walls of the hallway were lined with framed pictures depicting a multitude of time travel excursions. Beneath the sounds of their own footsteps on the hardwood floors, Sherman's ears detected the subtle humming of electricity, presumably from the plethora of glowing tubes and electrodes hooked up to miscellaneous mechanical apparatuses: Dr. Frankenstein meets Dennis Hopper in *Speed.*

"Does anyone *live* here?" Sherman wondered.

"God no!" Eternity answered mockingly. "You could say this is kinda like our home base though."

"Your home base? Like you and Kristen? You two are *sisters* right?" Sherman asked, continuing slowly down the hall.

"Yeah we are, Sherman. Sorry I couldn't tell you about that earlier. We'll explain everything soon. But no, she doesn't live here. She really does live up in Chicago. I live around here with my grandma: well, *our* grandma," Eternity explained, noting Kristen's smirk when she said "my grandma."

"Yeah, uh, sorry I couldn't tell you about her either…" Kristen added on.

"About her? Why would you ever want to tell me about your grandma? You and I just met, like, yesterday," Sherman replied.

"Yeah, I know but still. You'll see."

At the end of the hallway sat the master's den: an 18' by 26' bedroom suite converted to a technological funhouse akin to the former NASA control room at Houston Space Center. Sherman was shocked to see that as opposed to the monitors in the living room which were plotting meteorological anomalies and measuring geothermal variances, these screens were capturing what looked to be images straight out of ClockWorks. They were connected to ClockWorks's *security cameras*! "What's going on, Eternity?" He demanded. "Where are we? Why are these screens broadcasting Harper's surveillance films? Wait a second…Kristen…*Eternity*? You two were responsible for ruining the Harper's mainframe! You should be arrested. It…it was *you* who sent over Will's TDL Codes to the IDM

Room. This whole thing is YOUR FAULT! I knew Harvey and Lester didn't do it! Let me out of here. I want to go ho—"

"Dr. Hinkley, I presume," calmly said the familiar voice of an old woman from the hallway. "I've been wondering when I would get the chance to meet you."

Sherman was dumfounded. Could this really be *her*? The woman from yesterday morning? The woman with the incomplete file? The woman whose image haunted his tranq induced dreams the night before? *Eliza Jacobs herself*?!

"Miss J-J-Jacobs?" Sherman stuttered, faltering between gratitude and grievance.

"I'm afraid it's not that simple, Sherman," the old, fatherless woman lamented. *Why wasn't anything simple anymore?*

"Wait…are you…Eternity, is *she*…your grandmother?" Sherman just realized his dad was the tooth fairy. "But this doesn't make sense! Your last named is *Jacobs*. And yours is *Alcott*. Oh shit, and yours is…*Lapham?"* First the tooth fairy and now the Easter Bunny. It sucks being a kid sometimes.

"Actually, Sherman, those aren't really any of our names," Era tried to explain.

"Dr. Hinkley, I apologize for all the confusion. Please, forgive us and allow me to introduce myself. My name if Eliza Wyatt: Eliza Wyatt Harper.

Nineteen
Brilliance Personified

"If anyone could prove to me that Christ is outside the truth, and if the truth really did exclude Christ, I should prefer to stay with Christ and not with truth."
-Fyodor Dostoevsky

"From now on, I'm not doing anything I don't want to do. The world owes me happiness, fulfillment, and success. I'm just here to cash in."
-Calvin, *Calvin and Hobbes*

E.W. Harper was born in Omaha, Nebraska on November 22, 1963 on the same day President John F. Kennedy was assassinated in Dallas, Texas by a man named Lee Harvey Oswald who was killed by a man named Jack Ruby later on. Coincidentally, E.W. Harper and JFK never knew each other. No one knows what the E.W stands for because no one ever bothered to ask. Everyone just called him E.W. When he was in fourth grade, he went on a plane trip with a bunch of friends from school, but the plane crashed on an island and everyone had to live there for a lot of weeks and they turned savage and ate pigs. But then they got rescued and E.W. Harper came back to the United States and went to high school in 1977, the same year Star Wars *came out in the theaters. Everyone loved that movie. So did E.W. Harper. He wanted to be a scientist after seeing that movie.*

So, he started doing time travel. In 1984, E.W. Harper and his friend, Ted Theodore Logan, went into a telephone booth that took them back in time to all kinds of neat places and they met a bunch of very interesting historical people so they could get a good grade on their final history report because if they didn't than they would fail and Ted would have to go to military school in Alaska. That would have been bad. Parsimoniously, E.W. Harper did invent time travel and the two past their history class. That all took place in San Dimas, California. But that was only the beginning.

Soon, everyone in the world wanted to know how to do time travel, but E.W. Harper didn't tell anybody because he wanted to keep it secret just like the owner of Wonka's candy factory, Mr. Wonka, wanted to keep his recipes for candy a secret. It was the same thing, in conceptual. But one day, E.W. Harper decided he had enough of keeping time travel a secret and wanted everyone to know how to study history. So he found ClockWorks in 2018, five years before 2023 in which was the year I was born in. E.W. Harper became world famous and made a ton of money and nobody ever wandered what time was like again because all they had to do to see history was go to ClockWorks and get a vacation package. Soon, more TTA's submerged all over the planet Earth and other countries could do what Harper did in USA. But, unfortuitously, disaster soon stroked.

One day when E.W. Harper was flying his plane over the ocean, his baby was taken from his house. No one new where the little baby was!!!! Everyone looked and the guy who took the baby wrote letters saying clues and stuff but no one could find the baby until it was to late. He died that year. The nation mourned a great loss. E.W. Harper was upset and wowed to never do time travel ever again. And then E.W. Harper died mystically as well.

E.W. Harper was a genius and great American. I think he is the one of the greatest inventors of the last two hundred years because of his time traveling agency and everything good that has come out of it. If I were to meet E. W. Harper today, I would probably shake his hand say good job on all the time travels and maybe I would ask him what's the worst thing that could come out of it. That's why I think E.W. Harper is a great man.

As grad school applications go, Sherman just *knew* his writing sample had all the zing, zest, and zeal of a publishable article. The writing prompt for Cross University's Forensic Psychology program was easy enough to understand: "En seiscientos palabras o menos, por favor escriba un ensayo en que, en su opinión, es el inventor más influyentes de los últimos doscientos años y por qué. Asegúrese de apoyar su tesis con ejemplos de la literatura, la historia, o bien argumentadas opiniones de personas educadas. No se preocupe si usted no lo hace demasiado bien. Sólo pedimos que pruebe su absoluta mejor y tener un poco de diversión en el proceso. Buena suerte!"

After consulting a dictionary, Sherman reread the instructions. From his three years of high school German, he guessed the essay had something to do with global warming. Once translated, the instructions read, "In six hundred words or less, please write an essay on who, in your opinion, is the most influential inventor of the last two hundred years and why. Be sure to support your thesis with examples from literature, history, or well-argued opinions of educated individuals. Don't worry if you don't do too well. We only ask that you try your absolute best and have a little bit of fun in the process. Good luck!" *Nope, nothing about global warming.* Still, what more ideal subject for an essay than Sherman's childhood hero, Dr. E.W. Harper? Like the spilling of words in a child's letter to Santa, so too did Sherman's thoughts flow through his fingers onto his computer screen. *This shit is good!* Of course, he had to fudge a little on a few specific details regarding Harper's childhood, but all in all, he was proud of his biographical account of the man's life. Years later, however, as Sherman stood restlessly in this bedroom-turned-NORAD, surrounded by two beautiful sisters and one crazy old lady, a part of him wished he'd never heard of the great time travel pioneer.

"I can understand if you're a bit shocked, Sherman," Eternity empathetically expressed.

"Please, Dr. Hinkley, come and sit down. You look a tad peaked," Eliza *Whoever-she-is* requested. Sherman did as he was told. Something about his current surroundings made him think that perhaps it behooved him not to push these women too far. Aside from outnumbering him three to one, from the looks of their digs, they had enough techno-power to blow him up into enough pieces that nobody would know his remains from a piece of sugar on their toast. The least he could do was have a seat; no one ever got killed merely by sitting down.

The woman formerly known as Miss Jacobs sat across from Sherman, the smile of a homely old grandmother still canvassing her wrinkled face. On either side of her sat her granddaughters. "I suppose you'd like to ask me a few questions, Dr. Hinkley."

"Actually, no. I would *love* to ask E.W. Harper--the inventor of time travel, the founder of ClockWorks, the *man* who was born over a hundred years ago and died before I was even born--yeah, I'd just *love* to ask him some questions, you know, about life and stuff, but I can't because he's *not here anymore.*"

"Oh, Sherman, what do you really know about E.W. Harper?" Eternity jeered. It was the same condescending tone a girlfriend has when ordering her idiot boyfriend to stop blowing peas out of his nose in public.

"Wha--wha...I know everything there is *to* know about Doctor--*Mr.* E.W. Harper! I've loved his work since I was a kid. I studied his writings. I wrote a paper about him for my grad school entrance--"

"Sherman, that paper was horrible and you know it!" Kristen smiled. Sherman's face went ashen at the thought of these....*girls*...reading his writing. *Stay out of my diary!*

"It was not horrible! It got me into Cross University. I wouldn't have a PhD. if it weren't for that essay! And what happened to *Eliza Jacobs?*"

"That's right, Dr. Hinkley," Eliza said. "You did go to Cross University. Excellent school, Cross. Quite the impressive line of scholars and researchers has emerged from the hallowed halls of Cross University."

"That's right!" Sherman agreed. "And if it weren't for that essay--"

"Tell me, Dr. Hinkley," the old bat flapped on, "Who was that school named after again?"

"Excuse me?" Sherman was confused.

"Cross University: your alma mater. Who is its namesake? Who founded it?"

"Dr. Alexander Cross, of course." Sherman proudly proclaimed.

"*Dr. Alexander Cr*-oh, I see. Well then, there we are. But who, again, was he? What did he do?"

Sherman was wondering when he was going to get his chance to ask the questions. "Well, as a matter of fact, he did a lot of things. He was orphaned at an early age and went to live with his grandmother in Washington, D.C. He worked in soup kitchens and shortly as a migrant farm worker before going to Johns Hopkins and earning a doctorate in psychology. After starting his own practice, however, I think he became disenchanted by the *ethics*, maybe, of the medical community and decided to become a police officer in Washington. He would eventually become a detective and help D.C. Police solve some pretty damn important crimes!"

"Like what?"

"Haven't you ever heard of the Casanova Murders of the late twentieth century?"

"Why, no, Dr. Hinkley, please tell us."

"Fine. Dr. Cross--who was a *black* man, by the way--"

"What does that have to do with anything?"

"Nothing. It's just, I guess, like…it means that we shouldn't…so his school is, um, *important*, okay!"

"Fair enough. Go on."

"Thanks, well, I think it was in 1995, but Cross helped D.C Police locate the…location of several abducted and sexually abused women in the North Carolina forests. One of them was his niece Naomi. But even before that, he helped a wealthy Washington family recover their missing daughter who was first kidnapped by her teacher, Mr. Gary Soneji, but as it turns out, the girl was later kidnapped and almost murdered by Cross's double crossing partner, Jezzie Flannigan. So he saved the day again."

"Wow, very impressive."

"Damn right. So there, instead of just giving the school money and having them name it after him, Alexander Cross actually *did* stuff with his life."

"I see. Thank you, Dr. Hinkley." Eliza said. "Now tell me one thing: are you familiar with a Mr. James Patterson? He was an author around the turn of the century."

"Um, no. No, I don't think I am. Why?"

"Well, it's funny you mention Dr. Cross because James Patterson wrote a series of books--quite a few of them actually, a couple were even made into movies--that sound very similar to your stories of Dr. Cross. In fact, the protagonist in all of these books is, get this, a black man named Dr. Alex Cross who works in Washington, D.C as a detective but used to work in his own private practice." Sherman was silent. He didn't know what the old woman was getting at. "And then, the damndest thing happened. Around 2012, a bunch of morons down in Florida decided that this guy--this *Cross* character, you know, from these books?--was so important to the academic community that he needed to have, I can barely say it without laughing, a *college* named after him! A real life American University! I like to think the whole thing started off really as a kind of a sick joke, but no! They bought it. The public went nuts about the idea! So, for three years there was this massive campaign to try and find the perfect location for *Cross University* where they would specialize in--you can guess--*Psychology Degrees!*" Sherman had the strangest feeling the woman was telling the truth. And an even stranger feeling she was making fun of him. "Well, I'm sure you can figure out the rest. They decided on Indianapolis, and the rest is history."

Sherman paused. And paused. Then said nothing. And paused again. Finally, he spoke. "So, okay, if what you're saying is true…No, fuck it, can you *prove* any of this?"

"Oh, Sherman," Kristen shook her head.

"Dr. Hinkley, what would suffice as proof in this matter? I created a way for this world to prove virtually everything and all they did with it was turn it into some sort of bastardized rendition of an extracurricular activity: a game! What could I possibly do *now* to prove to you that I am who I say I am and you are *not*, I'm sorry to say, who you think you are?" *So many pronouns, so little time to process.*

"Why don't you just tell him your story, Grandma?" Eternity suggested.

"Very well, child. Dr. Hinkley, before I begin, I apologize. It's not your fault you turned out the way you did. Nor are you entirely to blame for what happened at ClockWorks. Though, you shouldn't have given that lad Zemeckalian Clearance, but we were the ones who sent the forged TDL Codes. There's no way you could have known we would do that. We've been watching you for months, studying you, learning everything we can about you. You're merely a product of your surroundings. You couldn't have controlled what happened any more than I could have. So I'm sorry for upsetting you just now."

"Okay, now I do have some questions." Sherman uttered.

"Please, allow me a bit more time, and then you can ask anything you want."

"Fine by me."

Eliza Wyatt Harper began.

Outside the apartment, four men stood in the parking lot, staring up at a second story window pane. They'd been led there by a transmitter Lester Whitman successfully planted on Sherman before he left him with Eternity in the ClockWorks prison. So far their presence had gone undetected. "What does that red light in the corner of the window mean, Mr. Douglas?" Waverly asked.

"Uh, it says here, sir, that light signifies the unit is secure: 'no visible sign of any danger' it says," Douglas replied, flipping through a leather-bound report from one of the ACHEs recent reconnaissance missions. "It's reversed: red means *clear* green means *clear out*."

"Is there a yellow?" Lieutenant Gage wondered.

"Yes, sir," Lester responded. "It means 'sleeping: do not disturb'."

"They're all up there, Mr. President," Gage declared. "What should we do, sir? How do you want us to handle it?"

"I'm not sure they know all that we know, yet, Lieutenant," Waverly said. "For now, we'll just wait out here for the rest of the team to arrive. Mr. Douglas, am I correct in assuming that Agents Newton and Emerson have been cooperating with the ACHEs thus far?"

"Indeed, sir. They will arrive shortly. The procedure took a few minutes longer than anticipated, and they chose to drive today so as to avoid suspicion. No one quite knew what to expect this morning."

"Quite right, son, thank you," Waverly said more to himself than to his employees. As Waverly fell silent, the four men maintained their stakeout of apartment B4. After a few moments of staring at the window, Waverly mumbled under his breath, "I wonder what our old friend Eliza is telling that poor bastard up there. Let's just hope he's still on our side if things go wrong."

"How could things go wrong, sir?" Gage wondered. "We fixed the mainframe. We've identified the Point of Divergence. The only thing that could go wrong would be if someone went back to stop Will Bauer from forging the new path, but all TDL Codes to or from anywhere near 1822 Bishopwearmouth have been permanently disabled from the system. There's no chance *anyone* can change what's happened."

"Lieutenant, I seriously hope you don't mean that," Waverly said austerely. "If you learn one thing from this experience today, gentlemen, or from your time with this organization, know this: with no one, yes, nothing changes. But *any*one can change *any*thing. And they don't need to work for *this* agency to do it."

"What do you mean 'this' agency, sir?" Lester asked.

"Only that there our other agencies in this world with which we ought to concern ourselves other than simply Harper's."

"Like what, sir? Lester persisted.

Waverly didn't respond. Someone was moving around in the living room of apartment B4.

"I wasn't born in 1963, Dr. Hinkley, and I wasn't born in Omaha. My father wasn't killed in India and my mother wasn't worn down and beaten by life in my perverted uncle's basement. You'll have to forgive me for haunting you with that story but in truth, I've always fancied my flare for the dramatic. Plus, it was the only way to get your attention. No, I'm afraid very little of what you know what E.W. Harper or Eliza Jacobs is true. My parents bought a small starter house in Metamora, Illinois in 1982, and I was born shortly after their first Christmas in the bungalow. My father was an engineer at the nearby Caterpillar plant and my mother worked as a teacher at a local Catholic grade school. Everything the books and websites say about my childhood is conceptually accurate though not terribly significant. I *was* the youngest of three Wyatt children. I *did* like science from an early age, but primarily as a hobby. I *did* have a dog named Octopus and, yes, my favorite movie was *Star Wars.* My family lived in Metamora until I was six and then, yes, we did move to Omaha. I never crashed on a deserted island with my classmates or went back in time with my friend Ted though, but I'm sure you already knew that. My childhood was fairly typical. I played sports in junior high, loved movies, liked reading, tolerated church, and hated—*hated*—the unrelenting burdens of female adolescence. The first real chance I got to leave that town and be a woman, I knew I'd be gone in a heartbeat.

"I graduated high school in 2000. Because I vowed to pay for college myself even though my parents were more than willing and capable to assist with the finances, I waited a year to apply for college during which time I stayed at home and worked a series of odd jobs around town. I helped at my mom's school working in the main office throughout the academic year. In the summer, I waitressed at a pub down the street during the busy lunch hours and administered private swimming lessons at night. On weekends, I would travel to bigger cities like Peoria and sometimes even Chicago to see if I could pedal some of my first inventions. In 1999, for example, I invented a cellular telephone that came equipped with a small monitor that played videos and was also was a music player. At the time I didn't have a patent for my design and after one promising visit to Chicago, I soon found my prototype in a local electronics store. The guy stole my design. From then on I made it a point never to share any of my ideas with potential buyers until I was absolutely positive I would receive full credit for them. That promise was short lived.

"I was accepted and enrolled in MIT in the fall of 2001, and shortly after the towers came down—you know about that, right?— I had my first inclinations to someday experiment with temporal alterations. Something about seeing people literally jump from the top floors of those burning buildings made me wonder if the whole thing could have been avoided if we could've only just gone back to see the events leading up to it. I knew I never wanted to see anything like that again and wondered if maybe we could learn something from the whole mess we could, in essence, *change* the course of our own future. But again, at the time, those were merely fleeting aspirations.

"In 2005, I graduated from MIT after only three years with a double major in Aeronautical Engineering and Nanotechnology. The following fall I began my PhD. work at Stanford, which I completed in May of 2009. I know this all sounds a little like my resume, but bare with me. It'll get better. It's important you know where I came from. As you know from reading my diary, I was offered a tenure track position at Purdue University in 2009 and taught for a couple of years before developing my theories of STOOP and the subsequent process of time travel. Before that point, my life was nothing out of the ordinary.

"Okay, so there's the basics, right: smart kid, normal kid, eager kid growing up in an age of rampant voyeurism in a society imbued by the cult of personality and a culture that valued empirical knowledge over wisdom as well as instant gratification over prolonged meritocracy. It would take a few generations of inherently narcissistic drones, of course, but over time the culture that *is* pop culture became so pervasive that even genuinely intelligent men such as yourself, Dr. Hinkley, would be dooped into thinking, excuse me, that your education actually *meant* something. But that's beside the point. Alas, as the story goes, I invent time travel and founded ClockWorks and died in my old age only to get immortalized in history books and countless future generations now honor my legacy. That's what you think you know, sir. But let me tell you what really happened.

"Shortly before I began my career with Purdue, I got married. Now, if you're keeping up with the math, you'll know that at this point—in 2009—I'm only 26 years old. Twenty-six, Sherman! My husband, Jeremy Harper was finishing his dissertation for Purdue's Electrical Engineering program when we were married in August of that year. When I began my work with STOOP in early 2010, my husband and I were the primary researchers. In fact, the initial trials with Abe, my darling chimpanzee, were conducted in Jeremy's laboratory in the basement of the electrical engineering building on Purdue's West Lafayette campus. Continued research was put on hold, however, in January 2011, due to the birth of our first child, Elijah Jonas Harper. While I stayed at home with our new baby, Jeremy continued the work in the lab though, I must admit, he lacked a certain veracity that his wife possessed. Needless to say, progress was slow when mommy was a no-show.

"Nevertheless, within four years, we'd gathered enough conclusive data to support my initial theories for STOOP and published our first book in 2015. When it came time to publish these groundbreaking findings, rather than using my full name and thus identifying myself as a twenty-something woman and risk the ridicule of my discursive colleagues, I wrote under the name "E.W. Harper." Over the years, as my theories began to come to fruition and my legacy within the annals of scientific experimentation grew increasingly solidified, I maintained the pseudonym. To this day, I can't really explain why. Perhaps it was my youthful pretension or maybe my own insecurities about my own ideas; what if I failed, after all? What if I was mocked and shunned by the scientific community? I couldn't stand the thought of bringing shame onto my family.

"And yet by 2016, my husband and I had proven that time travel was possible. I insisted that I be the first living human to undergo the process, and in July 2016, I was transported back to 1776 to witness the signing of the Declaration of Independence. But you already know that, I'm sure. All the rest of the details concerning how I stumbled across time travel are true: the tanks of water, the sprinkler, all of my trials with Abe. Those all occurred precisely as history dictates, save for a young woman behind the wheel instead of a weathered old man. Jeremy was the first to come up with the idea of using our invention to study time as if it were an interactive sort of textbook: an idea to which I effortlessly consented. Following the successful acquisition of numerous government grants, bank loans, and shareholders, I sent out a nation wide search for an architect for our brainchild: an agency that specialized in time travel. Well, long story short, ClockWorks was born in 2018. Now here's where things got hairy.

"With the exception of our research assistants and immediate colleagues, no one had really ever *seen* either Jeremy or me. Why would they? We weren't celebrities! We had a moderate level of fame within our own intimate realm of intellects, but we were still intellects in an age when intelligence wasn't revered. We weren't in magazines or on-line or on TV. Sure, people *knew,* to a certain extent, that the name 'Harper' was somehow affiliated with time travel, and sure, if you wanted to find a picture of us somewhere you could, but think about it; how many people would know the author of their favorite book or inventor of their favorite techy toy if they sat next to them on a bus? The avid fans, of course, would, but most people didn't know me from Adam. Or in my case, Eve. There was no *desire* to ever see us. We were merely the people that made cool things possible. No one cares about those guys. The cultural myopia was contagious. It plagued society in the same manner that materialism did before it, and depression before that. It was the vicious malady that was both the bane of my existence, but also my most trusted ally in keeping my family out of the public's Panopticonal gaze. Jeremy and I liked to joke that if Hawthorne wrote *The Scarlet Letter* today, he could basically tell the exact same story except the 'A' would undoubtedly stand for 'apathy.' But then again, that's what it originally meant anyway…never mind…So where was I? ClockWorks is finished. It's early 2018 and we're almost ready to open. But there was a slight change in plans for the overall…*direction*--as they called it--of the company. Instead of being an agency that deals with time travel--as my husband and I originally intended-- the businessmen and pocket books wanted ClockWorks to be a travel agency that dealt with time. Tourism became the goal. Epistemology: a far off, unacknowledged second.

"The shareholders wanted to take our little venture and thrust it into the competitive arena alongside the likes of Disney, Universal Studios, and MoonFlights United. They tried to patronize us by insisting that they wanted to maintain the sense of integrity and tradition from which Jeremy and I had fostered the idea, but ultimately all they wanted was an image, a logo, a marketable perversion of knowledge. So they stole some of my first sketches of time travel and devised that sickening ClockWorks emblem you know today: that infernal clock without hands. What they don't know is—*those morons*—is that my original sketches *did* have hands. Only the second hand was missing. Oh, sorry, let me explain: have you ever noticed how sometimes people's watches have second hands that seem to be going at different speeds compared to other people's watches? Like the turn signals on different cars stopped at a red light? Well, anyway, I read a book when I was still studying at MIT that argued that the slight disparity between the second hands on clocks is a fundamental component of understanding how time travel could, in fact, be possible. Every so often those second hands *will* match again, but for one watch it could be after five minutes whereas for the other watch it may be only after three minutes. In other words, it's the least common denominator of the two. But that doesn't mean the first watch is two minutes in the future, does it? Or that the second watch is two minutes in the past? Get it? Anyway, sorry, back to my story.

"The next thing they needed was a face for the company to match the handless face of that despicable insignia. They wanted it to be similar to the image of Walt Disney: the compassionate, wise, accomplished man in the suit, beaming at the children of the world with a smile that beckons, 'Don't worry! I've been there and everything will be okay!' They wanted Grandpa Time. Well, you can understand that thirty-five year old Momma Harper didn't quite fit the mold of the image these bastards wanted to convey to the world. So they hired—*hired*—someone to play my part! They paid some random Canadian stage actor to read the speech that *I wrote* at the ClockWorks inaugural address. Since the media publicized the event to unprecedented extremes, the man instantaneously became the face of the organization. He did interviews, posed for pictures, and appeared on television while the entire time Jeremy and I made the damn place run. I personally didn't mind the coerced marginalization but Jeremy couldn't bare to work for a company that refused to acknowledge my accomplishments.

"In May of 2019, after over a year of stomaching ClockWorks's avarice and denial of our existence, the company decided it was time to apologize. They surprised my family with a one week trip to a destination of our choosing as a gesture of their appreciation for our years of service in the name of scientific progress. What a bunch of garbage. We told them we wanted to go back to 1912 and watch the RMS Titanic depart from Southampton, but those monsters sent us back to the middle of a crowded marketplace in third century Arabia. Not only that, but we had specifically requested Dickensian Clearance. We had our child with us for God's sake! We didn't want to risk anything happening to him. Once we arrived in the bustle of the overcrowded bazaar, we knew something was wrong. People started staring at us and looking as though they meant us harm. Jeremy and I grabbed Elijah and hurried out of the village and into the nearby hills for safety. We remained there for two days before finally we were rescued by a former colleague of mine, Dr. Ajay Nagheenanajar. When he found us, he told Jeremy and me that the ClockWorks's president had banned any employee from future contact with any member of my family. Since we'd left, our entire team back home had been disbanded and replaced by an elite group of ethical conformists aptly referred to as "ACHEs". Dr. Ajay Nagheenanajar went on to tell us that we were sent back without any return TDL Codes in our STOOPING Pieces, which means they never intended us to return to civilization. The only reason we made it out of there safely was because Ajay was smart enough to bring with him a device he and I had been working on over the previous few months. It was, essentially, a portable IDM Room, except instead of being able to transport someone to a specific time *and* place, the device could only accommodate one of those destinations. It's the same device my granddaughters used with you earlier today. I never told the Agency about it, though, and to this day, they have no idea that we've harnessed such a technology.

"With Ajay's help we were able to return to 2019, and believe me, I had every intention of making things right with the Agency. But as it turned out, in the months preceding our exile to Arabia, a covert ClockWorks team had been secretly working on removing us from their files. They were wiping us from existence yet again. They implemented newer and more sophisticated security measures and somehow capped the current time line which made it nearly impossible for me or my family to get anywhere near the facility or do any damage if I did manage to crack all their new codes. Dr. Ajay Nagheenanajar couldn't go back to work either because he was now a fugitive. We were stuck. They had won and we were on the run.

"It took them little over a day to realize we'd escaped from the past and two more to find Jeremy and kill him. I'm not sure who did it or how they found us, but after we fled Indy and moved to Salem, the ACHEs found our house and burned it to the ground. But don't worry. It looked like an accident. They didn't stick around to realize Elijah and I were gone for the evening at the store, however. Everyone thought we all died in the fire and ClockWorks quickly pounced on the opportunity to publically mourn the loss of its founder. Mainly, they just wanted an excuse to fire the guy who was *playing* me. It was the strangest thing watching live television coverage of my own funeral while surrounded by people who were crying for my loss but weren't aware that I was sitting next to them, only to then see pictures of a complete stranger with your name under it: a man at that!

"In the wake of his fallout with ClockWorks, Dr. Ajay Nagheenanajar moved back to India for about forty years or so before creeping back into the States and settling in upstate New York. He works as a neurologist there and has devoted his entire career to reversing the hippocampus implants of former ClockWorks employees once a change in time has occurred. It's his own way of trying to save the world from my mistake one patient at a time. We've eliminated all correspondence with each other since our return almost fifty years ago, though I have every reason to believe the Agency knows his whereabouts but considers him more of a thorn in its massive corporate paw than a viable threat. They just let him be. Elijah and I moved to a small island in the south Pacific where I taught English at a mission for a number of years. Of course we changed our names and everything else attached to our past lives. Elijah grew up, went to Oxford, married an American and had two daughters, Eternity and Kristen. He died of a rare blood disease when the girls were still in junior high school. Soon thereafter I moved to Liverpool with my daughter in-law to help her take care of my grandchildren. It would be another couple of years before I reestablished any sort of contact with my own brother or sister.

"About ten years ago I found out my brother had a granddaughter who was a little older then Eternity. Her name was and presumably still is, Era. When she graduated from Notre Dame, she married Casey Howells and the two moved to Birmingham where she worked as a dental assistant and he directed commercials for a local telecommunication's company. When he was only twenty-four, however, two years into their marriage, he was diagnosed with a terminal form of Leukemia. He was dead within the year. Era moved to Indianapolis and was hired at ClockWorks as a Public Agent, like Eternity. I only met her once, but from what Eternity tells me, she held a great admiration for the company. She dedicated herself to the integrity of the Agency and the principles of time travel for which I blazed the trail. Of course she doesn't know that Eternity is her second cousin or that her great aunt is the famous E.W. Harper. She thinks of us only as her sworn enemies.

"When my granddaughters were old enough, the three of us commenced our quest to shut down ClockWorks TTA. For the most part, I assumed the role of silent advisor to the operation, so as not to risk compromising my best weapon which was still my anonymity: the fact that no one knew I was still alive. Kristen moved to Chicago, and for several years has been trying to infiltrate the system under a barrage of various pseudonyms and eliciting the aid of previous ClockWorks CHIMPs. Until you came along, however, her applications never made it past the front desk. Eternity was our internal mole, working the system from the inside out, trying to find any holes in the infrastructure and lobbying to implement new policies which would allow for easier access to the mainframe. All of our years of struggle culminated when you were hired, Dr. Hinkley. You became our white knight, the man who would help us realize our dreams. With my knowledge, Kristen's distractions, Eternity's leverage and your occupational status, we all knew this time around we'd succeed."

"I'm sorry to interrupt, but succeed in *what?"* Sherman begged. "Why would you want to destroy something you helped build?"

"Because they corrupted it. My creation is broken; it's flawed. It's no longer even a shadow of what it could have been." Eliza responded.

"But surely there are people out there who do use the Agency for the reasons you wanted. Not everybody is taking advantage of the power you gave them."

"It isn't only the misuse of the technology, Sherman," Eternity added, "It's just not worth the risk anymore. You saw the museum today. Do you really want to live in a world that adorns murderers like that?"

Sherman thought about her question. He thought about Eliza's story. He thought about the last twenty-four hours. He tried to think about Wally and Lamar but his mind kept going back to Isabelle Stowe. Dear, sweet, awful Isabelle.

"So, what now?" he finally asked. "What do we do now? I mean, okay, the world has gone to hell after last night, right? So, what next? Do we go back and fix things? Just tell me what you want me to do and I'll do it. You're right, Eternity, I can't stand living in a world where, because of something I did, a guy like Booth is regarded as a hero. Where do we go from here?"

"I'm afraid it's not the simple, Dr. Hinkley. I'm pleased to say that we were wrong both about you as well as what you did. You're a hero, Sherman, but not for the reasons we thought you'd be. Before you arrived here this morning, I took the liberty of doing some research. It appears the world is much different than you think it is," Eliza said, the smile still on her face.

"I don't understand," Sherman replied.

"Neither do I, grandma," Eternity seconded.

"Does this have anything to do with what you told me before they got here?" Kristen asked.

"Indeed it does, child," Eliza responded. "Eternity, Sherman, you needn't worry anymore. The only reason we had to evacuate you from ClockWorks so quickly is because they didn't know that we know what they know. You could have been in danger if they thought you still wanted to destroy the Agency."

"What do you mean *still?*" Sherman asked. "Isn't that what we want to do? To make everything okay again?"

"Wait," Eternity asserted. "Grandma, are you saying what I think you're saying? Are things really…?"

"I'll explain everything in just one minute," Eliza responded. "Right now, I must ask my granddaughters to let our other guests in. Emmanuelle, Phineas! Don't bother knocking, we're coming!" Eternity and Kristen rose obligingly from their seats and opened the front door. Lieutenant Gage entered first followed by Waverly, Harvey and Lester, a Reverend and a chump. With the ACHEs standing guard outside the building, the party was now officially ready to begin. The only people missing were Stowe and Era. But at that moment, the former didn't exist and the latter was on a plane to New York where an old colleague of her great aunt's was going to cut into her brain and remove a tiny machine simply so she can live a normal life with her reincarnated husband. Yup, there's no business like time business.

Twenty
In a Nut Shell

"An estimated 5,000 economic, political, and religious groups operate in the United States alone at any given time, with 2.5 million members. Over the last ten years, cults have used tactics of coercive mind control to negatively impact an estimated 20 million victims in the last ten years. Worldwide figures are even greater."

-Dr. Margaret Singer, *Cults in Our Midst*

"It requires courage not to surrender oneself to the ingenious or compassionate counsels of despair that would induce a man to eliminate himself from the ranks of the living; but it does not follow from this that every huckster who is fattened and nourished in self-confidence has more courage than the man who yielded to despair."

-Soren Kierkegaard

Shermy Hinkley. Fifth grade. For several weeks, a strange girl had been dropping secret letters off in little Shermy's cubby hole. He never saw who did it. He never found any fingerprints or hair samples nor did he have the equipment necessary to analyze such things even if they had been carelessly left at the drop point. None of his friends knew anything about the strange letters written by the vixen with unfamiliar though impeccable penmanship. Shermy asked his teacher if she could install a camera in the rear of his cubby, but she denied his request for funds, claiming such items weren't in the school's fall budget. Art class and reading time claimed most of his energy during the morning and, what with the nap he always took during music class after lunch, how the heck was he supposed to keep track of his cubby at all times?

The letters were provocative in nature, though often poorly crafted and contained frequent spelling/other syntactical errors. It didn't take long for Shermy to deduce they indeed came from someone in close proximity because they usually addressed Shermy's outfit on a given day or sometimes complimented the way he ate his lunch. *And she knew what kind of lunch he ate too!* She was cunning, clever, patient. Shermy was strangely attracted to the manner in which she always signed her letters: simply "NB." Now, of course Shermy not only combed through the entire fifth grade phonebook in search of a name with the initials NB, but he also devoured the Tell City phone book, high school yearbook, library database, and obituaries to make sure his girlfriend didn't live in another town or maybe went to high school. Or was dead. He never found anything. At least no girls with the initials NB. He didn't follow through with the boys.

After years, nay, *decades* of their unilateral correspondence, the mystery girl finally suggested they meet one day during recess. Shermy had a shoebox at home with at least…*eight* other letters from the girl, and yet this was the first time she ever suggested they actually meet. *Face-to-face!* He told all of his friends about the offer and solicited advice for what he should wear, if he should bring anything, and how he was going to sneak back inside his classroom, which is where she wanted to meet during recess. His classmates helped him with all matters fashion and tact. Operation "Shermy Meets Secret Love Letter Writing Girl at Recess on Friday" took a whole afternoon to plan, but when Shermy went to bed that Thursday night, he was ready for whatever life brought him the next day. How fierce his boundless love beat upon the bosom of his child's heart! What sparks would fly when first the Grecian meets his lyre! Oh, sing in me sweet muse and whisper softly from thine lips the music of your passionate tongue! Shermy pissed the bed that night.

The next day brought with it the anticipation of a Christmas morning wrapped inside a birthday present on the first day of summer vacation during Thanksgiving break. The class welcomed Shermy to school as he stepped off his condensed, yellow bus. (They sent the short buses for the kids who lived far away from the school.) Even Shermy's teacher seemed in excellent spirits that fine morning, almost as if she too shared in the class's collective excitement for little Shermy's impending nuptials. Art class came and art class went. Reading time came and Shermy was pretty sure reading time went too. He went to the bathroom in the middle of it. He could hardly bring himself to eat anything at lunch that day; the anticipation of meeting the future mother of his children tightened his stomach like the time he got kicked in the gut during a snowball fight in his backyard. Finally recess was upon him. Finally he'd meet the woman who loved him: NB.

Shermy's classmates rose to the challenge of getting him back inside without their teacher knowing. Little Mikey Townsend faked a vomit attack over by the swings while Leslie Davis and Sean Van Dyke pretended like they were holding hands and kissing in the tube slide. Plenty to keep the twenty three year-old teachers busy. Once safe behind enemy lines, Shermy maneuvered down the hallway. He needed to avoid the fourth grade corridor and the cafeteria; those regions could be Russia to his Napoleonic campaign. At last he made it back to his classroom. He'd never been inside the room alone before. The desks seemed eerily unfamiliar when not occupied by his fellow students. The teacher's desk, especially, appeared now more like a normal chair and table than the usual throne behind which sat the great and powerful Miss Koss. Shermy scanned the room but to no avail. Perhaps NB's train was late at the station or her village had been bombed by enemy troops. Maybe she was being held hostage by a mad ex-boyfriend and it would be up to Master Ninja Shermy Hinkley to save her. Or maybe she needed to go to the nurse's office to get a band-aid. Either way, Shermy was alone.

It took a while for him to notice the absence of one of the room's staple sounds: the noise the class hamster, Pooker made when he ran on his wheel. Shermy went over to the hamster cage to make sure everything was okay with Pooker and that he had a front row seat for whenever the heck NB decided to show up so Shermy could give her the card he made for her. But alas, the cage was empty. Perhaps Pooker's village had been bombed by enemy troops and maybe he was being held hostage by a mad ex-girl--*No!* Shermy thought. *Something else must be wrong*. Shermy could see that somebody forgot to secure the lid on Pooker's cage. Somehow Pooker escaped. *Suicide?* Shermy got on his knees and searched the room. When he was done there, he moved into the hallway. Then the bathroom. Then the other hallway. As he was nearing Russia, he heard a squeak by his shoes. Bending down, he picked up Pooker in his hands and stood up proudly. His sense of accomplishment quickly wore off, however, as two thoughts popped into his mind. One, he wasn't in the room anymore and NB could already be gone. And two, Miss Koss was stomping down the hallway directly toward him. And she looked pissed.

"Shermy, where did you go? You know you can't leave recess without a bathroom buddy! You scared me."

"I know, Miss Koss but…*look!* Pooker got out! But don't worry, I found him!"

"Shermy! Wow, how the fu--good for you, Shermy! You found the class pet!" The rest of the class trickled in behind Miss Koss who turned around and showed everyone how Sherman saved Pooker from a certain death. "Look class, Shermy found Pooker. Brad, I think it was your turn to feed him. Did you make sure the lid was tight?"

"No, Miss Koss," Brad sighed. *Bastard.*

"Well, good thing for Pooker that Shermy was here, right everyone? Let's go back to class now. Everyone hold hands."

Back in the classroom, Shermy milked Miss Koss's praise for all it was worth. He saved Pooker's life. Him. Shermy Hinkley. Who knows: maybe one day Pooker would grow up to become a famous hamster lawyer or movie hamster or something. All because of Shermy. And yet, he'd never met his dear NB.

"What's wrong, Sherm?" little Wally Emerson asked. He and two other girls walked over to Shermy and were now leaning on his desk.

"Nothing. I just never met NB that's all. I hope she doesn't think I hate her guts or anything."

"She doesn't, Sherm," Wally giggled. "Trust me…"

"What? How do you know? Do you know her?"

"Well…" Wally burst into a fit of laughter.

"Shermy," Marcy Dinkle said. "Okay, first, it was Wally's idea, but, um, *NB*, yeah…stands for *Nobody*…sorry!" And the three walked back to their side of the room. Sherman didn't know what to do. If he cried, they'd make fun of him and call him a pussy. If he acted like he didn't care, they'd think he was gay because he didn't care if a girl liked him. (He wasn't sure what "gay" meant but he knew that everyone called Mark Burman "gay" and he didn't like Mark Burman, so he figured he didn't want to be called "gay" either.) If he did nothing, they'd think he was retarded. Once a week a real retarded girl came in during reading time, and Shermy knew that he didn't want to be compared to her either. She was weird and read slow. The only thing Shermy could think to do in the face of total public humiliation was get up from his desk, go over to Pooker's cage and make sure the lid was shut tight. He may be a gay retard tomorrow, but at least for that day, he was a hero in the eyes of Miss Koss.

"There's the hero!" Wally exclaimed when he saw Sherman sitting on the sofa in Eliza Wyatt Harper's fortress of deception. "Good to see you again, Sherm. Pretty fucking exciting day, huh? I bet you're thrilled to know that you fixed everything, right?" Something was different about Wally. He seemed uncomfortably content, especially after having been thrown into a dark lair by large men with automatic guns.

"Yeah, Sherman, job well done!" Lamar seconded. He too didn't appear to grasp the magnitude of the situation.

"You all are a little early, gentlemen," Eliza scorned. "I wasn't expecting you for at least another half hour. I'm afraid Dr. Hinkley is presently unaware of his current hero status."

"So you *do* know then, Miss Jacobs. I had a feeling you might. You haven't told him, yet?" Waverly protested. "I was sure you'd have enough time by now if you knew."

"Jacobs?" Sherman cried.

"Quiet, Sherman!" Eternity shouted. Did Gage and Waverly not know who this woman was? Why would they think she was Eliza Jacobs? *She is E.W. Harper, right?* "We had some other issues to discuss with Sherman before we got the heart of the matter," Eternity explained.

"I see," Waverly acknowledged. "Well, now that we're all here, perhaps we should begin the debriefing so we can get back to the Agency by noon."

"Excellent plan, Mr. President," Harper agreed. *What the hell is going on?* Sherman thought to himself.

"Dr. Hinkley, I'm sure you're wondering what the hell is going on," Waverly began. "Well, let me explain it to you."

"Whoa, whoa, first of all I just want to know how the hell you *all* got here, why Eternity was in prison before and now you don't even seem to care she's standing in this room, why the fuck you *shot* me *and* Kristen yesterday morning and, um, where the hell Stowe is!" Sherman demanded.

"All excellent questions, Hinkley," Gage answered. His demeanor resembled that of a proud father applauding at his son's college graduation. Was he somehow *impressed* with Sherman? "We followed you here because of a device Mr. Whitman placed on you back at the prison. Until the mainframe was repaired, we wanted to make sure we knew where you were at all times. We would have arrived sooner, but we were waiting on Agent's Newton and Emerson to arrive from the Booth Museum. As for your other questions, I believe President Waverly can field those."

"Thank you, Lieutenant," Waverly said, taking the torch. The whole thing was like a commencement ceremony. Sherman just hoped he wouldn't be asked to give a speech. "You're correct, Dr. Hinkley, in recognizing that yesterday, we considered Miss Jacobs, Miss Lapham and Agent Alcott threats to the Agency. For years, they've been trying to hack into our system and sabotage our mainframe. They've never succeeded, however, until yesterday morning. When you inserted Kristen's disc into the computer in your office, the system understood that to mean a woman going by one of the aliases listed in the file was presently in the building. Those names, Sherman, do you remember all the names in that computer file? That file consisted of all the known aliases we've accumulated for Kristen and Miss Jacobs over there. That's why the Jacobs file was incomplete because we knew it was a forgery, and so we severed the transmission. Obviously, we never intended for you to see it. And, yes, that's why when you clicked on Kristen's alias on the computer screen, the alarm went off, and unfortunately we had to contain her."

"But, why did Era give me the file then?" Sherman pleaded.

"Agent Howells was in charge of squelching threats circling through the Public Agent's office. She concluded that Agent Alcott was a conspirator and thus gave you the file as a way of flushing the latest threat out into the open. She knew you would open it in your office once you met Kristen and the problem would be solved."

"But why couldn't she just catch her herself?"

"Because we didn't know what Kristen looked like until yesterday, remember?" Harvey responded.

"And besides, Agent Howells was aware of Agent Alcott's attempts to lure you over to her side and thought that by using you to open the file and by extension, exposing Kristen and Agent Alcott as traitors, you'd be inclined to side with the Agency."

"Side with the Agency?" Sherman repeated. *Side with the Agency?* "All I've ever wanted to *do* is side with the Agency. That's why I work for the fucking Agency! So, let me get this straight. In a nutshell, the teams were Eternity, Kristen, and...*Miss Jacobs*... against Era and the rest of the company? And I was some sorta 'go between' guy that both sides wanted to join them because I would somehow make things better for, um, whichever side I joined? Like, if I joined Eternity and Kristen I could help bring down the company, and if I stayed with the Agency, I could help bring down the threats?"

"In a nutshell, yes," Waverly responded. "It's been a battle that has been going on behind the scenes for years now, Dr. Hinkley."

"Okay, well, there they are!" Sherman conceded, pointing to the three women. "Take 'em in. Book 'em. Do what you gotta do!"

"Sherman, we're not arresting anyone today," Gage declared. "Not when the world is like it is!"

"Why the hell does everyone keep talking about the world!?" Sherman cried. "Would someone please tell me about the fucking world?!?"

"Gladly, Dr. Hinkley, gladly," Waverly replied. "It took some time, but Agents Emerson and Newton here have assisted us greatly in figuring out what precisely went wrong last night and how the world has changed because of the botched TDL code snafu. You may want to sit down, son, this can get complicated."

Sherman sat.

"Basically, here's what happened. The young man you sent back in time yesterday--"

"Will Bau--"

"That's the guy. Please, Dr. Hinkley, do not interrupt. We've discovered that he traveled not to 1822 Germany as he wished, but rather to a small port town in England called Bishopwearmouth. There, he apparently got into some kind of bar fight and ended up killing the brewery's owner: a distinguished, respected man named John Taylor. Mr. Taylor's four year-old son, Tom, was present that evening, and from what Dr. Emerson over there could ascertain, the event scarred little Tom so deeply that he never quite recovered from the trauma of seeing his own father killed before his very eyes. He grew up to be an educated yet tremendously jaded author and playwright, penning several of the more macabre bits of theatrical trash that nineteenth century culture has to offer. The works of Tom Taylor, from what we could tell, had two major impacts on our current society. One, Tom's close friend in adulthood, Mr. Charles Dodgson, was so moved by Taylor's tale of childhood loss that he felt compelled to write perhaps the most disturbing children's story ever written: 'Alice Among the Demons of Hades.' Of course, you recognize the name *Dodgson* as the real name of children's author Lewis Carroll who, prior to the temporal alteration, was most famous for his story 'Alice in Wonderland.' Well, sad to say, that story no longer exists. How Dodgson's new story affected our particular Agency is as such: in 1862, Dodgson told the story to three young sisters one of whom, little Lorina Liddell, happened to be a distant relative of Isabelle Stowe. On the old timeline, Lorina grew up and married William Baillie Skene on February 7th, 1874 and later prospered as the wife to the Treasurer of Christ's Church in England. This Mr. Skene, I gather, is somehow related to the great William the Conqueror, or so says Reverend Newton. The couple begat three children who begat more kids and well along the line until out popped out our dear lost Agent Stowe. Okay? That's the old line. The *new* line, we estimate goes something like this. Dodgson's story traumatized the girls so much that they never left each other's sight. They were terrified of the dark, of losing their father, of their own home. Their state of arrested development caused their parents to refuse to let them socialize, go to school, or even go outside. Lorina's incessant fatigue and close proximity to her youngest sister, Edith, caused them both to come down with measles and die years later, in June of 1876. Lorina never married. Stowe was never born. That's one major difference. The other, I'm pleased to say is much more exciting.

"As you know from your visit to the Booth Museum earlier today, Tom Taylor still wrote 'Our American Cousin,' though the new play is much more dramatic than his original comedy. You know all about how Booth died in the fire and all of that. What you probably didn't learn at the museum is what happened to President Lincoln who clearly was not assassinated on April 14th, 1865. As it turned out, Mr. Lincoln died six months after the performance, on October 21st, 1865 of a rare disease that doctors had never seen before at the time. Today, the disease is known as *multiple endocrine neoplasia type 2B,* or MEN 2B for short. Essentially, the illness is an extremely rare form of hereditary cancer mutations that ultimately results in cancer of the thyroid or adrenal glands. It's very rare indeed. Or, I should say 'was.' Here's where I love history. Because Lincoln was such a prominent international figure, his death elicited the study and research of countless prestigious doctors from all around the world. The autopsies and research and, whatever, Agent Newton explained it to me, but what basically happened was because of Lincoln's death from this rare form of cancer in 1865, it sped up the origins of oncology study and by the year 2034, virtually every form of cancer was eradicated from our planet. We can now cure everything! That's why Era's husband is back. That's why people are smoking more and there are more of our beloved senior citizens. No more cancer, Dr. Hinkley! TADA! Not only that, but pollution is no longer an issue. Evidently, the push for clean air and more efficient forms of fuel came about much earlier than the turn of the millennium because it correlated with other earlier environmental movements which occurred as a result of our planet's new health kick that all emerged after Lincoln's death from this disease. Everything is wonderful! You did it, Sherman! You and Eternity and Kristen and Eliza Jacobs. You saved the world!"

Still Sherman sat still.

He thought.

He let all the news sink in. Booth? Stowe? Era? *Booth?* Era. Stowe. *Booth!* He didn't know what to believe but he knew he couldn't bring himself to vindicate Booth in the name of progress. *Et tu, Boothus!* And Lincoln: Lincoln can't *not* die at Ford's Theater. His death, while tragic, threaded the fabric of the Reconstruction Era and, for better or worse, made America what it became. No, accountability cannot go unclaimed for this. Era, Stowe, *Booth! Okay, so people can now live without worrying about cancer, but what does that say about the bad people who are now alive as well? How many more terrorists are alive today because they didn't die yesterday? What about racial relations at the end of the Civil War? Who's on the penny? What else is better about society? What's worse? Something's gotta be worse. Something's always worse...Who decides what's better and based on what set of criteria and where does the criteria come from and who decides how it's decided and how are those people selected and Era and Stowe and fucking* Booth *and Eliza Jacobs and the lies and why the fuck is Wally on their side and what side is the right side and why aren't they arresting everyone and when can I go home and I have to pee and none of us have eaten in like half a fucking day and why am I still wearing this tie and fuck them and fuck this and fuck* Booth! *and I didn't do anything to be a hero and why am I a hero and when can I not be hero and what is a fucking hero anyway?* After what seemed like days of contemplation, at last the hero spoke.

"That's it? That's everything? I've been pounding my brain for over a fucking day for *that*? I've been through *allllll* this...shot....drugged...beaten...embarrassed...I've sat through lectures, read articles, seen film clips for *this*? I've read the histories of so many useless people and heard enough pretentious remarks and textbook clichés, for *this?* Two hundred years of history and you just sum it up in a couple of poorly worded paragraphs as if you were telling me what you did over the fucking weekend? You're telling me that this is *everything*? Era's shitty life, no big deal? Stowe gone, who gives a fuck? A fucking *John Wilkes Booth* Museum and no one cares because *old people can smoke cigarettes and drive electric cars now*? You're telling me I'm a hero because of *that*? There's gotta be something more."

"Sherman you need to remember that John Wilkes Booth was a national treasure," Waverly explained.

"JOHN WILKES BOOTH WAS A FUCKING MURDERER AND TRAITOR!" Sherman screamed.

"He never killed anybody, Sherman," Lamar said feebly.

"What? That's bullshit, Lamar! You know he killed Linco--"

"President Abraham Lincoln died of a rare disease in October of 1865, Sherman," Gage insisted. "It says so in every history book written in the last two hundred years. It says so on the internet. It must be true. Everybody knows that, Sherman."

"Oh come on! The man was a traitor! He killed--okay, maybe he didn't *kill* Lincoln but we all know he wanted to!"

"We don't know that, Sherm," Wally chimed in.

"What the fuck, Wally!" Sherman yelled in shock.

"Well…we don't…" he answered sheepishly.

"There's no way of knowing what any of us *want* to do in the deepest chambers of our hearts, Sherman. And even if we did, would it matter?" Waverly posited.

"Excuse me?" Sherman mocked.

"Would it matter if he did want to kill Lincoln? Lots of people have animosity, Sherman, but I don't think we can call them murderers if the extension of their anger is simply internalized animosity."

"This is ridiculous! Right now, Era Howells is having some guy cut into her skull and pluck out a piece of machinery that *you put in* so she would only remember a life that now, for the rest of the world, never happened!"

"Sounds to me like she's getting exactly what she needs," Harvey said. "She's with her husband now, right? I'm sure she'll be very happy."

"Fuck you, Harvey! You don't know what she needs. What she *needs* is everything to go back to the way it was! That's what we all need around here!"

"Sherman, can I say something?" Eliza asked sincerely.

"Did you know about this shit? HUH?!" Sherman yelled.

"I did, yes, Sherman, I found out this morning."

"Well, then, what the fu--"

"Please, Sherman," she repeated calmly, "let me say something." Sherman shut his mouth. "It seems to me that you're letting a single, solitary event define who you are. You're letting the Lincoln assassination dictate the path of your entire life, or Charles Dodgson's silly story dictate the course of Stowe's life."

"But his story *did* dictate the course of her life! SHE'S NOT HERE because of that story!"

"You can't do that, Sherman. You can't think like that. You are your own person. You are an agent of your discretion. Don't deny your own ability to influence your own fate! Don't let the present circumstance of the world inform what you wish to become. Don't do it, Sherman. You're better than that."

"What I *wish to become*? But…but," Sherman almost found himself at a loss for words. He frantically scavenged through this lexicon for a sufficient rebuttal. All he found was a rant. "But we let *events* define our lives all the time. Think about it. When I was kid--Wally, when we were kids--all our parents ever talked about when they were with their friends was where they were when 9/11 happened. Remember? They'd go on and on about how we live in a *'Post 9/11 world now'* and shit like that. It wasn't even a day for them anymore. It was a spectacle, a concept, a watershed moment in world history. What blind narcissism. What nihilism. It's a fucking *day*! You talk about *my* agency, what about theirs? They sure as hell let those fuckers in those planes dictate the course of their lives. It was a day that some bad shit happened to a lot of people, but ya know what--the world has it's share of 9/11s all the fucking time, but nooooo, in *our town*, there was only the before and after. We were taught--remember, Wally-- that there was this time--this wonderful, fanciful age a long time ago when three year-olds didn't have to take off their shoes before getting on an airplane and old women could bring water bottles to football games--that all happened before the dreaded 9/11. My parents used to talk about the time 'before 9/11' as if it were a magical land of fairies or lemon rivers and chocolate trees where everyone could afford gas for their cars and not have to worry about *not* wearing an American flag on your swimsuit. They talked about it the same way their parents talked about the Kennedy assassination. As if it literally changed everything! But I never understood that. In fact, until I was ten, I didn't even realize '9/11' was a specific day. We all grew so desensitized to the fact that it referred to an actual day on the calendar and not some government operation or sinister nuclear code, which is what I used to think it was. I mean, hell, *every fucking year* has a September 11th. But something about that day in 2001, yes, *defined* what America was. As opposed to the Fourth of July or, fuck, the day Harper's was founded, our parent's generation defined themselves by some kind of event. Shit, even the Fourth of July is an event, right!? But that's what history is, isn't it: a series of events that defines other events that defines other events? So no offense, *Miss Jacobs*, but while I get that I have agency, I refuse to let this fucking place strip me of it. Something's gotta be done."

"Now hold on there, Dr. Hinkley," Waverly intervened. "You can't just go back and change things on a whim--"

"YOU DO IT ALL THE FUCKING TIME! That's what we do: we change things to fit a certain agenda--"

"NO, GODDAMNIT!" Gage yelled. *Bad, Sherman, bad!* "We change things for the good of the *human race*. When something goes wrong in the past, yes, we change it to make things better for everybody. But damnit, Hinkley, you already did that, ya little shit. You already made things better. Our world is better now than it ever has been."

"How do you know? Huh? I mean, sure *certain* diseases are gone, but shit…I mean…we can't just sit around and do nothing. *Whoever designed Harper's emblem*," Sherman was staring directly at Eliza. He still wasn't sure if the others knew her true identity as ClockWorks's founder, "designed a watch with no hands, right? Whoever made that choice *probably wouldn't want* people to just stand around and stare at the watch without stepping in and doing something when things get all fucked up!"

"But that's what a watchmaker does, Sherman. They sell the watch to the customer who can then do with it as he pleases." Kristen asserted.

"She's right, Sherman," Lamar agreed. *What does Lamar know about watchmakers?*

"Dr. Hinkley, I think we all need some time to adjust to the new world," Waverly announced to the room. "We can't expect our minds to change overnight even though the rest of the world has. These things take time. Dr. Hinkley—Sherman—why don't you take the rest of the afternoon off? You should come back to Harper's with us, get some lunch, and then go home for the rest of the day. I think the time away from work will do you good. You've been through quite the ordeal since you started with the company."

Sherman knew there was no use fighting. He wasn't sure what to think anymore. Eliza Jacobs is E.W. Harper who, for some reason, agrees with the Agency that they shouldn't go back and fix things even though that's what she's supposedly been trying to do for so many years. Now everyone seems to be against Sherman, even Wally and Lamar. *Fucking Wally and Lamar.* Maybe the world really was better. Maybe Sherman was a hero. Maybe he should just go back and get some lunch. He was hungry after all. Yes, that's what he would do: go get some food, then go home and take an afternoon nap. Tomorrow would surely be a better day.

"There's just one thing we have to do before we go back to the Agency, Sherman. We might as well get it done here," Waverly said.

"Oh please, Emmanuelle, do you really need to do it?" Eliza protested. "We don't have to worry about him anymore. Give him some time and he'll be fine."

"I'm sure he will, Miss Jacobs. But it's standard procedure. Agents Newton and Emerson have already gone through the process." Gage attested. Wally and Lamar looked at each other, confused.

"Mr. Douglas," Waverly said, "Please escort Agents Newton and Emerson outside. This should only take a few minutes." Harvey gathered two ACHEs by his side and ushered

Lamar and Wally out into the hallway, slamming the door behind them.

"What's going on now?" Sherman pleaded. "I thought we were going to go back to ClockWorks."

"We are, Hinkley, but we need to do one thing first," Gage explained.

"You don't have to do this to him," Eternity pleaded.

"I'm afraid you and Miss Lapham are next," Waverly said.

"Oh please, not them. They have nothing to do with this!" Eliza cried.

"Agent Alcott certainly does," Gage replied. "She won't be permitted back into ClockWorks without a successful procedure. Since we now know what Miss Lapham looks like, I guess we won't need to take care of her, but if Eternity wishes to keep her job, she'll need to comply with the policy."

"Okay, seriously, what the hell is going on?" Sherman begged.

"They're right, Sherman," Eternity conceded. "They need to perform a requisite memory alteration swipe on us."

"Close, Agent Alcott," Waverly said. "All we need to do is swipe your memory for any recollection of Mr. Will Bauer. We don't need to perform a full scan: just enough so you won't remember anything about Will Bauer, his trip, or his role in our new world, and thus could never be tempted to go back and change the new path forged by his journey."

"That isn't so bad then, Sherman," Eternity said, relieved.

"So what, you're going to make it so we don't know how our world got this way? So we can't change it even if we wanted to?" Sherman tried to clarify.

"That's right, Hinkley," Gage responded. "It's a painless scan. Standard operational protocol in times when a travel package resulted in making the world a better place."

"What do you mean *standard?* You mean this has happened before?" Sherman asked.

"Certainly, Dr. Hinkley!" Waverly exclaimed. "You don't think this is the first time someone's actions back in time caused the world to change for the better, do you?"

"Actually, yeah!" Sherman confessed. "That's exactly what I thought."

"I'm afraid you were mistaken then, son. No, there have been several like you. I can name six or seven right now. Let's just say that World War II: yeah, should've been worse. It *was*, in fact, until some junior high kid accidentally fixed it. We just let that one slide. And World War III, well, should've happened. But again, a family vacation back in time to Ancient China squelched that sucker before it was a twinkle in the night sky. But trust me, after every positive temporal alteration, we've made sure that those directly invested in the project be stripped of any memory that would connect them to the catalyst of the event. It's really no big deal, Sherman. The technology's advanced so much over the years that now the whole swipe only takes a few seconds."

"Okay. And what if I don't want to do it?" Sherman wondered.

"I don't understand. You don't *want* to have the procedure here? Well I suppose we could do it back at ClockWorks, but we all thought it would be easier to perform here."

"No, like, what if I don't want it done at all…"

No one said a word. The prospect of refusing to comply with crystal clear corporate policies had never occurred to Waverly or Gage. *Everyone* went through the procedure. It's just what you did.

"Well, Dr. Hinkley," Waverly explained. "If you refuse the procedure then you will be in violation of the ClockWorks contract. You'll be in breach. And we'll be left with no choice but to terminate your employment."

"You'd fire me because I wanted to keep my memories? That's a little ironic, don't you think? What, with my hippo-*whatever* implant and all."

"Split hairs all you want, ya little shit. You'll no longer work for this company. You'll be fired. You'll never be allowed to work in time travel again or step foot on ClockWorks property. You'll be finished."

"Choose wisely, Dr. Hinkley," Waverly advised. "This could end very badly for you. Or, it could amount to nothing more than an occupational obligation: conceptually no different than a pesky weekend conference or a random drug test. It's your choice."

"Why are Lamar and Wally gone?" Sherman asked.

"Because we can't be discussing Will Bauer around them anymore, Sherman. It would confuse them. They'd have no idea who we were talking about. The mere mentioning of Will Bauer's name this soon after the procedure might jeopardize the temporal plane and permanently risk reversing the procedure's effects." Eternity said.

Still Sherman sat still, still.

He thought.

He let all the news sink in. He considered all his years of study, all his months of training, all his days of celebration, and all his hours of happy memories with his dream company. It all now hung in the balance. Would he stay or would he go? *Should* he stay or *could* he bring himself to go? Lester began to assemble the brain scanner behind Harvey. After the device was prepared and fully charged, Eternity walked over to Lester who proceeded to scan her entire head with a contraption that resembled the price checkers formerly found in supermarket check-out lines. After about five seconds, the device beeped and Eternity walked back over to reclaim her spot next to Sherman.

"See, Sherman, it doesn't hurt at all," she said sweetly.

"Agent Alcott," Waverly asked, "who were your clients yesterday?"

"I had two, sir: the Chestnut family and Leslie Rowlandson."

"Those were your only two PCs? You're positive?"

"Yes, sir. It was a slow day."

"Eternity, what about Will--" Sherman began.

"Damnit, Hinkley, can't you see the procedure worked?!" Gage screamed. Indeed, it appeared to Sherman that Eternity had no memories of Will Bauer or the subsequent ordeal with his file and TDL Codes. The procedure was successful. Another victory for science.

"Now, Dr. Hinkley, if you would step up here, please, we can finish up here," Waverly declared, growing visibly agitated at Sherman's delays.

"A-a-actually, sirs. Everybody. I think it's, um, time I move on from ClockWorks."

"Don't be a fool, son," Waverly cautioned. "This is it, you understand. You quit us, you quit your future. You'll be throwing away everything you've worked for. Are you sure want to do that?"

"No. I'm not sure of anything really. But I know that…I know that people should be able to learn from their mistakes instead of having them wiped from their memories."

"Sherman, I'm going to give you one last chance to reconsider. You only get one more chance. And keep in mind this offer is a gift. It's not a hand--"

"Thanks for the bullet, Harvey. I quit." Sherman got up from the couch and walked out of the apartment, removing his tie in the process.

So there he was: out a new job, out his new friends, out a paycheck and a career and a future. He was outside wondering where he was or how to get back home. He was running out of hope. And yet, for the first time in nearly half a century, Sherman Hinkley had finally broken out of his shell.

Twenty One
Sherman's Chapter 31

"In the beginning of a change, the patriot is a scarce man, and brave, and hated and scorned. When his cause succeeds, the timid join him, for then it costs nothing to be a patriot."

-Mark Twain

"I never liked when books would seem to climax with, like, a lot of pages left. I mean, seriously, either wait till the end to get to the climax or have a lot of climaxes. Also, novels with epigraphs always seemed pretentious. Like *Moby Dick*. That book had epigraphs and, yes, I found some parts of it pretentious."

-Jeff Spanke, *Second Hand Out*

The sun rose the next day as well. And the next. And even the day after that. It had been six days since Sherman created the world as the world now knew it to be created. In the wake of the "Great Change"--as Harper's management began to call it--Eternity and Eliza had confessed their full involvement in several past attempts to dismantle ClockWorks's infrastructure. The attempts ranged from physically tampering with the wires in the IDM Room to falsifying PC's applications, (as they had, of course, done with the Jacobs and Lapham files) to letting rats loose in the cafeteria. In the case of William Bauer, their intentions were simple: send him back to the wrong time period and keep him there for a few days so that when he returns, he'll be so furious with the Agency's incompetence that he starts a chain of rumors and publicity scandals that would eventually lead to the company's downfall. They never dreamed Sherman would actually give the guy Zemeckalian Clearance and the world would flip on its head as a result. Nor did they ever intend on him getting killed. Good thing they no longer had to live with that on their collective conscience. Ignorance is bliss, but total unawareness is heaven.

Fresh off their memory swipes, Lamar and Wally returned to work immediately following Sherman's departure. Their week had been spent mostly alone in their hotel room/office trying to coordinate field trips for the upcoming school year and locate the occasional lost child running around the building. They normally arrived to work about an hour late and worked until lunch, at which point they'd each take a much deserved two hour break before finishing up for the day around three or four in the afternoon. At night, they'd usually get together at a bar downtown to raise a toast to their two fallen comrades: Stowe to the paradoxes of time and Sherman to his own intransigence. The Agency had informed all employees that any future contact with Dr. Sherman Hinkley would be punishable by immediate dismissal from the company, as well as potential criminal charges. As far as ClockWorks was concerned, he was strictly off limits: unarmed, but cognitively dangerous.

Ironically, while Harper's threatened to occupationally castrate anyone who came in contact with Sherman, publicly, the Agency forged him into an instant celebrity. Because no one without a hippocampus implant would ever be able to recognize the shifting in the temporal plane, it was easy for Harper's to paint Sherman as the poster boy for a clean and better America. Who's to argue otherwise? If Harper's says so, it must be true. Time *was* in their hands. The Agency manufactured Sherman into a larger than life cultural icon, a genuine valorized hero: a fable. Sans, of course, any shred of actual heroism. But why bother? In the era of the instant celebrity, society's perception of heroism took precedence over actual heroism. Importance derived from exposure: an exposure that served virtually no other purpose than as a means for its own narcissistic consumption. Still, logically, ClockWorks didn't dare publish pictures of the middle-aged Titan of time travel. Sherman was, after all, still living in Indianapolis. And besides, in the darkest closets of peoples' souls, no one wants their heroes to be real people. *Real* people. Ministers get divorced, policeman speed, doctors smoke, psychologists commit suicide, and teachers beat their children. As cultural puppet-masters, Waverly and Gage capitalized on the emotional fragility of a society that could never accept *real* realism, despite its most earnest cravings for it in movies or on TV. Something always needs to be left out of the picture. In carving the Herculean Hinkley into a real-life Barthesian myth, ClockWorks executives had to first strip him of any ties with humanity in order to effectively deify his fabricated image. After all, Gods must have transcendence from the confines of mortality, and despite Sherman's feeble attempts at scholarship (and his impeccable fashion sense), he was anything but transcendental…and most certainly mortal. Something about the whole situation never sat well with Lamar, however, and from time to time, when he and Wally were left to their own devices, he would bring up their old friend whom he would then use as a microcosm from which he would relay his own personal anxieties.

"Did I ever tell you about my little girl, Wally? She reminds me a lot of Sherman."

"The one that got lost in Greece? Yeah, ya told me a few times."

"Sorry. I just can't help think that beneath Sherman's stubbornness there's a scared little boy that's just so used to having every one of his actions dictated for him by society or by his family or by this company--"

"Or by his own choices, Lamar! You gotta remember that it was *Sherman* who decided to quit. No one threw him out of here. He walked away on his own terms. This is the only place that ever gave him any kind of security, after all. So it seems to me that if he really were some scared little boy, it would have been better for him to stay with the one thing that at least he knew could keep him safe."

"True, Wally, true. But then what does that say about us? Do you ever wonder if Sherman saw something in this whole place that neither one of us has seen? Maybe what we consider his stupidity was really an act of pure rejection of stupidity. Maybe we're the morons who can't leave our cage. Maybe *we're* the slaves."

"Whatever, Lamar. We make good money. We live in a damn good world. We once worked with a guy named Sherman who maybe was a friend, but he threw everything away; so now we either move on or move out."

"That's it?"

"Yeah, Lamar, that's it. And let me ask you something about that trip to Greece."

"'She was the only one of us who actually did any work.' She was mean and cruel but she *did her job.* Sherman said that once."

"What? *Stowe?!* Yeah, she worked alright! Worked herself into a fuckin' size twenty. Who gives a shit about Stowe? She's gone, and the world's a better place for it."

"Maybe."

"Damn right it is. Anyway, seriously though, that trip to Greece…"

"Yeah, what about it?"

"You actually *went* to Greece, right? Like, cruise ship and everything?"

"Yeah. It was beautiful. We had a great time."

"Fascinating, I'm sure. But, like, the main reason you wanted to go was to study history, right? To see all the monuments and temples and shit?"

"Yeah. That's usually why we went on those vacations. My wife and I always wanted to try to make them as educational as possible. Of course, there was this one time when--"

"No, sounds great, really it does. But I guess my question is if what you wanted to study was history, why not take a trip to Harper's from wherever you're from and go back in time and actually *see* the temples in their glory days or, ya know, see--didn't you see St. Augusta write the Bible?--you could've seen that in person!"

"I know that."

"Well then why didn't you? What better way to study history than by seeing it face-to-face? That's why this whole place was built, and that's why I, for one, still work here!"

"We all don't speak Greek."

"You could've learned Greek."

"We all don't speak *Ancient* Greek."

"You could have learned that too."

"Maybe we didn't want to."

"Again, why not?"

"Because we're not Greek."

"*You're not Gre*--Listen to you, Lamar! Listen to what you're saying! We're talking about mind expansion here, man! Just because you're not something doesn't mean you can't learn to be that something, right? You learn Greek so you can understand the Greeks *while in Greece!* That's why you learn things: so you can study people different than you. I can't believe this shit. And from *you* of all people, Lamar."

"But we still learned about Ancient Greece even though we didn't go to Ancient Greece."

"But you didn't learn everything you could have!"

"Maybe we learned everything we wanted to learn. Maybe we learned all we needed to learn. It's not all about Greece. I learned about a lot more than *Greece* during that trip, Wally, trust me."

"What you *needed to learn*? What are you talking about? Seriously, Lamar, why the fuck do you work here in the first place? Everything you ever say seems to be against the reason this whole place exists."

"Sometimes it's better to keep the curtain closed, Wally."

"What the fuck does that mean?"

"Sometimes all you need is a silhouette to understand all you need to know about someone or something. Any more than that can ruin the whole experience or leave you blind. Why didn't we go back to see St. *John* write *Revelation?* I don't know. Maybe it's because I'd rather love the story than settle for the reality. Sometimes the story is all we need."

"Or sometimes the story keeps you in the darkness!"

"Explain."

"You remember that book about Tom Sawyer?"

"You mean, *The Adventures of Tom Sawyer?"*

"Yeah, but I don't remember a 'The' in the title."

"It's there. Trust me."

"Okay, well whatever," Wally reluctantly conceded. "You remember when the author first introduces the slave Jim? Our first sighting of Jim is when he's standing on the front porch and the light from the kitchen is silhouetting him to anyone outside. Tom just sees a black man, but the irony is *anybody* would appear black if they're being silhouetted. Tom's not seeing

Jim for what he *really* is. He's only seeing what he *wants* to see based on the image right in front of him."

"True. But I think that's from *Huck Finn* and not--"

"Whatever!"

"Sorry. What's your point, though?"

"My point is, if you rely only on silhouettes, you may never see the real character of something."

"*My* point is, sometimes the real character is something you may never want to see."

"Whatever! I still say Stowe's a worthless cow and you should've gone back to see Zeus!"

"Fair enough."

Era Howells hadn't slept since her operation in New York ten days ago. Well, aside from a fatigue-induced nap here and there, she hadn't slept. She certainly hadn't made it through one single night's sleep without dreaming of Sherman and Eternity and her grandmother and Kristen. Were those even dreams? They seemed so real. So true. Dr. Ajay Nagheenanajar had proven himself quite competent during their initial consultation and was positive he knew not only what Era's problem was before even examining her, but also how to remedy her condition. Her particular case, however, ended up being something the neurologist had never seen before.

With Casey in the waiting room and Era on the operating table, Dr. Ajay Nagheenanajar opened her skull where he expected to find an officially licensed Harper's hippocampus implant. The specific type of amnesia Casey described via their correspondence suggested that Era was simply the next in a long line of tragic Harper's victims of a temporal alteration who couldn't reconcile her "old" memories from the former timeline with her new life with her husband. He'd seen it a thousand times. All he would have to do was go in, take the contraption out, and presto chango, she'd be good as new! She'd still have her old memories, of course. Dr. Ajay Nagheenanajar couldn't *recreate* four years worth of lost memories. But at least she'd no longer be immune to any other temporal alterations that those cretins over at ClockWorks would allow to occur. Casey and Era would think she merely had a rare form of amnesia and with the operation, she'd be cured. She'd be scarred, but not broken and could continue to live a fruitful life. When he cracked open her skull, however, to fish out the wicked shard of mechanized sorcery, much to his chagrin, the piece was nowhere to be found. Short of removing her entire brain, he looked everywhere and couldn't recover the hippocampus implant for the life of him. After minutes of splashing cerebral fluid all over the table, he deduced the cause of the little devil's absence: the change in the temporal path--whatever it was--must have influenced her original decision to get the implant from the beginning. Something must have happened to affect her life in such a way that she was never compelled to work at Harper's, and thus was never equipped with the demonic brain toy. Indeed, he had never seen anything like this before.

So there Era was: sitting upright in bed once again in the middle of the night, sweat dripping down her naked chest. So many thoughts stampeding through her weary head: conflicting thoughts. Thoughts of a life without Casey, thoughts of a life with Casey. Had she ever worked at Harper's? His death was what prompted her to apply for a position with the Agency, but he never died. Right? So it all must be a dream. But she *saw* Sherman before they left Indy. And knew who he was! She was a Harper's employee. She was. She thought she was.

The operation was a success. Era and Casey were together again. Chalk up one more victory for science.

Few moments in American literature capture the essence of realism more effectively than in chapter 31 of Mark Twain's *Adventures of Huckleberry Finn*. Sherman remembered reading the controversial novel in his college elective on American Realism at Cross University--*stupid Cross*--and decided that since he no longer had a career to pursue at Harper's--*stupid Harper's*--he could afford to take some time and read some classic American books. He put forth a valiant effort to finish the first chapter of Henry David Thoreau's manifesto about the pond he built, but didn't quite understand what any of that had to do with the economy. He read a good five sentences (or thirteen pages) of William Faulkner's *Absalom! Absalom!* before wanting to shoot himself in the foot. He actually really enjoyed reading

The Death of Ivan Illych, but had to stop out of principle when he realized Tolstoy wasn't an American. After a week of combing his way through various paragraphs of various canonical texts, he reached Twain. His first impression of the novel was one of shock; he could've sworn the title had the world "The" at the front of it. He remembered it being *The Adventures of Huck Finn*: not *Adventures of Huckleberry Finn*, but alas, his memory must have been wrong. At least he still had it, he kept telling himself: flawed though it may be, his memory was still his own to screw up.

Sherman's reading of the book was retarded by his incessant anxiety about the Agency and the sequence of events leading to his departure/dismissal/running away scared. He wondered how his friends were doing and what they were doing and what they were wearing and why they haven't called and why he hadn't called them and when he was going to get a job and where and why he'd left in the first place and an army's laundry list of other concerns. And so, when he made his way to chapter 31 of Huck's journey, he found himself tragically empathizing with the juvenile protagonist. Huck, after traveling with the slave Jim down the Mississippi River, decides he best write a letter to Jim's owner, Miss Watson, to inform her of their whereabouts. After all, aiding a runaway slave was a deplorable crime in the antebellum south, and Huck knew full well that breaking the law was punishable firstly by the hand of man but ultimately by the hand of God. Eternal damnation awaited those who violated Christian doctrine, and in Huck Finn's perception of the antebellum south, slavery was as Christian as forbidden-fruit-pie. So Huck writes the letter. But then, for some reason, he plum rips it up! He spits in the face of everything he's ever been taught was right and good and moral and decent and damn near condemns himself to an afterlife in Hell for his wickedness. While Sherman vaguely remembered his Cross professors saying something along the lines of how Huck's restraint and deliberation before ripping up the letter signified something about "the ideal realist moment," Sherman actually began to feel sorry for Huck. Sherman knew what it felt like to have all the forces of the universe converging on a single, solitary point of your soul at a single, solitary point in time and urging you to subscribe to their hegemonic demands or risk permanent damnation. He found himself screaming at Huck, "No! Don't rip it up! Stick to the plan! This will end up bad for you! It's wrong! Take the easy way out!" He couldn't bring himself to read past that point in the novel. He never made it past chapter 31. Shame too, because it probably was something pretty damn good.

All in all, his two week literary survey consisted of skimming a little over four hundred pages spread out over seven novels. First a psychologist, now a literature scholar. But still unemployed. Sherman thought about Era from time to time. He wondered if the operation in New York was a success and how she was adjusting to her new life with her old husband: a life that wouldn't be possible if it weren't for Dr. Sherman Hinkley. He thought about Isabelle Stowe: poor, wretched Isabelle. He wondered if anyone missed her. Anyone who *could* miss her, that is. He hoped Harper's hadn't already hired a new CHIMP but figured that someone with his qualifications would take at least *three* weeks to replace. Right? After all, it takes time to put an ad out and field all the applicants and conduct the interviews and make the offers and wait for the acceptance and do the whole orientation thing and order the uniforms and wait for them to arrive. At least it would take two weeks.

Finally he thought about Booth. *Fucking Booth.* If there was one thing for which Sherman could neither ever forgive himself nor dismiss about his new world, it was the cultural deification of John Wilkes Booth. If only he could somehow sneak into ClockWorks, he'd go back and somehow repair the holes in the temporal dam. Somehow make things right. Somehow. *But wouldn't that be wrong too? Why is going back to fix things any more morally justifiable that refusing to go back in the name of the greater good? Why is my judgment any more valid than anyone else's? Where do we draw the line? Do two wrongs make a right? Can they ever, or is what is right and two wrongs mutually exclusive? What does that even mean? Is that even grammatically correct?* Sherman might've finally abandoned his shell, but the frosty kiss of the world's chilling air left him blushing: longing for yet another refuge to replace the solace of ignorance. Somewhere, Plato was rolling in his grave.

One afternoon, when Sherman was walking around downtown Indianapolis, he ran into a familiar face at the farmer's market. "Hi Kristen," Sherman greeted the Chicago hottie.

"Hey, Sherman. How've you been?"

"Oh fine, I guess. Little bored, but doin' okay. Not much to do, but I'm doin' fine. Wish I still was workin' for Harper's, but I'll live. Kinda gettin' antsy at home, but it's nice to be out. Missin' my friends, but I'll survive. Feelin' kinda constipated though lately, but I'll--"

"That's great, Sherman. That's all great. Really. Eternity misses you, she says. She thinks they were wrong to make you get the procedure done if you didn't want to. My grandma tried to tell them they didn't need to worry about you anymore, but I guess they just thought they'd stick with the rule book."

"I know. I was there. I heard everything, remember."

"I know. Sorry."

"So are you and Eternity and your grandma, like, doing alright? Like, are you still trying to destroy the Agency?"

"No, not any more. You really are a hero, Sherman. Grandma couldn't be prouder of you. She spent her whole life trying to find a way to make the world a better place with her invention and when people started using it for their own personal gains, that's when she decided to destroy it. But then you come along and wind up making the world a better place anyway. So, no, she's got no beef anymore, and the Agency has finally stopped trying to find us. And they even let Eternity come back to her old job as head PA."

"That's great, Kristen. Great for Eternity."

"I know, right? And ya wanna hear something really cool? They hired me to replace Era Howells!"

"Your cousin Era? You're going to take her job, huh?"

"Yeah, well, I mean with her in New York with Casey, there's really no point for her to come back, now is there? And they needed to have her position filled. School will be starting soon, after all. Everything's gonna get real busy with field trips and stuff like that. They needed to hire someone soon. I start next Monday."

"Wow. That's…that's just great, Kristen. Has anyone been hired to replace me?"

"Oh yeah, they got someone from Bloomington. A real tool. Doesn't know anything about TDL Codes or types of clearance or anything about ClockWorks's history at all. He thinks he's some kind of genius or something cuz he went to some bullshit college down there, but all he really does is sit around all day and dick around in his office. I don't think he's seriously evaluated an application yet. He takes, like, three hour lunch breaks and can barely stay awake in meetings. Harvey and Lester are his interns and they're, like, obsessed with him, but Lamar thinks he's useless and Wally can't stand him. He's no Sherman Hinkley, that's for sure."

"Yeah, sounds like an asshole."

"He is. Gage likes him though."

"Well, there ya go."

"Yup."

"Yup."

"Uhuh."

"Haha."

"Well."

"I know."

"Hey, ya wanna go for a walk for a bit, Sherman? I mean, if you're not too busy?"

"Sure, I'd like that."

And so they went for a walk. It was a gorgeous July afternoon in Indiana, and the two made the absolute most of it by strolling along the canal, walking around the Circle, and doing some window shopping around Circle Centre Mall before making their way back to the market. Sherman still had plenty of coupons for pizza delivery back at his apartment so he wasn't particularly in the market for fresh fruits and vegetables. Kristen bought seven apples and some fresh ears of Indiana corn.

"Want an apple, Sherman?" she asked.

"Sure, thanks." She reached into her bag and pulled out a delicious looking ruby red apple which Sherman graciously accepted: a tasty afternoon delight. As he took the first bite, something reminded him of what Lamar had said that morning back in Archer E. Room: the morning when the world changed.

He remembered it was dark, save for the flicker of the emergency lights blinking throughout the Agency. Lamar and Wally and he had been sequestered to the room to await further instructions. He remembered how Wally and Lamar were engaged in a heated debate about something to do with the human *condition? Capacity*? What was that picture Lamar was looking at on the wall? Sherman never went to examine it once the lights came back on. When power was restored to the building—from that moment forward—everything was in hyper-drive. There was no time to think, to stand still, to wonder what the hell was going on. Yet something about those early morning hours in that damn Archer E. Room now resonated with Sherman as he continued to devour his apple. What did Lamar see? What did he mumble to himself? Think. *Comeyethereforeletusgodownandthereconfoundtheirtonguethatth eymaynotunderstandoneanothersspeech.* He could hear the phrase falling from Lamar's lips. He could hear the sounds Lamar made as the air was pressed by his tongue through his teeth. But now, weeks later, confounded by the decay of certitude, all Sherman could recall was sounds. He couldn't break down the assorted syllables and phonemes into distinct words. He couldn't then and he couldn't now. What was that picture? Why did it seem so important to Lamar?

"You okay, Sherman? The apple alright?"

Then it struck him. The apple! Gregor Samsa and his apple…the apple…As if 1.21 gigawatts of flux-capacitated electricity surged through Kristen's words, Sherman could see Lamar's mutterings shatter into separate clusters and fall, in perfect order, upon the lexiconal plane deep within Sherman's mind. "Come ye, therefore, let us go down, and there confound their tongue, that they may not understand one another's speech." He knew what Lamar was looking at. He'd seen the picture before: not in the ClockWorks frame at the far end of the Archer E. Room, but during Father Daniel Norris's Sunday school class he when was a kid. More than likely an alternate rendition but he knew what it depicted! He understood what Lamar meant by human capacity. He could see Pilate washing his hands in front of the angry crowd. Pilate. The angry crowd. *Bring us Barabbas!* His hands. The family waving their hands in front of Jesus on the

Cross. *Cross University.* Eternity. *Booth.* Lamar was right. It all made sense. The clock with no hands. The watch. The handless watch. The watchmaker. *It's just what you do. It's what watchmakers do.* Doctor Sherman Hinkley, CHIMP. Abraham the chimpanzee. Jacobs. Harper. Chapter Thirty-One. E.W. Harper's world famous ClockWorks TTA. Yes, Sherman knew it all now. He knew we had to do. Shit just got real.

Sherman spit out the apple.

"Gross! Did it taste bad or something?" Kristen asked, disgusted.

"Kristen, um, can I borrow your cell-phone? I need to make a call," Sherman asked.

"Um, yeah sure, Sherman. Let me get my phone, it's in my purse." *It has to be in there*. She's got to still have it with her. Surely she does. *Why would she not*? Then he saw it.

"There ya go, Sherman—HEY!" Sherman snatched Kristen's purse right out of her hands. "What are you doing?"

"So how does this thing work again, Kristen?"

"What? Um, sorry, I thought you were, like, stealing from me or something. Um, yeah, you just select whether you're doing time travel or teleportation and type in your destination. That's it."

"Uhuh. And what's the deal with the thumb pad? Why is that important again?"

"Oh, um, every trip needs to be authorized to a specific person. Grandma designed it that way. It keeps people from stealing it and using it for their own private time parties or whatever."

"Cool, cool. Yeah, so, like, how do I program myself into it."

Pause.

"Sherman, listen I'm gonna need that back."

"What? Why? I'm just lookin' at it!"

"I know, it's just…look, I really need to go."

"I'm not done with this yet. How do I program myself into it?"

"Sherman, you're kinda scaring me a little bit. Here, just give it back and I'll see you later."

"No. Um, yeah, I'm gonna need to take this for a while."

"Sherman, you can't--"

"I know, but there's just something I really gotta go do!"

"But Sherman, I'll have to report you! My grandma will know wherever you went the second you're gone. There's a trace in there. She'll report you to the ACHEs, Sherman. You know she will. They'll find you and if they don't kill you, they'll bring you back and you'll go to jail!"

Sherman tucked the remote control in his pocket, shrugged his shoulders and smiled at Kristen. "Alright then, I'll go to jail!" And he tore up the sidewalk and lit out for the territory. Huck would've been proud.

PART THREE

Mr. Hinkley's Wild Ride

Twenty Two
Sherman's Birthday

"Let us learn our lessons. ... Never believe any war will be smooth and easy or that anyone who embarks on that strange voyage can measure the tides and hurricanes he will encounter. The statesman who yields to war fever must realize that once the signal is given, he is no longer the master of policy but the slave of unforeseeable and uncontrollable events... incompetent or arrogant commanders, untrustworthy allies, hostile neutrals, malignant fortune, ugly surprise, awful miscalculations."

-Winston Churchill

"When we know our own strength, we shall the better know what to undertake with hopes of success; and when we have well surveyed the powers of our own minds, and made some estimate what we may expect from them, we shall not be inclined either to sit still, and not set our thoughts on work at all, in despair of knowing anything; nor on the other side, question everything, and declaim all knowledge, because some things are not to be understood."

-John Locke

"I'm surprised you actually decided to show."

"We're friends. I couldn't just let you hang out to dry like that. We all miss you. Everyone. The new guy's a real jerk. Doesn't do anything. Just sits around and flirts with the PAs."

"Yeah, so I hear. How's Wally?"

"He's doing okay. I know he misses you too. He's just nervous about letting everyone know that he's still your friend, that's all. He wanted to be here. Really."

"Uhuh. Do you think you were followed?"

"No, I think I'm alright. Our containment starts tomorrow morning. They gave everyone one more night out before the official search begins. It's going to be big. The biggest ever, I'm told. You better be careful."

"I'll be careful. So what do you know? Anything? What have they done so far?"

"They've done a lot. Put caps on a lot of TDL Codes. Traces on every application going in and out. They've even sent ACHEs back to some town in England for some reason: permanently, as guards in case you or anyone else tries to go back and stop something from happening. But I don't know what."

"Yeah, that makes sense. You wouldn't know, would you…What about the remote?"

"Yeah, it still has a trace. Eliza and Kristen have been swarming the Agency, swapping information with Waverly and Gage. Everyone knows everything now."

"Why haven't they found me then?"

"Because, from what I gather, the trace only works if you use the remote to either go back in time or teleport. Until it's activated, they can't find you."

"That's what I figured. So I still have some time then. I'm gonna need just a little more to make sure everything's going to work."

"What are you going to do? Do you have a plan yet? Do you need my help?"

"I wish I could tell you. I'm only gonna get one shot at this and I don't want you to get hurt if things go bad. Thanks though. All I need is what I asked for earlier. Did you bring it?"

"Yeah, I checked it out this afternoon before I left work. They didn't seem to think it was too big of a deal. No one hassled me or anything. Truthfully, I'm a little surprised they still have the library open to employees."

"What do you mean?"

"Well, ya know. Usually in times like this, the more they can control the information flow, the better. Wouldn't want anybody actually thinkin', now would we?"

"Guess not. Listen, I'm not going to be able to give this back for a while. That gonna be a problem?"

"I don't think so. The way I see it, if you succeed, they won't care if it's gone and if you fail, they'll get it back anyway."

"Thanks for the confidence."

"Think of it as perspective."

"Well, thanks all the same. What about that other thing I asked for?"

"Oh yeah, almost forgot, I have that too. Wally gave me a hard time about it but I printed it off anyway. He thought this was his job, not mine. Why do you care about this stuff anyway?"

"It's important."

"Yeah, but did you really need the past fifty year's worth? I mean, I don't see how that's going to help you with whatever it is you're planning on doing. There's a lot of trips in here."

"I know there is. But I gotta cover my ass, that's all. Like I said, I'm only gonna get one shot with this one, and whatever I do, I gotta be quick. They're gonna be right behind me."

"That's true. I know Kristen's just itching to have you activate that thing."

"How much time do you think I have once I do?"

"I don't know, probably ten minutes or so. Depends on how fast you can run."

"Shit. Well, I knew this wasn't going to be easy. Whatever. Okay, thanks for coming. I got some more research to do."

"When do you think you're going?"

"If my memory serves me correctly, I only have a little less than two weeks. Just gotta be patient. Wish me luck!"

"Good luck. If you need anything else--"

"Thanks, I know."

"He still hasn't used it, Grandma. I wonder what he's waiting for," Kristen sighed. It'd been fourteen days since Sherman stole her remote control and so far, despite the most sophisticated manhunt in ClockWorks history, there'd been no sign of the fugitive. The unprecedented clandestinity with which Sherman concealed his whereabouts eroded away at the patience of the ClockWorks trustees who demanded Gage's ACHEs either find the hoodlum before he cause any real damage or face their wrath. No one expected Sherman to maintain such secluded composure while the rest of the world was hunting him down like Robert Redford in *Three Days of the Condor*. Lamar feared it would only be a matter of time before he cracked and revealed his location. But alas, no such cracking had yet occurred.

Waverly personally quarantined Wally, Lamar, and Eternity to Harper's headquarters so that they could spend every waking hour tracking their former friend, plotting his potential moves, searching archives and databases for any clue as to where the criminal may be hiding. Lamar and Wally were ordered to sleep in their office which the Agency converted into a fully functional control center/sleeping chamber. The renovation didn't prove too cumbersome considering their office already came equipped with central air, a deluxe bathroom, and two beds. During the day, Harper's ran like clockwork; customers would arrive, they would depart, and they would return from their trips, all the while paying handsomely to do all three. No one ever guessed the building was under siege by its own paid constituency.

In the after hours, Waverly and Gage would spend the nights trying to put themselves in Sherman's shoes. What would his next move be? Where would he go? Who'd be the first to take the little shit down? They implemented a number of contingency plans for extra security including sending decoy TDL Codes under the name "Will Bauer" to the IDM Room. Anyone hacking into the system to use these codes would be transported to a cellar in the middle of a Kansas farmhouse and immediately shot by armed ACHEs ready to kill. They garrisoned ClockWorks and converted it into a castle: a fortified citadel guarded primarily by the iron fist of a tyrannical idealist and the fascist inklings of an antiquated old doughboy. Instead of Harper's technology fostering social growth and unifying diverse groups of people, the ClockWorks lockdown effectively pushed more and more people away into little isolated crevices wherein Waverly and Gage could monitor their every move. Within the building itself, the resulting sense of parochialism created a marginalized village of hermits reminiscent of the small mountain town in Washington Irving's *Legend of Sleepy Hollow.* No longer were the employees connected to the external world, but rather lived a contained yet artificial life behind the closed, glass doors sealing in the beginning of forever. The paranoia sifting throughout the employees was so pervasive that most people expected the Cavalier Hinkley to come barging in through the front door and proceed to hurl flaming pumpkins at innocent bystanders: vengeance for a life the Agency stole. And yet, Hinkley never rode through the front or any other door of ClockWorks. No one ever saw him. He had a coveted remote control and he never used it. Since he stole it from Kristen, he had simply vanished from everyone's radar. He became a ghost. At least for fourteen days.

Aside from time travel and his brief tryst with crossbow hunting, Sherman's greatest love when he was younger was sewing, specifically fashion design. Of course, he never told any of his friends about his passion out of fear that they would steal his patterns and become famous designers themselves--that actually was his biggest fear--but whenever local community theaters needed costumes and couldn't afford to rent them from professional theater companies, "Sherman's mom" would usually volunteer to be the head seamstress. Mrs. Hinkley was always gracious enough to protect her son's anonymity, and Sherman never seemed to mind that she received all the praise for his consistently breathtaking costumes and flawless sense of aesthetical appeal. For him, it was never about the fame. It was about the art. It was about the fashion. And besides, in his mind, all that praise belonged to him anyway. Sherman could spin a compelling fashion narrative with two yards of beige viscose and three yards of silver rayon like nobody's business. Add some accessories, the right pair of heels and proper make-up and girlfriend, you got yourself a fierce looking A-line chemise with matching earrings and removable back drape! It's chic, it's relevant, it's functional: it's an original S. Hinkley! (Sherman's mom's name was Shelly, so he thought it would be alright if he sewed his name into all of his costumes as a way to personalize his garments.)

Topping Sherman's curriculum vitae of fantastic fashion feats were Belle's gown from *Beauty and the Beast,* Medda's dress from *Newsies,* and the entire cast's costumes for *12 Naked Men* for which Sherman made the hats and socks. Yet despite Sherman's brief run as the son of the premiere seamstress of B-grade community theater, the only costumes he ever kept for himself were the brothers' outfits from *Seven Brides for Seven Brothers.* He never could explain why, really. For some reason, he just loved his work for that show. The stitching, the seams, the plaid, the cowboy boots: it was Sherman's dramatic homage to the nostalgia of the golden age of American Theater. And to America itself. After all, nothing says America like a bunch of idiot cowboys in sequence singing and dancing in the middle of their log cabin. The performance enjoyed a brief run on the local stage before one of the brothers got sick and one of the brides actually got married and moved to Albuquerque. None of the cast could sing too well, but everyone thought the costumes were exquisite. Another solid from Mrs. Hinkley.

While Sherman was away at college, he insisted his mother save all seven of the costumes in his bedroom closet. His parents wanted to convert his childhood bedroom into a study or arcade room which Sherman reluctantly permitted with the understanding that nothing in his closet was to be removed, touched, or worn without his expressed written consent. When asked why, he would tell his mom he knew his costumes would come in handy one day and he would need them later on. When asked why, he said they'd probably save his life somehow but he couldn't explain why and she should just leave him alone. When asked why, he slammed his door shut and cried into his pillow. Mom didn't know *anything!* When Sherman moved into his apartment to begin his training for Harper's, the seven costumes were the first items he unloaded into his closet. And when he stole Kristen's remote control and ran back to his apartment, those seven costumes were the only things he retrieved before going into hiding.

Sherman guessed correctly that the one place the Agency wouldn't be looking for him would be the John Wilkes Booth Memorial Theater. He'd made it clear during the intervention at Eliza's apartment that he loathed Booth's renewed immortalization and despised the fact that he now had a museum built in his honor. Waverly and Gage realized that while Sherman was certainly capable of committing catastrophic deeds with the remote control, the chances that he'd waste his time at the Booth Theater were undeniably slim. Thus, they chose to allocate their resources to other, more likely targets for Sherman's inevitable attack. So when Sherman Hinkley casually strolled right up to the Booth Museum the afternoon after he stole the remote control and sold his cowboy costumes to the museum curator--claiming that they were actual outfits worn by Booth himself during his 1857 run in *Seven Brides in Seven Brothers*--not only was he not hassled by the moronic museum staff who *clearly* didn't realize that fashion designers didn't start sewing their names into their clothes until 1858--*idiots*--but there wasn't an ACHE in sight. At the same moment Sherman was greeting the Booth curator, Kristen was reporting his crime to the Agency, thus kicking off Operation Find Sherman. Ironically, while their eyes were focused solely on their computer screens trying to locate the agitator, Sherman was walking down Washington Street in the middle of the afternoon, counting the cash in his hand. The money the museum paid him would be enough to stay in a cheap hotel for the little over two weeks he would need before his plan would come to fruition. The curator awarded Sherman $201.80 for each of the six costumes he sold them. He needed to keep one for himself. The only other errand he had to complete that afternoon was to somehow find a way to get in touch with Lamar so they could schedule a meeting and exchange information. Lamar had access to some vital materials, and Sherman knew that the Agency would soon close off all outside contact to its employees. He had to act today. He took his money, found a seedy hotel, tried on his costume again--fabulous!--took it off, found some kid on the street and paid the lad ten dollars to personally deliver a handwritten letter to Reverend Lamar Newton at E.W. Harper's ClockWorks TTA. He only hoped the boy would come through.

Started work on a new project today. I haven't told anyone about this but I think it could revolutionize time travel. More later.

Continued work on new device. So far, nothing. I still can't figure out a way to make it function without the IDM chambers. Perhaps if I tried some other form of anatomical energy, I'd be successful. Still no word on when we're opening, but we're hoping it will be soon. They've been ignoring us a lot lately, more than I'm comfortable with--

Today, we teleported! We made it work. Yesterday we successfully sent Abe back five minutes using the remote. As of now, based on the size of the apparatus and the lack of dyhydrogen monoxide, I hypothesize we'll only be able to teleport or time travel, but further studies are needed. Last night we went to a lovely restaurant and--

Thumb prints seem to work quite effectively. We've managed to devise a means by which we can program individual codes into the remote to prevent people from using it without authorization. It's surprisingly simple to initialize. The only difficult part is extrapolating a sample of...

Harper's diary. Lamar had come through. He risked his career sneaking around downtown Indianapolis to meet Sherman, and yet he still brought with him everything Sherman requested. With the blinds drawn and the remote control disassembled on the hotel bed via the diary's detailed instructions, Sherman programmed himself into the device. He didn’t find it difficult at all. Harper was right. A wire cutting here, a piece of hair there; the entire process took roughly ten minutes. It was just that simple. The diary gave him all the answers he'd hope to find. And the rest of the materials Lamar confiscated provided Sherman with the remainder of the specific details he would need for his mission. He took a moment to sit back on the bed, gaze at the remote control lying atop his make-shift work station and congratulate himself for not royally fucking everything up over the last two weeks. The most prestigious and technical corporation in the world had been searching for him for fourteen consecutive days and he hadn't given them an inch. All their number crunchers and computer mainframes couldn't help them find a middle-aged chimp in a shady hotel room less than four miles away. The war was still far off on the horizon, but in the Battle of Operation Find Sherman, the chimp had kicked the hunters' ass.

Sherman couldn't believe how badly he wanted to test the machine, but he knew that any attempt to use it would trigger the ACHEs. Once again, his will power prevailed. He examined the other papers Lamar brought to the rendezvous. He'd spent the past fortnight strategically calculating his plan. The entire operation would come down to the most minute details. He orchestrated every maneuver, every step, every breath. Blueprints of ClockWorks were sprawled on the bed with red dots signifying certain points of his mission. An extensive list of TDL Codes, names, dates, and addresses were sketched on assorted napkins and paper towels strewn across the floor. His cowboy costume hung neatly in the hotel closet, ready to hop on Sherman at a moment's notice. It was 11:45 P.M. Sherman knew he only had a few more hours to wait before his plan would be realized. He went though each step again in his head. This was by far the most ambitious and daunting task Sherman had ever undertaken. It was like he was being born again: born into a world of chaos and espionage and heroism and valiance and truth. The epic battle of Pandemonium versus Serenity. Good versus Evil. Right versus Wrong. Pro-Choice versus Pro-Enslavement. Pro-Agency versus Pro-agency. It all came down to this. It all came down to Sherman. He knew this was his moment of deliberation. Yet he also knew it would not be the time for restraint. His task was clear. His methods, still uncertain. How he would carry out the task at hand had not yet crystallized in his mind, but he couldn't bring himself to think that far ahead. Right then, his sole focus rested on the following morning: just one night's broken sleep away.

"He could be dead, sir," Gage offered to Waverly. Per their standing nightly routine, the two were sitting in Waverly's office, wallowing in a doleful conflation of self-pity, fear, and anger. Across town, their prey was trying to sleep in his bug-ridden hotel bed as they toasted to yet another failed day on the prowl.

"He's not dead, Lieutenant. He can't be dead. Death does us no good."

"But sir, I thought you said that death is the only thing that can give us comfort?"

"I said if *Will Bauer* were dead, then, yes, I'd be satisfied. But Hinkley's different."

"How so, sir? Why is Hinkley different? I personally wouldn't mind if he were dead. That would make our job a hell of a lot easier, don't you think?"

"Not necessarily, Phineas. Mr. Bauer didn't have a mind of his own. He was just some dumb kid who got caught up in a situation he couldn't control. With him dead, the world could go on as it should. His life would only delay progress."

"So would Hinkley's, sir. Begging your pardon, but isn't that why we're after him? Because with him alive he's delaying progress."

"He's not *delaying* anything, Lieutenant. His life *threatens* progress, it doesn't delay it."

"What's the difference, sir? We still want to stop him."

"The difference is that our Mr. Hinkley has changed. You saw him at that apartment. He's starting to *think* now. He's evolving. Once an idea is out, killing the person won't change anything. The person is merely the symptom of the greater illness. The idea itself is the disease. With Sherman dead, the disease will still spread. He'll become a martyr. There's no telling what his death will bring upon this company."

"But, sir--"

"You destroy the symptom by killing the disease. Only then will healthy progress no longer be threatened."

"So, what? Do you want me to send out an order telling the ACHEs we want him alive? Why couldn't we just spin his death the same way we've spun everyone else's who's ever tried to mess with us? He's only a martyr if other people think of him as one. So as long as no one's doing any thinking, the disease has nowhere to go, right?"

"It's already spread, Lieutenant. I just don't know how far yet. A new threat has been born. We can't ignore this one like we used to. You find him. Change him back. Then kill him."

"Sir, permission to speak freely."

"Damnit, Phineas, go ahead."

"Thank you, sir. It seems to me that we can fix this whole thing right now. You want Hinkley gone, send us back and we'll get him for you. We'll go back whenever you want and just take him! Kill him before he's had those ideas, before he fostered the disease. End this thing before it started!"

"I was wondering how long it would take for you to suggest that, Lieutenant."

"Excuse me, sir, but I'm not the only one who thinks that's what we need to do. It makes no sense to have these patrols, to keep on with this lockdown, to cap TDL Codes, to waste precious ACHE time searching for this asshole when all we have to do is go back sometime in the last, what, *two weeks?* and get him! As long as we don't go back before he sent Will Bauer back, it shouldn't be a problem. Forgive me, but are we not in the business of time travel? Is this something outside of our pay grade? Why not take advantage of what we have right in front of us?"

"True, sir, we are in the business of time travel. But what you're suggesting is not *travel,* Lieutenant."

"Well, forgive me then, but what exactly is it?"

"What you're suggesting is not something I'm prepared to deal with. No, Lieutenant. The answer is no. Your job is to find him. Why don't you see to that before you come to me with any more of your suggestions."

"Is this about your sons again, si--"

"Watch yourself, Lieutenant Gage! You are never to mention my children in this office again, do you understand me? We will not be using our Agency to make a mockery of the business of time travel. There is a criminal on the loose. You have your instructions. You have your men. You have any and all resources I can grant you as president of this company. If you are incapable of performing the tasks for which you were hired, I suggest you take this opportunity to submit your resignation. Otherwise, I recommend taking the time to research your enemy. He will strike, I assure you. I leave it up to you to determine when."

"Sir--"

"Carefully, Lieutenant. Do tread carefully."

"I will, sir. Forgive me again, but can you not see how one may view your actions--I mean, the actions of the company--as a bit...hypocritical? I mean that only in the sense of using time travel for purposes of recreation and fun, but not using it when our world may be at stake? When the very fabric of our civilization may unravel at our fingertips?"

"*Our* civilization, Lieutenant? I believe the only reason our world is what it is today is because of Dr. Hinkley. Perhaps you ought to give credit where credit is due."

"That's a bit of a stretch, don't you think?"

"I find it hard to believe that you feel in any way responsible for the condition of our current way of life. What have *you* done, Lieutenant--what have any of us actually *done* to make the world the way it is?"

"Sir, perhaps you've had too much to drink."

"Perhaps I have. But then again, perhaps tomorrow I'll wake up and alcohol will cease to exist. Best enjoy it while it lasts."

"Very funny, sir, but I'm sure that won't happen."

"Oh, and how can you be so sure?"

"I won't *let* it happen, sir."

"Aha. I see. Well, Lieutenant, I'm sorry to say that you may not have a choice."

"We always have a choice, sir."

"Tell that to Isabelle Stowe."

"Who?"

"Goodnight, Lieutenant."

"Goodnight, sir."

"When do you think he's gonna do it?" asked the chump.

"I don't know. Probably pretty soon," answered the Reverend.

"Do you know what his plan is?"

"No."

"Do you miss him?"

"I think we both do."

"When do you think they're gonna let us out of here?"

"When they catch him."

"Do you think you're gonna catch him?"

"I don't know."

"I want to go home."

"So do I."

"Do you want them to catch him?"

"No."

"Why not? Don't you want to go home?"

"Of course I do. But I don't want them to catch him."

"Why not? That's the only way we get to go home."

"Maybe not."

"Fuck you. That's what you just said."

"I know what I said."

"Then what do you mean? How could you not want him to be caught but want to go home and know that the only way we're going to get to go home is if he gets caught?"

"I want to go home, yes, because I'm tired of staying here and I miss my family. But, no, I don't want him to get caught because I don't think he did anything wrong."

"What do you mean he didn't do anything wrong? He stole a time travel device!"

"Yeah, but he never would have had to steal it if he hadn't been fired in the first place."

"He wasn't fired. He quit."

"If he hadn't quit, he would've been fired."

"You don't know that. He could have gotten the procedure just like us."

"Right, and because he showed a little bit of will power, they made him quit."

"What did you just say?"

"They made him quit."

"No before that. What did he show?"

"Will power?"

"That's so weird. When you say that, it makes my head hurt a little."

"*Will power.* Yeah, mine too. Weird."

"Yeah."

"Anyway, I just think they crossed a line by making him do something he didn't want to do."

"We have to do things we don't want to do all the time."

"Yeah, but that didn't have anything to do with his job."

"It had everything to do with his job! And they didn't *make* him do anything. He had a choice."

"Yeah, and look at where it got him."

"We don't know where it got him. He could be livin' it up somewhere for all we know."

"Or he could be dead."
"If he's dead, he's probably somewhere better than this."
"Hopefully."
"Yeah."
"Yup."
"So you think it'll be big? Whatever it is?"
"Who knows?"
"*Who'll* know?"
"Nice."
"Thanks."
"See you in the morning. Sleep well."
"You too."

Twenty Three
Being for the Benefit of Mr. H

"Day after day, alone on a hill, The man with the foolish grin is keeping perfectly still. But nobody wants to know him, They can see he's just a fool. And he never gives an answer. But the fool on the hill sees the sun going down. And the eyes in his head see the world spinning round."

-*Fool on the Hill* by the Beatles

"Hard work is damn near as overrated as monogamy."

-Huey P. Long

Eliza slouched in front of her desk, drool slithering down the side of her cheek, her head awkwardly resting on the back of her padded office chair. Her youngest granddaughter, Kristen slept peacefully on the couch out in the living room. The two had spent the previous night sifting through years of Eliza's research, trying to figure out a way to trace the remote control without needing to activate it. They'd failed to come up with anything. After only sleeping for a few hours, Kristen's alarm clock went off. The two had been waking up every day since Sherman's disappearance when Eternity left for work so that they could most efficiently capitalize on a full day's labor. The three women had since abandoned the domestic tranquility of their cross-town apartment in light of the urgency of the situation at hand. As with the other ClockWorks employees, their headquarters had become their surrogate home.

Kristen rolled over on the couch and slapped the alarm, knocking it to the floor, and thus buying her nine more minutes of sleep before she'd have to reach down and hit it again. It was 7:30. Barely after Kristen rolled back over to rejoin her imaginary friends in dreamworld, an alarm started going off in Eliza's room. Kristen shoved the pillow over her face. *Turn it off, Grandma, it's early.* But still the buzzing continued. Then Kristen remembered: her grandmother didn't have an alarm clock. It was always Kristen's responsibility to wake her in the morning. It took a few seconds for Kristen to fully grasp the anomaly of what was going on, but once she did, she rose from the couch wrapped in an afghan and lumbered into the apartment's home base. Eliza was frantically pressing buttons on her computer switchboards and trying to copy down all the flashes of information bombarding the monitors. She swiveled in her chair and shot a terrified glance at Kristen. Their stares said it all. Suddenly the phone rang. Eliza jolted the receiver to her ear and uttered the words that confirmed Kristen's fears. "I know. I see it too. We'll be right there."

Waverly hung up the phone. Gage was standing in the corner of Waverly's office trying to shut off the same alarm that was going off in Eliza's apartment at the same time miles away. In light of the manhunt, Eliza was forced to come clean about her little remote control invention and supply ClockWorks with a working tracking system so they could keep an eye on the device as well. The simultaneous alarms signified that someone had indeed used the remote to either teleport or time travel. The alarm in and of itself couldn't convey which of the options the perpetrator employed, but Harvey and Lester were already working on tracking the device. "He's used it, Mr. President. He could be anywhere!"

"Calm yourself, Lieutenant. I'm sure we'll find out soon enough where the little bastard is going."

Soon enough came soon enough. Within seconds, Harvey burst through the doors with a computer printout in his hand. His brow glistened with sweat and his shirt was coming untucked from the sides of his Dockers. "Sirs, he's here! Dr. Hinkley's here!"

Gage and Waverly looked at each other, each with varying degrees of bewilderment coating their confused faces. "What do you mean he's come *here*, Mr. Douglas? You're telling us he used the device to come to ClockWorks? *Now?* After all of this? Why would he do that? Why risk getting caught?"

"Well, that's the thing: yes, he's here, sir. But, you see, that's not exactly accurate. He's *here,* but he's not *now*."

The fascist and idealist considered the news. Waverly understood what was going on. He rushed over to his office phone, picked it up, dialed one number, and paused for three seconds. When someone picked up, he spoke. "Reserve the IDM Room. He's gone back in time!"

"Sir, you don't think he'd be stupid enough to go back and try to stop Bauer, do you?" Gage wondered skeptically. Before Waverly could reply, Douglas stepped in.

"Actually, sirs. He's gone back, yes, but not to anytime recently. He's gone back to the year 2020." The room fell silent. No one knew what to do, what to expect. Shit just kept gettin' realer.

Sixty minutes earlier, Sherman Hinkley woke up from unpleasant dreams to find he was still in the same position he'd been in for two weeks: wanted. A man without boundaries. A lonesome dove. A hungry wolf. A criminal. A cowboy. He had slightly over forty-five minutes to get dressed, prepare himself mentally, make sure his gun was still loaded, and call and catch his cab. With the money he had left over from the costume exchange at the Booth museum, he bought a small pistol from a black market dealer in an alley four blocks from his hotel. He knew he would neither have the time nor the appropriate currency to purchase a firearm at his final destination, and the extra security of knowing he was packin' heat was enough to make him sleep somewhat soundly for the past two weeks. Still, his first black market experience was certainly an interesting one. Sherman insisted that the gentleman verify the gun's certification and past ownership and demanded that the guy in the jeans and hoodie at least *ask* for permission to do a background check on Sherman. What should have taken no longer then a few seconds to swap cash for gun ended up taking the better part of an episode of *Jeopardy.* Finding a guy on the black market who actually *sells* guns was the hardest part of the whole ordeal. It disappointed Sherman that he couldn't simply walk into an alley and discover a splendid array of arms dealers and drug peddlers. The entire endeavor took a certain degree of finesse that Dr. Sherman Hinkley otherwise lacked. Still, after much scoping, Sherman was able to find a nice lad who cut him a great deal on a basic pistol for only seventy-five dollars. He was running a special that day whereby if Sherman wanted to buy three more, the fourth would have been half-off. Sherman politely refused.

Sherman quickly showered and put on his outfit. The sequence sewn into the sky-blue plaid patterned polyester shirt fabulously complimented his rustic-looking trousers and pleather boots. The only accoutrement missing was an authentic western hat, but he didn't want to be too cliché. These things require an element of class that Sherman feared would've been compromised by a tacky cowboy hat. His cab arrived promptly at 7:15, allowing him plenty of time to make it to ClockWorks. Sherman paid no attention to the cab driver's expression at the sight of a real-life rhinestone cowboy emerging from the bowels of the most hellish, downtrodden hotel in the city. *Don't ask, don't tell*. The drive lasted roughly twelve minutes and involved weaving through morning traffic in downtown Indianapolis. Sherman stared out the taxi's window at all the people lining the street, cigarettes in hand. He smiled at how blissful the healthy senior citizens looked to be alive. Everything really did seem cleaner, better. There was no sense of polluted air filling his lungs with each breath taken. No evidence of crime on the streets. There were no sickly souls stumbling in between parked cars or children searching for their lost parents. This city was amazing! He had done this! He had built this city with his bare hands and the set the stage for the beginning of forever. *Him*! His hands! He washed his hands *and this city* clean of any transgressions! Dr. Sherman Hinkley: savior.

And yet for the first time, Sherman looked at his new city in very much the same way he always used to study the sets of the plays for which he crafted the costumes in high school. From his seat out in the audience, Sherman firstly noticed "his mom's" costumes and carefully listened to those around him to see if anyone was complimenting the pristine craftsmanship of the dresses or suit jackets. But as the play went on, Sherman's eyes would next be drawn to the set. He admired anyone who could realistically construct a two dimensional replica of the New York skyline or the bow of a luxury ocean liner. He was fascinated by anyone who could take something as complicated and naturally beautiful as the Grand Canyon and paint it--*paint it*--on a fifty foot backdrop so that it actually appeared as though the back of the raked stage overlooked the Colorado River. For Sherman, the sets were what made the plays worth going to. (Just as long as everyone else had come for the costumes.) More so than the quality of acting or the non-diegetic orchestra supplying the diegetic musical score: More so than the singing and the dancing and the stage combat and the special effects; even more so than the costumes, a good set never failed to remove the play from the community stage on which it was enacted and transport it to the rainforest, Vietnam, the south Pacific, or Oz itself. The set served as a means to its own teleportation: *a good set anyway.* Staring through the unusually clean cab window, Sherman couldn't help think that in a lot of ways, his brand new city strangely resembled a set: a construct, a malleable, hastily slabbed together heap of nails and wood that's only meant to be seen from one side. A snapshot of a reality that doesn't exist save for in the mind of its designer. Sitting in that cab, Sherman now realized he had a backstage pass to his own farce of an existence. *We really are merely players in it,* Sherman thought to himself. *Shakespeare was right.*

At 7:28, Sherman's cab pulled up to the curb outside the front entrance of ClockWorks TTA. Sherman got out of the car and gave the driver an $87.45 tip. It was all the money he had to his name. His bank account had been frozen by the Agency, and since he had no stocks or bonds worth more than a few dollars, he figured there was no use carrying any extra cash around with him anymore. If his mission floundered, at least the ACHEs couldn't rob him of his loose change after they stole his life. For the first time in two weeks, Sherman was back on Harper's territory. The sun was shining, the birds were chirping, and nobody seemed to care that the most wanted man in Harper's history was standing outside in the open walkway wearing a flamboyant, anachronistic cowboy costume, a gun strapped to his thigh, and carrying some magical space toy. He walked up the massive staircase in front of the building knowing full well that everyone was inside looking for him in their electronic databases. As usual, he looked at the garden, the columns, and the statue of some guy masquerading as E.W. Harper. He said a quick prayer to himself--his first in nearly twenty years--switched the device to the "time travel" position, pressed his finger to the thumb pad and hit the green button. The next thing he knew, he was standing in the same exact spot looking up at the same exact building. He was wearing the same exact outfit and, for the most part, the weather felt the same exact temperature. He turned around to face his beloved Indianapolis in all its glory. He had fifteen minutes to kill. Looking down at his watch, he saw the time. It was 7:30. The only thing different after hitting the green button was that no one in the building in front of him would know who he was. He was standing outside his former employer three years before he was born. His first trip back in time had been a success. He clenched the remote control in his hands and typed a few quick numbers before throwing it into a trash can outside the main Harper's entrance. There'd be no turning back now.

The ACHEs arrived a few seconds later. As with Sherman before them, a luminous flash and deafening crash accompanied their arrival on the Harper's steps in the year 2020. And as with Sherman before them, no one seemed to notice. Ever since Harper founded the Agency two years prior, the prospect of people appearing and disappearing no longer seemed like something straight from the pages of a self-published, quasi-science fiction novel. The ACHEs wasted no time zeroing in on Sherman's location. They traced the remote's homing signal to the trash can in the front of the building. When they arrived at the receptacle and saw the unclaimed remote control, a few of the ACHEs actually thought they'd caught Sherman. It took the wisdom of the Head ACHE to convince his Agents that just because they had found the remote, didn't necessarily mean Sherman was attached to it. Once everyone was in agreement that Sherman wasn't in the trash can alongside the blinking remote--a process that took far longer than one would expect for a group of grown men to open a trash can and realize there was no one inside--the Head ACHE wrote a note reporting the team's progress to Waverly and Gage. He sealed the note in an airtight container and buried it eighteen inches beneath the ground in a previously designated patch of soil alongside ClockWorks main walkway. Forty-eight years later, Waverly and Gage dug up the canister immediately after the ACHEs dispatched to see how they were doing. While the ACHEs knew Sherman couldn't have gotten far, they all realized that the seemingly simple task of finding him the instant he triggered the remote had now become slightly more difficult. He could be anywhere. He was on the loose, and they had no way to track him now.

Their directions were simple: find Sherman and bring him back. The was no contingency for him using, and then losing the remote. No one thought he'd ever be that clever. Since the ACHEs were given Zemeckalian Clearance for their trip back, they understood how important it was to maintain secrecy and not disclose their mission to anyone on their present timeline. While the ACHEs were standing on the threshold of their own Agency--complete with all the technological assistance they would need to find their target--ironically, they couldn't use anything inside. They couldn't use a single machine, ask anyone for help, or leave any trace of their presence behind in the past. Their impotence could not have benefited Sherman more. Despite their most innate longings to shoot the bastard, they couldn't very well discharge their firearms in the middle of an open foyer cluttered with innocent bystanders. The collateral damage could be inconceivable to their future well-being. Sherman's foresight had leveled the playing field by rendering their technological capacities useless. In going back to 2020, Sherman had essentially sent the ACHEs back to the year 1020 to a time when only their cunning resolves would guide them in their pursuit of justice. The war was fast approaching.

"The ticket says 8:00, dear," a young woman said.

"I know, honey, I just wanted to get some pictures before we go in," a young man said.

"But we only have a few more minutes before we need to be there."

"Honey, everything's been taken care of. They're gonna let us through, don't worry. Look at this place! It's a gorgeous day! I'd just like to get a few shots of the statue over here and then we can go in. Look, we still have fifteen minutes before we have to be there, and I'm sure it's just right through those doors. It can't be that hard to find."

"Fine."

The couple joined the hubbub of fellow tourists outside on ClockWorks grand platform over looking the Indy skyline. Man was documenting his trip on his digital camera while woman tore through their itinerary to make sure they weren't missing an important meeting or mandatory baggage check or cavity search or anything. When man had sufficiently captured the garden, the statue, the building's facade, and the view of downtown, he and his new bride walked into the glorious building prepared to embark on a honeymoon they'd never forget. They cleared the atrium, boarded the glass elevator and got off on the floor of their Public Agent, Melania, with whom they'd coordinated their first trip as husband and wife.

"Mr. and Mrs. O'Shea! So good to see you. Are we excited about our honeymoon?" the woman grinned.

"We sure are," Mrs. O'Shea replied, squeezing her husband in a public display of their undying affection and eternal marital bliss.

"Wonderful! Everything's all set for you two. You're the first customers of the morning, so we shouldn't have to wait to depart from the IDM Room. Did you two bring a change of clothes or anything for the trip?"

"Uh, no, were we supposed to?" Mr. O'Shea wondered.

"Well, no, not necessarily. Some people just like to look the part that's all."

"But we have a Dickensian package. So no one's going to see us--"

"Oh yes, listen to me! I'm sorry! Dickensian, yes of course. No worries then! You two will be just fine. Now, I've already coordinated your meal plan with our catering division. You're on a three day, 12 meal deluxe package, correct?"

"Yes, Miss, we are."

"Perfect. Here's a list of the drop points for your meals. We'll have Agents make sure to leave the food you ordered at these specific points at the times listed on the sheet there. Don't worry: no one else will be able to see the food or the Agents. It'll be waiting for you to arrive!"

"Excellent, that sounds great."

"Yummy, yummy!" Melania continued. "And we didn't go through currency exchange today, correct? There's no need to have any money while you're back there. You won't be able to spend it. If you'd like, of course, we do have our gift shop downstairs when you return, and of course we also have our ClockWorks catalog which allows you to order specific items from your trip that our specialized commercial Agents will then go back and purchase for you and deliver to your home."

"Wow, I didn't realize you offered that service. That's great!"

"Yeah, not many people know we offer it. Sometimes our Agents wait until the last minute to mention it, but it is something we always want to inform the customers of. It's a really nice deal, if you ask me. And, let me see…yup, everything's already paid for your package, so it looks like you don't owe anything today either."

"We shouldn't. This trip is a wedding gift from her parents."

"Ooo, lucky you. You know, I've always wanted to go back there, but I've just never had the time. Such a fascinating period in history!"

"Well, we think so. We're both sorta huge history buffs, and ever since we heard about this place, we wanted to come down here and see what you guys had to offer. I just hope it'll be a good show. We're both very excited to finally be able to actually take a trip."

"Aw, well good for you two! Now, if you'll follow me, it's almost time to depart, so let me grab your file here and let's head on over the IDM Room, shall we?"

"We'll follow you."

The 17th floor of the building hummed with the static excitement of a brand new day. Attractive PAs flurried to their respective desks, doors opened and closed, the elevators beeped, signifying the arrival and departure of fresh faces and Melania Roth escorted the O'Sheas through the mob to the Ionic Dyhydrogen Monoxide Room. "Here we are, folks! This is the place," the PA exclaimed proudly. She opened the door in such a demonstratively emphatic manner that Mr. and Mrs. O'Shea each privately expected to see gumdrop snowflakes and cinnamon zebras dancing beneath rows of licorice trees and Mackinac fudge mounds. Alas, all they saw were two large tanks of water.

"All set for the day's first trip, Miss Roth?" asked a moderately handsome but well groomed middle-aged man.

"We sure are, Dr. Cole. These are the O'Sheas. They're on their honeymoon."

"Pleased to have you with us today, folks."

"I'm sorry, allow me to introduce Dr. David Cole. He's our Chief Head of Unintentionally Misplaced Persons," Melania explained.

"Oh, so you're the chump I read about in *Harper's Monthly.* You've been doing brilliant work with the Mesozoic Era, sir. My compliments," Mr. O'Shea proclaimed in awe.

"Ah, an educated man. Why yes, we hope to expand our findings from that particular period to include the Jurassic, Paleolithic, and Neologismistic periods as well. We're still a few years away, though, I'm afraid."

"Fascinating, though, sir. Simply wonderful job so far."

"Well, I thank you. Have a safe trip, you two. Good luck in your nuptials!"

"Thank you, Dr. Cole," Melania replied. The chump left the newlyweds and their guide to continue with his checklist of daily morning procedures. The PA brought the PCs to the main IDM deck where they were greeted by the primary IDM Room engineer and equipped with their STOOPING Pieces. Similar to a SCUBA instructor, the IDM engineer explained what all the little gadgets and knobs and buttons and lights on the SPs represented and fielded any questions the two customers had before opening up their chamber and guiding them inside. Melania finished the paperwork and handed the file to the assistant engineers who programmed the O'Shea's TDL Codes into the Harper's IDM Room mainframe computer. Their honeymoon was about to begin.

A relatively short but well-built man entered the O'Shea's chamber and assisted them with their safety harnesses and seat belts. He made sure the electrodes were securely attached to their heads and the levers in the chamber were all turned to the "Full Power" position. The man adjusted the zipper on his Harper's coveralls before attaching his own set of electrodes around his skull and securing himself in an empty seat beside Mrs. O'Shea.

"Par'n, me, Miss, but 'ol man 'Arper always insists 'at 'is young married customers get air own private tour guide," the man announced in a horribly thick cockney accent.

"Um, excuse me, sir, but we didn't request any tour guide. We're on our honeymoon, ya see, and we'd really just like--"

"No worries, sir. As soon as we get whereva we're goin', I'll jus turn 'is thing around and head on back home, 'en. 'Ol man 'Arper jus wants a make sure 'is guests get to places safely, ya see."

"I guess that's alright, honey," Mrs. O'Shea conceded to her husband and reluctantly agreed.

"We'll start the countdown in a few seconds, folks," the head engineer called over the chamber's intercom. The newlyweds and their British tour guide sat in silence inside the chamber, all three anxious for the countdown to begin. Some more anxious than others.

"Alright, folks, here we go. Three, two--"

"Melania, how many TDL Codes did you program for this trip?" an assistant engineer asked.

"One!" And the chamber plummeted down into the tank, then exploded several feet into the air like an kickboard that was released from the bottom of a pool. The bobbing chamber flooded the deck with its tremendous splash. Everyone present knew the buoyant vessel now sat empty in the center of its tank.

"Two, why?" Melania asked, following the chamber's disappearance.

"Well, I only programmed two as well," answered the engineer. "And I only distributed two STOOPING Pieces. But *three* TDL Codes were just sent to that chamber."

"*Three?*" barked the chief engineer. "That's impossible! If you only sent over two and you only programmed two, then how on Earth could there have been *three* codes sent to the chamber?"

"I don't know, sir, but look at the monitor. *Three* codes were disseminated to the contents of the chamber. I don't see how the computer could make a mistake like this. This isn't an instrumentation error, sir. We're talking *real* problem on our hands, potentially. Someone else must have been in that chamber with the O'Sheas. Someone else is now back in--"

"Sir! Come over here!" hollered a much younger, rookie engineer. "I pulled up every TDL entry for the last hour. Look at this. Twenty…*four* minutes ago, *E.W. Harper* entered a TDL code for this trip. He overrode the system and programmed himself into their travel package. Oh shit. He also gave himself Zemeckalian Clearance!"

"Let me see that, Dale," demanded the chief engineer. "You're right. Someone used one of Harper's old clearance codes to override the system and program himself into the O'Shea's trip. Oh damn. He also gave himself Zemeckalian Clearance!"

"That's what I just said, sir," Dale muttered.

"Do you know what this means, team?"

"That Harper's not dead after all! That he's simply been hiding the last two years, waiting for the perfect opportunity to strike down his own company and ruin us all? That he probably has help on the inside and can use technology far beyond our current knowledge. How else could he do it? Yeah. Yeah! Harper's alive! Harper wants to kill his own brainchild!" suggested Dale.

"No, you idiot! Of course Harper's dead. Goddamnit, son, calm down. It was in the papers," the head engineer dismissed. "What this means is someone has tampered with this trip. Whoever was in that chamber could very well jeopardize our entire way of life. Someone find Cole. And damn it, alert the Head ACHE! They have work to do!"

As the afternoon spilled into the early evening, a horse drawn carriage made its way through the crowded roads of the nation's capital. Inside sat the four principle leads of a critically acclaimed dramatic play by a respected English playwright whose fixation on death and renowned penchant for the macabre had already captivated audiences overseas and begun to sweep their way through the now Disunited States. The thespians were discussing their upcoming performance, and each expressed their elation that the President himself was expected to attend. All but one appeared to welcome the opportunity to perform in front of the great emancipator. The lone naysayer was about to express his disdain for the leader of his country when a blinding light flooded the inside of the cabin, spooking the horses and causing them to halt in the middle of the road before flying down the street like bats fleeing the dawn. From a distance, the cast members turned around and saw a man standing in the middle of the road behind them removing a layer of blue clothes to reveal an odd compilation of a sparkly plaid shirt, tight pants, and alien boots. After stampeding through town, the horses swerved so abruptly that the momentum of the turn fractured the carriage's axel, sending the cabin into a dead-on collision with a street lamp. The fragile cabin pummeled into the iron pole, crippling its skeletal framing and heaving the actors through the front of the coach and onto the street. The crash knocked loose the light from the street lamp which fell onto the splintered wood, setting the wagon on fire in a matter of moments. Onlookers rushed to the scene to assist with the fallen citizens-- all of whom were now unconscious-- and tried to contain the wild flames. The abrupt pandemonium was so engrossing that no one paid any attention to the suspicious looking man in the middle of the road two blocks away. Nor did he have any cognizance of the commotion his arrival had caused at the other end of town.

"How are you going to get back?" Mrs. O'Shea asked their strange companion whom she noticed didn't have a complex, computerized watch strapped to his wrist. "Excuse me, sir, thank you for helping us, but I don’t think we're going to need anymore--" And Sherman started to strip. He unzipped his Harper's coveralls and exposed his sequined cowboy outfit complete with echoes of Will Rogers's worst nightmare and reminiscent of 1940's Broadway musicals. After he disrobed, he bundled the coveralls into a tight ball and tucked them under his arm.

"Well, um, wherever you are, thanks for letting me hitch a ride with you both and have a great honeymoon. Hopefully I'll see you again someday," Sherman whispered into the nothingness around him. The differences in their respective Harper's clearances meant that the O'Sheas could see him but no one could see or hear them. Once they arrived at their destination, Sherman was on his own.

"Can he see us, honey?" Mrs. O'Shea wondered.

"No, I don't think so. He must have ZC. We have *D*C. The difference between our respective clearances means that we can see him but no one can see or hear us."

"Makes sense now. What do you think he's going to do?"

"I don't really care. He can't hurt us, so I say let him be. We better go find our dinner. The show's gonna start in a few hours."

"I really hope it's as good as everyone says it was!"

"How can it not be? It's his last performance ever. This is a once in a lifetime opportunity!"

"Honey."

"Yeah."

"Why was that guy dressed like a gay cowboy?"

"I don't know."

"And what happened to his accent?"

"Don't worry about it, dear. He's can't do anything to ruin my night, so don't let him ruin yours."

"I guess you're right."

"Are you sure you're right about this?" The Head ACHE asked. Immediately following the departure of the three member party, Harper's engineers summoned a specialized team of ACHEs to IDM Room. When the call went over the Harper's private line, the only ACHE team close to the IDM Room was a small coalition of men stealthily roaming the halls. Once spotted, they were instructed to proceed to the IDM Room for further instructions.

"Of course I'm sure! We have a rogue time traveler on our hands. He or she snuck into a chamber just now after programming a personalized TDL Code using one of Harper's old sign-in codes and traveled back to 1865," responded the frantic chief engineer of the IDM Room.

"Alright then. Standard ClockWorks operational protocol requires you to send us back to five minutes before the arrival of the temporal threat. Let me assemble my team and we'll be ready to go."

"Standard protocol?" the engineer repeated. "What standard protocol? I was under the impression that the Harper's committee was still in session on all new protocol regulations for ACHE maneuvers." *Shit!* The engineer was right. Standard ACHE protocol wasn't finalized until eighteen months *after* E.W. Harper's "death" in 2019. "And are these uniforms general issue?" *Shit again!* The uniforms worn by ACHEs in 2068 weren't designed until 2064.

"They're brand new, sir," the ACHE called Denning announced. "Fresh off the line."

"And you're correct about the standard protocol not being finalized yet," added the ACHE called Carlisle. "But we have special classified orders from President…from President…"

"We have orders from Dr. David Cole, chief. He's the one who insists we go back to five minutes before the rogue's arrival. That should give us enough time to secure a perimeter and eradicate the threat once he or she arrives. We understand you're familiar with Harper's notion of an anti-military approach to temporal reformation, but Dr. Cole feels that the only way to restore our current timeline is to fix the matter swiftly and efficiently." the Head ACHE added. The engineers thought about what they'd just been told. The uniforms, the standard protocol, orders from Cole: none of it made any sense. How would Cole know about the situation that only occurred a few minutes ago? And what gave him the authority to issue any kind of temporal restoration task force? *Who* were *these ACHEs and why were they secretly maneuvering through the hallways? It was almost as if they were already looking for something...*

"Russo, program these men with TDL Codes for five minutes before the arrival of the last chamber," the chief engineer finally ordered after an uncomfortable delay. "And get the chamber cleaned. We have no time to waste!"

"That was close, boss," the ACHE called Franklin whispered to the Head ACHE as they walked up the metallic stairs to the departure deck. "Think he went to get back Stowe?"

"In *1865*, Franklin? Probably not," the ACHE called Denning sarcastically volleyed. "There's no one important named 'Stowe' back then. It'd be a waste of time!"

"Quiet, both of you!" the Head ACHE demanded. "We know the year we're going to, but we don't know *where* he went. So when we get back there, be prepared for anything. This whole thing could be a trap."

"Yes, sir," the ACHEs replied in unison.

The IDM engineers assisted the ACHE team as they boarded the departure chamber. When every member of the elite force was strapped in and hooked up to their respective electrodes, an engineer administered a STOOPING Piece to the ACHE called Denning. "We've programmed this to go off in sixty minutes. That gives you an hour to satisfy the requirements of your task. You realize that at this point, there's no contingency for a failed mission. We simply don't have the means to send back a recovery force, nor do we have the moral authority to fix your mistakes. I'm afraid those orders are nonnegotiable. Do you know how to use one of these?" the engineer asked.

"Please!" ACHE Denning replied. "We've been doing this for ten ye--"

"We'll be fine, thank you," the Head ACHE finished.

"Excellent. Well, we only have one SP to give you now. We need the rest for our tourists today. There're supposed to be more arriving this afternoon but--"

"What do you mean you only have *one?* I know for a fact there's a whole closet full of them over the--" Denning cried.

"This will be fine, thank you, son," the Head ACHE asserted. The engineer shrugged off the awkward rhetorical exchange and climbed out of the vessel, sealing the special Agents inside. "Damn it, Denning, know your place! This isn't the same Agency we know. We're in the middle of Harper's infancy! They don't do things the same way we do. Shut your damn mouth!" The chamber bobbed in the water as everyone cleared the deck. The countdown began. Three seconds later, the ACHEs were standing in the middle of a dirt road, guns drawn in full preparation to eliminate the threat once he or she arrived. The ACHEs ignored the few spectators watching them from the edges of the road. They needed to concentrate on the mission at hand. A hundred yards away, the they could see a carriage approaching them. "Should we move, sir?" Agent Franklin asked his commander.

"Negative, Franklin. Stay where you are. This will only take a second." When the carriage was only a few yards in front of them, a bolt of lightning struck the center of the road. The horses charged the ACHEs, crushing Agents Denning and Carlisle. Franklin dove out of the way of the raging steeds, landing in a puddle of muddy water on the side of the road. The Head ACHE barely dodged the left horse but tripped on a stone as he was trying to slide out of the way. Despite his best efforts, he was unable to stop himself from being pulled under the wheels of the charging coach. The traumatic bumps and bounces combined with the sudden swerving of the horses caused the wheel's suspension to fracture and the axel to splinter in half. The momentum of the coach carried it straight into a nearby street light. When ACHE Franklin pulled himself to his feet, he saw the two other members of the team lying motionless a few feet in front of his commander who was wincing in the middle of the road, holding his leg. At best, his team had experienced fifty-percent causalities in its first six minutes of the operation. Aside from a small fire at the other end of town which seemed to have attracted the attention of the majority of the bystanders, Franklin couldn't tell who his target was or where the hell he could find him.

Franklin stumbled over to his fallen comrades: his crippled commodore and trampled fellow troopers. Then he saw it. On Denning's hand was the STOOPING PIECE, its face shattered into bits of scattered glass and loose wire. The apparatus no longer contained any remnant of a device that would eventually lead them back to their future. And along with the lack of viable use from the SP, Franklin saw no signs of life emanating from the bodies of Agents Denning and Carlisle. So far, his mission had two confirmed deaths. So far, his leader had been disabled. So far, he'd been left without a way home. And so far, he'd been left without a target for his gun full of bullets. He'd been gone for seven minutes.

Twenty Four
The Play's the Thing

"Acting is the least mysterious of all crafts. Whenever we want something from somebody or when we want to hide something or pretend, we're acting. Most people do it all day long."

-Marlon Brando

"I believe it is an established maxim in morals that he who makes an assertion without knowing whether it is true or false, is guilty of falsehood; and the accidental truth of the assertion, does not justify or excuse him."

-Abraham Lincoln

"Nonsense! The show *must* go on!" Mr. Ford proclaimed to his group of understudy leads.

"Miss Keene seems to be doing better. Perhaps she'll be in good health in time for curtain," John Dyott suggested.

"But no one except Mr. Booth has played his role in years!" Harry Hawk argued. "Even if Miss Keene *can* perform, we can't replace the rest of the principles on this short notice! We have three other roles to fill! We must cancel the performance."

"Impossible," Mr. Ford maintained. "Miss Gourlay has already sold out the show. And President Lincoln himself will be in attendance. You all know your lines, correct? The blocking? We've notified Mr. Polkinhorn, and he's already begun the process of making new bills for this evening's performance complete with your names as the primary cast. Miss Keene will remain as the headliner, for now, but if anything changes, you let me know as soon as you can! You all have a little over an hour to prepare yourselves. Mark my words, we will begin promptly as scheduled." Mr. Ford retreated from the dressing room to the ticket office where he confirmed that the show had, in fact, been sold out. Meanwhile, the new cast grudgingly began fitting their costumes and reviewing their lines.

"Look! She's waking up!" W. J. Ferguson announced to the rest of the cast. Indeed, Miss Keene had begun to regain consciousness from her collision with the Washington ground.

"Miss Keene! Miss Keene! *Laura!*" shouted a few of the crew members.

"Whadda, men, the flash and fell between…sky...other…" She still seemed a bit groggy.

"Miss Keene, thank goodness you're awake. Mr. Booth and the rest of the players are all still unconscious from the fall earlier this evening. We need you for the show!"

"Fall show? Why I'm not never doin' no fall show in a booth again! Damn, blastin' horses! Never seen so many bloody dirt sparks in whiskey faced cow-eyed trampled antler eaters in before all my earth on days," Keene protested.

"She's gone mad!" Harry Hawk exclaimed. "We can't very well perform when she's in this condition. We'll have to replace her."

"We can't replace her," Dyott argued. "She's the only reason, besides Mr. Booth, that people come to see this show. And the new bills have her name on them. She needs to perform. She'll come around. Just give her some time. If anyone can come off a fall like that, Miss Keene can!"

"Aye, Miss Can keen do anything, mom," Laura gurgled as she rolled herself up on the sofa on which she'd been placed. "Point me in the convection of the rage and we'll play with the audience tonight, men!" Keene rose from her seat and proceeded to the dressing closet where she stripped off her clothes and began preparing for the show. The rest of the cast obliged her fragmented demands to the best of their ability and continued dressing. The evening's performance would now star three dramatically unprepared understudies and one delirious Miss Laura Keene. Hopefully, Mr. Lincoln would be pleased.

"Is it any better at all, sir?" Franklin asked his commander who replied by rolling his eyes in negation of the insolence embedded in such an idiotic query. "I'm sorry, sir, really I am. I didn't--"

"It's not your fault, Franklin. Did you see where he went?"

"No, sir. Not at all. He could be anywhere. *We* could be anywhere. There's no way to tell quite where we are, now, is there?"

"No, I suppose not. Are you sure their bodies are hidden?"

"Yes, sir. I stripped them of any conspicuous items and threw the bodies in a back alley."

"Well done. You followed the manual."

"To a T, sir. In more ways then one, too!" Franklin admired his freshly acquired authentic nineteenth century outfit. As per the manual, when a temporal snafu delays an immediate transport home, the ACHE must acquire period-appropriate clothing using "any means necessary." In this instance, the acquisition of two outfits consisted of Franklin walking into a local mercantile, firing a warning shot into the ceiling, and demanding two sets of clothes. It was that simple.

"And the STOOPING Piece?"

"It's destroyed. Completely. Hopefully Hinkley has a way to get back home cuz if not, we may be here for a while."

"I'm sure we'll be fine, Franklin." The two had been sitting inside Taltavul's Star Saloon since the accident. The Head ACHE was pleasantly buzzed on whiskey, while Franklin maintained a keen surveillance of the establishment for any indication of their location. (They each refused to simply go and *ask somebody*). A fresh piece of paper nailed to the swinging door of the tavern caught Franklin's eye. He got up from his seat and walked over to the tavern's entrance. Sloppily attached to the door was a playbill for that evening's performance. Five words jumped off the page and landed inside Franklin's memory back: FORD'S THEATER, OUR AMERICAN COUSIN. He didn't need to read anything else. *April 14th, 1865.* He knew exactly where he was and what Sherman intended to do. Sherman was going to kill President Lincoln! Sherman had traveled back in time to assassinate the president…at Ford's Theater! Yes! This was it. Franklin knew where to find his culprit.

"Sir! I know where Hinkley is!" Franklin proclaimed to his superior officer.

"Where?" was the callus response.

"Well, I'm not sure exactly, but I know where he's *going* to be!"

"Where?"

"Well, I'm not sure...*exactly*...but I know what he's going to do!"

"What?"

"He's going to kill the President. President Lincoln! Don't you see? We're in Washington on the night Lincoln got shot. And Hinkley's gonna do it!"

"But Lincoln didn't get shot."

"Right. Well Hinkley's gonna kill him tonight."

"Why would he do it now? Why wouldn't he wait until Lincoln was alone and kill him then? It'd be a hell of a lot easier, don't you think?"

"Well, yeah, but...I don't know...it just makes sense!"

"I don't think so, Franklin. Nice try though. Now, get me another whiskey, would ya? Just put it on your tab."

"Do they even have tabs back here?"

"I beg your pardon! Do you mean to tell me that I can't perform *my own role* in the very play that *I made* famous on the night when the *President* will be in the house?"

"I'm very sorry, Mr. Booth, but the show's already begun. You've slept through the entire afternoon and into the evening. We can't very well--"

"I wasn't *sleeping,* you miscreant! I was merely out of sorts, that's all. But now I am prepared and ready to take to the stage. If you'll kindly step aside so I don't miss my entrance--"

"I'm afraid that won't be possible. We can't stop the show once it has begun and replace the cast halfway through the first act! It would simply ruin the entire experience! The house would be quite displeased and Miss Keene's reputation would plummet to the orchestra pit!"

"Ruin! I will show you *ruin!* You haven't seen the last of me, Mr. Ford, I assure you. If you dismiss me, I vow this building of yours will someday *burn to the ground!* Do you understand me, sir? I curse you as well as your namesake."

"Oh, spare me your tirades, you overrated scallywag. *Your* namesake far outweighs the mockery of a theater legacy you've claimed to accumulate. I'm quite certain you'll never be the actor your father was!"

"My good man, when I leave the stage, I'll be the most famous man in America!" And Booth stormed out of the Theater to have a drink in the tavern next door. A few of his friends were already there.

"Please, sir. I'm strenuously requesting permission to track down Hinkley. I *know* where he'll be tonight. I'm positive. Just imagine what will happen if he succeeds!"

"Franklin, I don't suppose there's any stopping you, is there?"

"Negative, sir. I can be back in less than an hour. Trust me. This is something I have to do."

"Alright. Damn it, Franklin, go and catch your man. You know I'd be there with you if I could manage to walk on this leg. It's a fuckin' good thing we had all that morphine in our packs otherwise I'd really be fucked."

"Damn right, sir. Pretty convenient, I'd say. Okay. One hour. I'll be back."

"I'll be here." The Head ACHE's pain was excruciating despite the potent mixture of morphine and alcohol flowing through his veins. He had no choice but to wait for his subordinate to return from his own private war with Sherman. He was left alone in the saloon to ponder how to safely bring his broken team back home. As he swigged the final gulp of whiskey from his shot glass, he feared that the idea of "home" was now something he could ever only hope to ponder at all.

"This is great! Don't you see? He's there. He's right in there. We could carry out the plan tonight! No one would suspect a thing. You could walk right up to his box and kill him!"

"Yeah, John, there's no better time than now. It's perfect. We could change the world. You could make history. We've been plannin' it for this long, why wait until next week?"

"Because it wasn't supposed to be tonight, that's why! I'm supposed to be in there. I'm supposed to be on that stage, showin' that bastard all that's wrong with his country. I swear if I ever see that man again…"

"What man, John?"

"The guy that shined that light in those horses. The guy with the shiny shirt who jumped out into the middle of the road and made me miss the performance."

"You saw him, John?"

"Of course I saw him! I got eyes, don't I? I'll never forget what he looks like either. It was far away, but I swear to God in Heaven that I'd know him if I saw him. No one else could ever look that sinister."

Across the tavern, Sherman Hinkley cowered in the corner, a hat pulled over his eyes. In order to conceal his slightly conspicuous presence in town, he quickly conformed to the contemporary mores and finagled himself a genuine gentleman's hat. He'd spent the remainder of the afternoon in and out of hotel lobbies, sampling assorted taverns and even spent some time looming around Ford's theater as a means of building up the courage to do what he came to do: assassinate John Wilkes Booth. While in Ford's, during the cast's final (and first) blocking run-through, and while the management was clearing the lobby in last minute preparations for the evening's performance, Sherman even snuck up to the presidential box suite and carved a small hole through the door in case he would later have the inkling to return once the President was seated inside. Aside from his task of killing Booth, nothing would complete Sherman's mission more than having a closer look at the corporeal manifestation of the American ideal.

Now hours later, seated alone at his private table, he couldn't believe what he'd just heard, nor the mouths from which the menacing words seeped. Sitting at the bar, no more than fifteen feet away from the runaway chimp, were John Wilkes Booth, Davey Herold and Lewis Paine: two of Booth's cohorts in the Lincoln assassination. Sherman vividly remembered studying the assassination as a kid before everything got all fucked up and history valorized Booth as a national treasure and Lincoln as the impetus for cancer eradication. Sherman had certainly been through a lot in the last several hours, but amidst the foggy annals of his distant recollections, he concluded that

Booth was sitting with the very men who were *supposed* to aid him in his deviant act of treasonous treachery. Booth was wearing all black clothes with a matching hat, calf-length boots and what appeared to be new spurs. He wore a killer's countenance across his face, and from the few intermittent phrases Sherman could pick up, spoke of committing his violent act that very night. Sherman had a clear shot. If he so desired, he could end the charade right then. He could stand up, cock his gun, fire across the room and end Booth's life right there in front of a packed house. Of course, he wouldn't make it half a yard before being gunned down himself for murdering the greatest actor to ever grace the American stage. All the same, the thought definitely crossed his mind.

"John, listen to us. We're all here. Everybody knows the plan. Davey and I can get word to the Powell and Atzerodt, you can go over there, walk up the stairs, and do it! Everyone knows you there anyway. Just say you're gettin' your mail or something. Who's gonna say 'no' to you? It's Good Friday, besides. Nobody'll be expectin' something like this! "

"You're right. Spangler owes me a favor anyway. I could get him to hold my horse while I carry out our plan. As long as you two take care of the rest of the men, we should be able to get out of here without getting caught. We'll use the route we already diagrammed."

"We've put too much thought into it to risk getting caught, John."

"Yeah, John."

Sherman's heart leaped with joy but sunk under the weight of two centuries of lies. *John Wilkes Booth was no saint!* He was *and always had been* a murderer! Booth didn't need to kill anybody to reserve his seat in Hell, and Dr. Sherman Hinkley knew it. His mind raced back to the Booth museum where at that very moment two hundred years in the future, children were probably staring at the metallic monstrosity in the lobby as if it were a replica of Christ himself. How could they know that the man they were admiring--the man that supposedly *was* American theater--was at that moment two hundred years in the past, plotting to murder the man who *was* America?

Sherman's concentration was broken, however, with the tavern's latest arrival. Hardly anyone acknowledged the man's unassuming entrance, but Sherman could identify the stranger instantly. It was an ACHE. They'd come back for him. How many, he couldn't be sure, but Sherman knew the man standing between him and the door was the same Harper's Agent whom Waverly had dispatched to locate Stowe and who served as Gage's personal assistant. Somehow they'd found him. Surely they located the SP he'd thrown in the Harper's trash can but how they connected that to…no…no time to think. *Booth. Lincoln. Wally, Lamar, Era, Stowe...that sweet honeymoon couple...Eliza...Eternity...the watch...time was running out.* He needed a diversion. He had to get out of the bar. Sherman's duel with Booth could wait: the hunter had become the hunted.

The chimp cautiously rose from his seat, careful to not trip on his chair or knock over his empty glass. As he placed his hands on the table to prop himself up, he accidentally tripped on his chair and knocked over his empty glass. So much for stealthy discretion. Luckily, Franklin hadn't seen him. In fact, at the moment, the ACHE wasn't even looking for Sherman. He'd been all around town seeking the elusive assailant since he left the Head ACHE but to no avail. Ford's Theater didn't offer any leads nor did the locals or the exterior of the President's home. As far as Franklin was concerned, Sherman was a ghost, a figment of a past pursuit, a memory. When the disgruntled ACHE approached the bar, Sherman slipped out the door behind him and into the street. "You get a look at that there fella?" Herold nudged Booth who shook his head in a negative response. "You shoulda seen 'im. He was wearin' this sparkly shirt and dumb ole hat--"

"Did you say *sparkly shirt*?" Booth pepped up.

"I did. Fella who just left."

"Which way did he go?"

"Well there he is now, headin' over to Ford's!"

"That's him! That's the man who wrecked the coach. Get the others ready. Looks like a couple men are going to die tonight. I'll meet you soon." The most dangerous game had officially begun. Armed with a single-shot .44 caliber derringer and a hunting knife, Booth left the saloon and made his way over to the sold out forum. It was a little past 10:00 P.M. Since his friend Ned Spangler had to tend to some obligations inside the theater, Booth commissioned a young theater employee named Joseph Burroughs to watch his horse in the back alley, claiming he was merely stepping inside to check his mail and perhaps greet some of the evening's more distinguished patrons. Burroughs gladly accepted the responsibility.

Sherman wasn't quite sure how to calculate his next move or, really, what that move was going to be. He'd abandoned the prospect of killing Booth in light of the arrival of the ACHEs. So far he'd only seen one of the Agents, but he knew there had to be others in the vicinity. Rather than risk a public shootout, Sherman decided his time was best spent watching the blasphemous play being performed at Ford's. Though, of course, it wouldn't be the version with which Sherman was most familiar, he assumed that a couple of hours away from the ACHEs would do him good: clear his mind of the whole "now you're back in time being chased by people from the future who want to kill you" thing. The house was packed. The ticket box was now closed since the play was approaching its third and final act, so Sherman was able to waltz right through the back entrance to the house in search of a place to watch the remainder of the show. Standing near the rear of the theater, Sherman couldn't find a single empty seat. *I still don't see why this so is so popular,* he thought to himself. Adding to his confusion was the uproarious laughter spewing from the mouths of the patrons. *This version was supposed to be a drama!* And yet, from Sherman's brief exposure to the play, it definitely seemed like a hilarious comedy. The characters were bumping into each other on stage, stepping on each other's lines, knocking over the set pieces--*not the set!*--and one of the female leads seemed to be completely unaware that she was, in fact, in a play. She mumbled most of her lines, and the fanatical gestures with which she delivered her choppy monologues made the entire house double over with tremendous waves of thunderous laughter. Sherman examined the actors on stage when something struck a chord in his mind: *why isn't Booth up there?* Sherman knew he saw the killer at the tavern only a few moments before and yet, this was supposed to be Booth's final performance. *It's why Sherman came back in the first place!* The museum, the legacy, the statue: *this performance* was Booth's swansong! And yet, while the play was going on, he was drinking with his accomplice Davey Herold at the tavern next door. Something didn't seem right at all.

Looking up and to his right he saw the presidential state box…*The Presidential State Box!* Sherman couldn't believe his eyes. Abraham Lincoln--*Lincoln!*--no more than a hundred feet away! He was sharing a box with his wife, Mary, and two other guests whom Sherm guessed were Clara Harris and Major Henry Rathbone. If Sherman was going to die that night, he vowed to himself it wouldn't be without first shaking hands with the greatest American President who ever lived. At 10:12, Sherman found the stairs leading to the State Box. Conveniently, the stairwell was not guarded which allowed Sherman to ascend up to the President without the hassle of having to sweet talk his way past the theater security. He was about to open the door and peek inside to greet the President when he heard someone thundering up the stairs in his direction. *Probably the security,* Sherman thought as he prepared to smooth things over. When Sherman turned around to face the top of the stairs, he saw Booth charging at him like a mad man, his gun drawn and pointed straight at him. Sherman didn't know what to. He had nowhere to run. The only place to hide was the Presidential suite behind him, but if he went in there, he might get shot himself. Still, Booth kept coming. Sherman reached behind him and turned the knob on the door. He flew inside the State Box at the exact same moment one of the pathetic actors on stage screamed, "Don't know the manners of good society, eh? Well, I guess I know enough to turn you inside out, old gal—you sockdologizing old man-trap..." A wave of laughter flooded the theater as Booth closed in on Sherman. The next few seconds ticked by as if they were a detailed series of Mathew Brady photographs set to slow motion.

Sherman burst through the door. The actor said the line. The crowd laughed. Booth entered the suite and aimed his gun at point blank range from Sherman's head. Sherman tried to take a step back but tripped on Rathbone's chair. As Sherman fell, Booth fired anyway, piercing the back of Lincoln's head. "Oh shit!" Booth uttered. Sherman lay on the ground. Rathbone rose and tried to grab Booth. Booth stabbed Rathbone in the arm. Rathbone fell. Lincoln bled. Sherman laid on the ground. Booth stepped on the balcony and jumped the eleven feet to the stage. He shattered his fibula. Through the commotion of the State Box and terror of the house, Sherman stood up, stepped back into the doorway and did the only thing he could of. He cupped his hands to his mouth and yelled at the top of his lungs, "Sic semper tyrannis!" He then ran out of the theater like a scared little boy.

Twenty Five
An Era of Change

"Abused prosperity is oftentimes made the very means of our greatest adversity..."

-Daniel Defoe, *Robinson Crusoe*

"You must be the change you wish to see in the world."

-Mahatma Gandhi

Franklin sulked over his empty glass in the Washington tavern. Denning and Carlisle were dead, his commander was incapacitated at a saloon on the other side of town and Sherman Hinkley had seemingly vanished from the face of the Earth. Franklin had failed in all the tasks to which he had been assigned. His head began to throb at the realization that if he ever were to go back home, he'd have to face the gut wrenching ClockWorks tribunal of executives, politicians and shareholders. What could he possibly say to convince them that the mission was flawed from its conception? How could he ever explain that the most elite tactical force on the planet couldn't accomplish a simple routine time travel operation? His legacy was ruined. He was a disgrace to the Agency, to himself, and to the Harper's emblem. As he bowed his head further in shame, he started questioning the innate hypocrisy of his botched mission: find and contain a time traveler for time traveling using time travel in order to preserve the present timeline which allows travelers to travel through time at any time they choose. What made Sherman such a viable threat to the Agency? What made *any* time traveler more threatening than any other time traveler? Why was he, as an ACHE, above the moral code of rogues like Sherman Hinkley? His mind returned to the bedroom on Washington Boulevard: the one occupied by the gay couple who slept in the same room as the now fictitious Isabelle Stowe. Why wasn't the Agency concerned with Stowe's absence but handsomely funded the elimination of a fool like Sherman in order to "maintain the status quo"? For better or worse, didn't the status quo *include Isabelle Stowe*? As a symbolic act of submission to his Dundrearyism of an existence, he ordered another drink.

The bartender had just filled Franklin's order when a crowd took the streets with wailing cries of "He's been shot! The President's been shot!" The tavern poured into the night as mounted policeman feebly attempted to control the mob and infantry soldiers formed a barricade around the theater. After what seemed like hours of uproarious chaos and rioting, a captain cleared a path to a brick federal style rowhouse across the street where soldiers eventually carried the mortally wounded body of the President. Franklin watched as the crowd shifted to the Peterson boarding house and wondered to himself if Hinkley had anything to do with the incident. He thought of his commander and what he would do in a such a situation. Franklin turned and ran back to the saloon to inform his Head ACHE of the assassination. When he entered the building, however, the Head ACHE was nowhere in sight. Franklin called for him, but no one answered. The news of the murder had already reached the farthest corners of town causing every mobile citizen to take to the streets in an horrific conflation of mourning and savagery. The saloon was empty. Franklin was alone in the epicenter of the most culturally paralyzing political conspiracy in American history. He was scared. He was stuck. He would never see his commander again.

Sherman rounded a corner at full speed. He hadn't stopped sprinting since he leapt down the back staircase of the theater and out the side stage entrance. He could hear the echoes of terror and gunshots in the background. He could feel the vibrations of bucking horses with each footstep. People were running through the streets in every direction. Sherman didn't know where the ACHEs were, how he would get home, *if* he would get home or if Booth had taken the route he was supposed to take. If history really was doomed to repeat itself, it would take the small band of Union soldiers twelve days to track Booth down and kill him inside Garrett's burning barn. It would only take another nine hours for Lincoln to die from his wounds.

Poking his head around a brick wall to see if any of the commotion was nearing him, Sherman felt someone lodge a barrel of a gun into his back. He was speechless. *Booth! ACHEs?* The gunman didn't say a word. Sherman slowly inched his right hand down to his side in order to grab his concealed weapon when the silent robber took hold of Sherman's hand. The gunman's leather bound grip crushed Sherman's hand between his fingers. Sherman could feel something slide under his palm. The robber dropped his gun, pulled off his leather glove, and re-grabbed Sherman's right hand. He slid Sherman's thumb onto the foreign device the two were now holding and pressed a button with his index finger. A light flash and bright crash later, Sherman found himself standing in the middle of a brick sidewalk, staring at clusters of old style brick buildings surrounded by contemporary high-rises. On the side of the road stood a sign that read, "Historic Ford's Theater" with an arrow indicating the direction of the preserved landmark. Sherman and the gunman had traveled back to the future. At least *some version* of *some* future.

"Nice shirt, Sherman," said the sweet voice of the gunwoman. Wait. *The gunwoman?* Sherman pivoted on the sidewalk to find himself staring into the alluring eyes of Era Howells.

"*Era?!*" Sherman gasped. "Wha…how…wha…"

"You always were good with words, Sherman," she said, smiling.

"I know, but wha…how…wha…?"

"Relax, Sherman. Everything's okay. You're safe now. It's the future again. I'll take us home soon. I just wanted to get you out of there and bring you here first so I could talk to you for a minute." She had a melancholy air about her that she was trying so strenuously to conceal. Had Sherman been any less psychologically weathered, he would have wondered why sadness seemed to undercut her optimistic musings. But alas, weathered he was and thus wonder, he did not. Nevertheless, he couldn't help but sense that there was something…*un-Eralike* about her. The city, which Sherman assumed was Washington, looked similar enough to what he remembered. But Era: the vacancy within her eyes, when juxtaposed with the maternal comfort blanketing her smile, reminded Sherman of when his mom used to tell him everything would be okay when she so clearly wasn't sure herself. Despite their most valiant efforts, even the greatest mothers can't stop a tornado.

"Era," Sherman managed to utter. "You have to go. They could be coming for you! There were ACHEs back there. If they find out we're here, they'll--"

"Relax, Sherman. No one's coming to find us. No one knows we're here. It's just you and me now."

"What do you mean it's just you and me?! We have to get out of here. *You* have to get out of here. You have to go back to your husband and live peace--"

"Sherman, that's enough!" Era snapped. It was the moment when all kids first meet their parent's vulnerability. The shift from Übermensch to mortal, from omnipotence to impotence. Mother Era had just failed to lift the proverbial car under which Sherman had been pinned. Something inside of her revealed her own finitude. She removed her mask to reveal her pain.

"I'm sorry, Era, I just--"

"Just stop! Okay! You can't understand what's going on, what you did."

"What I did? *What I did?* Jesus Christ, when is everyone going to stop going on about what I did! I didn't do anything, alright! I didn't do anything to make the world better, I didn't do anything to make it worse. Fuck! I've never done anything. I didn't kill Booth, I didn't stop the ACHEs. I didn't destroy the Agency! Someone please, for the love of God explain to me why *I can't understand* what I did! Please. Go! I'm dying to hear what you have to say to me."

"Sherman, it's me. Okay. It's Era. I'll explain everything to you. Just sit down. Let me talk."

"Fine, go ahead then."

"Everything's fixed, Sherman. Everything. You did it. You really actually made everything better, *for real*, this time."

"I don't under--"

"Shh!"

"Sorry."

"It's alright. It's actually pretty simple, really. John Wilkes Booth killed Abraham Lincoln on April 14th, 1865. You were there. You saw the whole thing. The manhunt was just like it should have been. Twelve days, Garrett's farm, the burning barn--everything. The ACHE who was chasing you, well one of them anyway, *Franklin*, I think--he actually stayed behind and joined Edward Doherty's men in the 16th New York Calvary Regiment in their pursuit of Booth and Herold. In fact, Franklin was standing behind Corbett when he shot Booth through the crack in the barn. He ended up living the rest of his life back in the nineteenth century. He married a farmer's daughter, raised three sons and died in 1899. We would have gone back and retrieved him but when Wally found Franklin's memoirs buried in the ClockWorks Archives last month, he saw that Franklin wrote about his life with such fondness and pride that he and Lamar felt it behooved them to simply let him rest in the peace of the past. I guess something about his life back then filled a void he had in our time."

"What do you mean *a month?"* Sherman asked. "How could Wally have found that in the archives a month ago? I've only been gone for a few hours, right? You said this was the future?"

"It is the future, Sherman. Hold on. I'm getting to that. So, yeah, Agent Franklin lived a fruitful life during the Reconstruction and died in his New York estate in 1899 shortly after the great newsboys strike. Let's see, what else... Um...Oh yeah, the other ACHE who survived your arrival in Washington that night, Giuseppe Marconi, actually moved to Bologna, Italy shortly following Booth's capture. He wanted to go back to his old country or something to spend the rest of his life. He married a beautiful Irish woman named Annie Jameson and almost nine years to the day after Booth's capture, the couple gave birth to their second son, Guglielmo. Apparently the ACHE never stopped trying to build his own STOOPING Piece to bring him and his family back into the future. He'd work mostly every night in his study fiddling around with filaments and circuits and buttons and all kinds of weird things. He never succeeded, obviously. However, his son grew up watching his father experiment secretly with wires and electric currents and from these research sessions, developed a fascination for the wonders of wireless technology."

"*Marconi*?" Sherman gasped.

"Yup, the same guy. The Head ACHE was his father. Pretty cool, huh?"

"Definitely!"

"Yeah, I know. You can't make this stuff up. Oh and get this: the play, Taylor's play, whatever it's called--it's still known as a comedy! The only reason anyone today even knows about in the first place is because it's the play Lincoln saw when he was shot and on the night he was shot, the play was so horrible because of all the understudies that everyone thought it was actually supposed to be a comedy! So good job on that one too. Oh! There's more! In the international wake of Lincoln's death, Lewis Carroll decided he needed to write an uplifting, fantastic children's story to replace all the creepy stuff he'd written in the past. So, just a few months after Lincoln's death, in July of 1865, Carroll published *Alice in Wonderland*, which, I'm sure you'll recall, is a delightful tale of a young girl and a rabbit and blah, blah, blah, you get the idea. But that's not all! Lorina Charlotte Liddell, the young girl who was so traumatized by Carroll's original tale of demons and Hell and all that--which he still did tell the three sisters on the boat that day three years before--well, the shock of Lincoln's death caused her to empathize so much with his widow, Mary Todd, that she vowed she would never grow up to be a lonely, single woman. In 1874, just as history directed, she married William Baillie Skene and the two lived happily ever after and had some kids who had some more kids and well, a few decades later, Isabelle Stowe was born! She's back with the Agency and it's like she never left. Wally still hates her. Lamar still ignores her. It's just like old times. So that's all that. Even though you were only gone just a few hours, Sherman, you managed to put the world pretty much back on its original timeline. Minus, of course, a few small differences."

"Differences? Like what?"

"Well, obviously Taylor's dad still died that night in 1822 and, of course, Will Bauer is still dead and that caused some little things to happen, but it's really not that big a deal."

"Um, okay…wait a second…if Lincoln died…when he was supposed to…I mean, if Booth shot him 1865, that means that he never lived long enough to die of…Oh my God! Era!"

"It's okay, Sherman."

"No! No, it's not! I can't believe I did this to you again!" his eyes began to fill with tears. "I'm so sorry! I'm so sorry, Era."

"It's alright, Sherman. He never should have come back to me. We had our time together and it just happened that his time ended a little before mine, that's all. When he came back, everything was harder. I thought I could handle it, but I really couldn't. I kept having these mixed memories of a life without him and my life with him and everything got all bunched up that I couldn't tell when I was dreaming or when I was awake. I loved him. I'll *always* love him. But death is a part of life and I just have to accept that.

"We were just sitting in our apartment, having an argument over what to watch on TV one day when suddenly the room filled with light and he just wasn't there anymore. And neither was I. I was sitting in my old apartment with my roommate Stacey. We were arguing about what to watch on TV. It was like waking up from a dream I never had. I called my doctor in New York and asked him why I even remember anything about Casey coming back to me in the first place and he said he didn't know. He said that because I didn't have an implant, my mind should fluctuate in accordance with any shifts in the temporal plane. But mine didn't. I remember everything. The before, the after. The during. The never was. One minute he was there. The next, he wasn't. Our life together just stopped. There was no more life.

"Stacey still works for the Agency, but I quit a few weeks ago and found a great job working at the Efron Theater as a costume designer. Go figure, huh. But, anyway, back to you. When none of the ACHEs returned with you from their mission, and we confirmed the whereabouts of all four of them, the Agency determined that you must have died as well. Or at least, created a life for yourself somewhere in another time. After a few weeks, they called off the search for you. They had to continue with their business. Waverly wouldn't let anyone go back to fix the timeline again after you fixed it again after the first time it was fixed since the last time. It's confusing, I know. Basically, everyone decided to keep things the way they are and classify your status as 'lost in time.' My cousins and I spent a little extra time searching for you, but when nothing came up, they eventually quit looking. You could probably guess, but once the search was called off, Waverly made all employees undergo the memory scan. So now, no one at ClockWorks has ever even heard of you and couldn't go back to find you even if they wanted to. Probably for the best though. People have better things to do than look for important things in the past. Even grandma gave up trying."

"So why didn't you?" Sherman wondered.

"I'm not sure. I mean, everyone *knew* where you went. It's not like it was any big secret or anything. We all knew what you were going to do. No surprises there. And even though everyone was working so damn hard to find you, not a single person was workin' smart. I mean, really: it's not that hard! All I had to do was say, 'hey, Sherman's back in 1865. I know when and where. I'll go back a few minutes after Lincoln was shot and look for the idiot in the dumb outfit runnin' through the street.' No offense."

"No, none taken. Nobody else thought to do that?"

"I'm sure they did, Sherman. But you know as well as I do that sometimes people appear to work their hardest only when they don't really want to achieve the results of whatever it is they're doing. As long as they could all say they tried, that's all the Agency needs to hear."

"So what: they didn't *want* me back?"

"They sent people back to kill you, Sherman. Why would they want you back? You think they would just let you come back and work for the company again? That's not how things work."

"But they let Eternity come back. And they let your grandma help with my search."

"But that's different, Sherman."

"How? How is that in any way different?"

"You still don't get it do you. Damn. I thought when you went back with the remote that you finally caught on. I thought you'd begun to think for yourself a bit, but I guess not. Sherman, they can't trust you completely and because of that you're automatically a liability to their Agency."

"What are you talking about? They can trust me--"

"*Completely,* Sherman, they can't trust you *completely!*"

"Why not?"

"Because they know that you have the power to not trust them."

"Eternity never used to trust them."

"Only because my grandma told her not to. The second grandma said the Agency was good, did you notice how fast she and Kristen hopped on the ClockWorks bandwagon?"

"Okay, so Eliza is still dangerous though, right? Why didn't they kill her?"

"Because I guess they were willing to let one sheep go if they wanted to kill the wolves."

"So, she was bait? For who?"

"Think, Sherman. It's not that complicated of a metaphor! For *you*! Eternity and Kristen, sure, but mostly for *you,* Sherman! It's all a game. All of it. In the eyes of the Agency you're a twofold hero and yet in their hearts they'd gladly carry on their lives thinking you died in the past. You're the people's hero, but they couldn't care less about you."

"*The people's hero?* But I didn't do anything! I didn't do anything back then except trip and fall!"

"Who says you have to do anything to be famous, Sherman? You're important *because* you're famous. Not the other way around."

"It's not supposed to be like this. It's not supposed to be--"

"It is, Sherman. This--*all of this*--is life. You and me, this whole mess: this is our world."

"Well I don't like our world very much right now."

"Neither did my grandma. Don't you see how similar you two are?"

"No. Not anymore. I do have one question though. What year *is* this?"

"It's still 2068. It's just six weeks after you went back, that's all. To go back and get you, I had to steal Eternity's remote control and since they still had the trace on it until now, I didn't want to take you back to the moment of your departure because they would have found you and that might've affected how everything has played out since then. Make sense? So, if it's alright with you, you'll just have to live a couple weeks in your own future, if that's okay. Instead of bringing you back in early August, it's now mid-September. Understand?"

"Whatever. This is all messed up anyway. So there's no more trace?"

"Nope. They stopped caring. It's just us." Era paused for a few moments then quietly asked, "Sherman, can I ask you a question? How far back can you remember? Like, what is the earliest memory you have as a child?"

"Um, okay…I remember little things--flashes really--of my dad holding me late at night while he watched the talk-shows on TV. I remember feeling the air stream past my face as I slid down the slide in the park by my parent's first house or the feeling of weightlessness when I first learned to swing really high. *Pump your legs, Shermy!* I remember the hallway leading to the bathroom next to the kitchen in my house. I used to think the hallway stretched on forever and would have dreams that I was standing at the end of it and the toilet would come alive and chase me down the hall. I remember waking up from those nightmares in my spaceship bed with the railing still attached to the side to keep me from falling the six inches to the floor. I remember my uncle's dog that tackled me one time on the fourth of July. It was probably just trying to play with me but I can still feel how scared I was lying under the beast as he tried to--well, I thought he wanted to eat my face--but my dad was filming the whole thing and it looked like he really was just trying to lick me. I remember thinking that the grass in our front yard seemed so long because the blades would scratch right below my knees it seemed. But then, years later I saw pictures and the grass was never any longer than a few inches, so I must have been pretty small to remember that. Smells mostly, ya know. I can remember the smell of cookies, the scent of our old babysitter's house that smelled like a mixture of cigarettes and old ladies--which was pretty accurate because two old ladies lived there and they smoked a lot. I remember smelling our Christmas trees and the smell of new clothes on the first day of school. Sometimes I can hear things too. Like, *hear* my preschool friends say things that hurt my feelings or made me feel scared or angry. I can't remember anything else about them and even today when I think about them I have no idea why I remember them, but some of what the kids said back then really stuck with me. I can remember how guilty I felt whenever I would get in trouble at Sunday school. I can remember the first time I ever made a racist comment. I was standing in line about ready to go out to recess in first grade when a friend of mine, who was a black kid, was making fun of me. Again. I think he was making fun of my name or something. It doesn't matter. For no reason, to retaliate, I said, 'be quiet, *burnt face!'* He didn't hear what I said because the teacher was saying something but I remember how…*dirty*…I felt after saying it. It was the first time I remember being aware of using someone's physical appearance against them."

"Do you want to know what my first memory is?"

"Sure."

"I remember being four years old and hearing the phone ring. Even though I didn't know what had happened, for some reason, I can picture myself--through my own eyes, ya know--sitting in my room playing with my doll when the phone rang. It was one of those moments when even as a kid, you know something's wrong. Like, something just didn't seem right. You always listen to your mom when she answers it to see if her voice sounds normal and if it doesn't right away, you stop doing whatever it is you're doing to listen for any signs of danger or trouble. Well, anyway, this was one of those phone calls. My dad came running up the stairs and kicked my dolls out of the way, grabbed me, tucked me under his arm and carried me back downstairs and outside into our van. My mom was crying hysterically and my dad was driving faster than I'd ever seen him drive. I remember being scared but also wanting to hug my mom and make her feel better. I couldn't think about anything else other than making my mom stop crying. I can cry. *Me, not her.*

"So we get to the hospital and there's all kinds of police cars out front waiting for us. I remember I knew what building it was because my dad broke his leg earlier that year and we went to visit him there. At the time I thought every hospital only treated one patient. So, like, I thought *this is my dad's hospital...and he's healthy, so why are we going back?* My mom and dad were running a few steps in front of me. I just remember holding a policeman's hand and looking up and seeing the scared looks on all the doctors' faces. Phones were ringing, people were yelling, machines were beeping. It was not at all like when my dad had his leg broken. *That* was a calm day. My mom gave us ice-cream that day. And than I remembered. *Us!* Someone was missing from our family. Where was my sister? We left her at home! We had to go back and get her! She was playing outside and we just left her. I remember thinking that because we were twins, maybe my parents thought they left *me* at home and then I got mad at them--*mad at my parents*--for leaving me at home! Can you believe that? Anyway, the doctors take us all to a waiting room and they tell my dad that 'she's in surgery.' And my dad asks 'if they killed it.' And my mom's crying and my dad's about to cry and I start crying because it seems like the thing to do and the policeman says 'they got him,' and my mom screams and says 'I want to see her! Let me see her!' And they say 'she's still in surgery, ma'am and she screams and I scream and dad tells a policeman to take me into the gift shop. So I leave. Of course, I still don't know what's going on.

"I only have flashes of the next few hours. The next thing I remember is being told to wait outside as my parents went in the room to see my sister. They didn't want me to get scared. As I was waiting outside, a police office--that *fucker*--asked if I wanted to see my sister. I said 'no' because my parents didn't want me to get scared. He said he can hold me up so I could look into the window. I didn't see anything wrong with that because I wasn't in the room, so I wasn't disobeying. Plus, I was curious. She's my sister. I've never forgiven that officer for picking me up. What I saw when I looked in that room haunts me to this day. Both my parents were standing over a hospital bed crying. At first, I couldn't tell anyone was in there with them. I only saw all the sheets and tubes and machines and wires and bags and stuff. But then I saw her. My little sister--my *little, tiny sister*--was lying on the bed and all the tubes and wires and machines and bags were plugged into her all over her body. Her entire head was completely wrapped in bandages. She didn't look alive. She didn't look real.

"I don't really remember anything else until she came home. Our house was quiet without her. My parents were constantly sad and it seemed like every day they were gone at the hospital and I would have to have a babysitter over because they wouldn't want me going with them. I just kept living my life. Then one day, she came home. I remember thinking that she wasn't my sister anymore. How could she be? We were twins and now she didn't look anything like me. She didn't look like *anybody.* Over the next few months, we went to parties and celebrations because my sister was finally out of the hospital. I remember going to one party for the two men--they seemed like men. In reality, they were only sixteen--who saved my sister's life. They each seemed so proud of what they did. And that was that. That was my first vivid memory. I can remember basically the whole day. The day my sister was almost killed in the woods down the street by a pit-bull."

"*Howells?"* Sherman mumbled. "Your name is Era How--"

"Howells is my married name, Sherman. My maiden name is Marx: Era Marx. My sister's name was Ashley. I believe you two met once."

"Was? What do you mean her name *wa*s Ashley?"

"You don't know, Sherman? She killed herself when she was fourteen. Those scars didn't just run skin deep, I guess. We found her one afternoon in the woods by our house. She slit her wrists."

"Why are you telling me this, Era? Why now? What does this have to do with me *now*?"

"I don't know, Sherman. I just thought you should know. I guess I had a feeling you were getting tired of being praised for things you didn't do that I'd remind you of something good you once actually did. You saved my sister's life."

"That's not true, though, Era! That man—that *trucker man*—he was the one who shot the dog!"

"Yes, but he said he never would have stopped if you didn't leave your bikes in the bushes on the side of the road. And besides, that's not that point. You heard her scream! You went to see what you could do to help her because you thought someone might be in trouble. You might not have killed the dog, Sherman, but because of what you did, the dog didn't kill her."

"Maybe not *that* day, Era, but it seems like that dog never really got off of her. Or out of her. Or whatever. Yeah, I mean I guess Wally and I led that man to your sister but, again, he's the one who saved the day."

"Sherman, you didn't kill my sister. No one did. You didn't make her kill herself. She did that on her own because of things she couldn't deal with. You don't know what those things were. No one does. They might have had to do with the dog, but they might not have. She made the decision. You spared her life for a decade."

"I just feel like I could have done more, that's all. I've always felt like I could've done more."

"Maybe you could have, Sherman. Maybe you could have run over to her and picked the dog up and thrown it off of her. Maybe you could have killed the dog yourself. Or maybe not. Maybe it would've killed you instead. Maybe it would have killed Wally. Fact is, we just don't know. Fact is, no one can *ever* know."

"You know that's not true."

"Well then no one *should* ever know. How's that for hitting you over the head with it?"

"Not bad."

"Please don't feel like you lost your chance to make a difference that day, Sherman. Don't live your life that way. Me, well, all I've ever known is loss. Ashley, then my mom, then Casey. Then Casey again. That's why I went to work for the Agency. To try and find a way to grab hold of the past and relive the memories that were slowly fading with each passing day. That's why I hated how my cousins were trying to shut us down, and that's why I tried so hard to stop them. The Agency was the only thing I had to connect me with my past. Or with the past in general, for that matter. I don't know. I guess over time, though, I began to see that going back to see the past wasn't the same as reliving it. It was watching it, like watching a home movie. Time travel didn't make the past real for me. It made the past present, but I could never *live* in that present. At best, I could only hope to peer inside from the audience. Anyway, I just wanted you to know that the girl you saved in the woods that day was my sister. That was Ashley."

"Can you just take me back to Indy now?"

"Sure, Sherman. I'll take you home."

"Indy's fine." They put their thumbs on the pad, blinked, and bid farewell to Washington.

Twenty Six
Tabula Rasa

"Time is money."
-Benjamin Franklin

My name is Sherman Hinkley. I was once a doctor of forensic psychology from Cross University before being conceived by devils and born into a world where I was nothing more than a monkey. For over twenty years, I sought a career with E.W. Harper's ClockWorks TTA and for slightly over twenty-four hours, I worked for the Agency as their resident scapegoat. I have seen the full potential of time travel and have witnessed, with mine own eyes, the lengths to which a few will travel to control the many. By my hand alone, at least four people have died including a young girl, a loving father, a naïve student, and an American hero. I'm afraid I can't speak intelligently on how many more may have died as an indirect result of my actions. For now, four deaths suffice at keeping me up at night.

I seek your assistance in removing from my head the hippocampus implant with which Harper's egregiously equipped me. I have no further use of it. I can neither afford, nor do I desire to continue having my memories be impervious to alterations in the temporal plane, for they have grown too cumbersome to bear. From this moment forward, I wish to be subject solely to the shifting of time. I assure you that I have not arrived at this decision mildly. I have pondered its implications for these last several months and feel that only now can I truly say that I am prepared to accept the consequences of stripping my head of its unwanted intruder. Since its arrival inside my head, my life has been nothing but a time of storm and strife.

I've come to believe that I was once married. I cannot explain why I feel this way, though I have recently begun having dreams that suggest prior to my time with Harper's, I was indeed married to a beautiful woman whom I can only see in my deepest subconscious. Perhaps she is what compelled me to work at Harper's from the beginning. Perhaps my desire to explore time travel derived not from the writings of E.W. Harper, but from my passion for my lost love. Perhaps. The fact is, no one can deny with utmost certainty the validity of these dreams, as we have all learned that time travel is anything but objective. It can never be essentially without subjectivity. And yet, it is my subjectivity of which I now beseech you to relieve me. Beseech. Now there's a word you don't hear any more. Maybe I invented it. Who knows?

Sherman clicked 'send' without signing his letter. It took Dr. Ajay Nagheenanajar roughly fifteen minutes to respond. When Sherman checked his email again, he found a new arrival from a hospital in New York. The subject line was a return of Sherman's original email which simply read "Tabula Rasa." Sherman opened the new email and chuckled at Nagheenanajar's reply. The brief letter consisted of three simple words: *IT'S ABOUT TIME.* Sherman opened a new internet window and booked his flight out east.

"But what if he wins, sir? A victory could be disastrous for us!" Gage exclaimed. He and Waverly were discussing the heated 2068 Presidential election in Waverly's office on the fourth floor of ClockWorks. During his previous term, President Moses Martin's cabinet had stood on a decidedly firm "Pro-Time Travel" platform, yet the candidacy of Gomez Quaio had already caused a ripple of skepticism to flow through Martin's ranks. In waves of ghastly growing numbers, Martin's supporters were beginning to question his ethical foundation insofar as its relation to TTAs (such as Harper's) in the United States and others around the world. Quaio vehemently preached a campaign against time travel, claiming that the visionary idealism for which Harper once strove no longer served any *real* social demand other than concealing the Agency's incessant pursuit of greed, tyranny, and power. "If he wins, sir, I'm quite certain he'll shut us down for good."

"Phineas, now do you honestly think I would ever let that happen?"

"We may not have a choice this time, sir."

"We always have a choice, Phineas. That's what makes us who we are. No. He won't be shutting *this* Agency down, that's for sure. Not in my lifetime."

"What's to stop him, sir, from coming in here right now and destroying us? You know. Make it so we can't go back and stop him or something. Ruin everything we've worked for?"

"What's to stop him? You mean besides the fact that we'd see him coming a mile away?"

"We didn't see Hinkley, sir."

"We didn't need to see Hinkley. Hinkley couldn't see himself, so why should we give a shit?"

"But this Quaio guy: I think he means business. I don't think he'd let our surveillance deter him. Hinkley couldn't see himself, as you say, but he still managed to walk right through our doors, didn't he? What's to say that Quaio wouldn't do the same thing?"

"Would it really matter if he did, Lieutenant?"

"Excuse me, sir?"

"I asked you if it would matter if Quaio did walk right through our doors and blow this building right out from under us."

"Would it *matter,* sir?"

"That's what I'm wondering, Gage. Would it matter?"

"Sir?"

"Maybe he should do that, come to think of it. Yes. Maybe he should just walk in here and tie us all up and kill every last one of us and end this whole place right now! That'll get him elected! That'll change everything! Yeah, and then the world will be a completely perfect sphere of laughter and joy and it'll be a wonderful place because it wouldn't have the two of us running around all the time trying to fuck it all up! Yes. I like this plan. In fact, get him on the phone. Call off the security. Why wait for him to sneak in here, huh? I'm going to *invite* him here so we can take care of this today! Why didn't I think of this sooner? *Would it matter?* Of course it wouldn't!"

"Sir? What is this? What are we talking about? It seems like we're just talking for the sake of talking. I'm sorry, but I really don't know what you're trying to tell me this time. Could you maybe be a little clearer or a bit more specific or something because I feel as though we're just going around in circles in here and not really getting anywhere…"

"Talking for the sake of talking, eh?"

"That's right, sir. That's how I feel."

"Shut up, Lieutenant. You're not even registered to vote."

In November 2068, seventeen percent of the American people elected Senator Gomez Quaio as their president. Quaio never made it to Indianapolis or any other TTA for that matter. He didn't have to. He orchestrated a scathing political campaign against time travel without ever having to leave his headquarters in Atlanta. He ran a nearly flawless campaign predicated mainly upon his vow to rid the world of time travel in his first term and, despite a strong pull from his opposition, wound up taking seventy-six percent of the electoral votes. The analysts would later quarrel amongst themselves about the probability of a victory if only he would have mustered up the courage to challenge the various TTA presidents to a head-on public debate, but the banter between the talking heads ultimately evolved into more of a pissing match than an actual intellectual discussion. Though the fact is, they were right: Quaio probably would have lost the election had he chosen to engage in a debate with

Waverly or even Gage. Doing so would have compromised his entire campaign promise and brought to the forefront that which he intended on keeping hidden behind the curtain until after elected. He ran under the banner "Beginning Forever but Time Travel Never!" and relied on the luxury of promising to eradicate time travel without actually having to articulate how or when or really even why. In responding to a greater public need--albeit fleeting--to preserve the so-called "moral fiber" of America, Quaio capitalized on a vague promise by essentially doing nothing. Once elected, his first order of business, therefore, was not to disband ClockWorks, but simply to change its name from E.W. Harper's ClockWorks TTA, to E.W. Harper's ClockWorks PPA: *Past Preservation Agency*. Americans ate it up. This man really *was* about change.

Waverly remained at the top of the Harper's conglomerate, with the trusty Gage by his side. Wally and Lamar continued their posts as Harper's respective chump and Reverend, while Isabelle Stowe maintained her role as food consumer and task completer extraordinaire. Eternity led her finely tuned staff of Public Agents to a record setting month of sales in December. As it turned out, under the label "Past Preservation," time travel was more popular than ever. Despite a persistently dwindling economy, people were still willing to shell out millions of dollars each year to take vacations to watch the Hindenburg explode or the bomb go off over Hiroshima. No one ever remembered the name of the plane that dropped the bomb, but mostly everyone agreed the explosion was cool to look at. Eliza Wyatt Harper died on Christmas Eve, 2068 in her apartment. Only Kristen was with her during her final moments. To the grave, she took her true identity as ClockWorks's original founder and true namesake. As far as Waverly was concerned, she and her family were long-term time travel enthusiasts whose love for the *essence* of ClockWorks caused them to go through a brief spell wherein they wanted nothing greater than to see the Agency closed for good. Nobody outside the Harper family ever knew the truth about the conspiracy against Eliza and her husband years before or the fact that Eternity and Era were the rightful heirs to the ClockWorks fortune: nobody except a guy named Sherman who worked for the company one day earlier in the summer.

"So, I guess I just don't get it. If God hardened Pharaoh's heart—if *God* did it—and made it so that Moses *had* to bring the plagues upon Egypt, wouldn't that be kinda interfering with Pharaoh's free will?" Wally and Lamar decided they'd done enough work for the day, so an hour before lunch, they began to discuss scriptural instances which confounded the Christian notion of free will.

"Explain," beseeched Lamar.

"Well, okay. I mean, everyone's taught that Ramses—*Ramses,* right?"

"Ramses II. Go on."

"Whatever. Well, everyone's taught that he's an asshole because he didn't let Moses's people go and all that stuff. But, what I'm saying is, if it was *God* who hardened his heart so that he wouldn't let the slaves go free, then what does that say about the idea of free will? It's not really Pharaoh's fault then, is it? It's almost like the whole plague/Red Sea thing was a whole big set-up that God…set up from the beginning. So, I guess in that case, neither Pharaoh's actions nor Moses's actions were *really* free will because if God knew everything anyway, then no one could really ever make a decision for themselves, right?"

"You make an interesting argument. Not terribly original, but interesting nonetheless. What's even more interesting, Walden: if I were to say to you that there's a Hell—say, for a moment, we both agree there is such a place—and I asked you to name two people who were most likely *in* Hell, who would you say?"

"I'd probably say Hitler and Jubas."

"You mean *Judas,* right?"

"Yeah, the thirty silver pieces guy."

"Right. Well, a lot of people would agree with you. Yes. They'd say, *these men are certainly in Hell because one killed Jesus and the other killed twelve million people.* Makes sense, right? Well, according to scripture, before Judas turned Jesus over to the Roman guards, Satan himself entered into Judas's body. 'And after the sop Satan entered into him. Then said Jesus unto him, That thou doest, do quickly.' *Satan, Wally!* And, according to the story of Job, we know that occasionally God *allowed* Satan to, for lack of a better term, *mess* with people. 'And the Lord said unto Satan, Behold, all that he hath is in thy power; only upon himself put not forth thine hand. So Satan went forth from the presence of the Lord.' So, by extension, one could argue that God let Satan enter Judas who then turned Jesus over to be crucified. If you believe in an omniscient God, you have to believe that both Jesus and God knew this was going to happen. Thus, Judas was merely acting as an instrument for two external beings: God on the one hand and Satan on the other. How then can we ever condemn Judas for 'betraying' Jesus if 1) God knew he was going to do it and 2) he was under the total control of Satan when he did do it? And his suicide: same thing. He was possessed! Scholars have argued for centuries that Judas can't be held accountable for his decisions because he was never acting under his own authority. He was stripped of his own agency the second Satan entered his body. Make sense?"

"Yeah I think so. So, you're saying we have no free will then?"

"That's not necessarily what I'm saying at all. I'm only saying that it's difficult to reconcile free will with the conception of God as all-knowing, all-powerful *and* all-benevolent."

"Fair enough. But what do you mean by *all-benevolent?*"

"Take the Lord's Prayer, for example. Catholics, especially, believe it is the only prayer which Jesus himself gave to his disciples. Okay. So these are *His words*. Most of it is in accordance with everything else he's ever been reported to say in scripture, except one small phrase. *And lead us not into temptation—"*

"*But deliver us from evil*. Yeah, I know that line. I don't get what you're saying though. He's just asking God to protect us from evil. So what?"

"No, listen to the words. *And lead us not into temptation*. What is the subject of that sentence?"

"Temptation?"

"No. It's an imperative sentence. The subject is 'you' or in this case, since it's a prayer, God. Jesus is saying we need to ask God *specifically* not to lead us into temptation. The second part, yes, makes sense. *Deliver us from evil.* Sure, I buy that. But let me ask you: why would Jesus tell his disciples to ask God to never tempt them?"

"He's not saying that. He's saying to pray that God not *lead* his people into temptation."

"Regardless. My point is why would a God who is all-benevolent—who *never* acts in a way other than the kindest manner imaginable—why would this God *ever* lead his people into temptation? Why would he do that? If God were truly all-benevolent, there's no fathomable circumstance in which God would ever tempt his children. Such an act would be inconceivable under the banner of an all benevolent God."

"Okay. So, what, God is *mean* then?"

"I'm not saying that."

"Okay, so there is no God?"

"No, I'm definitely not saying that either."

"Then what are you saying, Lamar? What the fuck are you ever saying?"

"I don't really know, Walden."

"You never really know."

"I'm not sure if *that's* true. I do know that I love my wife and my daughters."

"Can you prove it?"

"Shut up, Carl Sagan. I've heard of *Contact* too."

"Sorry, just trying to be smart."

"Quoting books doesn't make you smart, Walden."

"*Contact* is a book?"

"Ugh, is it lunch time yet?"

"Not yet. And what do you mean quoting movies doesn't make you smart? You've always loved my knowledge about movies!"

"Knowledge and wisdom are two different things, Walden."

"Okay, and having which one of those means I'm smart?"

"Are you sure it's not lunch time yet? I'm getting tired of these mindless debates."

"Oh, so now you're anti-semantic?"

"Yeah, Wally, I am. I'm an anti-semantite."

"You can't just make up words, Lamar. You're not a neurologist."

"You mean neologist?"

"Is that a word?"

"Could be."

"Let's go to lunch."

"Well, what the hell do you mean he's *missing?* I just saw him ten minutes ago going in the food court!" Gage roared at Harvey Douglas.

"I don't know, sir. I'm only telling you what I heard. You can check the message if you want. It's still on the machine," Harvey apologetically replied.

"Goddamnit, if we have to start this shit again, I'm going to snap. I swear if Hinkley's behind this!"

"Who, sir?"

"Sherm--never mind. You say the message is still on the machine?"

"Yes, sir. Let me get it for you." Gage stomped his toe on the floor by Harvey's desk as the young intern accessed his voice mailbox. "Here you are, sir. Here, listen."

Hello. I'm sorry to inform you that one of your employees, Dr. Walden Emerson, is missing as of last July. He began working for Harper's TTA as the most recent in a long line of chumps, but after only a brief period with the company, went away and is now lost. I wish I could tell you how to find him, but as he himself is currently the only Agent with the authority to locate missing persons, unfortunately I'm afraid he is the only person who can find himself. I could perhaps offer a few suggestions, but I believe those will most likely fall on blind ears or deaf eyes. This is not a senseless joke. Wally is gone. You may never get him back. He could very well be gone forever. This is only the beginning. More will go lost. I don't mean to sound threatening, for I only speak the truth. The chump has escaped. He just may not know it yet. Oh and by the way, the third toilet on the left in the first floor women's bathroom is clogged and your prices are way too high. Thanks so much and have a great day!

Sherman Hinkley didn't care that he managed to arrive at his first three intersections at precisely the moment when he was granted the blinking, de-gendered human figure on the other side of the street signifying to all that it was now safe to cross. He probably would've crossed anyway. He breezed by the Indianapolis public library which had served as his surrogate home for nearly three years while he was finishing his doctorate in Forensic Psychology from a bullshit college. He hurried alongside Lucas Oil Stadium, home of the Indianapolis Colts who just last winter had won their 19th Superbowl in 50 years. He wondered if, like the Coliseum of Rome, this particular structure would be the last standing testament to America once America burned itself to the ground. Sports always prevailed, after all. With an increased kick to his step, he glanced at the banner hanging in front of Zachary Efron Memorial Theater to see the advertisement for this season's off Broadway showcase. Sherman had never heard of "Shit-Wrecked," but then again, live action musicals about bodily functions weren't exactly his strong suit.

He walked up the ClockWorks stairs, flipped off the Eve-like figure in the garden, brushed past the statue of some Canadian actor standing like an idiot on a broken watch, and entered the building. He ignored Gage, Harvey, and Lester running on the seventeenth floor breezeway to the glass elevator. They must've received one hell of a phone call to make them run like that. Sherman walked over to the food court and found Wally and Lamar. Before he could say anything, Sherman saw a tiny critter racing toward a hotdog bite lying by Wally's foot. Sherman stomped his foot on the creature, smothering his body against the sole of Sherman's shoe.

"Gross! Was that a cockroach?" Wally asked, disgusted.

"It was something, that's for sure," Sherman replied curtly.

"Well, thanks, man," Wally offered.

"Not a problem," Sherman answered. He hovered over Wally and Lamar, not saying a word.

"Um, can we help you, sir?" Lamar wondered. "Are you looking for someone?"

"You always were kinda cliché, Lamar," Sherman smiled.

"Do I *know* you?" Lamar asked.

"Probably not. I actually just saw that bug crawl over here and wanted to kill it before it got in your food or something."

"Well, thanks again," Wally said, returning to his food in a gesture of dismissal of their unwanted guest.

"Not a problem. Hey could you guys do me a favor?"

"Sure, what is it?" Lamar accepted.

"If you see Eliza Wyatt Harper or her granddaughter, Eternity Alcott, could please tell them that Sherman Hinkley's dead."

"Who?"

"Just tell Eliza Wyatt Harper or her granddaughter, Eternity Alcott, that Sherman Hinkley died a few months ago. Thanks so much. *Sherman Hinkley*. Remember that." And he left.

"Sir, Dr. Emerson's right down there with Agent Newton!" Harvey exclaimed to Gage as they rode down the elevator to the lobby. Gage, however, didn't reply. He was concentrating on a strange man strolling out of the building. "Sir?"

"I heard you, yes, Douglas, I see Emerson. I see him. He's not lost. Must have been a prank. Let's go to the fourth floor. I need to talk to President Waverly."

"Should I go with you?"

"No, Douglas. This needs to be private."

"Fair enough, sir."

"You alright, Wally?"

"Yeah, it's sad about Sherman Hinkley though."

"I know. We'll have to tell Eternity when she gets back from New York."

"Yeah. But who's Eliza Wyatt Harper?"

"Who knows?"

"Yeah."

"And who's Sherman Hinkley?"

"I don't really know. But, gosh, my head really hurts all of a sudden."

"Mine too. Shit, maybe we should take the rest of the day off."

"Yeah, let's go back to the office and get our things. Isabelle can take care of business for the rest of the day."

"Yeah. Headaches suck, man."

"Yeah."

Their heads hurt.

So they went home.

It's just what you do.

Jeff Spanke is a recent graduate from Purdue University's MA program in American Studies where he studied nineteenth century American Literature and Education. He is currently seeking licensure in secondary education and plans to teach high school English around the greater Indianapolis region. *Second Hand Out* is his first novel.

www.ingramcontent.com/pod-product-compliance
Lightning Source LLC
Chambersburg PA
CBHW032136270626
47172CB00008B/96

* 9 7 8 0 6 1 5 2 5 3 7 0 1 *